The Devil at my Heels

Charles Mossop

MuseItUp Publishing
www.museituppublishing.com

The Devil at my Heels © 2011 by Charles Mossop

MuseItUp Publishing
14878 James, Pierrefonds, Quebec, Canada, H9H 1P5
http://www.museituppublishing.com

Cover Art © 2011 by Delilah K. Stephens
Edited by Fiona Young-Brown
Copyedited by Valerie Haley
Layout and Book Production by Lea Schizas

Print ISBN: 978-1-927085-93-6
eBook ISBN: 978-1-926931-86-9
First eBook Edition * June 2011
Production by MuseItUp Publishing

THE DEVIL AT MY HEELS

◆

CHARLES MOSSOP

Dedication

For Louise, who has shared my life for the past forty-two wonderful years.

Acknowledgements

I wish to acknowledge with thanks the help of Marie Davies, Renee Otis, Abigail Beal and Jennifer Payton in the preparation of the initial manuscript. Grateful thanks are also due to Jim Sanders, a true aficionado of the mystery novel, for his careful and thoughtful critique of the draft prior to submission. In addition I am greatly indebted to Fiona Young-Brown and Valerie Haley, members of MuseItUp Publishing's editorial staff, for their invaluable assistance in the preparation of the final manuscript. Last, but most certainly not least, I thank Lea Schizas, Managing Editor of MuseItUp Publishing, for her advice and mentorship as I took my first uncertain steps toward a writing career.

AUTHOR'S NOTE

Apart from documented historical events such as the sacking of Rome in 1527, the Spanish Succession treaties and the D-Day invasion of 1944, the events described in this book are fictitious and the product of the author's imagination. Except for recognized historical figures, the characters portrayed are likewise fictitious, and if, through name, appearance, speech or behavior, any resemblance is found to any real person, alive or dead, such resemblance is coincidental and unintentional.

PROLOGUE

England: The Present Day

Dr. Michael Stuart, red-bearded and in his early fifties, closed the door behind the last of his dinner guests and sighed in satisfaction. *Thank heavens they've gone,* he thought. He went quickly to his study, opened the small, fireproof safe he kept under his desk and withdrew a plain brown file folder. Relocking the safe, he put the folder on his desk and sat down. *This is it,* he thought, looking at the sheet of yellowing parchment the folder contained. *The first definite proof in eight hundred years. That stuff will be worth a fortune, and the publicity will be incredible. Could get me a knighthood. When I publish this, we'll have to rewrite the history books. Thank you so much, good King John.*

He looked up and frowned as the sound of footsteps reached him. He rose, walked out of the study and stopped abruptly at the sight of a man in dark jacket and slacks standing in the hallway.

"What the hell are you doing here?" he demanded. "How did you get in?"

"Easy. You left the front door unlocked after you saw your guests off. Very careless of you."

Stuart heard the cold menace in the intruder's voice and suddenly realized the danger he could be facing. He strove to keep his voice steady as he tried to take control of the situation.

"Get out. Now."

"I want that parchment back. I only asked you to authenticate it; I didn't give it to you."

"I've told you. I've got it in safekeeping. I can look after it for you."

"*Bollocks.* You just want the glory. That document belongs to me, and I want it back."

Cold-fisted fear squeezed Stuart's vitals as in the dim light of the hallway he could see the intruder carried the heavy iron poker from the front room fireplace.

The man took a step closer.

"Give me that letter, Stuart. I'm through playing games."

5

A bead of sweat snaked coldly down Stuart's spine. *There's a phone in the study*, he thought. *If I can get in there I can lock the door and call the police. They'll believe me, not him.*

He spun on his heel and made a dash for the open study door. He heard a yell of anger and felt his shirt rip as a strong hand tried to hold him back. He stumbled, half turned.

"No!"

The heavy poker struck the side of his head. Its thunderous impact was the last sound he heard.

Chapter One

Winter, in the Year of Our Lord 1216, was a bleak time of bitter gales, snow and leaden, malevolent skies. The realm of John, King of England, racked by civil war and ruled by an inept and rapacious monarch was as cheerless as the weather. Everywhere, men and women of all ranks and stations lived in fear.

That turbulent, temporal world, however, seldom intruded upon the cloistered sanctity of All Saints Priory in southern Lincolnshire, nor did it disturb the quiet tenor of life for Prior Gottfried and his community of black-habited Benedictine brethren. The monks of All Saints measured the passage of time not by the travails of armies and the rise and fall of kings, but by meetings of the Chapter, the daily observance of the eight Divine Offices of the Church and the orderly annual cycle of work in the gardens, kitchens, workshops and scriptorium.

Prior Gottfried was a devout, scholarly man of nearly five-and-fifty years, tall, imposing and possessed of a calmly authoritative bearing. The thin hair ringing his tonsured pate was iron gray, but his dark eyes were as keen and bright as ever they had been, and his piety and sense of justice were renowned far beyond the confines of his isolated priory.

The stone buildings and enclosing wall of All Saints were situated on a low hill which, in addition to providing dry fields where the monks could grow their crops and graze their livestock, afforded an unhindered view across the flat marshland that surrounded it. Now, in the late afternoon of a bitterly cold day in February, Gottfried watched from the window of his private parlor as a troop of soldiers materialized out of the snow and approached the priory gate. He counted fifteen men with three heavily laden oxcarts. They struggled against the driving snow that flew wildly across the open fens, plastering the walls of the priory buildings until they looked like giant marzipan cakes.

Gottfried frowned, and wondered what their coming might portend. Were they king's men, or did they serve one of the rebellious barons? It looked too small and slow-moving a company to be a raiding party, but in these troubled times it was difficult to be certain of anything.

* * * *

The column halted outside the main gate of the priory, and one of its number beat the pommel of his sword upon the heavy wooden door.

"Ho there within," he roared above the whistling wind. "Open in the name of the king. Open, I say."

Three monks hurried into the snow, and lifted the great beam across the inside of the gate from its iron brackets. The ponderous door swung open allowing the men and their carts to move into the priory's public courtyard. Two of the monks unyoked the oxen, their breath smoking down their snow-covered flanks, and led them away to the byre, while the third ushered the soldiers into the guest hall. Their leather greatcoats and chain mail armor creaked and rang from the cold as they removed their heavy iron helmets.

Once the visitors had settled themselves onto wooden benches around a table before the blazing fire, Brother Cuthbert, the hospitaler, and his helper, a young novice named Robert, gave them dark ale, mulled to a bubbling heat by red hot pokers withdrawn from the fire.

After a long drink, the sergeant put down his leather flagon with a deep and satisfied sigh.

"God bless you, good brothers all. 'Tis truly an unkind evening to be abroad."

"But what brings you hither?" ventured Brother Cuthbert, a man noted as much for his curiosity as his devotion to God, as he refilled the sergeant's flagon.

"The king's business, Brother," answered the sergeant. "I crave an audience with the good Prior Gottfried."

Robert was at once dispatched to carry the request to the prior, and as he departed, the talk and laughter amongst the soldiers grew louder and merrier while the fire and mulled ale warmed their bodies from without and within.

"But, you are not all here, surely?" said Cuthbert, after completing another round with his ale jug. "I think your number lacks of three.

Where are the others?"

"On guard," answered a young soldier.

Cuthbert was about to inquire further, when Robert returned with news that Prior Gottfried would speak with the sergeant in his parlor when Vespers was concluded in half an hour. Robert was sent out into the snow once again, his sandaled feet well wrapped in wide strips of cloth, to carry comfort and sustenance to the unfortunates who remained outside standing watch over the contents of the three carts.

Back in the hall, the sergeant, a burly, thickset fellow of about forty, stretched his feet gratefully towards the fire and took another long pull at his ale.

Have a care, my friend, thought Cuthbert, *lest the half-hour leave you unable to stand, let alone speak with our prior.* But although he accounted for two more brimming flagons of mulled ale ere he was summoned into the prior's presence, the sergeant left the guest hall with steps both straight and firm.

* * * *

"*Pax vobiscum*, my son," Gottfried said to his guest, and then, lest the sergeant's Latin were insufficient, translated, "Peace be with you."

"*Et Dominus vobiscum*, Lord Prior," answered the soldier, rather to Gottfried's surprise.

"Pray be seated," said the prior, indicating one of the heavy wooden chairs.

The room was furnished in utilitarian fashion with several chairs, a stout table and many shelves of documents, and even one or two books. A small fire basket set on a low stone platform in one corner provided what little warmth there was, and a solitary candle standing in a plain earthenware holder on the table cast a flickering, orange glow over the chamber.

"You and your men are welcome, my son," said the prior in a placid voice.

"'Tis right grateful we are to you and your brethren, good Prior," answered the sergeant. "We are most kindly received and we give you hearty thanks for it."

9

Gottfried observed the sergeant while the man spoke, and noted the livid scar running the length of his face from his left temple to his chin. He saw as well the man's lower jaw was slightly crooked, no doubt broken by that same savage blow.

"We welcome all honest travelers as brothers in Christ," Gottfried said, "but I think you do not come to us this day by fortuity, my son. There is little of interest to men such as you in this part of the world, particularly at this time of year."

"Wisely spoken, Father Prior," said the sergeant, with a somewhat lopsided smile. "We come in the name of His Majesty King John, who begs a boon of you."

"His Majesty begs a boon of *me*?" asked the prior. "How can that be, my son? The king begs nothing of any man."

For answer, the sergeant withdrew from the breast of his red surcoat a folded parchment bearing the royal seal. He leaned forward and placed the letter into the prior's hand.

"Read if you will, and all shall be explained."

Still mystified, Gottfried broke the seal, unfolded the document and read its contents. It was written in Latin, in a neat and careful hand.

John, by the Grace of God, King of England, Lord of Ireland, Duke of Normandy and Aquitaine, and Count of Anjou, to our trusty and well-beloved subject Gottfried, Brother of the Priory of All Saints of the Rule of St. Benedict, and Lord Prior thereof: Greetings.

We do most earnestly desire of you and your brothers in Christ a solemn pledge of trust and fealty as befits good servants of your king. And we do further desire that you will find a safe and secure resting place in concealment and secrecy for those most precious and valuable objects, the regalia and riches of our realm and the sacred emblems of our kingship, which are carried to you this day by he who brings you these, our words, furnished with our seal. And it is our most express desire and instruction that you and your brethren will keep silent as touching this matter, both now and forever hereafter.

"Am I to understand, my son," asked the prior, looking up from the parchment, "that His Majesty seeks to entrust us here with certain objects he wishes us to hide?"

"It is even as you say, Father Prior," said the sergeant. "It is the king who speaks; I am but a soldier following orders."

"As a soldier surely must," observed Gottfried eying his guest. "But you are no common soldier, my son, any more than this is an ordinary matter. Your speech belies your appearance, as does the weighty charge that brings you here."

Gottfried leaned back in his hard chair and regarded the sergeant placidly.

"My good Lord Prior," declared the sergeant, "the matter is far from ordinary indeed. We have brought hither the regalia of the realm, as you have read, and this regalia be truly wondrous. Jewels, crowns, gold and silver plates and vessels, scepters, maces, orbs and many other such precious accoutrements of royalty."

The prior remained impassive, his expression betraying none of the astonishment he felt.

"As you rightly construe," the soldier continued, "I am no man-at-arms. I am Sir Gilbert Fitzhugh, and my estates and holdings lie in the north of this shire, in Kent and in Sussex. I am a sworn vassal of His Majesty, our liege lord, King John."

"But," Gottfried pointed out, "you come with a mere fifteen men. How is it that so few are sent to guard so great a treasure?"

"His Majesty is much beset by the armies of treasonous men, Father Prior," replied Sir Gilbert, "and more soldiers could not be spared. We trusted a small party would attract no great notice, and we came in this evil weather in hopes that thieves and masterless men would not be abroad. By God's mercy, we came safely."

Gottfried nodded. "Thanks be to God."

"I am bidden to convey these treasures hither," Sir Gilbert continued, "see them well concealed, and return to the king with report of it."

"But why, My Lord?" asked Prior Gottfried. "Forgive my weak wits, but surely there could be no safer place for the king's treasure than with the king's own army."

"These are fearful and dangerous days, Lord Prior," answered Sir Gilbert, "and His Majesty faces great trials. I warrant you know of that

11

thrice-damned so-called *Great Charter* which was forced upon His Majesty at Runnymede last year?"

Gottfried nodded.

"Well, the king does not intend to sit as idle as an apprentice while his Divine right of kingship is taken from him by knavish traitors."

Gottfried shifted uncomfortably in his chair. A copy of that selfsame Magna Carta had been sent to All Saints by Stephen Langdon, Cardinal Archbishop of Canterbury, and the prior beseeched God Sir Gilbert would not see it on the shelf close to where he sat. The charter guaranteed the preeminence of the Holy Catholic Church in England, and thus Gottfried had read it with care. Its secular provisions, momentous as they might have been, were of little interest to him.

"It is His Majesty's purpose," continued Sir Gilbert, "to crush his enemies and soon there will be great battles to fight. These treasures can no longer be kept safe by the king, and so they are to be hidden until this turmoil be ended and the king's enemies destroyed."

"But why here?" asked Gottfried.

"Where better?" replied Sir Gilbert.

The interview concluded and after the evening meal, Sir Gilbert and his men were lodged in the guest hall. Gottfried went to his own narrow bed and prayed to God for sufficient grace and strength to sustain him in this most extraordinary hour.

* * * *

At mid-morning the next day, after the office of Tierce, work began on the hiding place. Prior Gottfried instructed that no brother should go near the scriptorium without his leave, and under his supervision, the soldiers took up a large square of flagstones and began to dig a hole beneath the floor. The work was not easy, and by the end of the day, only scant progress had been made. The next morning they recommenced, and at midday finally breached a thick layer of hard clay and flint so that by six in the evening, just before the Office of Compline, a substantial excavation had been completed. The accumulated pile of soil and rubble was transported in buckets and barrows to a patch of disused ground behind the priory workshops.

On the third day, at Gottfried's bidding, Brother Eustace, the carpenter, delivered four dozen thick planks and six stout posts to the door of the scriptorium, along with a rule, scribing tool and several saws. He knocked, as instructed, when he was finished unloading, and departed before the door was opened.

The soldiers lined the bottom and sides of the excavation with planks and then carefully placed the contents of the three carts into it. One of the soldiers uttered a scrofulous oath, and hastily begged Gottfried's pardon, when a leather box split, spilling its contents into the bottom of the pit. Work halted for a time while the objects were retrieved, but eventually several posts were set up as vertical supports and planks laid on them across the top of the excavation. Then, following the addition of a layer of soil, the soldiers replaced the flagstones.

"God be with you, Lord Prior," said Sir Gilbert, swinging into his saddle as he and his men prepared to leave the following morning.

"And with you, my son."

"I pray I shall soon return to claim what has been left here."

"I pledge we shall keep it safe until you do," replied the prior, and blessed the soldiers as they marched out of the priory courtyard.

Gottfried waited until the gate was closed and barred before turning to the porter.

"Go and bid Brother Sacristan to summon all to the Chapter House. Let no one be overlooked."

The thirty-eight black-habited brothers, ten novices and numerous lay brothers and stewards filed into Chapter and stood in respectful silence in the cold building, the wind penetrating every small opening or ill-fitting doorpost. Gottfried entered and bade them be seated on the long wooden benches ranged around the walls, while he himself sat on a chair behind a substantial wooden table set on a low dais.

The prior let his eye roam over his assembled flock. Everyone present knew the contents of the three oxcarts had been buried beneath the scriptorium floor, but Gottfried alone knew the full truth.

"My Brothers," he said, his voice imbued with all the gravity and authority of his office, "what has been left here is not ours to keep, and by God's mercy it will soon be retrieved and returned to its rightful home. I straitly charge you all, on peril of your immortal souls that you tell no one what has befallen here. You shall tell neither new novice nor any person who lives outside these walls. I require each of you that you swear before God and this company that you will utter neither word nor syllable of this thing to any living soul save those here now."

One by one, they took the oath, and the air hung heavy with solemnity and high portent.

"Remember, each of you, what you have done this day," commanded Gottfried, in tones of irresistible moral and spiritual authority, as he rose from his place behind the table.

Chapter Two

The months of harsh winter finally yielded to a glorious spring whose blessed sunshine rejuvenated the winter-weary land. The thatching reeds of the fen country surrounding All Saints were released from their burden of snow and sprang up to become supple and green once again. Thatchers and their families appeared with sharp scythes, and as the men cut the sedge in broad, curving swaths, the women and children, their forearms wrapped in protective leather, built up heaping wagonloads of the long reeds to be taken away to repair the depredations of winter. At the priory on the low hill, the monks planted their vegetables and grains and drove their livestock out to pasture and pen. The well-ordered course of life went on.

The reawakened season brought no such pastoral peace and good order to the rest of the kingdom. Oppression and misery had become a way of life for the common folk. King John's subjects endured a precarious and uncertain existence. Marauding armies, whichever side they were on, lived off the land, took food where it was to be found and made murder, rape and pillage commonplace.

Prior Gottfried waited throughout the summer of 1216 for word regarding the reclamation of the hidden regalia, but none came. August brought news of the death of Sir Gilbert Fitzhugh, tortured and beheaded as recompense for his loyalty to a hated king, and in late October word came of the death of King John himself, struck down by a fulminating attack of dysentery at Newark Castle in Nottinghamshire.

On the night news reached him of King John's death, the prior sat alone in his candlelit parlor pondering what should be done. The king's letter lay on the table before him as he reflected that by now many outside the priory might know the secret of the regalia. Perhaps it was only a matter of time before some avaricious magnate or plundering army would come for it.

An October gale howled about the stone walls of the priory as if to pluck them from the very ground upon which they stood, but Gottfried paid it no heed. *Suppose others do come to steal,* he thought. *We would be powerless to stop them.* He looked again at the king's letter and considered destroying it, thus eliminating at least one clue to the secret, but he could not bring himself to do it. *There may yet appear a legitimate claimant who would possess the right to see the letter, and even if not, suppose the treasure were discovered accidentally and the letter destroyed. There would be no proof of the king's intent or of how the regalia came to be hidden. Sir Gilbert cannot speak on our behalf, and I and my brethren might find ourselves accused of stealing the royal treasure. How else could its presence and concealment be explained?*

"That is utter stupidity," he muttered aloud. "How could we few monks steal such things from the king himself? *But*, he reminded himself, *the danger is real, all the same.*

The prior made his solitary way to the Chapel and knelt on the stone floor before the altar to beseech God for guidance. He remained thus for several hours until the monks, summoned by the tolling of the bell, assembled shortly after midnight to celebrate Matins, the first prayers of the new day. Brother Bartholomew, the priory's keeper of accounts and daily records, helped him up onto his stiff legs, for the cold flagstones had numbed him to the bone. As Gottfried stood with his flock, listening to the ancient Latin prayers and benedictions, he felt a sense of calm trust enfold him, and before the Office was concluded, he had his answer. It was an uncomplicated and undemanding solution, and God gave it to him with the clarity of an epiphany and the glory of a revelation.

God told him to wait.

And so, ever obedient to Divine command, wait he did.

Days became weeks, weeks became months, and still no one came. No brigands invaded and no royal messenger arrived. All was silence, and it seemed as if the treasure were forgotten.

The good prior continued to pray for guidance, and the thought came to him one day that perhaps, in these times of instability and violence, God had placed the royal treasure in safekeeping at the priory until a strong and righteous monarch should wear the crown of England. Gottfried nurtured and cherished this idea, and gradually it grew in his mind into a conviction he believed had come from God Himself.

Nine-year-old Prince Henry, King John's son, although proclaimed king, would not rule in his own right until the age of five-and-twenty, and even then he may prove no better a monarch than his father. Would God choose such a king as that to inherit the riches hidden beneath the scriptorium? *No*, thought the prior, *never. The treasure will be reclaimed in God's good time by a king worthy of it in God's eyes.*

So Gottfried waited and his flock kept their secret, but in January of 1223, the prior fell ill and he knew within himself it was an illness unto death. After a lifetime of prayer, self-abnegation and devotion to God, he had no fear of dying, but cherished in his heart a blithe, calm expectation of eternal bliss.

By midsummer, Gottfried was often too weak to rise from his bed. The daily Offices of the Church were performed for him in his cell. While praying for his recovery, the good brothers prayed also for the repose of his soul, and sorrowfully prepared for his death, should it please Almighty God to gather him to His bosom.

But although his body failed him, Gottfried's mind did not. God answered his prayers once again. That answer, when at last it came, appeared in the form of one of the prior's own flock.

* * * *

Shortly after the burial of the royal regalia, Robert, the novice entrusted to Brother Cuthbert's tutelage, took his final vows and assumed his place as a permanent member of the community.

Robert, the son of a bondman tinsmith, had studied Latin and learned to read and write under Cuthbert's watchful eye, but it was Brother Adolphus, the priory's librarian and master copyist, who perceived the full magnitude of the young man's artistic genius.

Robert grew in grace and flourished as an artist, and Gottfried watched his progress and praised God that so gifted a brother had been given to All Saints.

"His work is breathtaking for its brilliance of color," declared Adolphus to the prior. "It is exquisite in its detail. His faith grants him Divine inspiration far beyond his years."

The entire community well remembered the day the great Stephen Langdon journeyed from Canterbury to Lincolnshire for the sole purpose of viewing one of Robert's earliest works: an illuminated copy of St.

Paul's epistle to the Romans. The Cardinal Archbishop proclaimed it the most sublime object he had ever seen, and carried the manuscript back to Canterbury to be given a place of distinction in the cathedral library.

Since 1216, death had reduced the number of brethren who knew the scriptorium's secret. New arrivals were never told of it. The old prior was confident those remaining brothers would likewise carry the secret to their own graves after he was gone, and thus he foresaw a time when no one would know of the buried regalia.

He called for assistance, whereupon two monks appeared and helped him sit up, his back against the stone wall at the head of his narrow bed. This position caused him difficulty in breathing, but he was determined to do God's will as he believed God had revealed it to him. He sent the two away after summoning Brother Robert, who quickly appeared and made respectful obeisance.

Robert was now twenty-two years of age, well-framed, although not tall. He was clean-shaven and the hair that circled his tonsured crown was dark and thick. His expression had a natural softness about it which, when combined with the unfathomable depths of his dark eyes, normally gave him a demeanor of calm serenity, but at this particular moment, his face registered both concern and curiosity.

Gottfried drew a deep and unsteady breath, but when Robert moved forward to offer assistance, he waved him back.

"My son," said the prior, "I have asked you here to deliver to you a most solemn charge."

"You have only to speak it, Father Prior," said Robert, spreading his hands before him, "and I shall obey."

Gottfried gathered breath once more and continued, his voice trembling in weakness.

"You remember the days of your novitiate when the king's men came?"

"Right well, Father," Robert declared, and then added quickly, "and as God sees me, I swear I have not spoken of it to any man."

"Peace, my son," said Gottfried, raising his hand a few inches from his bed. "All is well. But it is of those days that I would speak."

"I am listening, Father."

"My son," said Gottfried, "before I depart, I would know there is a record made of what was done in those times. I seek this in the hope that one day those things which were hidden will be reclaimed, and also as a testament to our faithfulness in the keeping of our oath."

"It shall be done, Father," Robert said. "Dictate it to me, and I shall record it."

"Not so," said the prior, his breath now rasping and labored, "lest evil men should one day read it. God has revealed to me another way, my son; a safer way."

"Then what must I do?"

"Brother Adolphus tells me you are at work on a copy of the gospel of St. John. Is that correct?"

Brother Robert nodded, and his eyes grew round with wonder as Gottfried delivered his instructions.

"Do you understand, my son?" he finished. "The illuminations must tell our story. The soldiers, the hiding place, but there must be no written word of it."

"I shall do it, Father Prior, just as you say," said Robert. "The gospel is nearly completed, but there remains room for what you describe. I shall make some sketches and bring them here to you."

"So be it, my son," answered the prior, "and now I beg you to call Brother Sacristan to me as you depart."

The sacristan came at once and Gottfried gave him a series of instructions to be carried out after his death, and then lay back, grateful he had done what was required. The truth of the scriptorium would be told, and the king's letter saved, yet both would be protected from the greed of unrighteous men.

* * * *

That night, Robert worked at his copying desk until the bell sounded for Matins. He destroyed many sketches before deciding on the final ones, which he carried to Gottfried for approval the next morning. The old prior was pleased and nodded in satisfaction.

"It is well, my son. Let it be done as you have shown me, with but one addition."

"Yes, Father Prior?"

"You must place the figure of a small crown just here," said Gottfried, pointing with a trembling forefinger to a place on Robert's sketch.

"A crown, Father?" asked Robert.

Gottfried said no more, so Robert returned to the scriptorium, puzzled, but obedient.

The manuscript upon which Robert worked comprised the entire gospel according to St. John as well as a series of suffrages, or prayers, addressed to the Saint himself. Each chapter and prayer began with an historiated initial, a large illuminated capital letter. It was within those and their surrounding decorations and embellishments that Robert would carry out Gottfried's instructions. *O God,* Robert prayed, *guide my eye and make steady my hand. If it please you that this be the last work of mine our blessed Prior will see, then I pray that with your help it will be the best of which I am capable. Thy will be done.*

"Is this the completion of the gospel, my son?" Brother Adolphus asked, bending over Robert's copying desk and interrupting his silent devotions.

"Yes, Brother Librarian."

"Splendid," beamed the old monk. "Splendid. And you will do the initials and borders, no doubt? Marginalia as well, perhaps?"

"Of course. All shall be done."

"Remember, my son," said Adolphus, raising his forefinger in admonition, "your skill is of God. Beware of man's vanity and of pride in your accomplishments. To God alone be the glory."

"Amen," said Robert.

Adolphus nodded, placed an affectionate hand on Robert's shoulder and moved away.

Robert took a piece of charcoal he had made in the burners behind the stables and carefully carved it to as fine a point as it would bear. With a deft hand and infinite care, he drew the outline of what he intended to create. After completing his sketch, so light and fine as to be almost invisible, he set out his three basic colors.

First came the carbon black called *atramentum,* or sable, velvet-like in its texture and requiring to be mixed fresh every day lest it set like stone in its pot overnight.

He crossed himself, loaded a fine brush with the sable paint and began the historiated initial of the gospel's final chapter.

"Well, well, good Brother," said a caustic voice from behind him, "and what is our prior's favorite illuminator making today?"

Robert started a little as the abrasive words broke his concentration. He raised the point of his brush from the parchment and sighed.

"What is it, Brother Julius?" he asked, without looking around.

The deep dislike Julius felt towards him had always been a mystery to Robert, and it tried him sorely. Christ-like forbearance and love were hard to feel when it came to Brother Julius.

"Why nothing at all," answered Julius with all the innocence of a devious child. "I merely inquire as to the work you do."

"If you must know," said Robert carefully, "I am finishing the gospel I have been preparing this twelve-month past."

"Ah," said Brother Julius, "so why does our prior take such an interest in you, I wonder? Why does he send for you and speak with you in private? I saw you. What secret does he share with you alone?"

"Father Prior remains interested in all that goes on amongst his brethren," said Robert, finally laying down his brush and looking around to see Julius regarding him with narrowed eyes and a firm-set mouth. A smallish man of nearly thirty with hollow cheeks and a long nose, Brother Julius was usually to be found in the priory kitchens. He seldom worked anywhere else, and Robert knew he had no legitimate reason for being in the scriptorium.

Robert felt Julius' enmity as if it was a palpable force. Many times had he humbly beseeched God to show him his fault that he might make amends to Julius for whatever wrong he may have unwittingly done him. God had not obliged, however, and eventually Robert came to regard Julius as a cross to be borne, a penance that must be done, albeit for an unknown transgression.

Julius stared at Robert for another few moments, and then, with a derisive snort, he turned and walked away. Even from the back, Brother Julius seemed to exude malice.

"*Pax vobiscum*, Brother," Robert called, and Julius stopped. Whirling around, he strode back to where Robert sat.

"There can be no peace with me as long as you are here," he hissed, putting his mouth close to Robert's ear. "You, with the gift of God in your hands. You, upon whom our dying prior still dotes. I damn you. Get you to Lucifer and burn eternally at the portals of hell."

"Good Brother—" Robert began, appalled at Julius' venom, but Julius was not finished.

"I work and sweat all the weary day in that hot kitchen while you sit here at ease painting pictures. I cut bloody meat, peel vegetables until my fingers ache, carry slops to the pigs, just as I have done since my father brought me to this miserable place when I was too young to protest. No one knows or cares what I do. If I fell into the cesspit, everyone would just piss on me without troubling to pull me out. But you…you are famous. Even the archbishop comes hither to see what you have done, you simpering little swine!"

Chapter Three

For the next three days, mercifully uninterrupted by the malignant Brother Julius, Robert labored on the historiated initial. He did not leave his wooden copying desk in the scriptorium except for meals and the Divine Offices, during which he prayed not only for the salvation of souls, but also that the ink would not harden before he could return to work. By the evening of the third day, he had finished the application of black paint and completed the sections in red and blue.

"Argent shall come next," he told Brother Adolphus the following morning, two hours after Prime.

"Yes, of course," nodded the elderly librarian. "You have made a most excellent beginning, Brother."

Robert had spent the two hours since Prime preparing sizing to make argent, the silver paint, in the priory's workshops behind the refectory. He boiled fish bones until they virtually disappeared, and the water in the pot became as white as milk. He let the liquid cool, strained it through a piece of muslin, and after examining its texture carefully, decided it would do.

Some copyists, who made their sizing from egg whites or shreds of vellum boiled for hours, declared that Robert's fishbone decoction often led to the growth on manuscripts of an unsightly fungus, but nothing of the sort ever marred Robert's work. He had learned to add a small cut clove of garlic to the boiling bones, a secret obtained from a copyist at the great Benedictine Abbey of Shrewsbury. Robert guarded the secret well, although few individuals ever ventured close enough to spy. When seethed with fish bones, the garlic produced so vile a stench that naysayers and the merely inquisitive stayed well away. Fortunately for all, the smell quickly disappeared as the sizing hardened.

Robert carried his pot of newly made sizing to the scriptorium, added a little water and silver powder, and began to brush the metallic paint carefully onto his parchment. It took steady, concentrated work to finish the application, bringing its surface to the smooth and lustrous sheen it required.

23

"Glorious, good Brother," murmured Adolphus as he followed Robert's progress. "Truly glorious, and a paean to Almighty God Himself."

The silver painting took all that day and most of the next, and was finished as the bell sounded for Compline. As he made his way towards the Chapel, Robert fell into step with several other monks, and unexpectedly found himself walking next to Brother Julius.

"Good even, Brother Julius," he said, but Julius did not answer. Robert noticed Julius smelled faintly of newly-baked bread, the warmth of that comfortable aroma contrasting sharply with Julius' outward demeanor. His eyes were like splinters of ice, his face as hard as flint.

As the brethren filed quietly into the Chapel, Robert blessed Brother Julius in obedience to Christ's exhortation to love one's enemies. *Julius is sent to try my faith*, he told himself, *and God shall not find me wanting when I come finally to stand before His judgment seat.*

As the monks formed two lines facing each other at right angles to the altar, the sonorous prayers of worship and devotion began. Robert saw Julius standing opposite him, tight-lipped and mute. The ancient and venerable Latin benedictions, chanted by the sacristan and answered in unison by the brethren, echoed and floated on the air within the Chapel, coiling around the carved stone columns and rising into the shadowed vault of the high roof.

The Divine Offices never failed to lift Robert to the very pinnacle of rapturous adoration, but they meant nothing to Julius it seemed. He bent an unwavering, malevolent stare upon Robert, and the memory of its malice haunted Robert as he lay in his small cell that night, begging God to help him love his apparently implacable enemy.

The next morning, trying resolutely to drive Julius from his mind, Robert commenced the two most difficult tasks in the illuminator's art: the making and application of gold paint and gold leaf. He approached Brother Adolphus and begged leave to take a piece of gold from the priory's small strong-room with which to make paint. Gold was supplied to the priory by the cathedral at Norwich, expressly for the use of copyists, and after selecting a modest lump he judged to be adequate, Robert went again to the workshops.

As with silver, gold paint consisted of nothing more than powdered metal mixed with a little water and sizing, but unlike silver, powdered gold could not be purchased. Robert took a large stone slab from a wooden shelf above the workbench and set it before him in a patch of sunlight entering the workshop through a narrow window. He needed good light to avoid losing any of the precious powder he was about to make, and he pulled back the full sleeves of his black habit lest any of it should find its way onto the coarse cloth.

The grinding stone had been given to All Saints by the Abbey Church of the Blessed Virgin Mary of Valle Crucis in north Wales shortly after the founding of that Cistercian community in 1201. All Saints prized the gift, for the slab was of the finest porphyry, the very best stone on which to grind gold. According to legend, it had been brought back from Jerusalem by a crusader knight and given to the abbey in gratitude for his safe return from war.

Robert worked patiently for several hours, rubbing the yellow metal back and forth across the slab's flat surface. Little by little, a thin film of luminous powder began to form, growing gradually into a small pile, glittering in the sunlight. Finally, with infinite care, he collected all the powder, so fine as to be virtually impalpable, and mixed it with water and sizing.

As he left the workshop, Brother Mark, the blacksmith, shot him a grin through the smoke from his forge and waved a muscular arm in farewell. Robert waved back and made his way to the scriptorium, well aware he must use the gold paint at once before it lost its smoothness and began to set.

This process was repeated for three days as Robert made and applied small amounts of gold fluid to his design. At length, however, the work was completed. The rich color in its intricate patterns of lines, circles and scrolls glowed against the other colors on the parchment. Brother Adolphus examined the work carefully and pronounced it exquisite.

"And now the gold leaf?" Adolphus asked.

"Yes, Brother," said Robert. "I must go to the workshop to prepare the mordant."

Mordant was the bonding agent forming the foundation for the gold overlay, which Robert planned to use to fill the larger spaces within the designs and painted scenes. Ordinary sizing became mordant through the addition of powdered white gypsum brought from Nottinghamshire, and two hours of work over his noisome boiling pot provided Robert with all he would need for that day. He returned to the scriptorium, and taking up his finest brush made from the softest hairs of the gray badger, he applied a thin layer of the mordant to the parchment where he would eventually place the gold leaf. Without the mordant, the gold would quickly peel off and disappear.

Robert made mordant and applied it to the parchment twelve times, each new application being laid on only when the previous one was absolutely dry. Then, with painstaking care, he burnished the mordant with a smooth piece of bone, meticulously polishing the surface until it resembled clear quartz crystal. So skilled was he in this technique that other copyists and novice pupils left their copying desks and gathered around him to stand in silent admiration and learn whatever they could.

With the mordant finished, Robert once more took pieces of gold and repaired to the workshop. At his sunlit bench, he set out layers of soft calfskin in a pile, placed a small lump of gold on top and covered it with four layers more. Then, after settling himself on a stool, he took up the heavy hammer Brother Mark had made for him by hollowing out the head of an ordinary wooden mallet and filling it with lead. Robert raised the mallet and brought it down solidly on the pile of leather, and so began the work by which the cube of gold would become flattened into a thin sheet.

Robert calculated he would need four such sheets, and when his right arm grew tired, he changed the hammer to his left hand without breaking the steady rhythm. Before long, however, and in spite of many changes of hand, he had to stop and rest. If the mallet were less heavy, the task would be less arduous, but would take much longer. He could not decide which was preferable.

After an hour, Robert saw Brother Julius enter the workshop and make for the forge. He carried an iron cooking pot in one hand and its large U-shaped handle in the other. He darted a sharp glance at Robert, but said nothing to him.

"This must be mended at once," he said to Brother Mark, who was hard at work on a new hinge for the priory's main gate. "It cannot wait."

Robert tried to ignore Julius, but his presence brought an oppressive sense of disquiet.

At length, Robert lifted the top layers of leather and examined the gold beneath. God be praised, it was almost ready. Too thick, and it would show creases when applied. Too thin, and it had a disconcerting habit of simply disappearing when touched, as if dissolving into the very air around it.

Another half an hour's work brought the gold leaf to the right thickness, and he got off his hard stool and gratefully rested his burning muscles. He strained the new mordant into a small clay jar, gathered up the pile of leather with its precious contents, and departed the workshop, leaving Brother Mark at work on the cooking pot with Julius looking on.

After the Office of Sext was celebrated and the midday meal finished, Robert returned to the scriptorium to apply a final and much diluted coat of mordant as an adhesive. Then, with the aid of a small wooden rod, a dry paintbrush and his own gently blown breath, he deftly positioned the finely beaten sheet of gold. He trimmed it meticulously and then sat back, heaving a prodigious sigh of relief. The first of the four layers was finished.

* * * *

So it was that after four months of steady work and unrelenting concentration, the illuminations and text of the gospel of John were finished. The initials, miniatures and geometric patterns were glowing combinations of paint and metal, rich in their display of color and executed with what Brother Adolphus described as *the skill of a master and the inspiration of God.* The blocks of black-lettered text were perfectly squared, the line spacing faultless and there was not a single broken word.

"The manuscript is an unrivaled triumph of the copyist's art," declared Adolphus. "God be thanked we are alive to see it."

Robert, however, saw more in his work than others. He asked himself if he had executed Prior Gottfried's instructions. Was the story told? Would the illuminations reveal the secrets of the scriptorium to those who looked carefully and understood what they saw? The only thing he did not understand was the placing of the tiny crown as Gottfried had instructed, but he asked no question concerning it.

The Gospel According to Saint John and Suffrages to the Blessed Saint was an undoubted masterpiece, but the satisfaction of its completion was overshadowed by profound grief at the death of Prior Gottfried on the feast day of St. Leo, April the nineteenth, 1224.

The beloved old prior was laid to rest in a sealed lead coffin, which was lowered by sorrowful hands into the grave in the Chapel yard while the assembled monks and novices intoned the ancient prayers for the burial of the dead. The priory bell tolled a mournful and solitary knell across the flat countryside, as the solemn Masses were celebrated for the salvation of Gottfried's immortal soul.

As Brother Robert crossed himself and turned with bowed head from the graveside, he felt bereft and alone. The only shaft of light piercing the darkness of his grief was the knowledge that before he died, Prior Gottfried had seen the finished gospel.

As soon as the work was done, the last of the gold applied and polished and the final letters of the text set down, Robert made haste to the prior's small cell. The old man lay open-mouthed and motionless save for his labored breathing. His chest heaved convulsively and the breath rasped and bubbled in his throat.

Three monks and the sacristan stood beside the bed, their heads bowed as they murmured prayers. As Robert begged leave to enter, the sacristan reached down and with his thumb traced a cross on Gottfried's forehead. The only light came from a single candle set in a wall sconce opposite the bed, and the sight and sound of the scene made Robert feel as though he stood already in the presence of death.

The sacristan, his face gray with fatigue after his long and sorrowful vigil, nodded and moved aside so Robert could approach.

"Father Prior," Robert said, kneeling beside the bed. "It is I, Brother Robert. Can you hear me?"

"He is very weak," said Brother Sacristan, almost in a whisper. "Do not tax him overmuch."

Gottfried made no response to Robert's words, and his labored breathing continued as before. Robert repeated his question, and this time there was a flicker of recognition in the dying man's eyes.

"I have brought the gospel, Father," said Robert, tears filling his eyes. "It is finished, and I have done as you asked."

He held the manuscript up and he could see Gottfried recognized what he was looking at. Robert showed him the historiated initials, the miniatures and the designs, and pointed out various particular details including the tiny crown, which he had executed in gold leaf. Gottfried nodded his head, but the movement was almost imperceptible. He took a deep breath and then managed to grasp Robert's wrist. His hand was cold, and the skin felt as thin as split parchment.

"I think he is trying to speak," said one of the monks, and Robert put his ear close to the prior's lips.

"It is well," whispered the old man. "I bless you, my son."

With those words, his face relaxed, he ceased his struggle for breath and died as his fingers slipped from Robert's wrist.

"He blessed me with his dying breath," said Robert, still on his knees. "He blessed me as he was carried to God."

The sacristan placed a gentle hand on Robert's shoulder.

"Go, my son, and pray for the repose of his soul."

The monks prepared the body for burial and, covering it with a linen sheet, placed it on a trestle before the altar in the priory Chapel.

"Our Prior," said the sacristan to Brother Mark as Robert and the other monks observed a solemn vigil, "instructed me that his mortal remains should be sealed in a coffin of lead, and I swore to him it would be so."

"And so it shall be," answered Mark. "I shall attend to it at once."

Robert and Bartholomew were summoned by the sacristan to assist at Gottfried's coffining, but before the lid was set in place, the sacristan turned to the two brothers and showed them an oilcloth packet, folded, tied and heavily sealed with red wax.

"Hear me, both of you," he said. "This was given into my hands many months ago, when the sickness first came upon our blessed prior. I know not what it contains, but it was his solemn charge that I place it with him in his coffin, and that you two bear witness that it remains unopened."

"I so witness," said Bartholomew, and Robert nodded, mystified, but profoundly moved by the solemnity of the occasion.

The sacristan crossed himself and placed the packet in the coffin under the dead man's right hand. The three monks then put the heavy lid into place, and Brother Mark was sent for to seal it shut with molten lead.

Chapter Four

All Saints being a daughter house of the cathedral monastery of Norwich, the Bishop of Norwich was its patron, and so a messenger was dispatched immediately upon the prior's death. The brethren did not anticipate the rider being long away, but he did not return for nearly three weeks. Brother Sacristan voiced concern for his safety, because the king's writ in England did not always run so far as to assure the safety of the highways and byways. At last, however, late in the afternoon of the nineteenth day, the messenger reappeared, the hooves of his sweating mount clattering harshly on the cobblestones of the priory courtyard. Brother James, the priory's chamberlain, and one of the office-holders now in temporary authority over the enclave, hurried forward and chided the young man, asking him where he had been for so long.

"We have been much concerned for your welfare, and your mission."

"The Lord Bishop was not at Norwich, so please you, Brother Chamberlain," answered the young man, sliding wearily from his saddle. "He and a great company of nobles and gentry were gone to Elmham Hall in Suffolk, and I did follow them thence and presented the letter as I was bidden. The Lord Bishop did not make haste to reply."

The chamberlain nodded. He knew the Bishop of Norwich maintained a summer retreat at Elmham, a fine residence built in the middle of a vast hunting preserve. He and his friends would be hunting by day and roistering by night. It was passing miraculous the messenger had seen him at all.

"The Lord Bishop bade me say he will be here in a three-month, for he must leave Elmham soon and return to Norwich for an assembly of the Cathedral Chapter. He must afterwards go to St. Benet's, and then he will come here."

Brother James nodded his understanding once again. The bishop was also abbot of St. Benet's, and in view of the revenue provided him by that office, he could hardly be expected to neglect it in favor of a visit to All Saints, which provided him comparatively little.

"Very well," said Brother James. "Get you to Brother Julius in the kitchens. You will have time for food before Compline."

As the young man led his horse away towards the stables, Brother James hurried to the sacristan with the news, which was later announced to the entire community at a meeting in the Chapter House.

"It is a mercy the bishop comes so soon," said the sacristan to the assembled community.

"Verily," agreed Brother Chamberlain, "and God be praised for it."

St. Benedict's Rule could not be wholly complied with if there was no superior. The brethren were in need of a leader, both spiritual and temporal, and felt adrift and lost without one. The sooner the bishop came to name a successor to Gottfried, the better it would be for all.

Brother Adolphus then rose and suggested Robert's gospel manuscript be displayed in the priory library.

"So wondrous a thing has never been created in England," he declared. "The Lord Bishop must see it."

"Is this not empty vanity, good Brother?" inquired James.

"Nay," answered Adolphus. "It is a glorification of God Himself. I made pilgrimage to Canterbury and Rome when I was a young man, and never did I behold so sublime a thing as this. I stood in the greatest scriptoria in Christendom, but before God I swear I never saw the equal of this work of our good Brother Robert."

As he listened to these words of praise, Brother Julius' bitterness festered like a cankerous sore. It was as if Brother Robert had become the very personification of everything Julius hated about his life as a monk.

Julius had not willingly taken the cowl. His domineering and tyrannical father had brought him to All Saints when he was a mere boy and *given him to God* in hopes of being delivered from an outbreak of a savage contagion that was decimating the local population. His father died of that contagion, notwithstanding his gift to God, and Julius, humiliated, concluded God had deemed him an unworthy offering. He had taken his final vows, although he regarded them as empty words, insubstantial and hollow. He dreamed of simply walking away from the priory, leaving the interminable toil, the stultifying daily routine and the unyielding discipline and regimentation. Three times he had actually tried, but fear of the unknown world beyond the priory walls had prevented him from going. He simply could not bring himself to walk boldly out through the main gate. He loathed himself for his weakness and fear.

Robert never accepted the accolades for himself when his work was praised. Uniformly, he gave God the glory, and always responded in a modest and self-effacing manner. The very piety of his bearing infuriated Julius all the more. It corroded his soul as lye burns the skin.

* * * *

As it transpired, the bishop did not arrive at All Saints for nearly four months, but finally, in early August, an emissary appeared at the priory gate and somewhat peremptorily bade Brother Porter tell the brethren to prepare for the bishop's arrival a week hence.

Immediately galvanized, the community turned to and began making ready. Under the stern supervision of the chamberlain, the best room in the modest guest hall was provided with what few comforts the brethren had to offer: linens and blankets, cushioned chairs and large candles made with heavy wicks to burn both slowly and brightly. Fortunately, the weather was warm and his lordship would not require a fire. Brother Peter, the cellarer, ordered the kitchens be prepared to entertain the visitors, and lists of requirements were drawn up to ensure the bishop and his retinue would have the food they expected. Fresh vegetables were gathered, meats brought in and casks of wine and mead obtained to augment the priory's supplies of plain home-brewed beer.

In order to be assured of sufficient funds for all this preparation, the brethren reluctantly decided—in spite of the hand-wringing pleas of the almoner —that disbursements to the poor of the surrounding countryside must be temporarily suspended.

"It will be but a short time only," said the chamberlain, "and we must show honor to the Lord Bishop."

"Dear Brothers," pleaded the almoner, "the good bishop is a man of God. He will understand that we cannot take bread from the mouths of the poor. He will follow Christ's example, as should we all."

Perhaps the bishop would follow Christ's example, but what

troubled the brethren was the distinct possibility he might not. A bishop took no vows of poverty, after all.

"Do not forget," reasoned the chamberlain, "the Lord Bishop has but lately come from his hunting hall where he doubtless dined on venison and wild boar and drank good wine. Cold mutton and boiled eggs with black beer would not likely be well received."

By the end of the week, all was ready, and on Sunday afternoon the bishop and his vast retinue appeared at All Saints an hour before Vespers.

The priory bell sounded a warning that the Episcopal party was in sight, and the brethren crowded through the gate to watch as the visitors drew near across the marshy flatland.

Were it not for the four heralds riding some ten yards ahead of the troop, bearing the brightly colored standards of the bishop's various ecclesiastical offices, the column might easily have been mistaken for a company of soldiers. All the riders in the procession's van, including the bishop himself, wore chain mail under their surcoats, and carried both dagger and broadsword with a confidence born of knowing how to use them. There were four heavily laden carts, each pulled by a yoke of plodding oxen, and behind them came a group of clerks, pages, squires, sundry other servants and lesser religious functionaries. In all, the company numbered nearly fifty and the good brothers stood aghast.

"God have mercy," wailed the cellarer, "we have not the wherewithal for such a multitude. What are we to do.?"

So great was the general consternation that no one answered at first, but at length the chamberlain spoke above the commotion.

"All is well, my Brothers. I perceive the Lord Bishop and his immediate party will lodge within, but the others will encamp in the fields. Do you see the wagons? They will contain tents, food and necessities, I am sure of it."

"I pray so," said Brother Cuthbert, crossing himself reverently.

Brother James' prediction proved correct. While the bishop and five or six others rode into the courtyard, the remaining members of the retinue turned aside and began to unload the oxcarts in preparation for making camp on the green hillside.

Pandulf, Bishop of Norwich, was a man of over sixty, strongly built with angular features and dark complexion. His long gray hair framed a face with an aquiline nose and deep-set sharp eyes. His voice was accented, for he was Italian by birth and had been sent to England by Pope Innocent III. Not only was he a papal legate and a cardinal, he had also served for a time as regent for the young King Henry III, King John's son, and thus the good bishop wielded much power, both spiritual and temporal.

"God be with you all, good Brothers," he said after dismounting and handing off the reins. "'Tis right glad I am to be here. The day is powerfully hot for traveling."

Brother James, the agreed-upon spokesman, made obeisance, welcomed their distinguished visitors and begged them to take refreshment in the guest hall.

"Aye, that we shall, Brother," the bishop said cheerfully. "That we shall, and our thanks be to you all."

Following a brief rest and a flagon of mead, the bishop celebrated Vespers with the brethren and spoke to Brother James as they left the Chapel.

"Tomorrow we shall apply ourselves to the matter which has brought me here, good Brother. Until then I wish to spend time in preparation and prayer."

Early the next morning, therefore, the chamberlain, sacristan, almoner, cellarer and the other office-holders were summoned into the Episcopal presence and consultations began. It was commonly held throughout All Saints that Brother James would be elevated to superiority, but as Brother Cuthbert observed to Julius and several of the brethren, "If the Lord Bishop has so decided, he is keeping deadly quiet about it."

Judas Iscariot can be our prior for all I care, thought Julius, *so long as Robert is not chosen.*

"Young Brother Robert could be our prior one day," said one of the group, and Julius cringed as Cuthbert nodded.

"Indeed he could. He is a man of great piety and humility."

God grant Robert is never named prior, Julius said to himself as he walked back to the kitchens. *I would rather be dead in purgatory than have to pay respects to that mealy-mouthed buffoon.*

* * * *

In the course of making his decision, Bishop Pandulf availed himself of the opportunity to study the priory's accounts, and for all his bluff cheerfulness, he showed himself a shrewd administrator. It behooved everyone he questioned to have correct answers swiftly delivered if they hoped to avoid a sharp rebuke.

It was in obedience to an instruction from the cellarer, therefore, who sought to satisfy the bishop's curiosity concerning broken kitchen implements that Brother Julius hastened to the workshop late one evening in search of the blacksmith. He stopped abruptly just inside the doorway as he saw not Brother Mark, but Brother Robert's black-habited figure bending over a fire basket preparing sizing fluid. Standing in the dimly lit workshop, Julius stared unblinking at Robert's back and loathing soured his mouth like an astringent herb.

I wish he were dead, he thought, clenching his teeth. *I would be rid of the pusillanimous little popinjay once and for all.*

Julius glanced about him and, seeing no one, moved softly to a workbench against the wall to his right. He picked up the hammer made for beating gold and felt a malevolent satisfaction at the weight of it in his hand. The half-darkness in the workshop gave Julius a feeling of security; a sense that he and Robert were alone in all the world and not even God Himself could see them.

He moved forward.

At that moment, Robert straightened his back and turned to face him, standing not three paces away.

"What is it, Brother?" Robert asked in surprise. "Is all well?"

"Is all well?" sneered Julius. "All is well with *you*, is it not? Gottfried saved his dying breath to bless *you*; everyone praises *your* work. *You* sit here at your ease boiling your stinking fish bones while I am sent chasing hither and yon to find bent spoons and broken pans."

"Good Brother," began Robert, "I beg you to believe—"

"And now," Julius interrupted, "I have heard you spoken of for prior."

"Prior?" Robert laughed. "Me? Surely you jest, Brother Julius."

"Don't you dare laugh at me," Julius shouted, seizing Robert's habit at the throat. "Get you to hell, you prating fool, and laugh at Satan if you can."

With a snarl of rage, Julius brought the hammer crashing down on Robert's head with all the strength he could command. The thunderbolt blow split Robert's skull from temple to crown and he fell dead onto the stone floor.

Breathing heavily, Julius stood over the inert form, staring down at the dead man's face, and he recoiled as he suddenly imagined he saw forgiveness in Robert's lifeless eyes. Horrified for a moment, Julius stepped back, and then hurled the hammer into a corner.

"I've finished with you," he exulted under his breath, "you and your forgiveness. I'm rid of you. Can you hold a paintbrush now, my fine sanctimonious friend?"

Julius looked about him again, but nothing stirred. He kicked the fire basket over and sent the pot of steaming sizing spilling across the floor. He watched as the hot coals slid and skittered over the stone flags, setting fire to sawdust and wood shavings. He turned and ran from the workshop, darting into the shadowy darkness in a corner of the cloisters and crouching behind a stone bench.

Stay silent, he told himself. *You have not been seen.*

For a short time, there was no sound, but then came an urgent shout. "Help ho! Fire! The workshop is afire!"

Chapter Five

When Julius heard the cries for help, his first impulse was to leave his hiding place and run towards the workshop as if in answer, but at once he checked himself. Arriving first might lead to questions about how he came to be so near and yet did not see the fire himself. Instead, he remained where he was until several of the brethren had rushed by, clamoring for buckets and a chain of men to be formed from the well. Merging into the crowd, Julius joined the chain and passed along wooden buckets filled to overflowing. As the empty buckets were sent back, they were dropped into the deep well, hauled up and sent on their way once again.

The alarms and tumult had aroused the soldiers and other members of the Episcopal retinue camped outside the walls. They rushed to join the fight.

After what seemed an eternity of buckets and water, a soldier took Julius' place in the chain and told him to rest for a time. Julius was exhausted, but ran to the burning workshop, desperate to know what was happening.

When he reached the scene of the fire, Julius was confronted by a vision from hell: flames filled the building; choking smoke billowed and churned in the twisting air. All was shouting and frenzy.

"For the love of God, keep it from the thatch," someone shouted, "or we may not be able to contain it."

As though in defiance of its enemies, the fire licked upwards and found the thick layers of sedge, igniting them with a crackling roar of triumph. Brother Mark, with a furious roar of his own, flung a ladder against the wall and almost leapt up it with a heavy bucketful of water. He hurled it over the burning thatch, and was quickly supplied with another, which he emptied the same way. The fire hissed its anger, and from his perch atop the ladder, Mark waged grim warfare with the remorseless flames. At one point, he left the ladder entirely and clambered onto the roof itself to beat back the fire with a wet sack, which had been thrown up to him. He bellowed at the devouring flames from out of the smoke and din. He swung the heavy sacking and struck at the burning thatch again and again, sending up clouds of glittering, ephemeral sparks.

"Down with you," he roared. "Down I say. In Christ's name, get you back."

The harsh orange glare of the flames cast leaping shadows across the ground and onto the walls of nearby buildings, as gradually the toiling monks and soldiers gained control. By about midnight, a halt was called, and the tired men stood and watched while the last embers were doused by a couple of the stronger young novices. Brother Mark descended to the ground and swung his arms to and fro to ease his aching joints and sinews.

"I did not know a man could climb up to hell," he quipped with a grin, his teeth white against his smoke-blackened face.

"God be praised," said Bishop Pandulf, who had done his share of work that night. "Methinks we have won."

"Aye, My Lord," said a soldier, his face begrimed and streaked with sweat, "but 'twas a close thing, withal."

There were murmurs of agreement from one or two about him, but the rest simply nodded, too exhausted to speak.

About half the roof had been saved. The stone walls were intact and the fire had been prevented from spreading, but the interior of the workshop was a black and smoldering ruin.

They have not found Robert, thought Julius with relief, *and when they do, they will believe him dead of the fire.*

By the time the fire was well and truly overcome, it was long past the hour for Matins, and Brother Mark turned to Bishop Pandulf.

"Well, 'tis safe enough now, I warrant. I shall venture inside and see if aught can be salvaged from my forge, although I do very much doubt it."

I could get away, Julius thought, fear tightening his throat, *but how to escape from this crowd?*

He began to edge away, but it was too late.

"God's mercy," called Mark from inside the fire-ravaged building, "there is a dead man here."

There was consternation immediately. A gasp of horror went up from the company as Mark reappeared carrying the charred corpse, its limbs stick-like where the flesh had been burned from the bones.

A hurdle was quickly brought from the sheepfold, and the monks carried the unrecognizable body to the Chapel where it was soon identified by a simple process of elimination.

"It is our good Brother Robert," said Adolphus, tears in his eyes. "He told me this afternoon he would go to the workshop to make sizing after Compline."

"The fire has exacted revenge for its defeat after all," said Brother Cuthbert, crossing himself.

"Not so," replied Bishop Pandulf, as he ended his examination of the body. "Not so, my Brothers. The fire did not take good Brother Robert. He died by the hand of man. His skull is well-nigh cloven in twain, and I declare before you all murder has been done here this night."

* * * *

Brother Julius went with his brethren to bed in the priory's dortoir, and lay in his small cell, rigid with terror. He thought of fleeing, but the Captain of the Episcopal Guard, William de Beaulieu, had posted sentries at every gate. The walls of his narrow cell seemed to close in on him, as if the very stones condemned him and sought to prevent his escape.

Later that morning, Lord Pandulf, in full ecclesiastical regalia with miter, gold-headed crosier and richly embroidered vestments, summoned all the brothers, novices and lay members of the enclave to the chapter house. Julius sat with his brethren, feeling monstrously conspicuous—as if his guilt were proclaimed upon a sign around his neck. He fought down the panic that rose within him as his thoughts raced in turmoil. *No one can possibly know*, he told himself again and again. *Had I been seen, I would have been denounced long since. I must simply be silent, and all this will pass.*

"God saw you," said a voice within him, and Julius suppressed a shudder.

"Hear me," said the bishop, and silence fell like a stone. "Robert, our brother in Christ, has been most foully murdered, and I declare

40

before you all there shall be no rest until the guilty one is revealed. Look about you. Is anyone absent?"

Heads turned this way and that, but no one spoke. Julius' heart hammered as if to break his ribs and he found it difficult to breathe.

Be still, he told himself. *Be still.*

William de Beaulieu entered the chapter house and made obeisance.

"Your report?" said Pandulf.

"Every gate remains closed and guarded, My Lord," said Beaulieu, "and there is no one within the priory walls save we here."

The bishop nodded.

"All those who encamp outside the walls are accounted for," continued Beaulieu, "and were within their tents until the alarm was raised for the fire, but I know naught of your own servants, My Lord."

"They were all with me between Compline and the time the fire was discovered" said Pandulf. "You have my oath upon it, before God."

Beaulieu made a small bow of acknowledgement.

"And was Robert seen at Compline?" Pandulf asked.

"Aye," said Brother Bartholomew. "He stood next to me."

"Then the culprit is one of these, My Lord," Beaulieu said, indicating the seated assembly.

"How is the mind to encompass such a thing?" said Pandulf. "So mighty and terrible a sin committed here, in God's community."

No one spoke. Julius strove to keep his face expressionless as cold terror gripped him still tighter.

"Stand at the door," said Pandulf, and Beaulieu, a large red crusader's cross on the front of his long white surcoat, walked across the chapter house and took up his position.

"My Brothers," said the bishop, his voice firm and clear in the small hall. "You have all heard. He who committed this vile sin against God and man, is here amongst us and must be found—rooted out, if need be—and punished. God sees the soul of he who is guilty and knows him by name, but we must seek him out in other ways."

He paused and regarded them all again with a penetrating gaze. Beaulieu shifted his sword belt as if to remind the brethren that he guarded the only way out.

"Let the guilty man come forth," shouted Pandulf, standing and raising his arms. "I charge you before God and all the Holy Saints, in the pure name of the Mother of God and in the name of her Blessed Son. Reveal yourself."

It was as if everyone had ceased even to breathe. No one made a sound, but Julius heard the voice within him once again: small and quiet.

"He speaks to you," it said. "He speaks to you."

"Confess," Pandulf thundered.

God preserve me, Julius prayed, and then cringed at his own effrontery. He had committed murder. Would God deliver him from punishment?

Terror overwhelmed Julius as water overwhelms a drowning man. He could not remain still. He could not remain silent. Spinning helplessly in a whirlwind of panic, he sprang to his feet.

"My Lord," he blurted in an impassioned voice, "it is Brother Julius who speaks. Forgive me, but none here could have done this dreadful thing. Brother Robert was beloved of us all. Surely it must have been some foul villain from elsewhere, for none here wished Robert harm."

"None Brother?" came the voice of Bartholomew. "Do you, of all of us, truly believe that?"

"I do believe it," said Julius, whirling to face Bartholomew.

"Then I fear you speak hypocrisy."

There was an immediate stirring amongst those present, and excited chatter broke out, but Julius spoke above the rising noise in a tone of injured indignation.

"What are you saying, Brother Bartholomew? I loved Brother Robert as truly as any here, and—"

"Hypocrisy," shouted Bartholomew, rising to his feet, the better to be heard. "Hypocrisy and lies!"

Julius stared open-mouthed at Bartholomew as the agitated talk died away.

"Many times I told Prior Gottfried, may he rest in the arms of God, what I had seen of your detestation and envy of Brother Robert," Bartholomew said, his voice filling the silence like a trumpet in Julius' ears. "I made note of it in my own writings as well. There are many here who knew of your hatred of Brother Robert."

Julius saw several heads nodding, and desperation seized him as if by the throat.

"Do you say I killed him?" he shouted.

Deny, Julius told himself. *You must deny all.*

"I do not say it," replied Bartholomew. "Only God sees the soul of a man. I say only that you did not love him as you claim. I call you a liar, not a murderer."

"It is you who lie," shouted Julius, "I—"

"Silence," snapped Pandulf, striking the table with the flat of his hand. "This is not a fairground. Stand before me, both of you."

The two black-habited monks left their places and moved forward to stand before the bishop's table, Bartholomew red-faced with anger and Julius pale and shaking.

Pandulf sat down, and addressed Bartholomew.

"Brother, do you make an accusation here, or merely point out a circumstance?"

"I accuse Brother Julius of nothing save hypocrisy and a lie."

"On what evidence do you rest your words?"

"The evidence of my eyes and ears."

"Then it is naught but hearsay."

"I spoke of it several times to the late prior, and he was much troubled."

"That may be true," said the bishop, "but it proves nothing. The blessed Gottfried is taken from us and cannot corroborate your words."

Julius felt his panic lessen.

"That is true, Lord Bishop," said Julius. "Prior Gottfried is dead, and I suppose Brother Bartholomew will say I killed him with a hammer also."

"A hammer, my son?" said the bishop. "What do you mean? How do you know Brother Robert was struck with a hammer?"

Panic rose once again as Julius searched for an answer.

"Well…what else could it have been?"

"Any number of things," said the bishop, and then his voice sharpened and his eyes narrowed. "Come now, Brother Julius. Do you know something of this affair which the rest of us do not?"

"I swear before God I do not, My Lord," said Julius, perjuring his immortal soul once again in his desperation. "Our dear Brother was murdered in the workshop, and thus to say *hammer* was but a manner of speech."

"God marks well the soul of a sinner," said the voice within Julius.

The bishop regarded Brother Julius steadily.

"Were you anywhere near the workshop when the fire broke out, Brother?"

Deny.

"No, My Lord," replied Julius. "I had no cause to go there."

The lie had scarce left his lips before Julius cursed himself for his blind stupidity.

"Not so," came the rather high-pitched and querulous voice of the elderly cellarer. "I sent you to the workshop myself to seek out tools from the kitchen which were to be repaired by Brother Mark. My Lord Bishop will recall inquiring after them."

"I do recall it," said Pandulf, nodding. "What say you to this, Brother Julius?"

Damn the old fool. Damn them all.

"I forgot," muttered Julius, barely above a whisper. "I did go, as Brother Cellarer says."

"You said you did not go, and now you say you did. You said you had no cause, and now we hear you were sent. You seem somewhat over-forgetful, my son."

"The night itself was a confusing and difficult time, my Lord Bishop," Julius said in a self-deprecating tone. "There are many things I may have forgotten."

"Well do you remember seeing Brother Robert in the workshop, then?" asked the bishop.

"Yes, and I left him alive…"

"And where did you go after leaving the workshop?"

"I was in the courtyard when I heard the alarm, and I made haste to help."

"Nay," said a monk from amongst the seated spectators. "I saw you running from the cloisters."

"As did I," shouted another.

"And I," echoed a third.

"The courtyard, the cloisters, what does it matter?" snapped Julius.

"I tell you I was nowhere near the workshop when the fire started."

"Your memory fails yet again, I fear," said Pandulf as if he were speaking to an errant child. "You do not know if you were in the courtyard or the cloisters, but wherever it was, you seem to be certain you were not near the workshop. Are you sure you were not there when the fire started?"

"Yes," stammered Julius. "I…I entered the workshop and saw Brother Robert boiling his sizing. And," he added, on a thoughtless impulse, "the hammer was on the shelf. I swear I did not touch it."

"Once again this hammer, my son?" asked Pandulf, as calmly as if he were asking for a goblet of wine.

"I mean…" Julius struggled for words, all eyes upon him.

"Yes, my son?" said Pandulf. "Speak. We are all listening with great interest."

Bartholomew's cold eyes pierced him as though to see into his very soul. The bishop's calm face seemed to swim before him, moving in and out of focus. The silence in the hall reverberated in his ears like the sound of a mighty waterfall.

With an explosive movement, Julius leapt past Bartholomew and raced for the door where William de Beaulieu stood. The bishop sprang to his feet shouting a warning, his chair tipping over behind him and banging onto the wooden floor of the dais. Two or three monks attempted to seize Julius' habit, but he wrenched himself free and pushed by. He was able to take only three more strides before William drew back his arm with studied deliberation and, stepping into Julius' path, struck him full in the face with his fist. Julius uttered a shriek of pain and shock, and covered his face with his hands. He staggered backward a few paces before collapsing onto the flagstone floor, blood spewing from his shattered nose.

* * * *

And so it was that Brother Julius departed All Saints three days later chained to an oxcart, his face bruised and swollen, to be conveyed to Norwich. Before leaving, the bishop proclaimed Brother James as prior, and his investiture was sanctified by a short and solemn ceremony in which James was declared by God's grace and the authority of the bishop to be *the first amongst these brothers in Christ here assembled; their lord and their servant, both.* A sense of order and familiar routine began slowly to supplant the upheaval and turmoil of the previous few days, and the brethren prayed such things would never be seen again within the precincts of their community.

Early on the morning of Pandulf's departure, Prior James and Brother Adolphus paid their respects and begged him to take Brother Robert's gospel manuscript to Norwich.

"It should go where it may gladden as many hearts as possible," said the new prior, "and do the greatest honor to the memory of Brother Robert and his Divine gifts. We humbly ask that you have it bound and placed in the cathedral."

After the two monks had gone, the bishop studied the manuscript they had left with him and sat enthralled by its beauty. *In very soothe*, he thought, *I have never before seen so miraculous and precious an object.*

He reached the final page and saw, at the bottom, Brother Robert had added a colophon, a short paragraph of his own, as many scribes were wont to do as a benediction, and had signed his name to it.

But, although the beauty of the work astounded him; as the bishop continued to study the illuminations, he became increasingly puzzled. A number of them towards the end were not what he would have expected. There were fewer representations of sacred and scriptural subjects than usual, and more scenes of a secular nature, of daily life and mundane, routine activities. The oddities were not many or glaring, may not even be noticed by most observers, but they were there nonetheless. And here was a tiny crown in gold, the symbol of temporal power. What message had Robert been attempting to convey? Why this strange departure from that which is normally seen? The bishop stroked the bridge of his nose thoughtfully for several minutes, but eventually gave a slight shake of his head and put the matter out of his mind. *It is enough to concentrate upon the glory of this work,* he concluded. *These small peculiarities do not truly signify.*

* * * *

Upon arrival at Norwich, Julius was taken in charge by the sheriff and an ecclesiastical court convened in the cathedral chapter two weeks thereafter. Julius vehemently protested his innocence, and made several vain attempts at prevarications and lies, but as the guilty verdict was pronounced upon him, he broke down and shrieked his hatred of Robert for all to hear.

At the order of the sheriff, and sanctioned as fit punishment by the bishop, Julius was locked, standing, in a narrow iron cage, and the cage suspended high above the market square against a buttress of the cathedral wall.

"If you be innocent," said the sheriff to Julius as the cage was locked, "our Lord will sustain you. But if you be guilty, you shall surely die."

The townsfolk railed upon Julius, calling him a godless murderer, and street urchins threw stones up at his solitary prison as thirst and hunger carried him inexorably towards death. At the end, he pleaded for forgiveness and begged God to take pity on him.

"God's will be done," said the good citizens amongst themselves when Julius at last fell silent. "So perishes a sinner."

As custom required, the cage remained where it was, and a dozen or more sharp-beaked black crows descended upon the corpse and tore at it for several days in a frenzy of beating wings and raucous cries. Julius' body soon became little more than a skeleton clothed in the tattered remnants of his black habit with the cowl over his grinning, empty-eyed skull.

Chapter Six

The Gospel According to St. John and Suffrages to the Blessed Saint was bound in heavy leather, studded and embossed with gold, and placed in the library of Norwich Cathedral where it was chained to its shelf alongside a number of other books, all similarly secured. Monks, priests and many other clerics and pious folk made visits to read it and marvel at the beauty of the text and its illuminations. The fame of the great book and its maker quickly spread far beyond Norwich, and soon Brother Robert became known as *Robert the Illuminator.* The Priory of All Saints was celebrated as the one-time home of that gifted man of God.

But the book began to acquire another, wholly unexpected, reputation: one that ultimately superseded the fame of its artistic grandeur.

Barely a year after its placement in Norwich, rumors began to circulate that all was not well with the great book. These dark tales stemmed from a story concerning a certain Brother Harold, an elderly monk who journeyed from the great Benedictine Abbey of St. Peter and St. Paul in Shrewsbury to view the wondrous work.

"It was well past dark, My Lord," Harold told the bishop in a querulous voice, "and I had but a single candle for light. I was alone, yet all at once, I was overtaken by an irresistible certainty that someone else was there in the library with me. It was a feeling much akin to a chill draught, or some sense of movement that I could not place or explain."

"And what then?" asked Pandulf.

"I cannot tell," Harold said, perplexed. "I know not how to convey it. I turned to see if perchance a door had come ajar, but all was as it had been before. Anon, however, by my troth, I saw something move. A black figure, as it were a monk with his cowl over his head. I called to him. I asked him who he was. And then, of a sudden, he, or it, was gone. The doors neither opened nor closed and the figure made neither sound nor sign. It seemed insubstantial. There, and yet not there. I have never seen its like before, and I pray I never shall again."

Bishop Pandulf listened intently and studied Brother Harold as he spoke. The old monk was obviously not given to hysterics. He was known to be a devout and temperate man of learning who, the bishop reminded himself, had come all the way from Shrewsbury to see the gospel; a long and dangerous journey, to be sure. His story had to be seriously considered, and yet it was hard to credit.

"You are quite sure of this, my son?" he asked. "It is a strange and troubling tale."

Brother Harold paused for a few moments, and Pandulf saw from the gravity of his expression he was measuring his words with care.

"I will swear upon the Holy Rood that I saw something, My Lord Bishop. But, alas, I cannot say with certainty what it was. Perhaps it was nothing. A shadow. A trick of the candlelight. And yet..." Brother Harold chewed his lower lip in thought for a moment and then simply shook his head.

The story flew as if with wings throughout the cathedral precincts and soon everyone, clergy and laity alike, was agog with fascination and fear.

"By the nails of the cross," said Pandulf to Beaulieu one evening as they sat in the withdrawing room of the bishop's well-appointed residence, "are we now to believe in ghosts and legions of hobgoblins? Do the spirits of dead monks rise to torment the living? We do not even properly know what Brother Harold saw in the first place."

"But could it not be," Beaulieu asked, "that indeed there is something amiss? After all, two men closely associated with the book are dead by unnatural means."

The bishop regarded him for a moment before replying.

"Just so, good William, and both those spirits may still be seeking repose. I do not deny there may be truth here, but let us not tremble like children cowering in their beds over what one elderly monk thinks he might have seen in a dark room by candlelight."

* * * *

For some months after Harold's experience, there were frequent sightings of the hooded black figure—always in the library at night and always it came and went without a sound. Eventually, fear of the apparition was so pervasive and powerful no one would enter the library at all once evening had come, and Brother Robert's masterpiece became universally known as *The Haunted Gospel*. Men still came to view it, but now it was as much for its supernatural attributes as for its artistic merit, and although after some eighteen months the glimpses of the wraithlike specter ceased, the book's notoriety did not diminish. On the contrary, it grew steadily and was much enhanced when, six years after its last visitation, the black figure appeared again. This time outside the library.

A priest of Norwich, known simply as Father Paul, one among the bishop's large body of supernumerary clerics, was found one evening, two hours after Compline, sprawled on the steps of the cathedral altar. The parchments he had been carrying were strewn about him on the stone floor, and the unfortunate young man was carried, insensible, to the infirmary. Upon returning to consciousness, he was fortified by a mixture of wine and honey prepared for him by the apothecary, and then questioned as to what had happened.

"I must speak to the bishop," was all he would say.

Accordingly, the young priest was summoned into the presence of Bishop Thomas de Blundeville and William de Beaulieu. The blessed Pandulf had been gathered unto God five years before in 1226, but Beaulieu served his successor no less faithfully.

"Now," said the bishop to Father Paul, "speak. What has befallen?"

"Were you attacked, Father?" put in Beaulieu.

"My Lords," blurted Paul, "I saw it. The figure of the black monk. He who is spoken of. The spirit of the haunted book."

Beaulieu and the bishop quickly crossed themselves.

"Go on," instructed the bishop.

"As I approached the altar," Paul began, fear filling his eyes at the mere recollection, "I looked up and there it was, over against the left side of the table."

"And what was it, exactly?" asked the bishop. "Describe it for us."

"A black monk, his cowl over his head. He turned and looked at me, but there was no face beneath the cowl. Only an empty blackness. Horrible, My Lords. Most horrible of sights."

Paul dissolved into near panic and the bishop, seeing he could tell them nothing more, dismissed him.

"Go, good Father," said Blundeville, making the sign of the cross in blessing. "Go in peace and do not be afraid."

"There has been no mention of this specter for years," said the bishop after Father Paul had gone, "and now it is suddenly here again and at the altar itself."

"I like this not at all," said Beaulieu, crossing himself again. "I prefer to fight an enemy I can see plainly."

"Calm yourself," said the bishop, "and let us think upon this as serious men. There was but little light in the cathedral, and a draught could have disturbed the hangings at the altar. Father Paul could have seen anything. Do not underestimate the power of suggestion or the creative abilities of a frightened imagination, much less a combination of the two."

Beaulieu nodded; his face still troubled.

"Nevertheless," said the bishop in a brisker tone, "something must be done. The townsfolk will hear of this visitation, or whatever it was, and when they do, tongues will wag. There will be much ado and general worriment. An exorcism may comfort the fearful for a time, but if this wandering spirit, if such it be, has truly been denied a place in heaven, I'll warrant an exorcism will not banish it for long."

"And so?" prompted Beaulieu.

"I think there may be another way," said the bishop, stroking his dark beard thoughtfully. "Another, and a better way."

The following morning, therefore, after a night of prayerful vigil, Bishop Blundeville sat down at his writing table and, taking up a raven's quill pen, began to write on a sheet of new vellum. The letter was not long, but he took much care over it and worked slowly. Then, summoning a clerk, he watched as the young man folded the letter and took up a ladle from its holder above a low flame. He tipped the ladle and poured a vivid pool of red sealing wax onto the vellum's edge so it could not be opened. Then, grasping his Episcopal seal and pressing it firmly into the wax, the bishop issued instructions for the immediate dispatch of the letter and what was to accompany it.

There, he thought as the clerk departed, *if this vaporous being be somehow bound to the book, then peradventure it will follow where the book leads.*

* * * *

And so it was that three months later, in a well-furnished private room in the papal apartments in the Vatican, His Holiness Pope Gregory IX looked upon the gift he had received from England and pronounced himself well-pleased.

"It is a noble work," he said to the assistant librarian, Father Bernard. "It is most wondrously wrought."

"With respect, Holiness," said Father Bernard, "I am told in private by the man who carried this book hither, that all is not harmonious concerning it."

"Indeed?" inquired His Holiness, with raised eyebrows. "How so?"

"He who made it was murdered by one of his own Benedictine brethren, who was himself then condemned and starved. And since that time, so it is said, restless spirits have visited the places where this book has rested."

"So," said Gregory with a slow nod, "let me see the letter from the good Bishop of Norwich once again."

Father Bernard handed over the letter, which had accompanied the book, and Gregory studied it before looking up.

"I see now the import of these words," he said, and read aloud, "*I pray this work and all connected with it may now find peace.*"

Pope Gregory considered the book before him on a large wooden table. He studied it, opened it to a number of different pages, the parchment leaves and thick leather binding creaking as he did so.

"Did you notice, Father Bernard, the illuminations towards the end of the book?"

"I have not seen them, Holiness."

"They are of a most fascinating character. Different from anything I have ever seen. Quite extraordinary."

Gregory studied the pages for a few moments longer.

"Yes, I shall accept this gift. If aught appears amiss, we shall investigate and act as God dictates, but until such time, if such time should ever come, the volume will be placed in our library. If God's peace be truly needed, surely it can be found there."

He ordered a letter of thanks to be prepared for the Bishop of Norwich.

"And also," he added, raising an admonitory forefinger, "prepare a letter of instruction to the librarian that this book be placed openly for all to see and read. If restless spirits do indeed attend it, let us know it plainly."

PART TWO
England: The Present Day

Chapter Seven

At ten o'clock on a late December Sunday morning, George Oliver Randall, Professor of Ecclesiastical History at St. Arthur University, Yorkshire, sat at his kitchen table reading the newspaper. He had eaten a light breakfast—since turning fifty the previous month he had become more conscious of his weight—and had just poured himself a second cup of coffee prior to doing battle with the crossword puzzle, when he heard the double-toned chime of his front doorbell.

"Who on earth…?" he said aloud, and letting the paper drop onto the table, went through to the hall.

"All right," he shouted as the bell sounded again, "I'm coming. Keep your wig on, whoever you are."

He reached the door and, taking a quick look through the side window, saw two men in dark suits standing in the porch. He ran his fingers through his rather unruly sandy-colored hair and opened the door.

"Yes?"

The older of the two visitors, a man of about forty-five, held up an identity card in a leather folder.

"Dr. George Randall?"

"Yes."

"Detective Inspector Thomas, St. Arthur Newtown CID. This is Detective Sergeant Joyce. We'd like a word, please."

"What about?"

"If we could just come inside, Dr. Randall?" said Thomas, his face expressionless.

"All right, if you must," answered Randall, mystified.

He led the way into the front room and invited the two policemen to be seated.

"What can I do for you?" he said. "The long arm of the law seldom comes calling on a Sunday morning. In fact, it never comes calling at any time."

"Are you acquainted with Dr. Michael Stuart?" asked Thomas.

"Yes, I am. Why?"

"Dr. Stuart was murdered sometime last night, sir," answered Thomas, his voice devoid of emotion, "and in order to eliminate you from our inquiries, I'd like to ask you some questions."

Randall heard nothing beyond the first sentence. He simply stared at Thomas, thunderstruck.

"But…" he stammered, "that's not possible. There must be a mistake, surely."

Some small part of his brain that continued to function more or less normally told him it was an asinine thing to say, but it was all he could manage.

"There's no mistake, sir," said Sergeant Joyce, a good-looking, square-jawed young man in his early thirties. "I'm sorry."

"But, hang it all," said Randall, still trying to grasp what he was being told, "I had dinner with him last night. I was there 'til gone ten o'clock, and he was very much alive when I left, I assure you."

"We'll make sure that forms part of your statement, sir," said Thomas, in a voice as smooth as polished marble, and equally as cold.

"My statement?" Randall blurted. "What are you on about? Are you saying *I* murdered him?"

"If, as you say, you were at dinner with him last night, sir," said Joyce, "then you're one of the last people to have seen Dr. Stuart alive. That doesn't make you a suspect in and of itself, of course, but for the time being you're a person of interest to us as I'm sure you can understand."

"Yes, but I…"

"We realize this has come as a shock," Joyce continued, "but it's very possible you can help us with our investigation."

Joyce's tone was less officious and more reasonable than that of his superior, and it brought Randall back down to earth. He took a deep breath and collected himself.

"Of course," he said. "I'll do whatever I can."

"Thank you, sir," said Thomas. "Now, how well did you know Dr. Stuart?"

"We're…we were…very close friends," said Randall, "and we

were colleagues for over twenty years."

With Joyce taking notes, Thomas questioned and cross-questioned Randall, beginning with details of the previous evening's dinner party.

"How many were present?"

"Four, plus Mike...Dr. Stuart."

"What did you talk about?"

"University matters, politics, that sort of thing, nothing earth-shattering."

"Has he ever mentioned anyone with whom he was having any sort of trouble or disagreement?"

"Not that I can remember."

"Is it possible he was engaged in some research or other investigation that could have brought him into conflict with anyone?"

"He specialized in the military history of the late medieval period, for heaven's sake; the weaponry in particular. I can't see that leading to anything, can you? Any secrets he might have uncovered wouldn't matter much now."

"Was he liked by his colleagues and students?"

"Yes, he was very popular."

"Has he ever been known to commit indiscretions with any of his female students, or his male ones, come to that?"

"Absolutely *not*."

"Was Dr. Stuart his usual self last night?" Thomas finished, after twenty minutes of questioning. "He didn't seem worried or distracted at all?"

"No," said Randall, "he was fine. In fact..." He paused for a moment.

"Yes?"

"Well," said Randall, "when I think about it now, I'd have to say he was more cheerful and animated than I'd seen him for some time."

"Did you ask him about that, sir?" said Sergeant Joyce.

"No, I didn't actually."

"So you can think of no one who might want Professor Stuart dead?"

"No, I most certainly can't," answered Randall. "And that's the absolute truth."

"Think carefully, please, sir," said Joyce, his voice sounding like a velvet glove after Thomas' mailed fist. "Anything you can think of might prove to be very important at this stage."

"Look," said Randall, beginning to feel a trifle exasperated, "I've answered your questions as straightforwardly as I can. You've come here and told me one of my closest friends has been murdered and I'm having a good deal of difficulty getting my head around that."

Randall jumped as the doorbell pealed again.

"I'll go," said Joyce, getting quickly to his feet and leaving the room.

Randall heard the door open and immediately recognized his daughter's voice. A moment later, a slender young woman entered the sitting room and crossed to him without so much as a glance at DI Thomas. She was not quite as tall as Randall's six feet, with shoulder-length fair hair, an oval face and wide-set brown eyes. Randall stood to meet her and she put her arms around his neck.

"Meg," he said. "You've heard then?"

"On the news," she said, her face still buried in his shoulder. "It can't be true."

"I'm afraid it is," Randall said, feeling her hot tears dampen his shirt. "These gentlemen are from the police."

"I can't believe it," she sobbed. "I won't believe it. It's awful."

"I'm so sorry, love," he said, giving her his handkerchief. "I know it's beyond comprehension, but there it is."

Thomas cleared his throat, and Randall turned.

"This is my daughter, Megan. Meg, Detective Inspector Thomas, Detective Sergeant Joyce."

"How long have you known Dr. Stuart, Miss Randall?" asked Thomas, his voice still as flat as a clock's face, and Megan looked at him blankly for a moment.

"Since I was a child," she answered, sniffing.

"And may I ask you to account for your whereabouts last night?"

"I was at the theater with friends," she said, dabbing her eyes with the handkerchief. "We went for drinks afterwards."

"May I have a name please? For corroboration."

"Er…Samantha Forest. She lives in York."

"That's enough I think, Inspector," said Randall, putting a protective arm around Megan's shoulders. "My daughter and I will be available for any further questions you may have in due course, but in the meantime we'd be very grateful if you'd leave us."

"You must understand—" Thomas began, but Randall interrupted.

"Good day, gentlemen."

Thomas hesitated a moment and then, turning to Joyce, jerked his head in the direction of the front hall.

"It's all right, sir," said Joyce as Randall started forward, "we'll see ourselves out. And please let us know if either of you plan to leave this area."

Joyce followed Thomas into the hall. A moment later Randall heard the front door close.

He and Megan sat together on the sofa and he put his arm around her shoulders again. At thirty years of age, Megan was the most precious person in Randall's life. Seeing her in such distress made his heart ache.

"Who on earth would want to hurt Mike?" she asked, turning her tear-stained face to him.

"God only knows, Meg."

"It's horrible," she said, wiping her eyes again.

"What's the media saying about it?" Randall asked. "I haven't had the radio or the television on."

"Well, just that he'd been found dead this morning and the police are treating it as a homicide, which is hardly surprising. Apparently, he was found by Mrs. What's-her-name, you know, his housekeeper, when she arrived to make his breakfast at about seven this morning. They interviewed her although she was pretty distraught. She said she knew something was wrong because the front door was closed but not locked. She found Mike lying in the hall. He'd been hit on the head but they don't know what with. His shirt was torn but there were no other signs of a struggle or of forced entry so, according to the news report, the inference is that he probably knew his attacker."

"Was anything taken?"

"They said nothing appeared to be missing, and Mike still had money on him."

"Dear God," breathed Randall.

Megan shook her head and sniffed.

"It doesn't make sense," said Randall. "I mean, someone walks into his house, kills him and then clears off without touching or taking anything? Whoever it was must have been after *something.*"

* * * *

Arriving on campus the next morning, Randall found the university in a state of shocked disbelief and deep sadness. As he threaded his way through the curious crowds milling about in the quadrangle, students and faculty bombarded him with questions, as though his close friendship with Michael Stuart somehow rendered him privy to inside information. He told everyone he could add nothing to what was being reported in the media, and finally reached the sanctuary of his office.

He sat down in front of his computer, and after opening an email folder headed *Mike Misc.* he found and read the message he wanted.

September 8th.
What ho, George:
Ever heard of a thing called the "Haunted Gospel?" I came across a reference to it in a Vatican document of 1356—a library inventory to be precise—and thought it sounded intriguing. Any ideas?
Cheers,
Mike

Randall had never heard of it, but he remembered Stuart telling him he thought he might try to track it down.

"How did you come to find the reference in the first place?" asked Randall.

"Oh," said Stuart in an offhand tone, "I was just following up on some stuff connected with Norwich Cathedral."

"Bit out of your line, isn't it?" grinned Randall. "You're usually more interested in armies and weapons, slaughter, mayhem, rape and pillage and other cheerful things of that ilk."

"Indeed," Stuart grinned back, "but this'll be a spare time effort. It just sounds interesting, that's all. I mean, why would a document be called *The Haunted Gospel*? Sounds rather mysterious don't you think?"

Over the ensuing weeks, Randall asked about the search once or twice, but Stuart said he'd had no time, and eventually the subject passed into oblivion until the end of the dinner party the night Stuart was killed.

"I've started to nose around a bit for that haunted gospel thingamabob," Stuart said as Randall put on his overcoat. "Haven't had much luck so far, though."

As he reread the message and recalled those conversations, Randall felt as if he somehow owed Stuart the completion of his quest. He resolved to begin the research and see if he could find the manuscript himself.

Randall was not a great religious believer–more of a skeptic than anything else–but even so, he was reluctant to accept dying meant the end of everything. In a somewhat vague sense, therefore, he hoped Michael Stuart would see what he was doing and be pleased.

"I'll do my best, old chum," he said under his breath. "I'll find it for you if I can."

DI Thomas' question of the previous morning drifted back into his consciousness: *could Dr. Stuart's research have brought him into conflict with anyone?*

Well, Randall said to himself, *if Mike was into anything dangerous, which is highly unlikely, it's not going to be a five-hundred-year-old gospel manuscript, now is it?*

Chapter Eight

The police investigation of the murder went exactly nowhere. Exhaustive forensic examinations at Stuart's house yielded no useful information, none of the neighbors had seen or heard anything, and Detective Sergeant Joyce confided to Randall that there were simply no tangible leads. Coordinated by Randall, Stuart's colleagues and friends clubbed together to offer a reward for information leading to an arrest, but that, too, proved fruitless. DI Thomas sent Joyce to question Megan, interviewed Randall again himself, and after checking alibis, confirmed they were both eliminated from the inquiry. Thomas immediately ceased all communications, but Joyce promised to keep them up to date. Randall was soon to discover the reason for the young man's interest in staying in touch.

The regular routine of the university was quickly reestablished, and at a faculty meeting three weeks after Stuart's memorial service, Dean Maxwell Thoroughgood tactfully broached the subject of a replacement.

"We must think of the students," he finished.

"Here endeth the earthly record of Michael Stuart B.A., M.A., Ph.D.," said Randall under his breath. "Murdered by a person or persons unknown, and soon to be replaced by someone as yet unidentified. Amen. Poor old Mike."

After a selection committee had been established, Thoroughgood, a moon-faced, rotund man of sixty, went on to inform the meeting that the university's Board of Governors was prepared to consider proposals for the creation of a permanent memorial to Stuart, and in that concept Randall saw an opportunity. He caught up with the dean in the corridor as the meeting ended.

"I've had an idea about something that could be done for Mike."

"Good," said the dean. "What are you thinking?"

"Well, it's not really a memorial in the sense of a plaque or a statue or anything like that," said Randall.

"Fine," said Thoroughgood. "Plaques and statues are out as far as I'm concerned anyway. No one ever reads the one, and the pigeons ruin the other."

"Exactly," said Randall, "but I think anyone who knew Mike would approve of my idea."

"Go on."

"Well," said Randall, "Mike had no family and I think everyone would agree I am...I was...his closest friend."

"The point, George?" nodded Thoroughgood.

"I was wondering what was to be done with Mike's papers. I mean all his office stuff and the material in his study at home. I know he left all his books to our library, but his will made no mention of his personal papers."

"Quite correct," said the dean. "And so...?"

"And so I was thinking that if someone went through his notes and so on, there might be enough material for a publication—sort of a posthumous recognition of his work, if you see what I mean. It wouldn't necessarily have to be long; it could just be the completion of some ongoing research or something like that."

"You know, George," said the dean, "that's a damn good thought. You're volunteering, I take it?"

"Naturally. I'm not a military historian, but I'm sure I can get help and advice from specialists if I need it."

"Have you any preliminary ideas?" asked Thoroughgood as they crossed the quad. "I mean, do you know of anything in particular he had on the go?"

"Yes, actually I do. Mike had come across a manuscript in the Vatican Library inventory of 1356 called *The Haunted Gospel,* and he became very intrigued by it. Said he wanted to find out what it was. I don't know if that will lead to anything concrete, but it's something to keep in mind. A place to begin, anyway."

The dean beamed his approval, his cherubic face fairly shining with pleasure.

"Well, I've never heard of anything called a *Haunted Gospel* myself, but I must say I'm very grateful to you for making this suggestion, George. I'll steer it by the vice-chancellor and the governors at their next meeting, and then see about letting you into Michael's office. There'll be a lot of stuff to go through and pack up, you know. All the files from his study at home have been moved into his office, as well, so the trustees of his estate can get on with selling his house."

"I don't mind the work," said Randall. "It's something I really want to do."

"I quite understand," said the dean. "This has been a tough time for all of us."

"And by the way," said Randall, "what about Mike's computers? Home and office."

"Ah, yes," said Thoroughgood. "The police took them both and set their forensic people to work on them. I'm told they got into all his files and even recovered a lot of deleted material as well. Don't ask me how. Both computers are now clean as a whistle; the one back at home for the trustees to deal with, and the other returned to us."

"But what about all his files?"

"Not to worry. They put everything onto disc," said Thoroughgood. "All his documents, emails, Internet history, the whole shooting match. Apparently there was nothing on either machine to help with the investigation."

"That's a pity, but can I get hold of those discs?"

"Of course. I'll send them along once your scheme is cleared."

"Thanks, Max."

"Oh, and you'd better put your proposal on paper, George," said Thoroughgood as he turned into his office. "The dear old governors don't think anything's important unless it's written down."

* * * *

A month later, Randall, assisted by Megan, began the job of packing up Michael Stuart's office. Armed with cardboard boxes and rolls of packing tape, they worked their way through his eight filing cabinets and the drawers of his desk. They filled box after box and carried them out to Megan's van.

After several hours work, they drove to Randall's house and deposited the cargo in the garage beside the pile of boxes from Stuart's study already packed by the trustees.

"My God, love," Randall wheezed as he surveyed the two piles of boxes, "It'll take forever to get through this lot."

"Poor you," smiled Megan. "I think if Mike knew what you were up to, he'd be having a good laugh about now."

"He knows," said Randall. "At least I truly hope he does."

Megan kissed her father's cheek.

"You miss him a lot, don't you?" she said, meeting his gaze from the depths of her expressive brown eyes.

Randall nodded, but said nothing. *Dear, perceptive Megan,* he thought. He smiled at his daughter, and thought again what a lovely young woman she had become. She was not flashy glamorous or Hollywood glitzy, she simply possessed the serene loveliness born of inward grace and gentleness of spirit. She had suitors by the cartload, but none of them ever seemed to last. *Perhaps,* he reflected, *that's partly because in addition to her loveliness she's highly intelligent and knows what she wants in life.*

Their moving work done, they went to dinner at a small Italian restaurant they both enjoyed and where they were well known. Their dinner conversation was pleasant, but Randall's thoughts kept returning to the boxes in his garage. Now that all his other possessions had been collected up, given away or sold, Michael Stuart's life was represented by, or reduced to, the contents of those cardboard cartons. They contained his life's work, and Randall was anxious to begin searching through the papers and files to isolate those that might hold promise in the search for *The Haunted Gospel.*

"Thanks for your help today, Meg," he said. "I'm grateful you were with me."

Megan smiled and patted his hand, but then he saw her expression cloud.

"I still can't believe it, you know," she said. "That Mike's gone."

"I know what you mean," said Randall. "I keep expecting him to come strolling into the office at lunchtime the way he used to. I can still hear him. *What ho, George. Victuals?"*

"How goes the work on the discs from Mike's computers?" Megan asked.

"I'm going through everything," said Randall. "It's tedious as hell, but I'm nearly finished. It's all routine stuff though. Bureaucratic bumf, administrivia, memos, reports, a lot of grant applications, that sort of thing. Mike wasn't big on computers really, at least not when it came to serious writing. He did that the old-fashioned way, by hand, if you can believe it. I haven't found anything to help me get a line on *The Haunted Gospel.*"

"That's disappointing."

"There's still nothing from the police," said Randall. "What the deuce are they doing, do you suppose?"

"I'll ask Tony for an update," she said, and Randall raised his eyebrows.

"Tony? Who's Tony, when he's at home?"

"Tony Joyce. You know, the detective sergeant."

"And how, pray tell," said Randall, "has he become Tony instead of Sergeant Joyce?"

"Er…well," said Megan, "when he called to tell me my alibi had checked out and I was off the hook, so to speak, he invited me to dinner."

"Did he now?"

"We've been out a couple of times, that's all. Nothing major."

"Well good for you," said Randall, "Joyce is a nice young chap."

Megan responded with a smile Randall could only describe as secretive.

* * * *

As it transpired, Randall's estimate of the amount of free time he would have proved overly optimistic, and it was not until late summer that he was able to make a solid start on Stuart's papers. In the spring, he had managed to take the obvious first step of contacting the Vatican to see if anything called *The Haunted Gospel* was currently listed in the library or archives, and the answer came back that there was nothing. The terse response also contained the information that a similar request had been received from a Professor Stuart at Randall's university.

On the last Saturday in July, therefore, he finally took the first box from the garage and carried it into his back garden where he had set up a chair and table in the shade of a gnarled and ancient apple tree, now heavy with the bounty of a warm and pleasant summer. The air was luxuriously soft and laden with the scent of lilies, roses and buddleias, all products of Randall's care and attention. Birds sang a brilliant chorus all about him and a cuckoo added its ethereal call from a copse of beech trees in a field beyond the high garden wall. Randall loved his garden and was a dedicated rose enthusiast. He reveled in the sights and sounds as the warm summer sun bathed all in brightness.

He stripped the tape off the box, the rasping sound temporarily silencing the birdsong, and began to study the first file he extracted: an unremarkable brown office folder marked *Agincourt,* which held nothing more than odd jottings, a couple of diagrams and a page of references.

He shuffled and skimmed his way through four boxes that day, but found no references to the gospel. The following Saturday he began again—inside this time, due to heavy rain—and in the second box of the morning came across a folder labeled *Document 2: All Saints Priory.*

He opened the folder and discovered only two sheets of paper. One was frayed at the top from having been torn from a spring-bound notepad and had only two things written on it: the date *1216*, and the words *King John letter authentic.*

What letter? Randall wondered. *From King John? To King John? About King John? What's its connection to All Saints, and is All Saints connected to the gospel? And whatever this letter is, why does it need authenticating?*

The second piece of paper offered no clues to the meaning of the first, only heightening Randall's mystification as he read the short sentence.

Ask George about Norwich and All Saints Priory. Vatican inventory: TNG (The Haunted Gospel, THG, only in 1356).

Chapter Nine

The weekend following Randall's discovery of file number two, Megan came round. They drank a glass of wine together in his front room as the afternoon sun sent aureate bars of light gliding through the windows. Randall's Scots terrier, William Wallace, lay snoring gently in a warm patch of sunshine on the carpet.

"Did Mike ever ask about Norwich or All Saints Priory?" Megan asked. "And what's all that other stuff about?"

"I haven't a clue," Randall answered. "He never asked me anything about Norwich or All Saints, and I don't know what he means by *only in 1356*. I've no idea what *TNG* stands for either. I've looked up everything I can think of that might apply, but I can't find anything that makes sense."

"Well then, what's special about the year 1216, apart from being the year after Magna Carta was signed?"

"Could be any number of things," Randall answered, "but Lord knows what Mike meant by it."

"We're stuck then," said Megan.

"In more ways than one, actually. That file was titled *Document 2*, and I went through all the boxes looking for document or file number one. Took me half the night, but there was no such file anywhere. Of course, there could be all sorts of explanations for it not being there, but it just strikes me as odd. Mike was meticulous in his research, so since there's a number two, I'll lay odds there has to be a number one out there somewhere."

"We know conventional robbery wasn't the motive for Mike's murder," Megan said, "but Tony says there's no sure way of telling if non-conventional things like letters or photographs were lifted. What if the killer took file number one? Who'd ever know?"

"No one," Randall agreed, "but who'd be interested in it anyway, unless they were searching for the gospel?"

"Exactly," Megan nodded, a serious expression clouding her brown eyes. "Assuming file number one *was* taken, and assuming it contained information on the gospel, it could be that someone thought that information valuable enough to kill for. This may be no ordinary manuscript you're looking for."

"Good point," said Randall.

"Maybe you should be a bit careful, Pop."

"Now hang on, love," he said. "Let's not get too carried away. For one thing, we don't actually know file one was taken, and for another, it's hard to imagine that an old manuscript could be as important as all that."

"Perhaps," Megan said, frowning slightly, "but I'll mention it to Tony anyway."

"You and Tony still an item, then?"

"I'm not sure we were ever an *item*, as you so quaintly put it," she said, "but we do see each other now and again."

"Just wondered," Randall said. "And speaking of Tony, are the police making any headway, do you know?"

"Well, there is something as a matter of fact," Megan said, "strictly on the q-t, you understand. They know what the murder weapon was."

"Where did they find it?" asked Randall.

"They haven't exactly found it, unfortunately, but when the trustees doing Mike's will were closing down his house and sorting out the furniture and so on, Mike's housekeeper finally got round to noticing the poker was missing and was able to describe the shape of it quite well. The pathologist confirmed that was almost certainly it."

"Cracked on the head with a poker," sighed Randall. "Poor old Mike."

"I know," said Megan. "It's an awful thought."

"Not a lot of help if they can't find it, though," said Randall.

"No," said Megan, "but getting back to the files…what is, or was, All Saints Priory?"

"A small Benedictine enclave in southern Lincolnshire. Nothing left of it now. It was flattened by Henry VIII and his commissioners. Not that it was worth much to him."

"Why would Mike be interested in it?" Megan asked, and Randall shook his head.

"No idea, Meg. It certainly had no military significance. Anyway,

Mike apparently found some sort of connection between it and *The Haunted Gospel.*"

"Well, what's King John got to do with All Saints then, and do you know what the *King John letter* refers to?"

"No, but stay tuned," said Randall. "I'll let you know if I find out."

* * * *

Later that evening, Randall went to his study and logged on to a subscription-only site which allowed him to search for ecclesiastical documents in a large number of separate archives, libraries, museums and private collections all over the world. He worked for several hours, and then each evening for the next week, but found no reference to *The Haunted Gospel* or anything similar apart from the 1356 entry at the Vatican.

Over the following weeks, he searched for a connection between King John and All Saints Priory, and came up empty there as well. He could find no mention of All Saints in any documents associated with King John, and no reference to any letter—extant or otherwise—that might link John to the priory.

I'm stymied, he thought, as he sat back in the capacious leather chair at the desk in his study. He lit his pipe—he always found it an aid to serious thought—and continued his contemplation as the study filled with aromatic blue smoke—aromatic to his nose at any rate. Megan said his pipe smelled like burning compost.

He ultimately decided to examine ecclesiastical records at Norwich dating from the reign of King John, and so the following day he secured a meeting with Max Thoroughgood in the dean's well-appointed office.

"So, George," said the dean, after the customary tea and biscuits had been brought in, "how goes the work on Mike's papers?"

"That's what I wanted to talk to you about," said Randall. "I've searched Mike's files but I can only find a passing mention of the manuscript I told you about. It's all very obscure."

"Ah yes," said the dean. "*The Bewitched Gospel* or something, wasn't it?"

"*The Haunted Gospel,* actually," Randall grinned. "I found a note in the files which hints at a connection between the gospel and Norwich —presumably the cathedral or the monastery. I want to nip down to Norwich and have a look through their archives and so on."

The dean's round face registered mild surprise, but he agreed to the proposal, and promised to clear it with the vice-chancellor.

"Good luck with it, George," he added.

Returning to his own office, Randall found a student awaiting him in a chair outside the door. The young man was tall and muscular, wearing jeans and a light windbreaker. He carried a leather folder and got to his feet as Randall approached.

"Dr. Randall?"

"Yes?"

"My name's John Archer, sir. I was wondering if I could speak to you for a moment. It won't take long."

"What can I do for you, Mr. Archer?" Randall asked when they were seated in the office.

"I'm in my second year," Archer began, "and I was in two of Dr. Stuart's tutorials. I'm aiming at a degree in military history, you see, but it's going to take me several years. Can't afford to study full time, I'm afraid."

"Frankly," Randall said, "to judge from your age, I wouldn't have said you were an undergraduate."

"No, Dr. Randall, you're right. I'm twenty-eight actually, but it took me some time to discover that I wanted to go to university. Seven years as a bricklayer finally convinced me."

Randall laughed.

"That'll do it every time. Anyway, Mr. Archer, I take it you're concerned about your studies now Dr. Stuart has…gone. Please don't worry. Transition arrangements have been made so your studies shouldn't be disrupted any further than they have been up to now."

"Oh, no, sir," said Archer at once, "that's not it at all. The university's been really good about everything since Dr. Stuart was… since Dr. Stuart died. No, you see, I thought a great deal of Professor Stuart—we all did—and I'm very interested in the kind of history he taught. He told me a few months ago that he'd like to look for a certain document. He called it *The Haunted Gospel,* and I offered to help. You know, literature searches, Web research, that sort of thing. I really wanted to find out about the document. I mean…with a name like that…."

Randall nodded.

"I know what you mean. Go on."

Archer paused for a moment.

"Well, with respect, Dr. Randall, the gossip on campus is that you've got all Professor Stuart's papers and so I'm wondering if by any chance you're going to take up the search. I hope you don't mind me asking."

"Not at all, and as a matter of fact I am, John," said Randall, warming to the earnest young man. "Your appearance is very timely. Dr. Stuart told me about the gospel as well, and I'm off to Norwich in a fortnight to try to pick up its trail."

Archer leaned forward in his chair, excitement showing on his face.

"That's brilliant," he said. "If there's anything I can do to help, sir, please let me know. It's like finishing a project Dr. Stuart started. In his name, as it were."

"My feelings exactly, John," said Randall with a smile, "and that's how the university views it as well. Thank you very much indeed for your offer of help, and I'll bear it in mind.

"Thank you, sir," said Archer as he rose to go. "I really admired Dr. Stuart, you know. He was inspiring and his knowledge of military history was incredible, and…."

Archer's voice trailed off, and Randall was touched by the young man's sincerity.

"Thanks, John," he said again, "and I'm glad to hear of your interest in history. It's been my lifelong passion."

Chapter Ten

As Archer had said, word of Randall's work on Stuart's behalf had spread across campus, and he was kept busy by a steady stream of inquirers wanting to know what the project was and how he planned to find the manuscript. He promised to keep people posted on his progress and two weeks later, he set out for Norwich.

He made a leisurely drive of it, keeping to the back roads and stopping frequently. He covered the distance in a day-and-a-half, arriving at his hotel on a warm afternoon in late August. He checked in and after dinner in the small restaurant, he called Megan.

"I almost didn't get here," he told her. "Nearly got run off the road by an imbecile in a minivan."

"Are you all right?"

"I'm fine, love," he said. "It was a little hair-raising, that's all. He came up behind me out of nowhere and cut me off as he overtook. I had to swerve and throw out all the anchors, but it was okay."

"Did you get his number?"

"No. I was too busy trying to stay on the road."

"Take the train next time."

"You'd have thought he did it on purpose," he said. "I'd have the bugger arrested and flogged."

"I don't think they do that anymore, do they?" Megan giggled. "Anyway, you're not hurt, and that's all that matters."

Randall spent the balance of the evening immersed in a spy novel. He seldom had time for recreational reading, but when he did, he enjoyed a bit of good espionage.

He was no stranger to Norwich, having done some research there a few years before. He was very familiar with the cathedral archives and felt pleased to be back when he arrived there the next morning. The archivist he had known previously had retired, and his replacement, whose name proved to be Donald Crowley, was about thirty years old, had somewhat unruly fair hair and displayed an easy-going affability.

"Anything in particular I can help you with, Dr. Randall?"

"Well, actually, I'm trying to get a line on a document called *The Haunted Gospel.* Ever heard of such a thing?"

"Never," said Crowley. "Where did it come from? Do you know anything about its provenience?"

"I know nothing more than a confirmation that it was in the Vatican archives in the mid-fourteenth century, and it's not there now. Some research done by a colleague of mine just before his death suggests a possible link to King John, and there might also be a connection to Norwich Cathedral or All Saints Priory, but at this stage, I don't really know."

"So it was created in England and somehow found its way to Rome, is that it?"

"I'm not even sure of that," said Randall.

"An interesting little problem," mused Crowley. "Let's see what we can do."

After a detailed catalog search with Crowley's help, Randall selected a dozen or so documents and books and settled himself at a small reading desk. He worked his way steadily through the material, but it offered nothing. He did find two letters from Bishop Pandulf written in 1216, but they dealt with mundane matters associated with repairs to Elmham Hall, and sundry other details of an administrative nature. He also found three papal missives to Pandulf regarding King John's dispute with the Holy See, but none of them proved useful either.

He did come across an intriguing piece of writing by one Wulfram of Norwich who described himself as a *Chronicler of the Many Travails of King John*, in which there was a single-sentence reference to Sir Gilbert Fitzhugh, one of King John's staunchest allies, and with whom Randall was very familiar. According to the chronicler—and this was new information to Randall—Sir Gilbert was sent by the king *to carry forth divers precious goods to another place.* The goods were not described, nor did Wulfram say where they were taken, so Randall paid it no particular attention beyond a passing interest.

Over the next few days, Randall, with Crowley's diligent assistance, moved forward from 1216, year by year. He made lists of possible leads, followed them up and checked sources. It was a slog, but it fascinated him. He found such searches exciting, and always learned a great deal from them. It was the thrill of the chase. He felt like a hunter, and when the quarry eluded him, it only heightened his determination.

By the end of the week, he had acquired nothing from his search beyond a sheaf of notes and a rather stiff neck. He took a break for the weekend, drove out of the city and went for long walks through broad fields and sunlit woods to clear his head. On Monday morning, he started once again and had, by that time, arrived at the year 1224. About three in the afternoon, he came upon a letter to Bishop Pandulf containing a marginal note that it had been delivered to Elmham Hall by special messenger. The letter told of the death of Gottfried, Superior of the Benedictine Priory of All Saints, and Randall happened to mention it to Donald Crowley that evening at dinner. He had struck up a friendship with the pleasant young librarian, and they often dined together. On this particular occasion, they were in a friendly little pub called The Saracen, busily engaged in the consumption of steak and kidney pudding and pints of stout.

"Oh yes," said Crowley. "All Saints. Home of Robert the Illuminator."

"Who?"

"A thirteenth century copyist," Crowley said. "He was a Brother of All Saints; very gifted, and particularly good at gold and silver work. There's a manuscript of his at Canterbury, one of Paul's epistles, and a couple of smaller items in the British Museum, I think."

"Interesting," said Randall, and then grinned at Crowley. "I wonder if he created *The Haunted Gospel.*"

"I doubt it," said Crowley. "He died at a very early age and I've never heard of anything he did being in Rome."

"But if Robert's work was so fine," said Randall, "it's not beyond the bounds of possibility that something could have got to the Vatican. Manuscripts did move about a lot."

"Yes, they certainly did," Crowley agreed.

"It's only speculation, of course," said Randall, after downing the last of his drink, "but speculation's about all I've got these days."

"That reminds me of something I wanted to ask you, George," said Crowley. "Michael Stuart never came here that I know of. He's not in the records. Never contacted us with requests for material or anything else. In fact, the only other person interested in the thirteenth century and All Saints was here almost a year ago. A bloke from the University of Surrey. So how the hell did Dr. Stuart get the leads you found in his file?"

"I haven't a clue," said Randall. "I can only suppose whatever research he did was carried out elsewhere or along other lines. Michael was a first class historian and might well have come at this problem in an entirely different way."

"Okay," said Crowley, "fair enough. Then did he have any more information you can use?"

"Well, that's the thing of it you see," Randall answered. "I don't actually know how much information he really did have. Remember I told you it looked as if he had two files, but I could only find the second one."

"And nothing on his computer?"

"Nope."

Crowley shook his head in mystification.

"I think about all I can do for now," said Randall, "is find out all I can about All Saints Priory in the thirteenth century. I've been concentrating on Norwich up to now and found nothing, so I'm going to investigate All Saints instead and see if I have better luck."

He spent a further week combing through many documents, but without significant result. There was mention of the priory in various letters and account books, but it was all within the context of the priory's administrative relationship to the cathedral monastery, and shed little light on the priory itself. There was a passing reference to the murder trial in September, 1224, of a Brother of All Saints named Julius and his subsequent execution, but there was no indication of whom Brother Julius had killed beyond the statement that it was *one of his brethren*.

There must be more information somewhere, Randall mused. *This is all too incomplete. Even the smallest enclaves almost always had someone who kept records of what went on. Surely there must have been a person doing that at All Saints. But if such a record was made and if it still survives, it's certainly not here. So the next place to look is the British Library.*

* * * *

At the end of the week, Randall and Crowley made arrangements to meet for dinner at The Saracen before Randall left for home. He arrived on time, but Crowley was uncharacteristically late. As he sat waiting, his mobile phone produced its customized electronic representation of the *William Tell Overture,* and upon answering, he heard Crowley's voice.

"George? Sorry to keep you waiting like this, but my mother's arrived unexpectedly from London, and I'm at the station to meet her. Is it okay if I bring her along to dinner?"

"By all means, Donald."

Twenty minutes later, Randall was introduced to Donald's mother, a slim, elegant woman in her early fifties with dark hair, a winning smile and fathomless hazel eyes that caught and held Randall's attention from the moment he saw her. He thought her one of the most attractive women he had seen in many a long year.

"Please call me George, Mrs. Crowley," he said. "Professor Randall is far too stodgy."

"And so is Mrs. Crowley," she retorted with a smile. "My name is Katherine."

"There have been great queens of that name," he said.

"Yes," she answered with a bright laugh, "and one or two of them came to a bad end."

"That's true, I'm afraid," he agreed with a rueful grin, "but thank you for not reminding me there was a king named George who went round the twist."

"Perish the thought," she said.

The evening's conversation continued in a lively vein, and Randall enjoyed Katherine's company immensely. He discovered she was an accountant and financial advisor who had founded the company where she worked, and had been divorced for several years. She was thoughtful, articulate and very knowledgeable. He paid no attention to the time until just after ten o'clock when Katherine unsuccessfully attempted to stifle a yawn.

"It's been a marvelous evening," she said, "but what with the train journey, the wine and all this good food, I'm afraid I'm fading fast."

"Of course," said Randall. "I'm sorry. We shouldn't have kept you so late."

"Not at all, George," she smiled, giving him her hand as she and Crowley prepared to go. "It's been wonderful. Really it has."

"Do you have a next step in the gospel hunt, George?" Crowley asked.

"Oh yes, I meant to tell you. I checked with the British Library and apparently they've got quite a bit of material on All Saints, so I think I'll give that a shot."

"Excellent," Crowley enthused. "That might be just the ticket."

"Will you be coming up to London soon, then?" asked Katherine.

"Yes, I expect so," answered Randall, holding her light summer coat for her to slip into. "I'd like to have a look at that stuff. Might I get in touch with you when I come?"

"Of course," she said, and retrieved a business card from her purse. "I shall look forward to it."

"One more thing," Crowley said. "There was a phone call for you at the library just before I left this afternoon, but when I said you weren't there, he just hung up without another word."

"That's odd," said Randall. "My daughter knows I'm here, and a number of my colleagues, but in either case they'd have left a message or called my mobile phone if it was urgent."

"It wasn't a woman," said Crowley, "but that's all I can tell you."

Not wishing to inject a discordant note into the evening, Randall passed the incident off with a shrug, but it puzzled him nevertheless.

Relaxing in his hotel room later, puffing contentedly on his pipe, Randall's thoughts were drawn irresistibly to Katherine Crowley. Since the death of his wife, Randall had never so much as looked with interest at another woman. Jennifer would forever be within his heart and soul, an indivisible portion of his very being, but he could not deny that in recent years he had experienced an increasing need for closer companionship and emotional support. As he sat by himself in his small room, a profound sense of loneliness engulfed him. He took Katherine's card from his shirt pocket and read it again.

Katherine M. Crowley, FACCA

Senior Partner
Crowley, Hamilton and Hove
Accountants and Financial Advisors

A lovely woman, he said to himself. *Very lovely indeed.*

* * * *

Randall spoke to Max Thoroughgood as soon as he returned to campus, and explained how things had gone in Norwich, and why he now had to go to the British Library.

"Perhaps ten days, Max, maybe less. Depends on what I find."

"You're dead keen on this business, aren't you?" remarked the dean.

"I'd like to see it through, yes," Randall said. "For Mike's sake."

"Speaking of which," said Thoroughgood, "the police are still scoreless, you know. There seems to be no evidence, no motive, no nothing. They're stuck."

"I know. It's damned frustrating."

"Now then, I almost forgot," said Thoroughgood. "Some chap called me wanting to know when you were due back from Norwich. When I asked his name, he hung up straight away. Wasn't overly polite about it either."

"Don't know anything about it," said Randall. "Happened in Norwich as well."

The two telephone calls retreated from his mind as for the next few weeks Randall concentrated on clearing away paperwork, rescheduling his tutorials to allow for his absence and making other preparations to depart for London. By the time he was ready, he had forgotten the calls altogether, but many months later he would say those unexplained and seemingly innocuous phone calls heralded the beginning of a difficult and dangerous chain of events unlike anything he had ever experienced.

He and Megan dined together at their accustomed Italian restaurant the evening before his departure, and over the cassata and cappuccino, he broached the subject of the unproductive police investigation.

"They're doing the best they can, Pop," she said. "Tony isn't happy with it either. There just isn't anything to go on at the moment. When they have something, Tony will let us know. I wish there was more they could do, but they're only human after all."

"What?" said Randall, raising his eyebrows. "The police? Human? I didn't think that was possible. Isn't there an act of parliament or something that says they aren't allowed to be?"

Megan glowered at him in mock anger.

"How are you and the good sergeant getting on, by the way?" he asked.

"Mind your own business," she said in a mischievous tone of voice.

"I think you like him," Randall teased.

Megan paused, and then flashed him a quick smile.

"I think I do too."

Early the following morning, Randall carried his small suitcase out to the waiting taxi, which took him to the station. It was a cool morning in autumn and his breath clouded a little as he stood waiting for the train. Two platforms over, a northbound express on its nonstop way to Edinburgh hurtled through the station in a blur of color and shiny metal, shaking the very ground. It disappeared, leaving behind it a churning turbulence in the thin mist, its thunderous sound seeming to hang, reverberate, in the air long after it had gone.

During the journey south, he reread parts of a book on thirteenth century ecclesiastical history, written three years before by a friend of his at Oxford. He refreshed his memory, not that it needed much refreshing, on the role of the English Church in the baronial wars with King John, the signing of Magna Carta, and the conflict between John and the Vatican.

He dozed a little, and when he awoke, he found the train rolling slowly into King's Cross. Outside the station, in the hurly-burly of London noise, streaming crowds and motor-driven pandemonium, he hailed a taxi and went to the Bestwycke Hotel, his habitual place of lodging. He wanted to call Katherine immediately, just to hear her voice, but was reluctant to disturb her at work. Mastering his impatience, therefore, he waited until after dinner before dialing her home number.

"Katherine, it's George."

"Hello, George," she said, the warmth in her voice lifting his heart, "it's lovely to hear you."

"I hope everything's still okay for tomorrow evening."

"Of course. I'm looking forward to it."

"So am I, Katherine," he said.

So am I, he repeated to himself as he hung up.

The next morning he walked the short distance up Euston Road to the British Library, turned left across the forecourt and went in at the main entrance. He presented his credentials, was informed that his place had been reserved as requested and the documents he was interested in would be brought to him forthwith. The archivist was a somewhat obsequious little man who fussed and bustled about and was full of *Yes sir, No sir,* and *How nice to see you again, sir,* and although Randall was not a man who liked bowing and scraping, he found this officious functionary rather entertaining.

When the documents were delivered, he was astonished at both their number and size. Although it had been a small community, All Saints had apparently contributed a good deal to posterity.

As he settled down at the desk in the small cubicle, the archivist reminded him in a most fastidious manner that he must always wear the white cotton gloves provided whenever he handled original parchments.

"It's the oils in the skin, you see, sir. I hate to bother you about it, but those are the rules and we wouldn't want to damage the documents or break the rules, now would we, sir?"

"Certainly not," said Randall, with suitable gravity as he stifled a grin.

"There's just one more thing," said the archivist. "There is another manuscript I'm sure you'd be interested in, but it's unavailable at the moment, I'm afraid."

"Well, next time, perhaps," said Randall, thinking he already had more than enough to be going on with.

"If there's nothing further you need, I'll leave you now, Professor," said the archivist, and bustled away leaving Randall alone in the tiny room with its temperature and humidity controlled ventilation and special lighting.

"Thank you," said Randall as the door closed and then, turning his mind to the task before him, he began to work his way systematically through the material on the desk before him.

By lunchtime, he had familiarized himself with the documents and organized them sequentially. After a quick sandwich at a nearby coffee shop, he was back by one o'clock and going through the ten or so recent publications that touched on All Saints Priory in one context or another. None of them were useful to him, and only one volume, a grindingly tedious tome on thirteenth century techniques of manuscript illumination, mentioned Brother Robert, saying: *Although his known works are only small in size, they are enough to demonstrate the magnitude of his artistic gifts. His work stands apart from that of his contemporaries by virtue of its boldness of color, its uniqueness of design and, above all, its brilliant mastery of the use of gold leaf and silver. In these skills Robert achieved a perfection of execution unrivaled before or since.* There was no mention of a gospel, haunted or otherwise, but reference was made to the rumored existence of larger works by Brother Robert, although their whereabouts were unknown.

Larger works, Randall said to himself. *I wonder.*

As he threaded his way along the crowded sidewalk on his way back to the Bestwycke in the late afternoon, he thought about the forthcoming dinner date with Katherine, and discovered he was actually a trifle nervous. He was desperately anxious for the evening to be a success.

Don't you dare make a pig's ear of this, he instructed himself.

At about ten to seven he went down to the foyer and very shortly saw the gold-liveried doorman pull open one of the ponderous glass front doors to admit Katherine. He went across to meet her as she came towards him, smiling.

"It's wonderful to see you again, Katherine," he said, presenting her with a single, long-stemmed red rose he had bought on the way back from the library.

"Oh, George," she said, "what a lovely thought. It's exquisite."

She leaned forward and kissed him quickly on the cheek and he smiled at her, feeling ridiculously happy.

He had reserved a table in a quiet corner of the Bestwycke's restaurant, and he ordered a good wine when they were seated. Katherine looked even lovelier than he remembered.

The evening proved to be most enjoyable. Their conversation deepened steadily until they were sharing their most personal feelings and convictions. The subdued lighting and elegant surroundings heightened the sense of intimacy and made the exchange of confidences seem easy and natural.

"Can I ask how your wife died, George?" she asked.

He put his wine glass down.

"Traffic accident," he said. "Ten years ago now. She was on her way to York and was hit head-on by a lorry. Driver had fallen asleep at the wheel. He wasn't badly hurt, but Jennifer was killed instantly."

Katherine reached out and took his hand in a simple gesture of empathy and understanding, which moved him profoundly.

"I simply can't imagine how you felt. It must have been hideous."

"It was that all right. I dreamed about it and about her every night for months. If it hadn't been for Megan I would have gone mad in very short order. And all the while she was supporting me she was dealing with her own grief all by herself. I didn't understand that until much later. I owe her more than I can ever repay."

He had very seldom spoken about Jennifer's death, but it seemed good and right to tell Katherine. It brought him a kind of release, almost a cleansing of spirit, which he found difficult to describe. In the ensuing months, he would come to regard this conversation as pivotal both in his relationship with Katherine and in providing a sense of closure he had not experienced before. He knew he owed his survival to Megan, but to Katherine he owed his liberation.

"And you told me you were divorced," he said. "Can you tell me about that, or is it too difficult?"

"No," she said, "it's fine. Sort of ancient history now, I suppose. My ex-husband, Gareth, apparently wanted a change of scene. He just up and walked out six years ago. Here today and gone tomorrow, as you might say. Or, more precisely, here this morning and gone this afternoon. I can still hear his voice. He got up from the breakfast table and picked up his briefcase the way he always did, but instead of giving me a kiss and saying 'See you this evening,' he dispensed with the kiss and said, 'I'm leaving you Katherine. I'm moving in with Judy Tremaine. I want to get started on a divorce as soon as possible.'"

"Good God," said Randall. "The bas…." He broke off, outraged but unsure of exactly what to say.

"Bastard is perfectly fine," said Katherine, with a bleak smile. "I called him lots worse at the time."

"And I suppose this woman is half his age?"

"Slightly over half, actually. She was his personal assistant, believe it or not, and they'd been having an affair for three years before he left. Sounds like a soap opera doesn't it?"

Randall merely shook his head in disbelief.

"She's very well constructed, mind you," Katherine added, in a pragmatic tone of voice, "if you like them top-heavy."

"I'm so sorry, Katherine," he said. "That sort of behavior is utterly beyond my understanding. I think it's the very height of arrogant selfishness. I'm old-fashioned enough to believe in marriage, and I see it as a commitment. I know there can be many reasons for ending a marriage, but cheating is heinous as far as I'm concerned."

"Well," she said, "he and Judy never did marry; they just live together."

"So no commitment," said Randall, and Katherine shrugged.

"Who can tell? They're still together, that's all I know. I'm a believer in marriage as well, and I thought Gareth was, but apparently not."

They talked until half-past ten, when Katherine declared she really must go. Her coat was retrieved, the doorman hailed her a taxi and she was lost to Randall's sight in the swirling, noisy turbulence of cars, headlights and red double-decker buses. He stood at the curb for a long moment, staring after the taxi, and then returned to his room. As he drifted into sleep, he heard her voice as she agreed to see him the following evening, and felt again the warm and lingering kiss they shared before she left.

* * * *

The remainder of his stay in London fell into a pattern of work each day at the library and dinner with Katherine each evening. As the days slid by and he searched document after document without result, he was tempted to think perhaps nothing more could be found. Whatever *The Haunted Gospel* might have been, it could well be lost and gone. But he clung to the belief that Mike Stuart must have made note of Norwich and All Saints for a reason. He just had to find the connection. *If the gospel was created here in England,* he asked himself, *how had it got to Rome, and what happened to it after that?*

On the ninth day, the punctilious little archivist brought him a book he had not seen before.

"Do please excuse me, Professor, but we've just had a real stroke of luck. This is the manuscript I told you about the day you arrived. I knew you'd want to see it. It was not replaced after the last gentleman saw it because it was in need of repair. I'm afraid he was a little careless with it. Most unprofessional indeed. Reprehensible in fact. We expected it to be away at the conservators for several more weeks, but fortunately it has been returned in time for you to have a look at it. The previous gentleman was here inquiring into All Saints as well, you know."

"And was his name Dr. Michael Stuart, by any chance?" asked Randall.

"It is not our policy to reveal the names of persons requesting access to our collection, sir. I'm sure you understand."

"Dr. Stuart was…has died," said Randall, "and he was a close friend and colleague of mine at my university. It is on his behalf that I'm undertaking this research—to complete the work he began. I would appreciate knowing if it was he, or if someone else is also engaged in similar work."

"Well, in the circumstances," said the archivist, dropping his voice to a conspiratorial whisper, "although I do hate to break the rules. Yes, sir, it was Dr. Stuart. I am very sorry to hear of his untimely demise."

"Thank you," said Randall, "and thank you as well for bringing me this text."

"You are most welcome, sir," said the archivist, and then added as he turned to go, "It's most interesting to think that no one had seen this book for years, and all at once two people have made use of it."

"How do you mean?" asked Randall.

"The book was placed in safe storage at the beginning of the war, and no one has studied it since it was replaced in the collection in 1947."

So, thought Randall as he watched the man bustle away, *Mike was here after all. At least that clears up one mystery, but it's not like him to damage the merchandise. An accident I expect. Anyway, if he did see this text, it may provide the connection I need.*

He put on his white cotton gloves and, with much creaking of leather and parchment, carefully opened the heavy old book. It appeared to be a set of records—accounts, inventories and the like—from All Saints Priory, but it also contained many pages of a personal journal interspersed between the official documentation.

Aha, he thought, *I knew there ought to be something like this somewhere.*

The volume proved to be the work of a certain Brother Bartholomew and covered many years of history from 1210 to 1251, presumably ending at Bartholomew's death. The black lettering was still easy to read and the Latin not overly sophisticated, so Randall made good progress through it. He took to skipping over the columns and lines of records after deciding he did not need to know that in June of 1218 nine pigs were slaughtered, or that on Midsummer's Eve of 1246 twenty-seven hundredweight of squared stone had been brought in from Northampton to repair the north wall of the refectory. *Interesting for future study*, he thought, *but not relevant just now.*

The journal segments proved to be a veritable window through time, which brought back to life the daily routine of the priory as experienced by one who actually lived it and reported on the lives of his brethren.

Shortly after lunch on the afternoon of his second day with the book, he found what he had been looking for. Brother Bartholomew chronicled the completion by Brother Robert of a manuscript entitled *The Gospel According to Saint John and Suffrages to the Blessed Saint,* and described it as a work of "extraordinary inspiration and artistry."

Randall spent the next day translating and transcribing the entire series of entries covering the gospel and then went on to read the personal history of Brother Robert as Bartholomew had set it down.

Good Brother Robert was a young man of profound piety and it is with sorrow I record that it was this very piety which set the seal upon his fate. Brother Julius, being a rancorous man of great malice and consuming bitterness so envied Robert his skill and grace that he allowed hatred to rule him above his duty to God.

Following the death of our beloved Gottfried, this Julius did set upon Brother Robert and strike him down. The blow was of such ferocity it clave Robert's skull, whereof he died. Julius then sought to hide his sinful deed through fire, and within the debris of that fire we discovered Robert's mortal remains. The Lord Pandulf, Bishop of Norwich, did with much care and fortitude uncover Julius' guilt and in Norwich Town, Julius was caged unto death.

So that must be the Julius I read about in Norwich, Randall thought. *He killed Robert the Illuminator. This is fascinating.*

He read on.

The Lord Bishop did carry with him to Norwich Cathedral the great gospel wrought by Brother Robert of which I have already written. Howbeit, in time we were told of strange appearances of restless spirits, which attended the book and caused no small disquiet amongst the good monks and nuns and the townsfolk of Norwich. So mighty did this disquiet become that after some years the Lord Bishop de Blundeville was minded to send the book to Rome as a gift for His Holiness in hopes the visions would cease. Doubtless, these wandering specters were the tormented souls of Robert and Julius, their unnatural deaths having afforded them no repose.

"*The Haunted Gospel,*" said Randall aloud in jubilation. "That must be it!"

That's how it got to Rome, he thought. *But where the hell is it now, I wonder?*

He turned again to the words of Brother Bartholomew to see whether any further clues might be forthcoming, but what he read next presented him with as tantalizing a mystery as he had ever encountered.

Brother Robert's work was much admired by beloved Gottfried before his death and he gave Robert a certain solemn charge, which was that he should tell the tale of this house's great treasure within the illuminations of the Gospel of Saint John. Gottfried did bind each one of us, brother and novice and layman alike, by sacred vow that we should not, upon peril of our immortal souls, tell how this treasure came hither, nor where it be hid. The nature of this wonder is unknown, even to me, and the full truth of it went to the grave with blessed Gottfried.

I have written what I may concerning these things, and now I leave them to the merciful care of Almighty God.

PART THREE
Italy: 1523 - 1527

Chapter Eleven

On the eighteenth day of November, 1523, Cardinal Giulio de' Medici, Knight of Rhodes and Grand Prior of Capua, was, in solemn conclave, elected pope, and took, as had six other pontiffs before him, the name of Clement. He had been a cardinal for a full ten years and had become a cleric of considerable consequence thanks mainly to his illustrious lineage which rendered him nephew of the great Lorenzo de' Medici, called *the Magnificent*, and cousin of Giovanni de' Medici who ruled the Holy Roman Church as Pope Leo X from 1513 to 1522.

That same lineage, however illustrious it may have been, contained a tiny irregularity, in that Giulio's father had not been married to his mother. His father had been killed in battle without having had the opportunity to attend to the finer points of social and religious convention. As young Giulio matured and eventually obtained clerical office, it became clear to his family that a way must be found to expunge this tedious irritation. Accordingly, it was deemed Giulio's parents had been betrothed—an uncertainty at best—and an ancient article of canon law was invoked to declare him legitimate. The Medici were nothing if not pragmatic.

Clement's immediate predecessor, Adrian VI, had been an ascetic, and his pontificate was a time of uncommon austerity. This abstemiousness had been a grievous burden to those cardinals and senior clerics who looked fondly backward to the almost profligate lavishness of Leo X, but their prayers were answered by the death of Adrian after only nine months on the Throne of Peter. Since Giulio had been the architect of most papal domestic and foreign policy enactments of Leo X —and with due regard to his family connections—he was elected pope a mere two months after Adrian vacated the position.

Thus it was that shortly after Clement's coronation, their Eminences Cardinals Cattaneo and Bartoli met inside the Sistine Chapel beneath the great ceiling fresco completed by Michelangelo Buonarroti eleven years before. After praying at the altar, the two crimson-robed prelates retired to Bartoli's private apartments where they settled themselves into well-upholstered chairs before being served wine and an assortment of sweetmeats.

Cattaneo, a fat, thick-set man of forty-five, drank deeply from his silver goblet, helped himself liberally to sweetmeats from the plenteous tray on the table, sucked each pudgy finger noisily in turn and regarded his companion quizzically.

"Well, Eminence, what think you to our new pontiff?"

"Now then, my friend," replied Bartoli, stroking his white spade beard, "you know full well that Clement's election was by God's will. Who am I to speak upon it or upon him?"

Cattaneo's round belly shook as he chuckled.

"Spoken like the canny politician you are. But, look you, although he wears the shoes of the fisherman, he is a temporal lord withal. Speak upon that if you cannot speak upon the other."

Bartoli exhaled slowly, blowing out his thin cheeks.

"I know not," he said finally. "There is much to which His Holiness must pay attention with Emperor Charles and King Francis in continual confrontation."

"Yes, but will he pay attention?"

"I daily urge him towards it, but already I have the impression he may not be a man of decision."

"Quite so," said Cattaneo through another mouthful of sweetmeats. "Those very words begin already to be whispered about the halls and cloisters. And His Holiness not two months crowned."

"Our first concern must be Charles," continued Bartoli, after a sip of wine. "He would value papal support against Francis of France who denies his right to the title Holy Roman Emperor. Francis also denies Charles the lands in France he, Charles, inherited from his father in lawful line of succession."

"Indeed," said Cattaneo, "these two earthly kings are sworn enemies, but what of this support desired by Charles. Does he want an army from us? Or money to pay mercenaries?"

Cattaneo's thick fingers sought out the sweetmeats once again as Bartoli pursed his thin lips in thought before replying.

"As you know, Charles was more than active in his advocacy for Clement's election, and he may well request men-at-arms or money in return. However, he has also let it be known he desires an alliance with the Medici of Florence, Clement's own kinsmen. We know not what he may ask for, but I trust him not one whit. He is an ambitious ruler who lusts after power."

"But," put in Cattaneo, "would support for Charles be so bad a thing? Suppose His Holiness were to supply an army for him, and perhaps even enlist the aid of the Medici, could that not lead to a final victory for the emperor and end this incessant bickering and fighting?"

You are a fair politician yourself, my friend, Bartoli thought as he watched Cattaneo fill his mouth with food once again, *in spite of your great size and prodigious appetite.*

"Possibly," Bartoli nodded, "but what eventuates if Francis should be the victor? The sack of Florence perhaps? The end of the Medici? Even a French army in Rome itself? I am loath to take the risk, especially since we can safely assume the Lutherans will not flock to the papal standard. Francis will have their help, of that we may be certain."

"No doubt," agreed Cattaneo. Bartoli heard a sharpening in his voice and saw his tiny, dark eyes begin to glitter in his fleshy face.

"Lutherans," snorted Cattaneo. "Heretics. A canker in the body of Christendom. Self-styled reformers with their perverted liturgy and boorish worship, their coarse German hymns and self-righteous protestations of faith and piety. They are every bit as dangerous an enemy as any rampaging army. Pope Leo once told me he thought Martin Luther nothing more than a benighted heretic of no significance. I shall do my best to see Clement does not make the same error."

Bartoli nodded, well knowing his friend's views on Protestantism.

The two men talked for a further hour before Cattaneo, expressing thanks for kind hospitality, heaved his massive bulk from his chair and delivered himself of a thunderous belch. He stood for a moment, collecting himself after the effort, a monumental figure in his cardinal's crimson vestments, and then took his ponderous leave.

Bartoli sat on alone in his comfortable room, turning over in his mind the question of the Holy Roman Emperor. *Can an alliance with Florence actually be brought about,* he wondered, his thin face narrowing into a worried frown, *and even so, would it be wise policy? With it, Charles' power would be stupendous. How, then, are we to support him, for support him we must—somehow. Any attempt to oppose him would be calamitous.*

* * * *

"The Vatican and the Papal States will conclude an alliance with King Francis of France," said Pope Clement in October of the following year. "To do otherwise would be sheer stupidity."

The red-robed cardinals seated around the table in the pope's private chambers stared open-mouthed in astonishment, and no one spoke until Bartoli rose slowly to his feet, a grave expression on his lean face.

"With utmost respect, Holiness, I beseech you to reconsider this course of action. Think what may happen when the Emperor Charles hears of it. He is certain to regard it as a betrayal of his support and trust. Perhaps, God forbid, even as an act of war."

"Be seated, Eminence," Clement chided, as though remonstrating with a rebellious child. "The emperor's power and influence increase daily, and how better to protect ourselves from that power and counterbalance that influence than through an alliance with France? I deem this wise and prudent. Can you not understand it?"

Bartoli resumed his seat and reached for a goblet of sack to calm his tattered nerves. He sought to marshal his thoughts for further arguments as every instinct he possessed clamored within him against this plan, but as he prepared to speak again, Cattaneo's voice was heard first.

"Holiness, if you please. It is known the King of France has been supporting the Protestants in the German states, and surely this is heresy. Are we to ally ourselves with the impious? Stand shoulder to shoulder with the ungodly?"

Clement shook his head and smiled.

"My dear Cardinal Cattaneo, you are the voice of our conscience as always. I have heard of these dealings with the protestant princes, but they are merely maneuvers against the Holy Roman Emperor. Francis does not pursue a policy based on faith or doctrine; he follows only a simple military strategy."

"Forgive me again, I beg," said Cattaneo, "but ought we to abandon faith and doctrine in favor of military advantage? Has the mortal now become more to us than the immortal; the temporal more than the spiritual?"

Clement's eyes grew dark with anger.

"Eminence," he snapped. "Have a care how you speak."

"Holiness," Bartoli began again, but Clement raised an imperious hand.

"Enough. I am resolved upon this. I adjure you all to trust that God's will has been made plain to us and that we do His bidding."

Clement was not a tall man, but the richness and color of his papal vestments bestowed on him a bearing and presence which outweighed his stature as he rose from the table.

"Mark what I say," he declared before withdrawing. "This thing will be done."

"We are confounded," Bartoli said after the door closed behind the pope. "In all my sixty-two years I have not seen the like of it. For a year past, he will not turn his attention to anything, and now, of a sudden, from we know not where, he shows himself determined upon an act of the most supreme folly."

"And at first we thought him indecisive," observed Cattaneo, almost under his breath.

"God help us," said another of the cardinals, crossing himself, and heads nodded. "I pray God for protection against the wrath of Emperor Charles."

"And I pray for protection against the malicious and Godless heretics in the north," added Cattaneo, and the heads nodded again.

"Is it truly so dangerous?" asked an elderly, white-bearded cardinal. "Cannot there yet be some reconciliation between Charles and the French king?

Bartoli sighed.

"Francis has been an aggravation to Charles for years now. Although surrounded by the Holy Roman Empire on the south, the northeast and the east, Francis has sought by every possible means to menace Charles' holdings, both from without and within. As good Cattaneo has pointed out, Francis has been sending his agents into the

German states to agitate for the ascendance of the protestant princes and to spread political and religious disaffection. For the last two years, his representative, Antonio Rincon, has been urging the King of Poland and the Voivode of Transylvania to threaten Charles on his eastern frontiers. I have no doubt the wrath of the emperor will fall heavily upon us when he learns of this reckless and injudicious alliance."

* * * *

After leaving his council, Clement observed the prayers and benedictions of Vespers and then seated himself at a large desk in one of his private rooms. The room was spacious and well- appointed with chairs, low tables and several gold candelabra. A few minutes later, a lay steward entered with a lighted taper and made obeisance. Clement nodded and the man moved quickly about the room lighting candles, finishing with the large reading candle at Clement's elbow.

As the man departed, Clement reached for a large, heavy book, leather-bound and studded with gold, which rested on a corner of the desk. This book, brought to him several months before in response to his request for a gospel to study, was titled *The Gospel According to Saint John and Suffrages to the Blessed Saint,* and it had become his constant companion. The suffrages inspired him, and he loved the story of his Savior's life on earth. In addition, he found the illuminations wondrous, and he marveled at the colors and brilliant workmanship.

The uniqueness of the illuminations had, in fact, arrested his attention when first he opened the book. He saw buildings and monks hard at work in a scriptorium. There were men digging, presumably in a garden, although they looked more like soldiers than monks. The illuminations were a prosaic representation of the quiet and well-ordered life of a spiritual community, and it brought him a sense of peace to look at them and study the sacred text. It frequently left him yearning for release from the oppressive weight of his pontifical responsibilities.

He found the volume intriguing for another reason as well. His interest stemmed from what he had been told the day the book had first been delivered to him by Father Piero, a priest assigned to the library.

"It was sent to Rome from England, Holiness, as a gift to the blessed Gregory IX nearly three centuries ago. We still have the letter which accompanied it from the Lord Bishop of Norwich."

"The book seems not much used for its being so old," Clement observed, and Father Piero nodded.

"There are few who wish to open it, Holiness, because of the stories that surround it."

"Stories?" inquired Clement, raising his eyebrows. "What stories?"

"It is noted in our records that the Benedictine monk who made the book was murdered by one of his own brothers in Christ, and the guilty one was then condemned and executed. Then, later…"

The young priest hesitated before saying, "Perhaps I should not have brought it to you, Holiness. It was not wise. I beg your forgiveness and your permission to return it to the library. I shall bring you another gospel."

"No, no, Father," said Clement, "pray continue. You have made a beginning, and you cannot leave me in ignorance. Come now, I insist."

"As you wish, Holiness," said Piero, with a slight bow. "When the book was received into the library it was recorded under the name of *The Norwich Gospel,* but I have also seen it referred to in our lists as *The Haunted Gospel.* "

"Haunted?" echoed Clement. "How can that be?"

"It is noted that after the murder and the death of the guilty one, the book was visited by spirits who took the form of Benedictine monks. They were seen many times and in more than one place."

"Here in Rome?"

"No, Holiness. Nothing has been seen here—or so I am told."

"Then we may assume, may we not, Father, that these perturbed spirits, if spirits they truly were, are now at rest. I shall keep the book. Thank you, Father Piero. Go in peace and have no fear."

Clement now recalled that conversation as he opened the gospel text, and wondered if the stories could be mere fantasy.

"Who can know the truth of such mysteries?" he murmured to himself.

After reading and meditating on several of the suffrages, Clement closed the book and rested his hand on it.

Such an odd story, he mused. *Spirits and visitations. And yet I find truth in this book; God speaks to me through the words on its pages. I trust it as my guide and Divine counselor, in spite of what may be said about it.*

Chapter Twelve

Charles V of Austria, Holy Roman Emperor and King of Spain, brought his fist down upon the table beside him with such force the gold goblets and silver platters jumped and clattered.

"God damn him. That miserable little pontifical poltroon has made a treaty with Francis. By the nails of the holy cross, *I am betrayed.*"

Charles leaned back in his chair, breathing heavily; his face empurpled with rage and indignation. He crumpled the sheet of vellum bearing the short message in his fist and flung it across the room.

"I gave him my open support," he growled, snatching up his goblet. "I spoke for him to the Spanish cardinals. I pledged myself to his service, and now, barely a year after, he allies himself with my enemy. I can hear Francis laughing all the way from Paris. This is unspeakable and treacherous villainy."

Charles was but four-and-twenty years old and had been Hapsburg ruler for a mere five years, but he had already proved himself a strong leader. Long fair hair cut straight across the brow framed his face, and the look of youthful innocence in his deep-set eyes gave little hint of the formidable intellect which lay behind them.

He glowered at the courtiers who stood in silence around him.

"God's blood," he shouted, "I will not have it."

Charles drank again; his anger still as hot as a refiner's fire, but his mind was already clearing as fury began slowly to give way to shrewd calculation. He began, as was his habit once anger subsided a little, to seek a practical solution to the problem before him.

"We must have a balance," he said, as much to himself as to those around him. "Clement is a milksop to be sure, but he is a Florentine Medici withal and must not, therefore, be underestimated. Thanks to his new alliance, Francis will have the power of the Vatican at his back and perhaps even a Florentine army at his side, so where, then, are we to find our ally against Rome? Who is to stand at our side? Where is the balance?"

No one spoke. Charles sat silent for a time, and his anger rekindled.

"After all I have done, Clement treats me thus. He *knows* I sought an alliance with him, and now he throws my strategy onto the dung heap and estranges me from the Medici. But I swear before God I shall ere long have both Clement *and* Francis to bend their knees before me."

Charles swept a cold gaze around the assembled nobles, commoners and functionaries who together formed his court and his eye fell upon the Marquis of Pescara. *And I know just the ally to help me subjugate my old enemy and my new one,* he thought with satisfaction: *the Family Colonna, Pescara's kinsmen. They hate the pope and France as much as I, if that were possible. There is our strength. There is our balance.*

The young emperor unexpectedly smiled at the company and spoke in lighter tones.

"A pox on all French kings and Roman popes, my lords and gentlemen. They are but stupid moths and I a bright candle. They seek to extinguish my flame by the fluttering of their feeble little wings, but they approach only to be burned and fall as dust. Let us feast and dance, for I perceive all will yet be well. Come." He stood and beckoned. "Bring food and wine aplenty. Where are my musicians? Let us be merry and drink to the damnation of our enemies."

The hall at once became a-bustle with frenzied activity. Servants made haste to the kitchens and others to find drummers, lutenists, crumhorn, and sackbut players. Torches were lit in wall sconces, filling the air with the acrid smoke of burning pitch, tables were rearranged and fresh straw brought in for the floor. Charles, standing in the midst of this swirling busyness like a lone rock in a fast-moving river, called his valet to his side.

"Tell My Lord of Pescara that I would speak with him."

When the marquis appeared and bowed, the emperor led the way into a small antechamber concealed behind a heavy Flemish tapestry depicting a mighty Arcadian battle between demigods and centaurs. Once the thick tapestry fell back into place behind them, the two men could not be overheard.

The marquis was a Neapolitan nobleman of highborn Spanish heritage, but at that particular moment Charles was more interested in his wife's family. Pescara was married to the beautiful and gifted Vittoria, daughter of Fabrizio Colonna, Grand Constable of Naples.

"So," said the emperor, "Francis is now in league with the Vatican and may bring Florence and the Medici against us as well. What say you, My Lord?"

Pescara's eyes darkened.

"I say treachery, sire. Base treachery."

"I take it, then, we may rely, when the time is propitious, upon the full support of your wife's family as we move to repay that treachery?"

"I pledge it, sire," replied the marquis. "The Colonna will have no French king in Italy, nor will they countenance the duplicity of this Medici pope. The Vatican must be brought to heel, aye, and crushed beneath it if need be. Your Majesty shall have whatever support is required, and by your leave I will speak with my father-in-law upon the matter at once."

"Do so," the emperor nodded, "but beg him to stay his hand until I give the word. Whatever is to be done must be done with diligence."

"As you command, sire."

"Where is Francis now, My Lord Marquis?" Charles asked with a thoughtful frown. "Do you know? I have had no recent reports."

"He continues his assay into Lombardia, sire. He has taken Milan, as we expected."

"Yes, that is hardly a surprise," mused Charles. "So what will he do next? We have a garrison at Pavia, less than fifteen leagues from Milan. Will he turn thither or ignore it?"

Pescara was about to reply, but Charles continued.

"What is his strength?"

"At least twenty thousand, sire," said Pescara. "Or so say our spies."

"Composition?"

"Light and heavy horse, Swiss pikemen, mercenary and levy foot soldiers."

"Siege guns? Field artillery?"

"Presumably, sire, but I am not certain of the numbers."

"They outdo us in cavalry then," said Charles, and Pescara nodded.

Charles pondered the problem as methodically as a scholar and with the coolness of a born strategist.

"Francis will lay siege to Pavia," he said at length. "I judge him to be no great tactician, but even a blind idiot would see Pavia must be taken if a permanent hold is to be gained in Lombardia."

"Then he must be stopped, sire," said Pescara. "We dare not risk French control of northern Italy now that Francis and the Vatican are allies. Austria herself would be threatened."

"Indeed so," said Charles, "and it would then take our whole army to safeguard our southern flank. Yes, Pavia is the key that unlocks the door to Lombardia, but Francis shall not have it."

"The city cannot withstand a siege for long," Pescara said, and Charles nodded slowly.

"Very true, My Lord Marquis, and it is therefore vital that we break our enemy's strength outside the city, before he can breach its walls and use those same walls against us."

Charles placed a hand on the marquis' shoulder and his eyes glittered with fierce resolve as he spoke.

"Make preparations My Lord, for we march to Pavia's aid with all speed. I would see this Frankish king brought down, and if that double-dealing excuse for a pope falls with him, I will shed no tears."

"I go immediately," said Pescara, with a bow.

"And pray do not forget your pledge as touching the Colonna," said Charles, as the marquis reached to push aside the tapestry.

"Never fear, sire. You have my oath upon it. When you need them, the Colonna will be at your side."

Pescara departed and in a moment or two, Charles pushed aside the thick tapestry and reentered the hall himself. He saw before him a scene of great animation: the musicians tuning their instruments, serving wenches and lads scurrying hither and thither arranging tables, setting out food and drink and laying clean linen. The members of the court were no longer in evidence, having departed to change into finery more suited to a night of revelry, and to call their wives and daughters from their reading and embroidery and bid them make ready as well. His Majesty had ordered all to be merry that night, and merry they would all most certainly be.

The music and dancing lasted until long past midnight, and the emperor, having vomited both violently and voluminously on the table after a surfeit of meat and drink, was carried to his bedchamber, pale and groaning. Once on his bed he fell into a stupor from which he did not rise until late the following morning.

He awoke an hour before midday in as foul a humor as any could remember, and declared to his valet that his mouth tasted like a cesspit and his head was about to burst. The apothecary was sent for and in spite of being roundly cursed by the emperor as a useless quack, he managed to administer a sleeping draught that transported Charles once more into the arms of Morpheus, from whose slumberous embrace he did not emerge for a further twenty-four hours.

Upon waking, his head was much improved. Charles sent for Pescara, but was informed the marquis had departed.

"And news arrived from Pavia yesterday, sire," said his valet.

"What news?"

"The French march on the city."

"Why was I not awakened?" shouted the emperor, struggling out of bed amid a great flailing of sheets and blankets. "Why was I not told of this?"

"We tried, Majesty, but the sleeping potion."

"God damn the sleeping potion, knave. Has Pescara gone to rally our troops?"

"He has, sire. In fact, he departed before the revels ended, bidding us tell you he would set out for Pavia himself as soon as our army is made ready."

"I knew Francis would turn on Pavia," said Charles, breaking the thin sheet of ice on the water in his washbasin. "We shall have him now, pray God."

And so, by the beginning of February, 1525, the army of Spain and the Holy Roman Emperor under the command of the Marquis of Pescara reached the ancient university city of Pavia and prepared to break the siege laid by the French.

* * * *

"What in the name of the Blessed Savior is all this commotion?" demanded Pope Clement, jarred from a sound sleep early on the morning of March the third. His servant of the bedchamber, Brother

Ricardo de Firenza, was hammering on the door and shouting.

"Holiness. Please."

"All right, all right," called Clement, sitting up and gathering the bedclothes around him. "Enter and be at peace, please God."

The door banged open, jarring Clement yet again, and causing him to clench his teeth in shock. The young servant made haste inside in a fever of anticipation wholly beyond his normal habit.

"His Eminence Cardinal Bartoli is come, Holiness."

"And could he not wait until the sun was risen upon us?" asked Clement. "Why comes he before cockcrow?"

"There is news from the north, Holiness."

"Why did you not say so?" snapped Clement. "Send him in, and be quick about it."

Bartoli walked into the room, his thin face gray with fatigue and lined by worry. He spared not a glance at Firenza, but made his reverences to Clement and begged forgiveness for the disturbance.

"I trust your news warrants the disturbance," said Clement. "I do not customarily conduct business while in bed."

"This matter is urgent, Holiness. Urgent and unhappy."

"Well proceed with it, then."

"There has been a great battle at Pavia, Holiness, and I regret to say the French were defeated."

Clement shut his eyes for a long moment and shook his head as though to shut out what he had heard. His grand alliance with France that was to have protected the Church from domination by the Holy Roman Empire crumbled into pieces before him. He saw the Vatican and her treasures lying helpless before the onslaught of marauding imperial troops led by a vengeful Emperor Charles intent upon a bloody retribution. The very thought of it sickened his stomach and froze his heart.

"Holiness, are you all right?" asked Bartoli, breaking into the dismal train of Clement's thoughts.

"Be seated, Eminence" Clement said, in a tone of weary despair. "Be seated and tell me the rest."

"A messenger has arrived with a letter from Tiercelin, Commander of the French Light Horse," said Bartoli, settling himself into a chair at

Clement's bedside, "and with your Holiness' permission I will summarize what he has told us."

Clement nodded, his face expressionless.

"The battle began on the twenty-third of last month," said Bartoli. "In the evening to be precise. The imperial army opened with a fierce attack on French positions around the northern wall of the Mirabello Park—a hunting preserve, Holiness—with the clear intention of breaking the siege lines at that place."

"Eminence," interrupted Clement, "I am neither soldier nor tactician. Tell me only what is important in this calamity."

"As you wish, Holiness," said Bartoli. "Francis was captured. His army is in disarray. Tiercelin writes there has been no comparable slaughter of French nobility since the English victory at Agincourt a century ago. There is nothing to stop the emperor now."

Bartoli paused, his gaunt features strained.

"I am sorry, Holiness. Would that I could bring better word."

Clement sighed.

"I was told Francis employed German mercenaries," he said. "What of them?"

"Both Charles and Francis employed them, but those in the pay of the emperor were commanded by Constable de Bourbon, and showed no mercy to their fellow countrymen who were incompetently led by French captains."

"But," faltered Clement, "what of Francis' Swiss pikemen? Proud soldiers. Surely they…."

"Cowards all, Holiness," snorted Bartoli in a bitter tone. "They hesitated and vacillated, and in the end broke ranks and fled the field, followed hotfoot by whatever remained of the French army."

"Alas," murmured Clement. "We are ruined."

"I give Francis his due, mark you," added the cardinal, raising a finger, "for he was in the thick of the fighting, and had the very horse shot from beneath him. So says Tiercelin himself. But he was captured by the emperor's troops and is even now on his way to Madrid."

Clement twisted the blankets in his hands like a frightened child. *What is next*, he asked himself. *Charles can demand the crown of Italy if he chooses.*

Clement sighed again. Farewell his dreams of a masterful and astute foreign policy. Farewell his hopes for peace. *How can this have happened,* he wondered. *I have surely been betrayed,* he thought, and anger welled up within him.

"France's shame is our shame also, Eminence," he said with unwonted harshness. "How is it possible that you permitted the papal throne to find itself in this sorry plight? Did you not encourage me in my plans to join with France? I have been deceived by those closest to me, those to whom I have given my solemn trust."

Bartoli stared open-mouthed in horror.

"Holiness, with the greatest respect," he began, but Clement waved an imperious hand to silence him.

"Be gone," he snapped. "Leave me."

Bartoli, his lips compressed in impotent fury, rose, made perfunctory reverences and departed.

As the door closed behind the cardinal, Clement reached for the illuminated gospel of John, which lay on a table beside his bed. He cradled the heavy volume in his hands for a few moments and then, turning to the suffrages, fell at once to urgent, if not desperate, prayer.

* * * *

Upon hearing the news from Pavia, Emperor Charles ordered feasting and rejoicing in celebration, and the entire court descended into such a state of blind debauchery as had not been seen in a twelve-month. Vat after vat of wine was opened, spirits of every description flowed as water, and the casks of sack were beyond enumeration. Everywhere there was prodigal extravagance, and the men and women of the court donned their finest satins, silks and jewelry to honor the occasion.

Merrymaking for the emperor himself, however, did not begin at once. First, as always, there were practical matters to be considered.

Surely, Clement must now see he has thrown the dice and lost, he thought. *Perhaps if reconciliation with the Vatican could be effected, we might yet hope for an alliance with Florence and the puissant Medici. A guarantee of Florentine independence in return for the crown of Italy without hindrance from the See of Rome might be enough to settle the matter. That would keep His Holiness where he belongs: within the walls of his spiritual domain and well out of the way of men with more worldly work to do. I shall send emissaries to the Vatican, but we still have our pact with the Colonna if His Holiness proves obstinate or fails to appreciate the fragility of his position.*

"And when all this is concluded," he chuckled as he rose from his chair by the fire, "Clement shall crown me King of Italy. I warrant that will twist his bowels for him."

Charles left his chamber and walked to the hall where the revels were already in full spate, well satisfied with his plans. The huge room was ablaze with candles and torches when he entered and waited for the tumult to die down as his presence became known. While the music faltered to a stop and dancers looked around inquiringly, he crossed to a dais against the far wall and the crowds parted like water before a ship. The only sounds were the rustling of gowns and cloaks as all present bowed and curtsied when he passed.

Reaching the dais, he seated himself and surveyed the glittering scene. All eyes fixed themselves on him expectantly.

"Come, my lords and ladies," he called, "let us have a galliard and a goblet of the best wine for all, for I am well pleased."

The musicians struck up the lively measures of a galliard, and the dancing began again amid cheers and applause.

"I vow His Holiness does not celebrate overmuch this night," said Charles to one of his nobles, an elderly man in the final stages of inebriation, and the man guffawed through a mouthful of roast beef.

"God rot all popes, Your Majesty," he managed to reply before lurching away and disappearing into the crowd of revelers.

Chapter Thirteen

A year after the battle of Pavia, a year during which the Vatican languished in a state of fear and uncertainty, a letter finally arrived from Spain for Cardinal Bartoli. The letter was from Marguerite d'Angoulême, King Francis' sister, who had gone to Madrid to negotiate her brother's release, and Bartoli broke its red wax seals impatiently.

Your Most Gracious Eminence, he read, I write to inform you that yesterday there was concluded here a treaty upon which I and others have labored these many months. By its terms and provisions my dear brother, his Sovereign Majesty, is at last set at liberty. I praise Almighty God for His great mercy in delivering Francis from his humiliations and oppressions at the hands of Emperor Charles, but I fear Francis grows and nurtures a burgeoning hatred for the emperor, and I dare not think of what revenge may now be in his heart.

Nevertheless, I beg that you will read the following description of the treaty and convey to His Holiness the import of what has been done. Francis has set the seal of France to this parchment and after payment of a manumission in token, he will be a free man once more. The further terms are these:

My brother renounces his claim to the crown and title of Holy Roman Emperor and accepts the right of Emperor Charles. The lands and territories of Burgundy have been yielded to Charles as true inheritance and Francis has abandoned his suzerainty over Flanders and Artois. But of far greater moment and danger to you all is the provision under which Francis renounces all his claims to lands, titles and preferments in Italy and agrees to withdraw all his soldiers, both levy and mercenary, his cavalry and cannon, from Italian soil. The Emperor Charles was jubilant over this victory, as well you may imagine, but I fear what this may mean for His Holiness and for our Holy Mother Church, for Charles bears His Holiness great ill will, as you know right well.

As Bartoli finished reading, a young lay brother knocked on the door and announced the arrival of Cardinal Cattaneo. That worthy cleric waddled into the room with a smile on his fleshy face and his little eyes sparkling with curiosity.

"Well, my friend," he said sinking into a chair, which groaned in protest, "I am told you have received a letter from Spain. Word travels quickly in these troubled times. Does it concern King Francis?"

"Read for yourself," said Bartoli, handing him Marguerite's letter.

Cattaneo read the letter slowly, the only sound in the room being his labored, rather hoarse breathing.

"So," said Cattaneo when he had finished, "now we stand entirely alone do we? Such is the price of injudicious alliances."

"Our position is indeed a little delicate," said Bartoli, "but God may have granted us a keyhole though which we may squeeze and so escape this prison."

Cattaneo regarded his friend narrowly.

"How so?" he inquired. "What devious little scheme have you dreamed up now?"

"Charles desires an alliance with the Florentine Medici, does he not?" said Bartoli.

"So we heard, and I doubt he will have changed his mind."

"And His Holiness is still a Medici," said Bartoli. "So perhaps we may assure the safety of Holy Mother Church in return for Clement's sponsorship of such an alliance."

"But look you, my friend," said Cattaneo, handing back the letter, "we have considered this before. A Medici alliance would make Charles the most powerful ruler in Europe, and His Holiness would never countenance such a thing."

"Indeed," nodded Bartoli. "With the Medici at his side, Charles will bestride Europe like a colossus, but he knows a Medici army would never support him should he march on Rome. To attack us, therefore, would make shipwreck of his coveted alliance, weaken him and turn the Florentines and their supporters irrevocably against him."

"I do not understand," said Cattaneo. "Would not the Florentines support us now if Charles should attack?"

"Probably not," said Bartoli. "At this moment, even they could not prevail against Charles. His armies are overwhelming. The only way the Medici can protect us is from the inside: within an alliance with Charles. Without an alliance, they have no influence over him. And, importantly, we will also obtain information on Charles' activities through Clement's kinsmen."

"Surely the emperor will see through this plan of yours? He is no fool."

"Indeed he is not," agreed Bartoli, "yet he has a flaw which we can exploit, and that flaw is his towering ambition. As you said yourself but a moment ago, a Medici alliance will give him mastery over Europe. It will be his final move in the chess game he plays. He will be unable to resist it. Charles is not the master of his ambitions, my friend; he is their slave. The alliance will give him what he desires, and will end this continual warfare. And it will protect us at the same time. My aim is security, peace and stability."

"That is all very well," said Cattaneo, "but how are we to persuade His Holiness of all these things?"

Bartoli sighed.

"At this precise moment I confess I do not know, but I am convinced it must be done. If we cannot secure our safety through force of arms—and clearly we cannot—then we must achieve it through other means."

"You play a rare game of chess yourself," said Cattaneo with a throaty chuckle, but Bartoli shook his head.

"Not I alone. This game is one we must all play together."

Cattaneo crossed himself and passed a thick hand over his pouched face.

"Does His Holiness know of that letter?"

"Not yet. Tomorrow."

"I must be away," grunted Cattaneo as he heaved his ponderous body out of the chair. "But pray tell me before I depart, Eminence, which do you fear most, the threat from Charles, or the unpredictability of His Holiness?"

Bartoli shook his head and made no reply.

* * * *

In council the next morning, Bartoli read the letter aloud to Clement and the assembled advisors and then provided his own appraisal of their situation and his proposed solution. There were cries of alarm, agreements and disagreements, pleas to God and much genuflection amongst the cardinals, but His Holiness seemed remarkably unperturbed. He listened to Bartoli's plan for the alliance between Charles and the Medici, and his response was wholly unexpected.

"God's will be done," he said with a calm gaze around the large table. "I shall pray to the blessed St. John. He, by God's mercy, will show us the way."

Clement adjourned the council and went into seclusion. Days became weeks but the council was not reconvened. No word came from Clement, and Bartoli's repeated requests for an audience were declined.

"Does His Holiness do nothing but read?" Bartoli fumed to Cattaneo one evening. "The servants tell me he buries himself in that book day after day. It reminds me of a child facing into a corner in hopes the world will be different when he turns back."

"Is prayer so bad?" asked Cattaneo.

"Of course not, but ask yourself this: is what he does true prayer? How is God's will revealed to him through the John gospel? His Holiness tells us only that his supposed prayers have been answered in some mysterious manner."

"God Himself is the greatest of all mysteries, my friend," said Cattaneo, "and He will reveal Himself in His own way and time."

"And now I hear His Holiness has begun to receive and dispatch messengers. With whom is he communicating, and to what end? Worse yet, I am told privately that emissaries came recently from Charles seeking a reconciliation through an alliance with the Medici, exactly as I had hoped, but Clement sent them away."

"And have you now come to trust the emperor, may I ask?"

"Not necessarily," said Bartoli, with an impatient wave of his thin hand. "There is no harm in listening to what he has to say. It is simple prudence to explore every avenue that may be open to us."

These thoughts were Bartoli's constant companions until Clement at last summoned his council to explain what God had revealed to him through the Blessed St. John. Bartoli listened in horror-stricken incredulity.

"Holiness," he blurted when Clement had finished, "I beseech you in God's name. This is utter madness."

"Come, Eminence," said Clement with an avuncular smile, "such drama. Be less strident, I beg you. The new alliance I have described will afford us the protection we so desperately need. It is the answer we seek. Surely that is plain."

"Forgive me, Holiness," said Bartoli, striving for greater calm while yet retaining an urgent tone. "Can you not see this strategy will lead to further war, to more needless bloodshed. We know the King of France makes a mockery of the Treaty of Madrid and repudiates its terms. He goes to war yet again. To support his cause as you did before is to invite Emperor Charles to lay waste to all Italy, and France will be powerless to help us. It can only be folly to continue this policy of support for Francis. Charles has sought reconciliation, and surely your Holiness must see that our salvation lies in that reconciliation, however it may be achieved, rather than in further military adventures."

Clement regarded Bartoli narrowly for a few moments and when he spoke, there was a warning edge to his voice.

"Do you presume to tell me what I must see, Eminence?"

Bartoli looked down at the tabletop.

"No, Holiness, I only try to point out."

Clement raised a hand and looked around the company.

"Francis need not feel any obligation to honor a treaty forced upon him at the point of a sword, and I have told him so. And as for reconciliation and Charles' request for a Florentine alliance, you may be sure I will never treat with a man possessed of such surpassing and ruthless ambition as he. His offers are a sham; he seeks only to enlarge his power. It is we who will ally ourselves to Florence, not Charles. I adjure you all to hear me well. It is not only we who fear Charles' warlike heart and rapacious spirit. On the morrow, I depart for the city of Cognac where I shall meet with emissaries from Florence, England, Venice and France, and together we shall swear our united support for Francis against the emperor. We must do this to prevent the very catastrophe to which Cardinal Bartoli refers. This is God's will. The blessed St. John has revealed this to me through my prayers and earnest supplications."

* * * *

"It is as you said," Cattaneo observed at dinner later. "He relies wholly upon that ancient book from England."

"It has become his holy text," nodded Bartoli. "His obsession. Within that gospel, he believes he finds answers to whatever troubles him. By reading it, he declares God Himself enlightens him through the words of the Saint. He believes himself divinely directed in all matters of theology, dogma, administration and foreign policy. Yesterday, I even overheard the stewards whispering and laughing that His Holiness will not piss without first consulting St. John."

Cattaneo snorted with laughter before drinking deeply of Bartoli's good red wine.

"I ask again, should we not be glad our pope seeks God's guidance?"

"Of course, of course," said Bartoli. "His Holiness is the descendant of Blessed St. Peter and is nearer to God than all other men. I know. I am no novice."

"Well then?" asked Cattaneo, his little eyes as innocent as a child's.

"His reading of the book is not the prayer he declares or believes it to be," said Bartoli, a note of exasperation in his voice. "It is a mere fascination with the words on the page. He believes he finds his answers there, but I do not believe those answers come from God. His study is nothing more than empty contrivance. He does not seek direction, only justification for what he already believes or has decided upon. Remember how, after Pavia, he turned upon us all and accused us of allowing, nay, persuading, him to make the first alliance with France? He did not blame the words of his book for the catastrophe; he blamed us. We, who advised him against the very course of action he insisted upon and which led to disaster."

Cattaneo grunted and wrinkled his pudgy nose.

"So," said Bartoli, "it is that book which is the source of much of our trouble."

"It is said the book was visited by restless spirits," said Cattaneo.

"Yes, but none have been seen here."

"Well," said Cattaneo, "if what you say of His Holiness be true, this once-haunted volume governs him and all the rest of us as well."

"And perhaps," added Bartoli with a grimace, "to judge from what we have seen of late, the spirits who once attended upon the book, though no longer choosing to be seen, work evil against us even now."

Cattaneo crossed himself hastily and reached for his wine.

"I shall make one final effort to dissuade His Holiness from following this fearful path," said Bartoli, "but I hold out little hope of success."

Bartoli's assessment was accurate.

"It is God's will, Eminence," said Clement as he prepared to depart the following morning. "Your obstinacy on this matter is misguided. Let us pray it is not heretical as well."

Standing in the window of his apartment an hour later, Bartoli watched helplessly as Clement left for Cognac with a large retinue of servants, scriveners, cooks, miscellaneous clerics, his confessor, three hundred mounted men-at-arms and a hundred halberdiers. He shook his head as he observed Clement carried with him the heavy leather-bound volume from which he would no longer allow himself to be separated.

There is but a single hope left to us, Bartoli thought. *It is possible the allies will be unable to reach agreement on the terms of their proposed treaty, and in the face of that, His Holiness will turn to reconciliation as his only course.*

Several weeks later, however, to Bartoli's despair, word came of the signing of the Treaty of Cognac by which France, England, Florence, Venice and the Vatican were bound together into an alliance henceforth to be known as the League of Cognac.

* * * *

To the surprise of no one at his court, Emperor Charles greeted the news of the League with a display of incandescent fury. Already enraged at Francis' perfidy in repudiating the Treaty of Madrid, the news of yet another military alliance against him drove Charles to the very limits of his endurance.

"And Rome has joined this accursed League, to boot," he roared.

He flung a silver chalice across the room and gave vent to so creative a tempest of oaths and blasphemies that noblemen recorded it in their journals and ladies whispered about it for days thereafter.

"We need have no fear of this League of Cognac, sire," said Pescara, approaching the emperor, albeit cautiously.

"I do not fear their paltry alliance, for God's sake," Charles growled. "They may do as they please. If they array an army against me, I shall destroy it."

"Then pray be at ease, sire."

"At ease?" exploded the emperor, seizing another goblet, and Pescara took a hasty step backward. "When I am betrayed by Clement yet again? When he has once more thwarted my plans for an alliance with the Medici? When he spurns my offers of peace and reconciliation and flouts my good will? How am I to be at ease?"

Charles glowered at Pescara and those around him.

"Never fear; I shall humiliate this praetorian pope. He shall dance in the palm of my hand and then I shall crush him like a grape, but not before he crowns me King of Italy, which I swear before God I will make him do ere long."

Eventually the angry storm abated, and Charles' mind turned to strategy. *This*, he thought, *is the moment to unleash the Colonna. They will be the instrument of my revenge and victory.*

The Colonna, an offshoot of the extinct lineage of the Counts of Tusculum, were a large and ancient family that took its name from its great fortress castle situated a few leagues southeast of Rome in the Alban Hills. From this medieval fastness, the Colonna administered their vast lands and prodigious fortune. They had for centuries opposed the power and influence of the Holy See in Italy, however in spite of numerous wars and persecutions, the family survived and prospered. The Colonna were in such frequent conflict with the Vatican that many Roman citizens came to regard their excommunication and subsequent restoration as almost predictable annual events like Easter and Christmas.

Charles knew the Colonna had grown resentful and rebellious in recent years, thanks to an increase in papal influence, and were impatient for action. This was the moment for which he had been waiting.

"My Lord Marquis of Pescara," he said, "come hither, and the rest may leave us."

The noblemen and functionaries of the court departed, and Charles waited until he and the marquis were alone.

"Speak to your father-in-law," he said. "Tell him he will oblige me greatly should he choose this moment to assert the independence of his family. He may harry the Vatican to extremity if he wishes; I shall not complain."

"It shall be done, sire," said Pescara, with a bow.

* * * *

Throughout the summer, therefore, under Charles' watchful and contented eye, troops fielded by the Colonna steadily intensified their raids into the Papal States, snapping at the heels of the Vatican like a sharp-toothed terrier. Here a manor house was pillaged, there a tax wagon looted, elsewhere a town sacked or a village burned. These attacks, as fierce as they were unpredictable, became a constant aggravation to the pope's political advisors, but His Holiness, obsessed by the need to protect the Church against Emperor Charles, had little time to devote to what he summarily dismissed as lawless brigands and thieves. In vain did Bartoli and the others attempt to impress upon Clement the threat posed by the Colonna.

"Would that they were no more than lawless brigands, Holiness," Bartoli said, "but they are a powerful family, long dedicated to independence from the Vatican. It is obvious they are in league with Emperor Charles. There is in all likelihood a much larger strategy in play than a few isolated forays into papal domains."

"We will come to terms with the Colonna," Clement declared, "when we are secure against the military adventures of Charles. The Colona are but fleas, while Charles is a scorpion. Through the League of Cognac, we will cage the scorpion. Then we shall squash the fleas. I am persuaded the Colonna will come to realize friendship with us is a more desirable state of affairs than an alliance with Charles. God tells me this through the words of the gospel."

As if to prove God and the gospel correct, the Colonna ceased their raids and in the midst of an August downpour, their emissaries appeared at the Vatican.

Clement greeted the news with jubilation. He congratulated himself warmly and repeatedly on the astuteness of his prediction.

"They have come to sue for peace," he exulted at Bartoli. "I knew it, but you doubted me, did you not, Eminence? That was unwise and unworthy of you and no doubt you now acknowledge your error. These bandits fear the League of Cognac, as well they might. God be praised."

Bartoli smoldered at Clement's insult, but held his peace.

His Holiness ordered the ambassadors be given dry clothes, and be treated as honored guests.

"They shall sup with me this night," he said. "Meanwhile, bid them rest and be comfortable."

Still glowing with self-satisfaction, Clement entertained the six representatives of the Colonna to a feast of bacchanalian extravagance. Meat and drink were everywhere in abundance, music played and choirs sang benedictional prayers and anthems of praise. Cardinal Cattaneo, smiling and greasy-fingered, was a man in paradise, but Bartoli and many others chafed at the sight of such a feast given in honor of those who had so lately been the enemies of the Holy See, and in truth probably still were.

"For centuries they have promoted the interests of the German emperors," said Bartoli, "and now they come to Rome to do what, I ask you? Make amends? Make peace? I think not, my Brothers, I think not. I smell treachery and deceit in this, and I see the knavish hand of Charles in it as well."

"I wonder if Cardinal Colonna could tell us anything," mused a young cardinal, and Bartoli snorted in indignation.

"Ha! The good Pompeo, our blessed vice-chancellor, elevated by Clement himself. The man is no straighter than the hind leg of a dog, and certainly no cleaner. Talking to him would be worse than a waste of time, but I wager he is in the thick of whatever this conspiracy may prove to be. The Colonna have always deemed it prudent to have an ear and an eye and a faithful reporter here within the Vatican."

"The true menace," put in an aged and white-bearded French

cardinal, "is the gospel to which His Holiness is dedicated. If I had my way, I would see that book at the bottom of the Tiber."

"My Brothers," cried another, scandalized, "it is a sacred text, the word of God as revealed to Blessed St. John who walked with our Savior here on earth. How can so holy a book possibly be an evil influence?"

"Because the uses to which it is put are decidedly unholy," Cardinal Bartoli shot back, his voice sharp as splintered glass. "To pray to be shown the will of God is one thing, but to choose your own road and then contrive a means of claiming God's guidance, is entirely another."

* * * *

By the middle of September 1526, Cardinal Bartoli saw the clouds of war menacing the Vatican like the anvil-topped thunderheads of an autumn storm. Bartoli and those of his colleagues who shared his fears spent hours in desperate conference and implored Clement to exercise prudence and restraint in his dealings with the Colonna. It was as if His Holiness had withdrawn from the world of men. Each day he walked the corridors and apartments of the Vatican in a state of irrepressible euphoria. He had prevailed, or so he apparently believed. His strategy in joining the League of Cognac had been vindicated. Even the powerful Colonna had come to him with offers of peace. Those proud Colonna were even now sitting regularly at his table, dining with him and drinking his health and longevity. Pompeo Cardinal Colonna was his friend and ally, and all the arguments, warnings and importuning of Bartoli and the others could not move him a hair's breadth from his comfortable complacence.

Bartoli wanted to wring his hands in rage and frustration over Clement's blithe refusal to understand their true situation, but on the nineteenth of September, it was done for him. As the sunset tinted the dome of St. Peter's red and gold, an exhausted and terrified young rider hurtled into the stable courtyard, his horse all but spent.

"They come," he gasped, almost falling from his saddle. "They come. The army of the Colonna marches hither."

Chapter Fourteen

"How can it be?" Clement moaned. "I simply do not understand."

His Holiness sat in his private rooms staring in disbelief at Cardinal Bartoli who had hastened to give him news of the attack.

"Surely it is an honor guard of some sort," Clement said in sudden enlightenment. "They come to present us with some gratuity in recognition of our new-found peace. That must be their purpose."

"Would that it were, Holiness," said Bartoli, "but it is not so. The messenger tells us they come in armor and full battle array. There are foot soldiers and cavalry."

"Siege cannon?" asked Clement, his eyes round with fear.

"No," answered Bartoli, trying to keep the bitterness from his voice. "There is no need. The city is open to them since your Holiness ordered our forces to stand down."

"But," Clement tried again, "their emissaries spoke of peace. You heard them yourself."

"Vipers, Holiness. Deceitful serpents."

Clement bit his lip.

"What shall we do?"

"You must escape, Holiness. Your safety is of the first importance."

Although no great admirer of Clement as a pope, Bartoli was utterly dedicated to the papacy as an institution ordained of God and to the Church as God's instrument on earth. The preservation of Clement as the present embodiment of that Divine purpose was therefore imperative.

"I have summoned the Swiss Guard, Holiness, and they will be here anon. They will escort you to safety and—"

"No," Clement interrupted, a slight quaver in his voice. "I shall meet this army and entreat them to withdraw. We have made peace with the Colonna and they will recognize it. They are come under a misguidance of some kind. I am sure of this," he finished, taking up the gospel from the table at his elbow and opening it.

Bartoli was unable to contain himself. He stood aghast at this bland denial of deadly truth.

"Holiness," he blurted, "are you both blind and deaf? The Colonna were never to be trusted. They were and they remain dedicated to the German cause. They are implacable enemies of the Holy See. It has been so these three hundred years and more. In God's name, can you not see what is happening here? All this is planned by the Holy Roman Emperor. I implore you to accept this and make haste away. We know not what this army intends. They may seek your life, Holiness. I beseech you to flee."

Bartoli's entreaties were in vain; Clement remained obdurate.

He instructed Bartoli to order the Swiss Guards back to their stations and peremptorily dismissed the cardinal, telling him he wished to pray and was not to be disturbed until the army of the Colonna was at the city gates.

Bartoli, black despair and foreboding filling him utterly, said nothing. He made obeisance and went to do as he was told.

* * * *

When the menacing host reached the city, a steward gave Clement the news, and the papal carriage was made ready to carry His Holiness out to parlay with the commanding officers.

Clement rose and prepared to go, but it was already too late.

Allowing nothing to hinder them, the Colonna and their troops flooded into Rome like the legions of Lucifer. The papal forces, hopelessly outnumbered and in disarray, valiantly attempted to forestall the onslaught, but were swept aside and scattered like dry leaves before a hot wind.

A dozen men with drawn swords confronted Clement as he left his rooms. They seized him with rough, contemptuous hands and thrust him out into the street amid jeers and hoots of derision. His mind in a turmoil of confusion and horror, he was bundled into a donkey cart and conveyed to the fortress castle of Sant'angelo which the invaders had captured unopposed. He made an incongruous figure in his papal robes clutching John's gospel in his arms as the cart jolted and bumped through the narrow streets. Soldiers threw rotten vegetables and stones at him and shouted for his head. As he fought to keep his balance, Clement felt betrayed and monstrously alone. Where were his allies? Where was the League of Cognac? Where were the Florentines, his own kinsmen?

As the pope was paraded through the city like a jester at a fair, chaos overtook the Vatican. Cardinals, bishops, priests, monks, nuns and novices, servants, grooms, footmen and cooks scattered for their lives as the Colonna's men rampaged through the rooms and corridors. Paintings and sculpture were destroyed, tapestries slashed, while silver and gold objects of all kinds were seized and thrust into sacks.

All day the pillage continued and when darkness fell, a thousand blazing torches revealed wagons and oxcarts rumbling through the streets carrying off the plunder. Even inside his locked room deep within Sant'angelo, Clement heard the shouts and cheers of victory as the invaders began to disperse and withdraw from the city. Rome itself had been left almost untouched, but the Vatican stood looted and empty.

"A plague on all popes," the soldiers shrieked. "Long live Emperor Charles and the glorious Family Colonna."

A day later, when all was quiet, the castellan of Sant'angelo unlocked the door allowing Clement to be taken back to the Vatican. He stood, wretched and alone, amid the ruin and desolation of his once-comfortable apartments, and wept.

* * * *

"Charles continues to deny any complicity in the Colonna's atrocities," said Bartoli to Cattaneo one evening in December, as they sat on hard wooden chairs in Bartoli's bare apartment. "But I say he lies. He has been diligent in his attempts to exploit our weakness. He threatens and bullies, he masses his troops, now here, now there. Thanks to his victory at Pavia, he has total mastery of the north and he demands territorial concessions from us, even reparations. I am at my wits' end."

"Charles' warlike stance has finally forced His Holiness to negotiate with him," said Cattaneo, "and surely that can be no bad thing. Might not those negotiations afford us some stability and security?"

Bartoli exhaled a long breath and shook his head.

"I doubt it. I have tried to help him, but he will not heed my advice. He is like a tree in the wind, blown this way and that by his own indecision. At one moment he speaks of a truce, while at another he waxes lyrical about his belief that the League of Cognac is preparing a stupendous army to destroy Charles on the battlefield. He negotiates, he breaks off negotiations; he simpers like a girl and then threatens as if he were master of all Europe."

Cattaneo was unable to respond, his mouth stuffed with sausage, and Bartoli suddenly chuckled as he took a sip of the cheap wine his steward had purchased at a nearby inn.

"I swear the imperial representatives know not which way to jump. They cannot keep His Holiness in one place long enough to achieve anything."

"Perhaps, then, he has more cunning than we give him credit for," said Cattaneo, licking his fingers industriously. Bartoli's ephemeral good humor evaporated.

"Not so. It is his precious gospel once again. However, it seems on this occasion he cannot find the direction he seeks, and each time he reads and prays, he finds a new answer. He trusts none of us since we advised him, as he has chosen to construe it, to make the first alliance with France."

"So," said Cattaneo, taking up a goblet of wine and barely suppressing a belch, "how lies the land at present, then?"

Bartoli sat back in his wooden chair—soft velvet upholstery was but a memory—and folding his hands over the silver crucifix that hung from a heavy chain around his neck, he spoke with measured deliberation.

"I truly believe we stand in peril of our lives."

Cattaneo paused, the wine goblet half raised, and stared at his friend in unmixed shock.

"Let me explain," said Bartoli. "It is a tangle and at this moment I know not how it is to be resolved so long as His Holiness continues to play hoodman blind with the enemies that threaten us."

Cattaneo blinked his tiny eyes and breathed heavily.

"The Emperor Charles, himself, is still in Spain," Bartoli said, "yet he wishes to press his claims here in Italy. However, my informants tell me he has insufficient revenue to raise a large enough army. He has, therefore, turned to his ally the Tyrolese Condottiere, Georg von

Frundsberg, who has mortgaged his houses and castles, all his other possessions and even sold his wife's jewelry to raise nearly forty thousand gulden. With that, he has retained the services of some ten thousand men-at-arms. Now, I ask you, why would von Frundsberg do that?"

Cattaneo looked blank for a moment, and then said, "For a future reward of some kind, I suppose."

Bartoli spread his hands and inclined his head.

"Of course. And what could that reward be, do you think?"

"I do not know."

"Rome," said Bartoli. "They will plunder Rome. And when they do, it will make the attack on the Vatican by the Colonna look like a children's game. Charles will have his final revenge upon Clement; he will establish his suzerainty over Italy and all without stirring himself from Madrid or spending a single Spanish ducat of his own money."

Cattaneo swallowed hard and went a little pale.

"Are you sure of this?"

"I have just received news that last month von Frundsberg crossed the mountains and moved in force towards Brescia. Once there, he made common cause with Alfonso of Ferrara who made him a present of several of his heaviest siege cannon. You can be certain he does not intend to hunt rabbits with them."

"Alfonso is no lover of His Holiness," muttered Cattaneo. "I am sure he was only too pleased to be of assistance."

"Doubtless," said Bartoli, his voice as dry as old straw, "since both Medici popes have done their humble best to depose him."

"Surely," said Cattaneo, waving a pudgy, white hand, "we can field an army greater than a mere ten thousand men."

"I have not finished," said Bartoli. "Von Frundsberg and his Lutheran rabble have crossed the Po, and have lain waste the farmlands of Lombardia. They moved on to Milan and there met Constable de Bourbon who commanded the German mercenaries at Pavia. The Constable has almost incalculable wealth—some say he is the richest man in all Europe—and was created Duke of Milan once the French troops had been driven from the city. He, too, has been raising an army for the emperor."

Bartoli took another mouthful of wine, grimaced slightly, and continued.

"That is all I know at present, but we can assume the Bourbon will unite his army with that of von Frundsberg, and together they will march on Rome."

"But," said Cattaneo, "what of the League of Cognac? Their combined armies would surely be sufficient to——."

"There is no time for the League to act," Bartoli interrupted. "They can do nothing for us."

"Have you told His Holiness of this?" asked Cattaneo.

"Indeed I have," answered Bartoli, "and he does nothing but hug his gospel to his heart and dither like a small boy who cannot find his chamber pot."

* * * *

Many months after that conversation, after Rome had been ransacked and pilloried, and Cattaneo lay dead, Cardinal Bartoli sat writing at a plain wooden table in a bare room in the castle fortress of Sant'angelo. A small candle guttered at his elbow, casting a meager light. A tray of food sat untouched on the floor beside his chair. There was no sound in the stone-walled chamber save the steady scratch of his quill. Through the act of writing, he sought to purge his memory of the horrific images that invested it, and expiate the sin he had committed.

I was correct, he wrote. Would that I were not. At the beginning of February, Constable de Bourbon marched out of Milan at the head of an army and allied himself to the German commander, von Frundsberg. Together they fielded an army of over twenty-two thousand men. They moved eastwards along the Via Emilia, ravaging the countryside and visiting ruination and death on the innocent folk of that region.

His Holiness, by now overcome with dread, read his English gospel of John for many days before begging the Viceroy of Naples to arrange a truce so that we might be delivered from our enemies. A truce was made, but we discovered to our dismay His Holiness had agreed to pay sixty thousand ducats to clothe, feed and pay the German army of von

Frundsberg. Our treasury was dangerously depleted.

His Holiness declared his prayers answered, and the danger passed. Against all entreaties to the contrary, he dismissed the Roman army and, with what little money remained, paid the soldiers, and bade them return to their homes. I implored the Holy Father to maintain the army, reminding him of the attack upon the Vatican last year. Alas, he would not listen to me. He declared again that God, through the gospel of John, had revealed the truth to him. The city guard was thus reduced to a paltry three hundred men.

When the army of the Bourbon heard of the money paid to the German troops they howled in rage. The men were so incensed against their hardships and against Rome that the Bourbon had of necessity to inform His Holiness on March the nineteenth that the truce was at an end after a mere eight months. He declared he could no longer control his men.

In his customary fashion, the Holy Father passed more hours each day in prayer and in the study of his gospel. He would not be disturbed, and thus we who endeavored to take some practical measures to save the city were denied an audience.

The day of May the sixth, brought our ruin and called down upon all Rome such a calamity of torture, plunder, rape and murder as to make all Christendom quake.

The enemy poured in upon us like a hideous tide, and what few defenders there were, including our ever-faithful Swiss Guards, were cut down with a ferocity frightful to behold.

His Holiness, I and twelve other cardinals, as well as numerous other persons of various rank, managed to find safety in the castle of Sant'angelo, that selfsame place wherein His Holiness had so lately been confined by the Colonna. The renowned sculptor, the great Benvenuto Cellini, took command of the fortress' cannons, and proved himself a most able and gallant soldier.

The fighting on the ramparts was monumental, but before the day was spent, the enemy was master of the city, and so ceased his assault on the castle.

The protestant heretics stabled horses in St. Peter's and every church was defiled and ransacked. Among the dead was my dear friend, his Eminence Mario Cardinal Cattaneo, who was killed as he tried to reach Sant'angelo.

His Holiness watched the sack of the city from Sant'angelo's towers. He clutched his gospel to himself and beseeched God with wails and cries of despair to show him what he should do, but answer came there none.

Bartoli reached for another sheet of vellum, crossed himself twice and bowed his head for a moment before dipping his quill and beginning to write once again.

* * * *

On the sixth day of the sack of Rome, a young soldier named Gerhard Zeller walked along a dusty street close by the fortress of Sant'angelo. There was rubble everywhere and on either side of the narrow lane, he saw the smoldering ruins of houses and small shops. Here and there, human and animal corpses lay amongst the broken bricks and shards of stone, and as he picked his way along, the smell of smoke and putrefying flesh soured his nostrils and sickened his stomach.

As he rounded a corner, he caught sight of another soldier approaching wearing a sleeveless leather jerkin and chain mail.

"Greetings," said Zeller as they met.

"Greetings," answered the other man. "And where are you off to, may I ask?"

"To the city gates and then home," said Zeller. "I have had my fill of this butchery and destruction."

"'Tis no butchery to kill papists and idolaters, friend. It is the just work of true Christians."

"We are all the children of God," said Zeller. "Luther himself says so."

"Oho," said the other with a mocking laugh, "a theologian, are you? Well, theologian, I say death to all Catholics and ruination to their gaudy, sin-filled churches."

The man thrust a cloth bag he had been carrying into Zeller's hands.

"Here, theologian, tell me what this is if you can."

"It's a book," said Zeller, peering into the bag.

"I can see that for myself. It's full of pictures as well. Can you read, theologian?"

"Only German," said Zeller, "and this is in Latin."

"Then I'll take it back," said the soldier. "I can start a fire with it tonight."

He grasped the bag, but Zeller pulled it away.

"Likely it is a holy text. It should not be destroyed."

The man regarded Zeller narrowly before drawing a dagger from his belt and holding it before Zeller's face. Zeller saw dried blood on the blade.

"Perhaps you are a priest in disguise, theologian. Perhaps even a cardinal or the thrice-damned pope himself."

"I am a Bavarian Lutheran," said Zeller, "and I have sworn my loyalty to Emperor Charles. I want no papal armies in Bavaria. The pope may rule those who wish to be ruled by him, but neither he nor his church shall rule me."

The man stared hard at Zeller for a few moments, and then shrugged.

"Then I wish you joy of your holy text, theologian," he sneered, and walked on down the desolate and deserted street.

PART FOUR
England: The Present Day

Chapter Fifteen

"So there it is," said Randall, looking at Megan and Tony Joyce who sat opposite him in his living room on his first evening back from London. "That manuscript of Robert's would appear to be *The Haunted Gospel* all right, but I haven't the foggiest idea of what this treasure thing Brother Bartholomew speaks of could possibly be. He doesn't say how it's explained in the gospel's illuminations either, just that it's there. Pictures of whatever it is, I suppose. But it certainly seems as if there's something more here than we originally thought."

"And I take it all these documents are genuine?" asked Joyce, in a rather official tone of voice, and then grinned as Megan told him to stop being a policeman if he possibly could.

"They most certainly are genuine, Detective Sergeant," said Randall, mimicking Joyce's tone with a laugh. "There's no doubt about that."

"Has there ever been, or have you ever come across, any other references to any sort of treasure or such like at All Saints Monastery?" asked Joyce. "Even legends or stories?"

"All Saints was a priory, actually," said Randall, "and I've never heard of anything of the kind. All Saints was a very minor house, you understand, and apart from Robert the Illuminator, has no real claim to fame."

"Well," said Megan from her place next to Joyce on the sofa, "what now?"

"I'm going to try and trace the manuscript," Randall said. "It's clear Mike had found out something about it that he thought was important. I presume it was this treasure business, whatever it may be. The archivist in London said Mike had studied Brother Bartholomew's journal and accounts book."

"When was that?" asked Joyce.

"I didn't ask, but the archivist said Mike had damaged the book slightly and it had to be repaired. The repairs took some months, so it looks as if Mike saw the book shortly before his death."

"Was the archivist sure it was Dr. Stuart?"

"Yes. It would have been recorded. Anyone given access to original documents of that sort has to have credentials and is always logged in and out."

"I think I'll ask Thomas to have that checked in any case," said Joyce. "You never know. This treasure thing may have a bearing on Dr. Stuart's murder. Money's a powerful motive."

"It doesn't have to be gold, or money or anything of that kind, though," said Randall.

"Doesn't it?"

"Not at all. Treasure to a thirteenth century monk could well have been the bones of a saint, a splinter of wood from the True Cross, a vial of water from the River Jordan or the Lake of Galilee. Not necessarily anything we'd define as objects of great value."

"I see," said Joyce, "and yet it's hard to think that Dr. Stuart would have got excited about non-monetary treasure."

"We don't know that he did," put in Megan. "He probably didn't know what the supposed treasure was, any more than we do."

"True," answered Joyce, "but since he was a military historian, I wonder why else he'd become so interested in a medieval religious text?"

"There could be any number of reasons," said Megan.

"Quite," agreed Randall, "but whatever his reasons, he did find the references to *The Haunted Gospel* in Bartholomew's journal at the British Library, just as I did. So he certainly knew of the treasure's existence."

Joyce nodded.

"And," Randall added, "Mike would certainly have known that if this treasure were of the precious metal or gemstone type, it wouldn't automatically be his to keep even if he did find it. Under the 1996 Treasure Act, he'd have to report it to the proper authorities. He'd get some monetary compensation if a museum or some such place decided they wanted whatever it was, but the objects wouldn't simply be his to sell privately for whatever he could get."

The evening drew to a close and Megan announced she would have to go. Joyce rose and offered her his hand with a smile. She took it with an answering smile and was still holding it when Randall brought her coat. Randall kissed Megan on the cheek and after Joyce gave his hand a vise-like shake, he saw the two of them off. He went upstairs to bed and fell asleep wondering what the future held for his daughter and her handsome young police officer.

The next morning, Randall saw Max Thoroughgood and filled him in on the research in London. He told the dean about All Saints, Brother Robert and the gospel, but decided he wanted more information before mentioning the so-called treasure in case the whole thing began to sound too much like a remake of Peter Pan.

Later that day, Randall got in touch with his contact at the Vatican and asked if the archives currently listed any manuscripts attributed to Robert the Illuminator or Robert of All Saints, and was told they did not. Hardly surprising, he thought. Mike would probably have found *The Haunted Gospel* himself if it had been sitting in Rome under Robert's name waiting to be discovered.

He sent an email to John Archer asking him to come and see him. The young man duly appeared the following afternoon.

"Thanks for coming in, John," said Randall. "I was wondering if you'd be interested in earning a little money."

"I certainly would, sir," said Archer, brightening visibly, "and I could definitely use it about now. What would you like me to do?"

"Well," said Randall, "it wouldn't be a huge amount, I'm afraid, but I do have a little research funding available, and you once asked if you could help in connection with that manuscript Professor Stuart discovered in the *Biblioteca Apostolica Vaticana.* Remember?"

"Yes, of course. Do you know where it is now?"

"No, but I had a stroke of luck at the British Library."

"Do they know about it?"

"Not exactly, but I think I've traced its origins. I read a text written at All Saints Priory in the thirteenth century that makes reference to a gospel of John created by one Brother Robert the Illuminator, a famous copyist of his day. There's an example of his work at Canterbury and a couple in the British Museum."

"Then what about the haunted part?"

"Well, it appears poor old Robert was murdered by another monk of All Saints who was tried and then stuck in a cage and starved to death. That was the method of choice for execution when it came to clerics, you see. The gospel was taken to Norwich Cathedral, and then later sent to Rome because it was reputed to have been visited by the ghosts of the two dead monks."

Archer stared for a moment.

"My God, that's it for sure. That's terrific, but how do we find *The Haunted Gospel* now?"

"Well, I checked with the Vatican, of course, and they say they have nothing cataloged under that name or under Brother Robert either, so they're out of the picture. However, what I'd like you to do, John, is contact dealers and see if any of them have ever heard of anything called *The Haunted Gospel*, or any work of Brother Robert of All Saints that might be in private hands. It won't be too arduous. There aren't that many dealers who concern themselves with documents of that kind or age. It will take a bit of sleuthing, though, to identify the right dealers to approach."

"I can do that all right, sir, but I wonder why it isn't still in the Vatican archives?"

"Anything could have happened to it," said Randall. "However, if the manuscript is still extant and buried in someone's private collection, it might be almost impossible to find. The dealers are a good starting point, though."

Archer left with profuse thanks and earnest promises to begin work immediately.

Randall undertook a search of his own, concentrating on museums, galleries and academic institutions, and he spent the next two days on the Internet compiling a list of the people and organizations that might have a line on a thirteenth century manuscript. He also listed several personal contacts who were specialists in the history of the Church in Italy and set himself a schedule to work his way systematically through all the names he had accumulated.

He picked up the phone and called Katherine. He had wanted to call her immediately after he returned home from London, and wondered if she might feel he was trying to push her towards a relationship she was not quite ready for. True, she had said she would look forward to seeing him again, but the very intensity of his feelings for her somehow led him to doubt, to question and wonder. Could he love again, and could Katherine love him?

Damn, he thought, as her phone rang again and again. *She's not in. What do I leave for a message?* He paused in indecision and was about to replace the receiver when he heard her voice.

"Katherine Crowley speaking."

"Hello, Katherine, it's George. Look, I really want to see you again. Soon, if that's all right with you."

* * * *

On Friday of the following week, Randall took an afternoon train to London and taxi to the Bestwycke. Megan asked him why he was going again so soon; had there been some sort of breakthrough in the search for the manuscript?

"Er…no, not exactly," he said, and deciding obfuscation was pointless, added, "The fact is, Meg, I've met someone who's become rather important to me, and I'm going to see her."

Megan launched herself into his arms with a squeal of delight.

"Oh, Pop, that's absolutely brilliant. I'm so happy for you."

They sat down and over the next twenty minutes, she made him tell her everything about Katherine, and tried to extract from him a promise to bring her home as soon as possible.

"She sounds charming," she said, "and I want to get to know her."

"Now hang on," he said. "It hasn't gone quite that far yet."

"Doesn't matter. I want to meet her."

"You don't think your old Dad's too ancient and decrepit for such gallivanting about, then?" he asked.

"Oh, I'm all in favor of gallivanting," she said with a laugh. Then she took his two hands in hers, her expression serious. "Follow your heart, Pop; that's what you've always said to me, isn't it?"

"Thank you," he smiled.

"Were you worried about what I might think?" she asked. "About

Mum, I mean."

Dear, perceptive Megan, he thought.

"Yes I was, rather."

"Well don't be," she said. "You've been alone ten years, and if you should love again it wouldn't mean for an instant that you'd forgotten Mum or that she wasn't important to you anymore."

As he lay in bed in his room at the Bestwycke that night, he thought again of that conversation. Had Megan been seeing something in him he had perhaps not fully appreciated for himself? The emptiness in his existence was no longer there, and he felt a sense of completeness for the first time in a decade.

Katherine came to the Bestwycke for lunch the next day. Afterward, they walked through Green Park in the declining afternoon sunshine of the late summer's day. The great trees seemed to surround and enclose them and Randall relaxed, feeling far away from the tumult of traffic and the surging crowds of hurrying Londoners.

Towards evening, they sat on a bench and surveyed the vistas of green grass before them, speaking little but spending long periods in companionable silence.

"Katherine," he said, turning to face her.

"Yes George?"

"Katherine, I just want to tell you how much—"

At that precise moment, a pigeon, flying unseen high overhead, let go a dollop that landed with a loud and startling smack on the pavement not ten inches from Randall's shoe. In his state of heightened concentration and emotion, it sounded to him like a pistol shot.

"Good God," he blurted.

Katherine dissolved into peals of helpless laughter. Randall was suddenly speechless.

"You lead a charmed life," she managed to gasp.

"Damn thing," muttered Randall, feeling as if his dignity had been affronted, but Katherine's laughter was too infectious to resist and the absurdity of the situation dawned on him. They laughed together as he shook his fist skyward at his avian attacker.

"I thought the blitz ended years ago," Katherine said as they regained a modicum of composure.

"Where's the bloody RAF when you need them?" he said. "That was undoubtedly a German pigeon and there isn't a Spitfire in sight."

"So, anyway," she said, "what was it you were about to say?"

"Oh…er…well," he tried, but the moment had been irretrievably lost. "I was going to suggest we find somewhere for dinner."

She regarded him for a moment with her luminous hazel eyes.

"Why not my flat?"

"Your flat?"

"Don't look so worried," she laughed. "I'm fairly good in the kitchen. And," she added, "I took the precaution of investing in two very fine filet steaks for precisely this eventuality."

His heart literally missed a beat. She had actually planned for this already.

"That sounds marvelous, Katherine. Thank you."

After a short taxi ride, she ushered him into a large and tastefully furnished flat on the fifteenth floor of a new building.

"My humble abode."

"It's lovely. It really is."

"I'm so glad you're here, George," she smiled.

"So am I," he said, and kissed her.

"Come into the kitchen and talk to me while I do the dinner," she said.

She asked him to open a bottle of wine and pour them each a glass, and he leaned against the black granite countertop while she prepared their meal with competent efficiency. He fixed the salad while she grilled the steaks and all was soon ready.

They ate at a small, round table situated in a dining alcove surrounded on three sides by large windows affording a panoramic view of the city. Randall declared he had never had a meal in more wonderful surroundings.

"Nor with such wonderful company," he added, and she reached out and took his hand.

"Careful, Professor," she said with a mischievous smile. "Now I've got you, I just might never let you go."

After dinner, she put a Mozart CD on the stereo and they sat drinking wine and talking. It was past midnight when he finally and reluctantly made a move to go.

"The time has come, the walrus said," he told her with a smile.

"To speak of many things?" she answered, finishing the famous quotation, but turning it into a question. "I thought we'd already been doing that."

"Indeed we have," he said, "but I mean it's time for me to be going."

She fixed her hazel eyes on him.

"You can stay you know, George."

His thoughts raced through happiness and excitement, but then came to rest on sudden nervousness. When Jennifer died, he had been forty-two, well-proportioned and very fit. Now, a decade later, he had put on a little too much weight and had long since given up the hiking and climbing he and his wife had so much enjoyed. Katherine's invitation conjured up a disturbing vision of himself standing naked before her, a soft-muscled, middle-aged man with a slight paunch, and she, slim and elegant, looking at him and wondering why in God's name she had ever thought him attractive, let alone invited him to share her bed. Worse yet, and he shrank from the thought, he was not sure he would be able to give her the physical pleasure he wanted to: the pleasure she was no doubt anticipating. It was ten years since he had made love, and he no longer had much faith in his staying power. For a tumultuous moment he considered declining her invitation, and then became aware that she was looking at him with raised eyebrows.

"I didn't actually expect you to seize me and carry me in triumph to the bedroom, George," she said, "although I wouldn't have objected if you had. But I was hoping for at least a modicum of enthusiasm."

"I'm sorry," he said. "I was…I mean…."

"George," she said, "you haven't been with anyone since Jennifer died, have you?"

He shook his head.

"And I've been alone since Gareth ran off with little Miss Two-buckets, his ever-so-personal assistant. I love you, George, and I don't want either of us to be alone any longer."

Their lovemaking was warm, passionate and completely satisfying. Randall, cradling Katherine in his arms, drifted off to sleep in a state of bliss and utter contentment.

$$* * * *$$

When he returned home, Randall had to run the gauntlet of Megan's expectant curiosity and field her questions about his weekend in London.

"Did you enjoy yourself, Pop?" she asked with a conspiratorial smile.

"Yes, Meg, thank you," he answered. "Katherine is a wonderful companion."

"No, I said did you *enjoy* yourself?"

Why make a secret of it, he asked himself.

"Yes, I did. "

"Good on you," she grinned.

Chapter Sixteen

It was not until October that Randall returned his attention to the gospel. The new university term had begun and he had commenced tutorials. There were some particularly bright sparks amongst his students and he looked forward to a stimulating and interesting year. The bleak evenings of autumn drew in towards the even bleaker evenings of winter, and the weather chilled into raw winds and steady rain: a climate well suited to the desolation in Randall's soul as he missed Katherine more and more. He went to see her as often as he could, but wonderful as those visits were, they made it harder to endure the times they were apart.

On one such wet and windy afternoon at the end of the month, Randall's phone rang and he heard the voice of John Archer.

"Good afternoon, sir. Sorry to trouble you, only I was wondering if I could see you sometime soon about the work you gave me to do. I would have called a lot sooner but I've been pretty bunged up with stuff for the new term."

He and Archer met the following morning and the young man handed over a report on a CD-ROM.

"I've listed every contact I made," said Archer, with a worried look, "but the upshot of it all is I didn't find anything really definite or useful at all. Nothing. I mean, no one's heard of anything called *The Haunted Gospel.* Lots of people knew about gospel manuscripts—there's a ton of them out there it seems—and all sorts of other biblical stuff, but there was no mention of anything haunted or anything to do with All Saints Priory."

"That's what I was afraid of," said Randall, with a rueful smile at the young man.

"I'm really sorry, sir," said Archer. "I wish I could have been more help."

"Well," said Randall, "I'm beginning to think the whole search is a long shot. I've identified the gospel, I know who created it and how it got to Rome, but I'm not sure how we trace it from here."

* * * *

Determined as Randall was to discover the gospel's history, events that autumn conspired against him. He was slated to be the keynote speaker and to deliver a paper at a conference in London in mid-December, and he had done almost no preparation for it. He was annoyed at himself for having allowed this situation to develop. It was not at all his style.

One mid-November night he stayed in his study well past midnight, his smoldering briar clenched between his teeth, He was hard at work on his paper, which he had entitled *Monarchy and Theocracy: Towards an Understanding of Public Policy Development in Twelfth Century England.* His aim was to present an entirely new way of looking at the political relationship between Church and State in the 1100s and he was oblivious to everything but what he was doing. It was as if he were transported back to the twelfth century himself.

Having composed and written one of the most salient points in his argument, he sat back in satisfaction, took the reeking pipe from his mouth, stretched, and at that moment experienced what he later described as the shock of his life.

The window directly in front of his desk exploded inwards. The windowpane disintegrated into a thousand flying shards of splintered glass as a heavy stone burst through it and crashed onto his desk. It bounced off onto the floor with a loud thud, narrowly missing him and smashing his computer monitor as it went. Randall sat dumbstruck and so completely stupefied he did nothing for a few moments. Then, galvanized into action as though released by a spring, he leaped to his feet and sprinted for the front door.

"Bloody hooligans," he roared, as he ran down the front path, his face bleeding from a laceration he had not even noticed.

"I'll have your guts for garters! Where the hell are you?"

He stood on the pavement looking up and down the deserted residential street, trembling with shock and fury. Lights came on in the surrounding houses and one of his neighbors hurried out into the chilly darkness to see what was amiss.

"Kids I suppose," growled Randall. "Must have seen the light on.

Little buggers."

In spite of his protests, the police and an ambulance were summoned, and soon his house and front garden were illuminated by a cluster of flickering blue and red lights.

"It looks like Christmas already," Randall muttered.

A young paramedic examined the wound on his cheek, and although there was still some bleeding, pronounced it small and not requiring sutures. After allowing a white sticking plaster to be put on the cut, Randall prescribed himself a generous tot of brandy as a recuperative which he settled down to drink in his front room. The two policemen who had arrived with the ambulance saw the spectators off to their homes and then followed him inside. As they prepared to take a statement from him, Megan, alarmed and white-faced, hurried in.

"Oh my God," was all she could say at first, but then, composing herself somewhat, managed to ask him if he was all right.

"I'm fine, love," he said as bracingly as he could, "but what are you doing here? How did you know something had happened?"

"I came with Tony," she said. "They called him as soon as the 999 came in."

Detective Sergeant Joyce appeared, preventing Randall from making further comment.

"You all right George?"

"Yes thanks, except for this cut on the face, but—"

"There's no sign of anyone," Joyce interrupted, "and none of the close neighbors heard or saw anything, but we'll canvas the entire street in due course. We've found where he got the stone from and where he stood to heave it through the window. It seems there was only one person; or at least there's only one set of footprints in the flowerbed."

"What's all the fuss about?" said Randall. "I'm sure it was just some local clod. How did you hear about it, anyway? It's hardly the crime of the century."

"I asked the local nick to let me know if anything untoward was reported in or around this neighborhood," Joyce said.

"Whatever for?" Randall asked, and Joyce shrugged.

"Oh, call it instinct or something like that, I suppose. Ever since you started talking about this treasure possibility in relation to the gospel manuscript, I've been a bit edgy. There's been one murder already, don't forget."

"The treasure *again*?" said Randall. "I thought I explained about that."

"You did," said Joyce, "to us. However, someone else may have a different point of view."

"That would mean someone else has found out about it," said Randall, "and I can't see how they could have without reading Bartholomew. And the chap at the British Library said Mike and I were the only ones to see Bartholomew in decades."

"Be that as it may," said Joyce, "I think this little episode tonight shows us it's better to err on the side of caution."

The two constables reappeared, one of them carrying the heavy stone projectile in a large plastic evidence bag as carefully as if it were a newborn baby. Joyce instructed them to get it to forensics as quickly as possible, and then he sat down next to Megan on the sofa.

"You could have been killed, Pop," Megan said.

"Tosh," said Randall. "Stupid prank, that's all."

"Well," said Joyce, "I'd rather be safe than sorry, and until we get a better line on who killed Dr. Stuart, I want to keep an eye on everything."

An unexpected wave of weakness swept over Randall like a cold, clammy wind as he envisioned what might have happened had he not been sitting back in his chair at the moment the stone was thrown. His stomach knotted, and he felt slightly ill.

"Would you get me another brandy please, Meg?"

She refilled his glass and resumed her place next to Joyce.

"What are you actually saying, Tony?" she asked.

"I'm saying that even if it sounds implausible at this stage, someone else might have found out about the treasure—be it real or imaginary—and they're after it themselves. I think we should be very careful for the time being. Have you told anyone about it George, apart from us?"

"Katherine knows, but I haven't told anyone else. Treasure hunting sounds rather far-fetched, so I've kept it quiet."

"Good. Stay with that plan."

"Mike knew about it," said Megan. "He may have told somebody."

"That's true," nodded Joyce, "and there's nothing we can do about

137

that. Anyway, I'm now working on the assumption that whoever killed Dr. Stuart probably did it on account of that treasure thing."

"I still want to go on looking for the gospel," Randall said, and Joyce chuckled.

"Yes. I knew this wouldn't put you off. Be careful, and try not to make the search too public. I mean, don't involve more people than you have to."

"Tony," Randall said, "a lot of people on campus already know what I'm up to. I've even employed a student to do some legwork for me. It would look very odd indeed if I suddenly stopped talking about it. Furthermore, apart from library research, the main method of tracking down ancient books and manuscripts is by talking to people. It's no different from your line of work in that respect."

Joyce was silent a moment.

"Fair enough. I understand. But don't mention the treasure, or whatever it is."

* * * *

Within a week, the window was repaired, and Randall was back at work on his conference paper in front of a new flat panel monitor. The police confirmed the stone had come from the front garden rockery, and Randall waxed more than eloquent when he saw one of his prize rose bushes had been broken by the vandal.

"It's my Lord Mountbatten, dammit," he complained to Katherine a few days later during an evening telephone conversation. "I'll bet it was an envious member of the Rose Growers Association.

"I trust that's all it was," she said.

"Oh, and by the way, Tony thinks we shouldn't tell anyone else about this so-called treasure of All Saints."

"Oh dear," she said, "I'm afraid I told Donald."

"I shouldn't think that's a problem," Randall answered. "Ask him not to broadcast it, though."

* * * *

By early December, Randall was ready for the conference and had even managed to devote a few hours to his contact list in the gospel search. He ran into John Archer on campus one day as the two of them hurried to escape a heavy downpour being driven across the open quadrangle by a wind that seemed cold enough to have come straight from the high arctic.

"It's just as you found with the dealers, John," he said. "No one's heard of the blasted thing."

"Sorry, sir."

"Never mind," said Randall. "I've lots to keep me busy just now anyway."

"Have a good Christmas, Dr. Randall," said Archer, offering his hand.

"Thank you, and you too, John. Good luck with the Christmas exams."

Randall finished his remaining administrative work, and a couple of days later took the train to London where he headed for Katherine's flat —his now customary lodging. The city was in its festive garb and the shops were busily attempting to outdo one other in the annual Yuletide ritual of separating shoppers from their money.

He had purposely arranged to arrive in London four days prior to the conference in order to allow time to meet old friends and colleagues, and he spent many hours in pleasant conversation with them. He also took the opportunity to put out the word that he was looking for any information available on a thirteenth century manuscript referred to as *The Haunted Gospel*, however no one knew anything about it. He was a little disappointed, although not surprised or discouraged.

He stayed in Katherine's flat, but she was only there for two days before leaving for Berne to meet an old friend for a Christmas holiday, which had been arranged many months previously. He felt very much alone without her, in spite of how busy the conference kept him.

His keynote address and paper were well received and Randall was pleased with the outcome of the conference. Once the closing ceremonies were complete, he made a foray out into the busy streets to do the last of his Christmas shopping. By seven o'clock in the evening, he was laden with parcels and wondering where best to find a taxi back to the flat.

As he threaded his way along the crowded pavement, he suddenly found himself being strongly propelled by unseen hands out into the road.

"Hey, what the—?" he managed to shout, before stumbling down the curb, dropping his parcels and sprawling headlong. A horn blared somewhere very close by as he felt an excruciating pain consume his left arm. His head struck the road with a stunning impact that reverberated within his skull, and he knew no more.

Chapter Seventeen

Randall's Christmas was decidedly less than merry, in spite of its being spent with Megan. His arm was sealed in a grossly uncomfortable and inconvenient cast, and supported by a sling.

Not wishing to shock Megan at the sight of him in an injured condition, he telephoned her after being discharged from the hospital. He briefly explained his broken arm and asked her to meet him at the station and bring Tony Joyce with her.

As promised, they were waiting and promptly whisked him off to Megan's house where, she announced in a tone that brooked no denial, he was to stay until fully recovered. The three of them sat down in the living room, and Megan asked about the accident.

"I think Tony's right," Randall said. "There *is* something going on."

"What do you mean?" Joyce asked.

"I mean I didn't fall off that curb by accident. I was pushed."

Megan uttered an exclamation of shock.

"I was afraid you might say that," said Joyce.

"I didn't want to think you were right," said Randall, "but I've no choice now. I feel as if I've got the devil at my heels."

"Did you report the incident to the police?" Joyce asked.

"Yes, and they came to see me in hospital. Didn't take me seriously, though. Probably thought I was just some dotty old academic with a too-vivid imagination. They said I'd probably just been jostled by the crowd and lost my balance."

"Oh, God," breathed Megan, "this is all getting out of hand."

"Did you see anything of him at all?" asked Joyce, compressing his lips.

"Not so much as a glimpse."

"Hardly surprising," said Joyce. "In those crowds with all the Christmas lights, the noise and confusion, a bloke could simply be swallowed up and disappear."

"What about surveillance cameras," Megan asked. "They seem to be just about everywhere these days."

"The police checked that out while I was in hospital," answered Randall, "and they have good pictures of me falling into the road, but there were just too many people and too many headlights to see anything more than that."

"Well, well," said Megan, "isn't it marvelous? All that money gone on fancy equipment, and where is it when you need it?"

"Okay," said Joyce. "I suppose this is as good a time as any to give you my piece of news as well, although it only adds to our problems, I'm afraid."

"Now what's going on?" Megan asked, apprehension clouding her eyes.

"You remember when you were at the British Library, George," Joyce said. "You found out Mike Stuart had seen the Bartholomew book?"

"Yes."

"Well, I said I'd check that out. I took it to Thomas and after a bit of coaxing he put in a request. Unfortunately, it was assigned a very low priority for some reason so it took forever to get done, but I've just had a call to say the person signed in at the library was Dr. Michael Stuart."

"Right. That's what the archivist said," Randall nodded. "So what's the problem?"

Joyce gave a rueful chuckle.

"The problem, George, is that the person signing in as Stuart did it two days after the murder."

There was a momentary silence before Randall and Megan spoke almost in unison.

"Two days after?"

"Two days. It seems none of the staff can remember exactly what the fellow looked like," Joyce went on, "but the register shows he provided a letter of *bona fides* from Dean Maxwell Thoroughgood. I spoke to Thoroughgood, and he confirmed having written such a letter for Dr. Stuart about three weeks before his death. He faxed me a copy."

"Well I'm damned," said Randall.

"Didn't anyone notice the name and connect it with the murder?" asked Megan.

Joyce shook his head.

"Apparently not. I'm afraid the murder didn't get much press in the nation's capital. Posing as Stuart was a risk, I grant you, but a calculated one, and it seems he got away with it."

"You know what?" said Randall. "This means that if Mike knew about this treasure thing—and we don't know for certain he did, of course—he must have found out about it from another source. He didn't read Bartholomew after all."

"Could there be another source out there somewhere?" asked Megan.

"Oh, I imagine so," Randall answered. "The fact that we haven't heard about it doesn't mean it doesn't exist."

"Well," said Joyce, "I think we can be sure that the imposter at the library was Dr. Stuart's murderer."

"Look," Megan interjected, "since the murderer read Bartholomew *after* killing Mike, he must have an additional source as well. That is, if the treasure was the motive for the murder."

"Or," Randall added, "Mike had told him about it and about his plans to go to the British Library."

"That's more likely," said Joyce with a nod. "Our man kills Stuart and takes the dean's identification letter so he can continue the search himself. That's confirmation Stuart knew his attacker, as if we needed it."

"I'd say so," agreed Randall.

"Who was Dr. Stuart talking to about his search for the gospel, George?" asked Joyce. "Do you know?"

"Well," said Randall, exhaling and blowing out his cheeks, "he told me about it, and for all I know may have talked to many others as well. And he did mention it to at least one of his students, John Archer, the one I had working for me. But Mike never mentioned anything to me about Norwich or All Saints Priory, and certainly never said a word about a treasure."

"He wouldn't have, would he?" Megan said. "Not if he was after it himself."

There was a brief pause, and Randall finished his drink.

"So I assume I'm the target now Mike's dead. Is that it?"

"I think so," said Joyce. "You've got to be very, very careful from now on. He's tried to get at you twice already. If this treasure legend has any basis in fact, it could well be that our man's found out a little more about it than we have, and it's something more valuable than holy water or some saint's wisdom tooth."

"I find it hard to believe in hidden treasure," said Randall, "especially if it's nearly eight hundred years old. It's all too much like looking for the Holy Grail."

"Well it seems someone believes in this particular hidden treasure," said Joyce, "and he'll remain interested in you so long as you continue looking for the gospel. I think that's the way to flush him out."

"I'd rather you just dropped the whole damn thing," Megan said, but Randall shook his head.

"Megan does have a point you know, George," said Joyce in his most professional tone. "We can't insist on your cooperation. There's obviously some danger here."

"At the beginning I wanted to find the gospel for Mike's sake," said Randall, "and I still do. Now it appears continuing the search could lead us to his killer, which is even more reason to press on. Do you see that, Meg?"

Megan smiled, albeit wanly, at her father, and nodded.

"I get it, but it's still frightening."

"Who knew your travel plans to London, George?" Joyce asked.

"Anyone and everyone," he answered. The conference is a major annual event, and when I was asked to be keynote speaker, it was reported in the campus newspaper."

"I see," said Joyce, "but it's just occurred to me that we have a new angle to consider."

"Which is?"

"Which is…that if we assume whoever shoved you into the road is our man, then he's known enough about you to know where you stay in London, and was watching you closely enough to follow you out shopping."

"Oh wonderful," said Megan. "This is getting worse by the minute."

"We'll get him, I promise," said Joyce. "And no one else is going to get hurt if I have anything to say about it."

Megan responded with a brief smile, but did not look convinced.

"So, George," Joyce went on, "we'll want to know whenever you notice anything odd, out of place. Particularly someone following you. Anything at all, no matter how vague. And, of course, we don't want to tip our man off, so you'll have to go about your business in the normal way. Just be extra observant."

* * * *

Randall stayed with Megan until after New Year's. He was eventually released from his cast at the end of March, the doctors having kindly informed him to his intense irritation that it had taken the bones a little longer to knit due to his age.

By spring, when his teaching duties lessened somewhat, he decided he had time to recommence work on his list of contacts to see if he could tease out any new information on the gospel. There had been no further untoward incidents. He was apparently not being shadowed by anyone, and as summer drew on, he felt more relaxed.

Throughout the summer, as time allowed, he worked his way through the balance of his list and came up empty-handed once again. Thanks to Brother Bartholomew, he had verified the existence of the manuscript, confirmed its origins, uncovered the background to its journey to the Vatican and its link to the probably apocryphal treasure at the priory, but now it appeared he had done all he could. The trail seemed stone cold. The gospel was certainly in Rome in 1356 and apparently vanished into oblivion sometime thereafter.

"Like all roads," he said to Megan, "this one has led to Rome. The problem is, I can't find where it goes after that."

Chapter Eighteen

"Good morning, Max," said Randall, encountering Dean Thoroughgood outside the dean's office on a chilly and damp October day. "Just the man I want to see."

"Morning, George," said Thoroughgood. "What's up? You look like the cat that ate the canary."

"I've got a lead on *The Haunted Gospel*," Randall replied with a grin. "Looks solid, too."

"Well, that's good news," said Thoroughgood. "Come into the office and tell me what's been going on."

"It goes back to the beginning of this term actually," Randall began, as he settled into a chair in front of Thoroughgood's vast, polished oak desk. "I got a call in mid-September from an old mate of mine at the University of Southampton. Fellow called Alfred Baines. He and I were at Oxford together as undergraduates, back in the Early Neolithic. We used to call him Heinz. You know, Heinz Baked Baines."

Thoroughgood looked blank, and Randall hurried on, reminding himself that Thoroughgood was a very bright chap, but not so quick with words.

"Well, never mind. Anyhow, I'd been chatting with him at the conference in London just before Christmas last year and he promised to see what he could do. Apparently, he's discovered a bloke in Milan, a Dr. Silvio Farina, who specializes—if you can believe it—in the history of the Vatican Archives. Baines says he knows more than anybody about what was in the archives, when and for how long. It turns out he's heard of the gospel manuscript. Baines isn't sure of the details, but this fellow's become very interested in the thing. I thought I'd pop down to Milan and have a chat with him. If I'm lucky, we may be able to find out what happened to the manuscript after it disappeared from the records."

Thoroughgood shot Randall a dubious glance and made a fussy little noise with his tongue.

"So you want to go to Milan?" he said. "In the middle of term? I'm not certain the vice-chancellor will be very keen on that idea. She wasn't best pleased when you beetled off to the British Library last year, you know. Why don't you just telephone this chap? Send him an email or something."

"No, no, Max," said Randall. "I thought I'd go down there over Christmas with a friend of mine. Make it an excuse for a sort of short winter holiday, you see. No expense to the university."

"Now, I damn well know you're up to something," said the dean. "I've never known you to spend Christmas anywhere but at home with Megan."

"The times they are a-changing, my dear dean," said Randall with a smile, as he rose to go. "The times they are a-changing."

Changing they certainly were. Randall and Katherine had begun to discuss a shared future. He had not proposed to her, although he fully intended to at some point, yet there had arisen between them an understanding that they would be together. The practicalities, however, were challenging. Katherine lived in London, Randall in Yorkshire, and they each had careers, which kept them where they were. Nothing had been resolved thus far, but Randall was determined to find a solution.

After talking to Thoroughgood, Randall confirmed the travel dates and immediately called to invite Katherine to go with him: an invitation she received with surprise and delight.

"I know Milan's not really a Christmas destination," he said. "You're supposed to go to Garmisch Partenkirchen or Cortina or somewhere like that, but we can have a wonderful time anyway."

"It's perfect," she said. "I have a friend in Milan who used to work in our London office a few years ago. She's the one I went to Berne with last year, remember?"

"Of course."

"She's been on at me for ages to come and see her. She's delightful, and I promise she won't get in the way of our holiday."

Randall thought Christmas would never come, but come it eventually did and on December the eighteenth, they left a rainy, fog-shrouded London on an Alitalia jet filled to the rafters. They were squeezed into their seats, jostled and pushed about by crowds of voluble Italians and although Katherine didn't seem to mind, Randall found the flight very tedious.

Katherine's friend, Christina, statuesque and raven-haired, met them at Malpensa Milano International Airport and drove them through the older parts of the city to the Hotel Carlo where she had arranged a room for them at a ridiculously low rate.

"Carlo owns the place, you see, and we do his books," she explained with a laugh. "We keep him out of jail, and he knows it. I told him what I wanted and, *eccola,* an excellent room."

Randall and Katherine spent their first day relaxing. The weather was cool, but not unpleasantly so. They window-shopped and strolled the busy streets until noon when Randall allowed that his feet were killing him. They went into a small *trattoria* they happened upon near their hotel and sat at a round table with a red cloth on it, close to the front window.

"Do you think this Professor Farina here can help find the gospel?" Katherine asked, working on a plate of ravioli.

"I don't know. I hope so, though."

"Donald always asks how you're doing when I talk to him. I've told him all about your progress."

"Donald's a good friend," he smiled.

"But there's still no progress on finding Michael's killer?"

Randall shook his head.

"Does Tony Joyce still think there's a possibility the killer will try to scare you off again?" she asked. "Or worse? It's not a very comfortable thought, George."

Randall put down his glass of Chianti.

"Tony is beginning to think, albeit cautiously, that whoever this bloke is, he might just have given up. And I'm inclined to think that's right."

"Why?"

"Three reasons. First, I think whoever it is has realized that even if he does stop me somehow, he can't go out after the manuscript without giving himself away. You can't search for it in secret."

"All right."

"Second, I think he's probably figured out that I was being used as a lure and he sees the danger in making a move with us on special lookout."

Katherine nodded.

"And third?"

"Lots of people know I'm still looking for the gospel, and yet nothing's happened since the London incident this time last year."

"Well, I certainly hope you're right," she said, "but I'm not entirely convinced."

"Now listen," he said, "if I'd thought there was even the remotest risk, I certainly wouldn't have invited you to come here with me, now would I?"

* * * *

The next morning, Christina called for Katherine and the two of them vanished for a day of sightseeing. Randall went to his appointment with Dr. Silvio Farina, Professor of History at the ancient and venerable University of Milan.

Dr. Farina was a man of about fifty, sharp-eyed and thin of face, and gifted with irrepressible good humor. He grasped Randall's hand warmly in both his, and in quite good English invited him to be seated. His office was commodious and well furnished with a large desk, two comfortable armchairs, numerous filing cabinets and long wide shelves piled with books, papers and assorted folders.

"Welcome to Milano, Professor Randall," he said, beaming.

"Thank you," said Randall, "and do please call me George."

"Ah, George. Thank you so much."

Randall was anxious to know what Farina had found, but the cheerful Italian was apparently in no hurry. Randall sat through an interval of small talk accompanied by large cups of unspeakably strong coffee, before Farina came to the point.

"So, my friend, I have solved your little mystery I think."

"I beg your pardon," said Randall, somewhat taken aback.

"Your haunted gospel," said Farina, with a broad smile. "I have found him."

"Really?"

Could it be this easy, Randall wondered.

"Well, that is to say, I don't actually know where it is today, but I have what I think will be helpful information. Please to relax yourself and I will tell you the story."

"Please do," said Randall, barely managing to suppress his seething impatience.

Farina gulped down the last of the vitriolic coffee in his cup, smacked his lips noisily and began.

"When the good Dr. Baines sent me an email regarding your search, I was at once most excited because, as I told him, I myself have also seen the 1356 reference to *The Haunted Gospel* and wondered at its meaning. I have never had time or reason to pursue it, but now here was an opportunity. After speaking to you about this visit and reading in your email of the connection to, how do you say, Nor-which…?"

"Nor-itch," Randall supplied.

"Ah. Well. I read of the connection to Norwich and I wonder if there may be some reference to that place. Indeed, there are many. I go back and back and back," said Farina, dramatically turning over imaginary pages with his hand, "and so I come to the reign of Pope Gregory IX. There is a notation in the Vatican documents—no date unfortunately, but I estimate it must be in the 1220s—that a gospel has been received as a gift for His Holiness from the Bishop of Norwich. I cannot recall the name just now, but it sounded French."

"Thomas Blundeville," Randall supplied again. "I told you about the Bartholomew journal, didn't I? The gift to the pope was mentioned in there, although the pope was not named, nor was there a date."

"Yes, yes, thank you, George. So here is the main thing. The manuscript, a gospel of St. John, is entered at that time into the records of the Papal Library as *The Norwich Gospel,* and once I saw that I was on my way. That volume, *The Norwich Gospel,* is referred to many times in later inventories, and only once, in 1356, is it called *The Haunted Gospel.*"

Randall's mind flew back to the note he had found in Michael Stuart's file. *TNG,* he thought, *The Norwich Gospel. THG, The Haunted Gospel, only in 1356. That's what Mike must have meant. But how on earth did he find that out?*

"This is incredible," Randall said, "but how can we be sure it's the same manuscript?"

"Aha," said Farina, raising a finger, clearly enjoying himself hugely. "Everything can now be revealed, my friend. To begin with, there is no reference in 1356 to a Norwich gospel at all, even though it appears in 1355 and 1357. But there is more definite evidence than that, and it comes straight from the time at which the manuscript arrived in Rome. At the time of Gregory IX, the Vatican Librarian was a Spanish Cardinal named Alphons of Madrid, although that is no matter to us. What is important is that he had as his assistant, a young priest, named Father Bernard. This Bernard later became Bishop, Archbishop and finally Cardinal, and may have become pope but for the fact that he was sent as Papal Legate to Constantinople where he met not only the reverend doctors of the Eastern Rite, but the plague as well. He never returned to Rome. However, that is also of no matter to us."

"But what about—" began Randall, not caring much about the personal career of Father Bernard.

"Of course, of course," said Farina nodding vigorously. "While at the library, this Bernard was responsible for cataloging all books, manuscripts, documents and so on. His writing and his name are everywhere in the records of the time. Now, this Bernard made a special notation next to the name of *The Norwich Gospel* saying that wandering spirits were said to visit the book wherever it was to be found, and that it was sent to Rome in hopes of quieting those restless souls. His Holiness accepted the gift on those terms, and that all coincides with the words of your Brother Bartolomeo, does it not?"

"It certainly does, Professor Farina," said Randall. "That's brilliant."

"*Piano, piano,*" said Farina waving his hand. "There is more. *The Norwich Gospel* is recorded in all the inventories of which I have record —except 1356, which I have already explained—until 1524 when we find a note saying the book has been taken from the library for the permanent use of Pope Clement VII. For the next three years, it is noted as being part of the library, yet not in the library, so to say. But all such references disappear after the year 1527, and I am very sure you know what happened in that year."

"The sack of Rome," said Randall.

"*Esattamente.* Exactly."

"I'll bet it was destroyed," Randall said.

"Perhaps," said Farina, "but as I say, whatever happened to it, it is never recorded again after 1527, either in or out of the library."

"Well," said Randall, "we know a lot more of its history at least. This is a marvelous job Professor Farina. I can't thank you enough."

"But I fear I have found your book for you, only to lose it again."

"I'm not so sure about that," said Randall. "Let's think about it for a moment. The sacking of Rome is very well documented indeed. There's any number of diaries, journals, letters and other things describing the event, and perhaps, just perhaps, there is mention of the library or its contents or something like that. Clement VII survived the attack, so perhaps he kept the book with him and, if so, it may surface somewhere else, in spite of its disappearance from the library records."

"A good consideration," said Farina. "A number of Church officials took refuge with His Holiness in the Castle of Sant'angelo. If any of them wrote down their observations, and if those documents have survived, they might be the place to start. But it will be tedious work, I think."

"Never mind," said Randall. "I love this sort of historical detective work. But I know a hell of a lot more now, thanks to you, and I have a definite direction in which to look."

"Perhaps I can be of further help," said Farina. "To begin with, I will see if we have anything here, and then I have a good friend at the University of Pavia who has done much research on this time period and on the famous battle which took place in that city. I will contact him and see if he can suggest anything."

Having politely declined Farina's offer of another cup of his corrosive coffee, and after profuse thanks, Randall departed with Farina promising to be in touch again before Christmas.

Chapter Nineteen

Before he and Katherine left Milan, Randall had several telephone conversations with Farina's colleague in Pavia, Professor Rossi, and by the time he returned home and the winter term had begun, he felt he was hot on the trail of the elusive gospel once again. He invited Megan and Tony Joyce to dinner and told them how things stood.

"So," he said, "between what Farina and his chum at Pavia have given me, I've got my work cut out for me. Rossi is writing a book on the sack of Rome and he has a mountain of stuff. All kinds of original documents and goodness knows what else. Speaks good English and reads Church Latin as easily as a telephone book. He's studied Clement VII extensively. Says he had a long career in the Church, but made a series of strange and inexplicable decisions—mainly in the area of foreign policy—that caused a lot of trouble for everyone. He got himself caught in the middle of the conflict between Francis I and Emperor Charles V and could never make up his mind what to do about it. All that's well known, of course, but Rossi's got so much more detail on everything than I've ever seen. He's extraordinary."

Randall paused for a mouthful of tea.

"Apparently," he continued, "Clement was given to justifying his odd decisions by saying God had revealed His will to him and he was simply doing God's bidding. At any rate, I have lots of material and Rossi has promised to keep his eyes skinned for any reference to either *The Haunted Gospel* or *The Norwich Gospel*. Meantime, I'm going to go through what he's sent me and follow up some of the other leads he's suggested."

"No further mention of buried treasure, then?" inquired Megan.

"Not a squeak."

"And still no incidents of any kind?" asked Joyce. "No trouble, strange happenings or anything?"

"Nothing at all. I'll bet he's given up."

"Well," said Joyce, "stay vigilant anyway, just in case. You haven't told anyone else about the pirate's treasure, have you?"

"No, indeed," said Randall, grinning.

Megan turned the conversation in a new direction.

"So Pop, are we to take it that all remains well with you and Katherine?"

"Yes, you are," Randall answered, and then decided one good question deserved another. "And what about you two?"

Tony opened his mouth to reply, but Megan got there first.

"Tony still has his flat, but we pretty much live full-time at my place these days."

"Well Tony, my lad," said Randall, "it appears as though you've done it. Congratulations."

"I'm sorry?" said Joyce, looking mystified.

"For a number of years," said Randall, "my daughter was widely celebrated for her lack of interest in men, but it seems there was a weak spot in the defenses and you found it."

Tony smiled and reached for Megan's hand.

"Since we're on the subject, I'd like to tell you that I love Megan very much."

"Glad to hear it," said Randall, with mock seriousness. "Have you told Megan?"

"Constantly," Joyce said, with a smile.

Megan's radiant answering smile warmed Randall's heart. Her happiness was evident, and he was immeasurably pleased.

"I think this calls for champagne," he said, "don't you?"

Joyce demurred saying he had to drive, but Randall grinned and told them they could stay the night.

"It's snowing like buggery out there anyway," he said. "It's no night to be driving. I'm quite sure you would agree with me in your professional capacity, Detective Sergeant?"

"Oh, of course," answered Joyce with suitable gravity.

Randall produced a bottle of his best, popped the cork and proposed a toast to the two of them, and Megan responded with a toast to Katherine.

"And when on earth are we ever going to meet her?" she asked, but all Randall would say was that he was working on it.

Tony and Megan retired to the spare bedroom and, after checking the doors, Randall went up to bed himself. As he lay in the dark, he contemplated what he had come to call his new reality. Within the space of a year-and-a-half, both he and his daughter had met someone and fallen in love. She vowed she never would, while he thought he never could. *The wheel of fate runs in strange directions*, he thought. *If it weren't for The Haunted Gospel, none of this would have happened.*

And Mike would still be alive.

* * * *

Over the next several months, Randall employed his limited spare time in following up numerous leads and reading the many background references provided by Professors Rossi and Farina. He became an expert of sorts on the sacking of Rome, Pope Clement VII, the Colonna family, Constable Bourbon, King Francis I of France and Charles V of Spain, the Holy Roman Emperor. In the course of this work, he came across a number of references to Pope Clement's habit of consulting the scriptures for guidance, and could not help wondering if it was *The Haunted Gospel* he read. It had been signed out to him, after all. He also encountered frequent references to a Cardinal Bartoli, and in early May, he emailed Rossi inquiring about him.

It is a great pity (Rossi replied) that no work of Cardinal Bartoli has survived. It is well known that he kept diaries and journals but I know of none still extant. As you have no doubt realized, he was one of Pope Clement's principal foreign policy advisors and took refuge with him during the sacking of the city. He was a central figure in the events of that time, and I am sure he could have told us a great deal if his writings had come down to us.

In his reply, Randall offered to conduct a little research project of his own to see if any of Bartoli's writings could be located, and Rossi responded with best wishes for good luck, but added there had been many such searches in the past, and all had been unsuccessful.

It was virtually certain Cardinal Bartoli would have chronicled so monumental a catastrophe as the sack of Rome, and Randall was

155

reluctant to accept that everything had been lost.

If any of Bartoli's writings have survived, he reasoned, *they obviously aren't in any well-known library or museum, so they're probably buried in a private collection somewhere—quite possibly belonging to someone who is unaware of their significance.*

He retrieved the list of private dealers and agents compiled for him by John Archer, and sent an email to all those in the British Isles as a start. He received a positive reply two days later.

"It's a dealer in Edinburgh, if you please," he told Katherine by phone. "Nice chap, name of Trevor McIntosh. Finding him so soon was sheer luck, and nothing else. The gods were smiling on me. McIntosh said my email stirred an ancient memory. He went back into his records, and hey presto, there it was. It seems that in 1996, he was approached by a certain Lord Kentsmere—of whom I have never heard—who was facing some rather stiff estate taxes following the death of his father. His lordship had decided to sell his father's collection of old books and manuscripts to raise the necessary funds and asked McIntosh to handle the sale. The collection had to be evaluated and cataloged, of course, and in the process of that, McIntosh came across a seventeenth century compilation of Vatican foreign policy documents of the previous one hundred years or so. One of those documents, he recalled, was an eyewitness account of the sacking of Rome written by a cardinal. McIntosh got in touch with the buyer and found he still owned the manuscript, and it turned out to be Bartoli. I could hardly believe it. It was so absurdly simple."

"George," Katherine asked, "how do you know that document has anything to do with *The Haunted Gospel?*"

"I don't. However, given who Bartoli was, I think if anyone can tell us about the gospel, it's likely to be him. Whether he does or not is an entirely different matter, but whatever the case, the gospel disappears from all records after the sack, so this is all we're left with. Rossi nearly went apoplectic with joy when I told him I'd found a Bartoli manuscript. He couldn't believe it either."

"All right," said Katherine. "I suppose a shot in the dark is better than no shot at all. Do we know who bought this thing by Cardinal Who's-it?"

"Indeed we do," said Randall. "Thanks to the altogether remarkable Mr. McIntosh, bless his kilt and sporran. The buyer and current owner is a Viennese financier named Wolfgang Brauer. I've put in a call to him and he says he'd be happy to let me see the document and translate it."

"When are you going?" Katherine asked.

"In two weeks. Can you come?"

"I'd really love to," she said, "Vienna is such a beautiful city, but it's a madhouse at work and I just can't get away."

* * * *

British Airways deposited Randall, laptop computer in hand, at Vienna International Airport after a short and uneventful flight from London, and he took a taxi to the Hotel Maria Theresa in the Kirchberggasse where he was to reside for the next two or three days. The taxi drew up at the hotel's wide, flag-lined front entrance, and a liveried porter hurried forward to open the door. A bellboy materialized as if from nowhere and, before he knew it, Randall was swept into the opulent lobby, checked in and escorted to his room.

He slept well that night. At eleven the next morning, as arranged, he presented himself at the home of Wolfgang Brauer which occupied the entire second floor of an elegant eighteenth century building near St. Stephens Platz and the Cathedral. He was cordially received by a butler, shown into a spacious drawing room and offered coffee pending the return of Herr Brauer who, he was told with profuse apologies, had been unexpectedly detained at his first appointment of the day.

Randall settled himself into a comfortable leather armchair, took a sip of what proved to be excellent coffee—a welcome contrast to the caustic brew he remembered drinking with Professor Farina—and contemplated his surroundings. The room was large and furnished with expensive antiques. There were ornately carved and inlaid chairs and tables, oriental porcelain vases, age-darkened paintings on the walls and a fireplace of deeply sculpted white marble. The room bore an atmosphere of refined and prosperous elegance, and clearly demonstrated its owner's sophistication and discernment.

After a wait of some forty minutes, Randall heard approaching footsteps outside the door and got to his feet. Brauer entered a moment later wearing a dark business suit, blue silk tie and heavy gold cufflinks. He moved quickly to where Randall stood and put out his hand, a broad smile on his face. He was short, a little rotund and had a neatly trimmed white moustache. Randall reckoned he was eighty if he was a day.

"My dear, Herr Doctor," he boomed in strongly accented English, "welcome to my house. I am so happy to meet you. Please forgive me for keeping you waiting."

Randall made appropriate sounds of deprecation, and Brauer invited him to outline the reasons for his interest in Bartoli's testament.

"I did not know this Cardinal Bartoli was a man of such particular distinction," he said, when Randall had finished. "Up until I heard from you, Bartoli's document was a very minor item in my collection. I acquired it as part of a larger purchase and gave it little attention. It is a plain manuscript, without illuminations, and as I told you on the phone, it is only about five pages in length. I have never had it translated. However," and here his blue eyes sparkled, "if, as you say, it is the only writing of this cardinal known at this time, it may have a value beyond what I considered."

"Well," said Randall, "that depends to some extent on the contents. If it's merely mundane material of no particular historical significance, its value will lie only in its age and uniqueness. However, its value will be much higher if it tells us something we didn't know before."

"*Ja*," said Brauer with a smile. "We shall see."

"Although," Randall put in, unable to resist, "in either case you might consider donating it to a university. Mine, for example."

Brauer threw back his head and laughed a deep, rich peal of mirth.

"Well done, Herr Doctor," he said. "Well done."

Brauer insisted Randall join him for lunch, and after beef stroganoff and an excellent claret, he conducted him to the study. The butler brought in a folder containing the manuscript and placed it on the desk.

"I sincerely regret to say, Herr Doctor, that I must go out yet again and I doubt I will return before this evening. But please make yourself absolutely at home and complete your work. Everything is here: Internet, phone, fax, and photocopier. Use whatever you need. I shall be most interested to read the translation."

After thanks and handshakes, Brauer departed and Randall seated himself, booted up his laptop and went online. He called up his various Internet translation tools, created a file and set to work.

The Bartoli testament was closely written in Latin on four-and-a-half small sheets of vellum, now dangerously brittle with age. Randall handled them using a clean handkerchief and took great care to treat them gently. He made a mental note to advise Brauer they were in need of attention if they were to survive much longer. He was a little surprised that a collector of Brauer's caliber would have allowed a manuscript of that age to go unattended, but Brauer had said he thought the writing insignificant.

The black ink was still strong, however, and apart from some stained patches and minor difficulties deciphering Bartoli's handwriting, the work was not especially arduous. The majority of the document contained nothing substantially new, merely describing the sack in May of 1527, and the events leading up to it, but one sentence arrested Randall's attention immediately; a sentence in which Bartoli referred to Clemens reading "his gospel of John from England."

That's it, he exulted. *It must be. Surely there couldn't have been more than one English gospel of John Clement was reading. It has to be The Haunted Gospel. But what the hell happened to it?*

Randall returned to his translating and sat stunned as he read Bartoli's final paragraph.

On the sixth day of the sack, while we yet remained within Sant'angelo, I went to see His Holiness but found his chamber empty. His John gospel lay before me unattended upon a table and, God forgive me, I took it hence, hidden in a bag. Dressed as a common citizen, I ventured out into the streets and there gave the gospel to a passing soldier. He showed little interest in it, but in the end took it saying he would use it to kindle a fire. I saw no more of him, for I made all haste back to Sant'angelo, grateful still to have my life. His Holiness wailed and wept in rage and sorrow to find the book gone, but I held my peace while all Sant'angelo was searched and searched again. My sinful deed marked the end of that most unfortunate and troublesome book, and we are no longer beset by it. Would that it had never come to Rome. I stole it, and although I rejoice to see it gone, my sin weighs heavily upon me. Can a sin be committed in the cause of a righteous intent? Can the sin of one man be extenuated if it be committed to ease a burden on many? I know not. I beseech Almighty God for forgiveness. Mea culpa. Mea maxima culpa.

The gospel was gone. Burned in a fire by a nameless soldier. The search was finished.

Thanks to Pope Clement's faith in it, Brother Robert's gospel had influenced the course of European history, but that very influence had brought about its destruction. Randall felt bereft. He had cherished the hope and expectation of seeing the gospel, touching it, and uncovering the secret of the illuminations, but now it was all over. With a sharp pin, reaching down the centuries from 1527, Cardinal Bartoli had burst the bubble, and Randall felt as if he had been cheated.

Well, Mike, old chum, he said to himself, *I know what happened to your haunted gospel, but that's the end of it now. Whatever or wherever that great treasure is, it's gone as well.*

Chapter Twenty

Carl Otto Hoffman, citizen of Munich, cloth merchant, patriarch of a numerous family and unyielding servant of the Holy Catholic Church, sat uncomfortably in his finely appointed carriage as it lurched and jolted through the cobbled streets of his native city. He was in dreadful pain.

At fifty years of age, Hoffman was one of Munich's most respected men of business. Prodigiously rich, he lived in a house so large and ornate that visitors to the city often mistook it for a royal palace.

His wife, Maria, eight years his junior, was still beautiful in spite of spending nearly all her seven years of marriage to Hoffman in the production of children as if by a timetable. She had been a widow and Hoffman a widower when they were married, and it was generally believed that he intended to wear her out with childbearing as he had worn out his first wife.

Herr Hoffman believed with unshakeable certitude that since God was undoubtedly masculine and ruled His world absolutely, so mortal men ruled their world, including and especially women, in like manner. A woman's purpose in a man's world was the making of children, the heirs and successors of men. His first wife had given birth eleven times and six children had survived. Maria, who had had no children by her first husband, a sickly fellow with a constitution no stronger than wet paper, had just given birth to a healthy baby boy, her sixth child, and the previous five were all still living. Hoffman declared himself well pleased with her performance as a dutiful wife.

The carriage with its white wheels and blue and gold coachwork crashed heavily into, and then out of, a more than usually large pothole as it rounded the corner into the Bergstrasse where Hoffman's house stood. Putting his hand on his right cheek, he groaned. He had a rotten tooth and he was returning home from his place of business to meet the surgeon who had decreed it would have to be drawn. The pain of the abscessed molar was now sufficiently hideous as to overcome his fear of its removal, and he was anxious to be home and have the ghastly operation over with.

As the carriage drew up outside the house, the two footmen who had been standing above the carriage's boot jumped down, unfolded the step and stood respectfully aside while their master alighted. The groom, who had been sitting with the coachman on the box, had already run up the seven stone steps and given a mighty pull on the metal handle which rang a bell deep within the bowels of the house. The porter soon appeared and flung wide the two brass-embossed wooden doors, each deeply carved and brightly painted.

The butler, Peters, made haste to welcome his master and after a deep bow and respectful words of greeting, informed Hoffman that Herr Josef Zeller waited upon him in the morning room.

"Ach," said Hoffman. "That miserable little man. Lutheran! Why now, in Jesus' name? Is the tooth drawer here?"

"Yes, sir. He is in your dressing room. Shall I inform Herr Zeller you will not see him today?"

"No, no," mumbled Hoffman, rubbing his swollen cheek gingerly. "Perhaps by some miracle of grace he has come to pay the money he owes me, although I very much doubt it."

The butler announced him and Hoffman, a tall, squarely-built man with a fair complexion and pale blue eyes, walked somewhat unsteadily into the elaborately furnished room. Standing before him he beheld a worried-looking man of about forty-and-five years, short, thin, without hat or wig.

"Well?" snapped Hoffman. "Are you come to pay or are you not?"

"Herr Hoffman," pleaded the visitor, "I swear I will pay all I owe, but I beg and implore you to give me more time."

Hoffman sat down heavily in the nearest chair and put his hand to his face again. Of all times this was the worst in which to request his charity or understanding. His rotten tooth ached beyond all imagination and the pain was so overpowering as to make him feel ill. It was as if some fiendish torturer were drilling into his upper jaw with a sharp steel auger. He was for a moment afraid he was about to bring forth his breakfast, but fought off the clammy wave of nausea.

"Are you well, Herr Hoffman?" inquired Zeller, looking more

worried still.

"Of course not," snapped Hoffman. "Do I look well? Now what is it you want, as if I needed telling?"

"Your generosity in allowing me more time to repay you," said Zeller in a wheedling tone of voice.

"Always you ask for more time, Zeller," Hoffman said, his words now slurred as the swelling in his mouth impeded the working of his tongue. "I have been fair with you, have I not? You bought cloth to the value of a thousand thaler and that is all I ask you to pay. I do not practice usury. I am no Jew."

"I know, I know," wailed Zeller, wringing his hands. "But as I have told you, my former partner has cheated me. He has stolen all the capital of the company. I can barely feed my family. All the money I have is devoted to reestablishing my business and my reputation. Once that is done, I will be able to pay you everything."

"Have you nothing to sell?"

"I have sold most of my furniture and all my wife's jewelry already, and all I have left are two objects which have been in my family for generations. One is a painting of my ancestor, Gerhard Zeller, and the other is an old book, which it is said Gerhard acquired almost two centuries ago in Rome. To sell them would cause great sorrow to all of us."

The word "book" caught Hoffman's attention for a brief moment, but Zeller was continuing.

"I am doing everything I can to avoid the shame of public bankruptcy, for such a thing would destroy my reputation and business forever. I have been left with enormous debts thanks to that scoundrel, and I must rebuild my business or I shall be completely ruined."

"So you keep telling me. You are as boring as plainsong, la, la, la."

Hoffman stood up, swayed a little, grasped the back of the chair to steady himself and groaned.

"How much is that book worth? The one you just mentioned?"

Zeller's face registered abject misery.

"Please, Herr Hoffman," he implored.

"Get out," snapped Hoffman. "I shall consider what to do with you when I can once more think clearly."

"Thank you Herr Hoffman," said Zeller, bowing deeply. "I am most grateful. You are a generous and—"

Hoffman waved Zeller away impatiently and made as much haste as he could to his dressing room where a thin man with a bony and lugubrious face awaited him. Held firmly by the surgeon's two assistants, Hoffman bellowed in agony as the decayed molar was wrenched from its putrescent socket.

"It did not break," said the surgeon examining the tooth. "It will not be necessary to probe for the root."

Hoffman thought the wretched fellow sounded disappointed.

Hoffman's valet helped him to change as the three men of medicine departed with smiles and a promise to send an accounting of their charges. Then the injured man lay on his bed and waited for the unspeakable pain to abate. The surgeon had left a soporific draught and Hoffman swallowed it, choking on its vile bitterness, before drifting into a drugged slumber from which he awakened in the late evening.

As he opened his eyes he saw, albeit dimly, the face of his wife as she bent over him.

"Is it a little better, husband?" she asked. He could do nothing but grunt in response.

Fully recovered over the next ten days, Hoffman returned to his shops and warehouses and took up the conduct of his business as a general conducts a military campaign: with care, cunning and absolute determination. He bought and sold cotton from Egypt, wool from England and silk from merchants who traded eastwards from the Mediterranean and into shining Cathay itself. He dealt in Flemish lace, finely embroidered fabrics from Italy, linen, French taffeta and velvets of all kinds and colors. He even bought plain felt from a one-eyed Turk with gold teeth, and resold it at enormous profit to shoemakers who used it as lining in winter boots.

Since Hoffman's business interests spanned Europe, his commercial success was dependent upon there being at least a modicum of stability amongst the patchwork of states, kingdoms, dukedoms, principalities and palatinates which comprised the region. As the century waned, stability had become dependent upon the answer to one, overriding question. Everyone, everywhere, wanted to know who would succeed to the throne of Spain.

Charles II, the present king and a Spanish Hapsburg, was in failing health and had no heir. Every time he dwelt on it, Hoffman became acutely aware that if the question of succession could not be resolved through diplomacy, war might well eventuate. War would be disastrous for business. Given the delicacy of the situation, he believed it imperative that he keep abreast of all developments, for, like a general, he knew the value of good intelligence.

He was much availed in his efforts to unravel the tangled skeins of political intrigue by the fact that his eldest daughter, Hildegard, had married—entirely by her father's contrivance—Georg Richter, the son of a prominent jeweler and nephew of none other than Herr Johann Richter, Ambassador of Bavaria to the court of Louis XIV of France. Georg maintained a continuous correspondence with his uncle, and every scrap of information thus obtained was dutifully transmitted to his father-in-law.

Hoffman often congratulated himself on the soundness of his decision to ally himself with the Richter family. Not only had the marriage provided the means for obtaining information, it had also provided someone with sufficient wit to discuss it intelligently. Georg, though only five-and-twenty, possessed a sharp and agile mind and Hoffman much enjoyed conversing with him. As well, young Richter had shown himself admirably industrious at home. He and Hildegard were about to make Hoffman a grandfather for the third time.

And so it came about that on a particularly cold evening late in the year, the two of them sat before a log fire in Hoffman's front parlor drinking mulled apple cider and discussing the latest news from Paris.

Richter sat opposite his father-in-law, his blue eyes keen and bright, savoring his warm cider. He wore white doeskin breeches, lace at his throat and a bottle-green coat, which Hoffman observed to be very well cut from expensive cloth.

Richter drained his tankard and smacked his lips appreciatively.

"I bring you good news, sir. A treaty is signed concerning Spain."

"Indeed?" said Hoffman, his face immediately alight with interest. "Pray tell me all. Alliances have changed once again, I perceive."

"Yes," said Richter, with a broad smile. "The inconstancy of political alliances is extraordinary. Upon my word, I believe only the weather changes more frequently these days. But if I may have another tankard of this truly excellent cider, I will be pleased to tell you what I have heard."

Hoffman bellowed for a serving girl who appeared almost at once bearing two pewter tankards of cider on a wooden tray. Richter thrust a poker into the fire and the two men settled back in their chairs once again as he began his narrative.

"I am told by my uncle that the question of Spanish succession is answered by a treaty concluded between Louis and King William of England. It is known as the Treaty of Partition, and by its terms the lion's share of Spain and her possessions and territories will go to Bavaria's own Electoral Prince, Joseph Ferdinand, who will become king of Spain."

"It seems a decent enough compromise, does it not?" Hoffman nodded. "The French dauphin has a claim to the Spanish throne by marriage, but uniting the French and Spanish empires is anathema to England as well as to the Dutch."

"Precisely."

"On the other hand, the Holy Roman Emperor, Leopold of Austria, has a similar claim, but England and France strongly oppose Leopold's acquisition of the Spanish throne since it would bring about the union of the German and Spanish branches of the Hapsburg family, thus creating a dangerous imbalance of power."

Richter inclined his head in assent.

"Very well," continued Hoffman, "but I am not so much a lackwit as to think such a compromise was struck simply out of righteous good will and amity. What was the price?"

Rising from his chair, Richter withdrew the poker from the fire and plunged its ruby tip into each of the tankards in turn, causing the cider to hiss and splutter. He stoked the fire vigorously, sending an iridescent hail of sparks soaring up the chimney before handing one tankard to Hoffman and resuming his seat.

"Ah yes," he said, his head on one side and a mischievous smile on his lips. "The price. All things have a price, have they not?"

"The value of something obtained for nothing is usually exactly that," said Hoffman. "I wish to know what was paid to oil this accord, for men who sign treaties today would as lief go to war tomorrow if there is insufficient oil to smooth their paths to peace."

Richter chuckled.

"You are a philosopher, sir."

Hoffman gave a good-natured grunt, and Richter continued.

"The French dauphin is to receive certain Spanish territories, notably Naples and Sicily, and Milan goes to the Archduke Charles, Emperor Leopold's son."

"Very neat," said Hoffman.

"Indeed it is," agreed Richter. "It was in Charles' name that Leopold claimed the throne of Spain, as Louis claimed it for his son, the dauphin. Thus, everyone is kept happy."

"Buying off the fathers by enriching the sons," observed Hoffman, sipping his cider. "And they call it diplomacy."

"Essentially, yes," agreed Richter.

"But what of William of England?"

"It is said he is the happiest of all. He now has the gift of a fragmented Spanish empire and the House of Hapsburg remains divided."

"Excellent," Hoffman nodded. "Excellent."

War had been averted, and for that Hoffman was devoutly grateful and profoundly relieved. Business and family decisions, long held in abeyance, could now be made. His plans had been prepared for months, and he refined them as winter gripped the city ever more tightly.

By the time the new year of 1699 began, the weather had become as cold as could be remembered. For weeks on end, snow mantled the countryside, while bitter winds rattled the bony branches of bare trees and shrieked down city streets like demons from the netherworld.

Safely protected from the cold, the Hoffman dwelling was always comfortable and its inhabitants well fed. It carried on its accustomed way of life with scant regard for the plight of the poor. In the worst of the frigid weather, Hoffman did not go to his places of business but remained at home before his fire sending messages, instructions and exhortations to his numerous minions. His presence at home, however, greatly disordered his household.

In spite of his abiding belief in the propriety of large families and his own army of offspring, Hoffman was no great lover of children, and showed them little affection. His notion of fatherhood was limited to impregnating his wife as frequently as physically possible and then more or less ignoring the resulting beings until they could be made good use of. Daughters were there for the making of marriages advantageous to his business, sons for working in that business, and when not old enough for either excellent purpose, children were to be kept out of the way.

Thus, when he was at home, the legions of his family had to be kept quiet and, above all, out of sight. Only at the evening meal would he see those children old enough to be out of the nursery and even then, they were required to sit silent at the table, eat decorously and speak only when spoken to.

Hoffman had himself been raised under a regimen far more stringent than this. His father, Otto, had sat in absolute dominion at the head of the supper table with a cane by his chair, and Hoffman could remember many occasions when he had been dragged from the table by the scruff of his neck and beaten mercilessly for some perceived infraction of good manners or household rules. His mother was powerless to prevent these beatings and many were the times he had heard her cries of pain and terror as she herself was beaten.

At the age of fourteen, Hoffman stole the key to his father's strongbox, took five thaler and ran away from home, leaving a letter for his mother begging her to forgive him and not to worry. He fled to Munich where he talked his way into a job in a cloth merchant's shop. Once hired, he had the effrontery to ask for an advance on his wages because his money had long since run out and he had not eaten for three days. Fortunately, Herr Zimmer, his new employer, laughed, cuffed him playfully about the ear and then, throwing him a few small coins, told him to go and buy himself a meat pie.

Within ten years, Hoffman had his own prosperous business growing and spreading like wild ivy, and when, years later, he heard Herr Zimmer's wife was dead and the old man himself ill and all but blind, Hoffman went to his house, gave him money and paid for his upkeep and care until his death.

"Why do you do this?" Herr Zimmer asked one day.

"For the meat pie," Hoffman answered.

While he disciplined his children rigorously in various ways, he seldom resorted to the cane and never touched his wife in anger. He accorded Maria the measure of dignity associated with her status as the wife of a wealthy man, and believed it was her place to show the children affection, his to show them authority. He was now about to exercise that authority and would begin by informing his wife of the decisions he had made.

* * * *

One day in late January, Maria Hoffman and her husband sat in the parlor after sharing a midday meal before the fire—something they did occasionally when he was at home. Frau Maria Hoffman had been a tall and shapely woman of thirty-two when Hoffman married her. She was celebrated for her beauty, fair-haired and green-eyed, and many a man envied Hoffman his young and voluptuous wife.

He seldom confided in her, rarely discussed business, and usually confined their conversations to matters of the household or harmless gossip about their friends and acquaintances. He almost never asked about the children unless one or other of them was ill, but she sensed today might be different. There was something on his mind.

Maria had come to understand her husband well during the years of their marriage. She saw him as a lonely figure in spite of his family and prosperous business. Maria imagined him as a solitary being, isolated in a teeming world. She had loved him when they married, and perhaps she loved him still; she was not entirely certain. Maria felt sorry for him, of that she was sure.

"What are you thinking, husband?" she asked, deciding encouragement might be called for.

Raising his eyes, Hoffman looked at her, appearing surprised she had divined his purpose. She looked at him expectantly, and waited in silence.

"I am thinking of my daughter, Helga," he began. "She will soon be fifteen and she is not yet betrothed."

"She is young, husband," Maria said. "I beg you to let her remain a child a little longer."

"Fifteen is not young," he replied. "She is well into her years of childbearing. Her childhood is passed and an alliance must be made."

An alliance, thought Maria bleakly. *Not a marriage, not a bond, not necessarily even a friendship, but an alliance.*

She thought of Helga: shy, sensitive and pretty, always happier to sit alone with her poetry books than be with her brothers and sisters. Maria could not bear the thought of that innocent young creature leaving her home forever to live as wife and bed partner to goodness knows who.

"Herr Wilhelm Kopf has a son, Peter," her husband continued. "Kopf is comfortably fortuned and his business interests will be of value to me. Now that the question of the Spanish succession is settled to the considerable advantage of Bavaria, it is time to plan for the future. Kopf imports leather goods from Madrid and weapons and armor of fine steel from Toledo. Between the two of us, this trade could be much expanded."

Maria heard nothing beyond the first sentence. She tried to prevent her face from showing her revulsion at the thought of a marriage to Peter Kopf. Her whole being rose in rebellion against it.

"But, good husband, everyone knows Peter Kopf is remarkably weak of wit. He is a young man in his body, but a feeble child in his mind. A marriage to him would be unthinkable."

"Peter's wit, or lack of it, is not my concern," said Hoffman. "I intend to do business with his father, not with him. We must pray Helga's children will partake more of her wits than of his."

Children!

Maria sat aghast, staring at her husband. She felt physically ill at the hideous image of Helga being subjected to the fumbling sexual explorations of that blithering boy.

I will not allow it, she thought, her initial horror now replaced by cold fury. *He cares nothing for his daughter. This is pure avarice, and I will not have it.*

"Such a marriage would be a travesty, an offence before all earth and heaven," she said. "How can you even think of it? Your own dear daughter, wedded to that object?"

"Enough," said Hoffman. "Inform Helga and I shall speak with

Herr Kopf. I am determined upon this and I will have no opposition from you or anyone else."

Maria turned imploring eyes upon her husband and almost shuddered at the coldness of his expression.

"Peter Kopf is what he is by the will of God," Hoffman said. "It was not I who made him so. By God's grace, he may be cured of his infirmities. I shall pray for it."

Maria folded her hands in her lap and lowered her eyes.

"And who, then, shall pray for Helga?"

"Ach," said Hoffman, rising from his chair and waving an impatient hand. "God preserve me from the bleating of maudlin women."

He strode quickly from the room leaving Maria in a tumult of anger and fear. Helga was a child of her husband's first marriage, but she loved all the children and saw Helga as a girl of pensive and gentle disposition. If she came to marry, it must be to a man of intelligence and sensitivity, not a mewling cretin.

Maria had never defied her husband; she had obeyed him in all things, but this marriage was an abomination she could not countenance. *It will not be a marriage*, she fumed as she mounted the wide, carved wooden staircase to the upper floor of the house. *It is an obscene mockery, to be done for the sake of Spanish gold.*

"Or thirty pieces of silver, perhaps," she murmured under her breath as she reached the landing, "for the betrayal of an innocent child."

She sought the sanctuary of her private withdrawing room where, by strict rule, not even her personal maid would enter unless requested. Settling herself with her feet up on a purple velvet chaise, she quieted her tumbling thoughts and carefully weighed the position in which she found herself.

After nearly an hour, she rose and straightened the folds of her long white gown. She had resolved to make one final attempt to persuade her husband to abandon his plans, but if he proved intractable, she had conceived a scheme to thwart his purpose. The sheer audacity of it made her tremble.

* * * *

Later that week, a carriage drew up at the imposing front entrance of the Hoffman residence. Its two horses were blanketed against the bitter weather and their breath smoked down their flanks as they were reined to a stop. The coachman was little more than a shapeless heap of coats and scarves with a small opening from which his eyes peered in manifest misery.

Summoned by the pealing of the large brass doorbell, Peters opened the door just wide enough to admit the visitor and then shut it quickly. Once inside and divested of his heavy overcoat, scarf and hat, the newcomer was revealed as Georg Richter. Hoffman, seated at his desk, received him in the study and bade him be seated.

"I shall be with you presently."

"Upon my word and honor," said Richter, stretching his hands and feet out to the blessed warmth of the fire, "I wonder if this damnably cold weather will ever end."

"Well what in God's great mercy brings you out in it, then?" asked Hoffman replacing his white goose quill pen in its silver holder and joining Richter by the fire.

"I fear I bring grave tidings, sir," said Richter. "His Highness, the Prince Elector, is taken ill. The physicians can neither name the malady nor divine its cause or cure. There is concern for his life."

Hoffman stared at his son-in-law.

"But if he should die" and here Hoffman crossed himself, "which God forbid, who takes the Spanish throne?"

"Exactly," said Richter. "Once news of this illness reaches the courts of Europe and England, the chess game will begin all over again. All will seek to gain advantage in the event he does not live."

Hoffman groaned inwardly. The hydra head of war, so lately put to rest, rose again with all its attendant horrors. War would bring commerce to a standstill and woeful tax levies would be imposed to pay for it all. Business would be ruined. His golden dreams of a profitable partnership with Herr Kopf would be as dross.

"Let us all pray for the life of his Highness," he said, crossing himself once again.

"Amen," said Richter.

For the next ten days, all eyes were turned towards the Elector's Palace. Messengers came and went, black-coated and white-wigged physicians with long faces and melancholy expressions entered and departed. Apothecaries were summoned—even an Italian religious mystic was observed arriving at the palace—and the Prince Elector's confessor took up residence in case he should be needed quickly.

On the eleventh day, there came promising news at last. Soon it was being noised throughout the city that his Highness had begun to amend. It was said he grew stronger, he had been cupped and bled again, the evil humors were abating and all citizens were exhorted to thank Almighty God for his Highness' deliverance from the threshold of death.

Carl Hoffman's gratitude to Almighty God knew no bounds.

"We are saved," he enthused to his son-in-law. "The treaty stands."

"It seems so," said Richter, "but let us hope this is not a temporary recovery only. The physicians availed him naught, do not forget, and if there should be a relapse...."

"Nonsense," said Hoffman, with great confidence. "Never say it. I am sure he will recover completely and permanently. And now I can return my mind to the matter of my daughter. It is imperative that her marriage proceed at once, and the business partnership be established. I am not the only merchant in Munich to have thought of expanded trade with Spain, but I intend to be the first to achieve it."

Chapter Twenty-One

The Prince Elector made a recovery of sorts, but his illness left him weakened to the point of almost perpetual debilitation. At first, it was believed this weakness would quickly worsen and cause his death, but such was not the case. His condition remained unchanged, and his physicians eventually concluded he would, in all likelihood, live out his God-bestowed span of years in a state of chronic enfeeblement. This situation caused increasing concern over the Prince's capacity to ascend the Spanish throne if ever the ailing Charles II should deign to die. The future of Europe, therefore, appeared to rest upon the frail constitutions of two sick men: one unable to die, and the other unable to recover.

Her husband's preoccupation with the political situation had afforded Maria precious time to finalize her plans, but all too soon, the respite was ended.

"Wife," said Hoffman one evening. "I wish to acquaint you with a decision I have made regarding Helga's marriage. The times are uncertain, but those willing to take a calculated risk can sometimes turn uncertainty to advantage. Herr Kopf and I have agreed to act now and not wait in idleness as do our competitors. Swift action at this moment might well yield greater profits later on."

Maria bit her lip in anxiety as she steeled herself for a final attempt at dissuasion.

"Good husband, can you not see what this will mean for dear Helga? Can you not have her to marry a true man who will be a husband to her, rather than this weak-witted boy who can be neither lover nor companion? I beg you to search your heart and reconsider. I implore you not to condemn Helga to a life of bitter misery and emptiness."

"I have told you," said Hoffman, "I will have this done. Herr Kopf and I are in complete accord as to the value of our partnership, and to secure it safely Helga must marry Peter. Paper contracts can be torn up at will, but the ties of marriage are indissoluble. Helga will make her own life as all wives must, and the alliance with the Kopf family will add much to our prosperity."

"Prosperity?" echoed Maria. "Have you not money enough already that you sentence your own daughter to a purgatorial existence for the sake of a few thaler?"

"Now look here, wife," said Hoffman, rising to his feet. "I will have no more of this. You will prepare Helga for her wedding and I shall arrange time, place and dowry with Herr Kopf. And," he added, with a smug smile as he moved towards the door, "the dowry will be all the smaller for Peter's being what he is, so we are advantaged on all sides, are we not?"

Maria rose and faced her husband. She was outraged and infuriated.

"Be silent, woman," Hoffman shouted as she prepared to speak. "I command you. Have done."

Maria stood trembling. She was appalled a man could possess so malignant a rapacity that he would treat his daughter as if she were a chattel or a commercial property. She watched her husband's tall figure stride from the room, and renewed her silent vow to prevent this fearful marriage. All she could do now was appear to acquiesce, follow her husband's instructions and bide her time. Later that evening, therefore, she told Helga of her forthcoming betrothal.

"I do not even know this Peter Kopf," Helga cried, her eyes brimming with tears. "I cannot marry him."

Maria took the sobbing girl in her arms.

"All will be well, my lamb, I promise you before God. No harm will come to you, but you must trust me. What you and I must do for now is prepare for your wedding as your father wishes us to do."

Helga nodded and although Maria longed to tell her more, she dared not. A thoughtless word could spell disaster, and Helga would then be beyond all help. Maria knew the success of her strategy hinged upon all things appearing normal to her husband until the last possible moment, and until then she could only pray Helga would have the fortitude to do what was necessary.

"Holy Mary, Mother of God," Maria prayed aloud, kneeling before the altar in the small private chapel adjoining her dressing room. "Forasmuch as thou art a woman, I beseech thee to help me. I entreat thee to save our gentle Helga from this barbarous marriage. Holy Mary, Mother of God, in the name of thy Blessed Son, our Savior, hear my prayer."

Maria prayed far into the night and at length, her cheeks tear-stained and her knees stiff and sore, she struggled to her feet and went to bed, exhausted.

* * * *

Three weeks later, on a mild and soft afternoon in late spring, Hoffman, Maria and Helga seated themselves in a small anteroom adjacent to the ballroom in the Kopf family home. Helga sat rigid on a velvet chair, her hands clasped tightly in her lap, and Maria's heart ached for her. She had concealed the truth about Peter as long as she could, but before they left home that day, she had taken Helga aside and spoken to her with utmost gentleness.

"Listen to me, my child. I must tell you the full measure of what is to happen today. Would that I could do otherwise, but I cannot."

Helga stared at her in panic.

"You promised I would not marry."

"And you shall not," said Maria. "However, I must reveal the truth about Peter Kopf before you see him."

"What is it? What truth?"

"He is a cretin, a simpleton, with the mind of a little child."

Helga went deadly pale. She put her hand over her mouth and for a moment Maria thought she was about to vomit.

"I beg you not to be afraid, my dear," she said. "Remember what I have promised. You must govern your emotions and, above all, make no scene. Everything depends upon that. God will give you strength, and all will yet be well."

The sound of the chamberlain's staff striking the floor of the ballroom brought Maria abruptly back to the present.

"My lords, ladies and gentlemen," the chamberlain called, his voice rising above the dying laughter and talk of the assembled guests. "The betrothal is announced this day of Peter, son of Wilhelm and Eloisa Kopf of this city, and Helga, daughter of Carl and Maria Hoffman of this city."

A footman in gold livery opened the door of the anteroom. Helga and Maria followed Hoffman into the ballroom amid what seemed to

Maria a stunned silence. Ragged applause finally broke out as they were shown to the long head table where Peter and his parents were seated.

Helga appeared before the gathering dressed in white, a slight young figure, slim and delicate, her face hidden behind a veil. Peter Kopf was arrayed in buff-colored breeches and blue velvet doublet with a white linen cravat at his throat. He laughed and clapped his hands as he looked this way and that around the vast room.

Hoffman and Kopf together announced the wedding date for a month hence, and then Helga's veil was lifted by her future husband with a good deal of assistance from his father. Maria glanced at her husband during this performance and saw him watching with complete impassivity, his mind no doubt full of happy reflections upon future gain.

"We will see no children, I vow," chuckled a guest within Maria's hearing, "unless Herr Kopf himself does the honors."

Maria cringed at the words, but had no time to dwell upon them. She looked anxiously about the room for her friend, Elizabeth Schuler, and having found her, caught her eye. Frau Schuler nodded in return, and Maria drew a silent sigh of prodigious relief. That was the agreed-upon sign. All was now in readiness and the rest was up to her.

At the conclusion of the banquet late in the evening, the pair exchanged betrothal rings. Helga placed an emerald and diamond encrusted gold band on Peter's finger, and it was apparent to all that Peter was completely unaware of what he should do in return. Eventually, after a painful interlude during which Peter stared helplessly about him and then dropped the ring he held onto the table with a peal of mirthless laughter, his mother rose from her place and swept to his side, picked up the ring and helped him slide it onto Helga's trembling finger.

"Please forgive him," she said to the silent guests. "He is very nervous, you see."

There was a murmuring amongst the crowd, some awkward giggles and nervous coughs, but Maria held her breath for what she had warned Helga would come next.

"Peter," said Frau Kopf, turning to her son. "Will you not kiss your betrothed?"

The boy gaped emptily once again. Custom required the bridegroom to take the lead; Helga could not kiss him first, even if she had wished to, and so she simply waited. Peter began to admire his new ring, turning it in the candle light and grinning and giggling with delight.

Another agonizing pause ensued: a dreadful, lingering silence during which time stood still. The only sound in the mirrored room was Peter's child-like prattling, until even that died away.

Please, sweet Lord Jesus, prayed Maria, *deliver us all from this torment.*

An end to the mesmeric stillness finally came when one of the company, evidently more resourceful than the rest, raised his glass.

"My friends, a toast to the young couple. Drink with me to Helga and Peter."

The guests answered the toast with enthusiasm, and Maria sighed with boundless relief. Throughout the entire episode, Helga had stood expressionless, and Maria watched her in admiration. *That's my strong one*, she thought. *That's my good little soldier.*

Proceeding homeward at the end of the evening in their commodious and comfortable carriage, Hoffman allowed himself well pleased with the day's events.

"You see, wife," he said, "all is not so bad. Peter Kopf may not be an ideal husband, but Helga will have an agreeable future notwithstanding."

"As you wish, husband," answered Maria, her lips compressed.

"Ach," said Hoffman slumping back heavily on the leather seat. "I am sick of your nonsense. The family Kopf is rich; Helga will want for nothing."

"Nothing, save a husband," answered Maria, her face wooden, while Helga sat silent at her side, her eyes downcast.

Hoffman coughed suddenly and drew in a quick breath.

"The pain in your chest again?" asked Maria, and he nodded, grimacing.

"You should see a physician."

"Not likely," he snorted. "Charlatans, all of them."

The two pairs of white horses drew the carriage on through the darkened streets, the rhythmic clatter of their hooves echoing off the walls of the tall, narrow houses. Maria, unable to calm her ragged nerves, went over her plans again and again, desperate to be certain nothing was overlooked. One mistake, one unforeseen chance, could spell disaster. *There is one thing left undone*, she reminded herself, *and I have but a month. There must be a way....*

Upon reaching home, Hoffman disappeared into his study without a word and Maria made haste to get Helga into the privacy of her withdrawing room. By the time Maria closed the door behind them Helga was in a storm of tears.

"I would rather be dead," she wept. "I swear before God."

"Hush, now, hush," Maria soothed. "You will be safe."

"He dribbles," she sobbed. "He makes game of his food and I swear he pissed himself after dinner. I caught the stink of it."

"Come and sit down, my dear," said Maria. "You did well, and I am so proud of you. Try to calm yourself."

They sat together on Maria's chaise and she took the young girl's hands in hers.

"The only way to prevent this marriage," she said, "is for you to leave this house without your father's knowledge."

"You mean run away?"

"Yes, in a manner of speaking."

"But I cannot. I have nowhere to go."

Maria smiled at her stepdaughter.

"I have arranged a place for you to go, a place where neither your father nor the Kopf family can touch you. You may be able to return home in a few years, but I cannot promise that."

"Is there no other way?"

Maria shook her head.

"None. If you stay here, the marriage will certainly take place."

Helga raised her red-rimmed eyes to her stepmother's face.

"God grant that I may die before ever I marry Peter Kopf."

"Then listen well to me," said Maria, and unfolded her plans. In a month, Helga's life would indeed change, but not in the manner her father anticipated.

Helga blinked in amazement.

"Henceforth we must be vigilant," Maria finished, "lest we give ourselves away. If your father suspects our design, all is finished. I have friends who are willing to help us, and we must protect them as well. I was minded not to tell you until just before the wedding day, but after today I could not bear to see you in such torment."

Helga hugged Maria.

"Is it true?" she asked. "Really true?"

"It is all arranged," smiled Maria, "and I believe you will be content in that life."

"I know I shall," said Helga, her pale blue eyes glistening with tears once again. "Thank you, stepmama."

"Away to bed with you then," said Maria, but hardly had Helga departed when the reverberations of the doorbell echoed and reechoed through the darkened house. From below came the sound of running feet. Maria went out into the upstairs passage and looked down over the carved mahogany balustrade into the cavernous entrance hall. She saw the porter outlined in a pool of pale yellow light cast by the single candle he carried as he opened the front door. A figure hurried into the foyer and she recognized the voice of young Richter.

"*Calamity!*"

* * * *

The Prince Elector, Joseph Ferdinand, had collapsed and died after a state dinner. The physicians could not say why. All Bavaria mourned. His funeral procession wound its way through the streets of Munich to the muffled measure of a hundred black-draped kettledrums, while helmets and halberds shone in the afternoon sun as brigade after brigade of troops followed the catafalque in final homage. A column of lancers wearing brass-embossed steel breastplates formed the rearguard, their horses brushed and burnished like polished ebony. Crowds of silent citizens lined the streets and bade farewell as his Highness was laid reverently to rest amongst his ancestors of the House of Wittelsbach. By order of Ferdinand's father, an honor guard of twelve soldiers, their sabers drawn, stood before the tomb for a full month.

The Prince Elector's unexpected death plunged Hoffman into a state of consternation. Helga's marriage was immediately postponed in deference to the period of mourning, and Maria was consequently obliged to alter the arrangements made for her stepdaughter's deliverance. As it happened, however, the delay proved most opportune in providing Maria with the final piece to her puzzle.

She knew those to whom she would entrust Helga's care following her escape must be recompensed in some way. A sum of money was usually given, and Maria had secretly planned to sell some of her jewelry, but she soon realized that to raise a sufficient amount she would have to sell almost all she possessed, and that would be impossible. *In any case*, she thought, *money, once spent, is gone forever. If I do not offer money, then I must offer a true treasure instead, but treasures have I none.*

Her answer, when it appeared, came from an unexpected source.

* * * *

"Herr Zeller, sir," Peters the butler announced as Hoffman sat in his study.

Zeller, in high agitation, almost ran into the room without waiting for Hoffman's permission or invitation. He clutched to his chest a large parcel wrapped in cloth and tied with cord, knotted and sealed. He began to blurt out his story at once.

"I must speak to you Herr Hoffman. It is most important and I have but little time."

Hoffman was much less than happy to see his visitor. The recent death of the Prince Elector had rendered the partition treaty useless, placed the Spanish succession in question, raised the specter of war and, most grievous of all, threatened the normal course of legitimate and profitable commerce. Now, on top of all that weighed upon his mind, here came this miserable little Lutheran weasel no doubt to snivel and whine about his continuing inability to pay his debts. The mere sight of the man caused a sharp pain in Hoffman's chest. His heart missed a beat and he coughed before speaking.

"Well?"

"I am lost," Zeller wailed. "Ruined. Disgraced."

"Still, or again?" asked Hoffman.

"I have failed, Herr Hoffman. I cannot save my business. My creditors are taking all I have and I am a bankrupt. I cannot bear the shame."

Hoffman detested such blubbering shows of vacuous self-pity and brusquely told Zeller to state the purpose of his visit.

"I come to bid you farewell, Herr Hoffman. I am using the last of my resources to take my family to Innsbruck. I cannot stay in Munich."

"I must remind you—" began Hoffman, rising to his feet in alarm, but Zeller interrupted.

"I bring you this," he said, thrusting the cloth-wrapped parcel out towards Hoffman. "It is the last thing of value I possess. All else has been taken, but I have saved this for you. Take it, I beg you, in cancellation of my debt. I must leave many creditors unsatisfied; I would not have you to be one of them, Herr Hoffman."

Hoffman grunted, thinking this was not the declaration of honorable intent it purported to be. While Zeller's other creditors were likely simply to write him off as a scoundrel and forget him, Hoffman would hound him to the uttermost dungeons of hell, let alone Innsbruck, to retrieve his money, and he had made sure Zeller knew it.

"What is this, then?" asked Hoffman, pushing the parcel back towards Zeller.

"Allow me," said Zeller, rapidly breaking the red wax seals and unwrapping the bundle. "It is the ancient book of which I once told you. Centuries old and very valuable. It is all I have left to my name, Herr Hoffman, and I ask you to accept it."

Valuable or not, the gift was a masterstroke. Hoffman firmly believed that men of substance such as he should also be men of learning, and to demonstrate this virtue in himself— in lieu of formal schooling—he had accumulated a large and diverse library. He had collected the classical writings of Plato, Aristotle, Pliny, Cicero and Hippocrates, along with works of philosophy, theology, casuistry and natural science. He prized these books as symbols of his social and intellectual standing, although he had read hardly any of them. True, he had tried this book or that from time to time, but his studies had amounted to very little. However, his library remained his most treasured possession, notwithstanding its lack of use. This book, so old and venerable, would be the jewel in his collection.

"It is made by hand, you see," said Zeller, "and the mark of the

Vatican Library is here on the first page, just above my own family name. The book has been rebound since then, but you can still observe its fine illuminations and lettering. According to an inscription at the end, it was made by a man named Robert."

Hoffman looked at the thick brown leather binding of the book and felt its weight. The spine was reinforced with engraved brass straps, but his eye was drawn to the four gold studs on the front and back covers. Each was round and richly decorated with the coat of arms of Bavaria. He opened the book and the parchment creaked in protest as he turned the pages, admiring the still-brilliant colors of the pictorial illuminations and geometric designs.

"It is a gospel," continued Zeller. "St. John's gospel, with suffrages to the saint appended."

"It is very fine," said Hoffman. "A beautiful object."

"Then you accept it in payment?" asked Zeller with desperation in his voice. "My debt is expunged?"

Hoffman could not take his eyes from the old volume. Not only did he genuinely admire its craftsmanship, he was also envisioning the pride with which he would show it off to his friends. *Congratulations, sir,* they would say. He saw himself hailed throughout Munich as a man of great refinement and culture. He crossed the room to his desk and returned with a sheet of paper, which he tore in half and gave to Zeller.

"The note you signed. All is settled."

Zeller clutched the torn pieces of paper and departed with vast relief writ large on his haggard face.

As soon as Zeller had taken his leave, Hoffman claimed ownership of the book by writing his name and the date on the first page below the name of Zeller, thereby marking the volume as part of his private collection.

* * * *

"How did Herr Zeller obtain it?" Maria asked later that day in the library as her husband showed her the book.

"From Rome itself," Hoffman said. "It will make a most excellent addition to my library. No one in the city has so old a volume as far as I

183

know, and it is nothing less than a gospel life of our Blessed Lord. I am surprised that Lutheran heretic Zeller even kept it under his roof."

"Even Lutherans read the bible, husband," said Maria.

"Ha! So they do indeed. But they spurn the sacred Latin of Holy Scripture and read their heretical bibles in ordinary German as if they were nothing more than bills of fare in a beer hall. They defile the word of God."

Maria believed in the supremacy of the Holy Catholic Church, but stopped short of sharing her husband's condemnation of Protestantism.

"Should we not value Christian deeds above liturgy and dogma?" she asked.

Hoffman glowered at her.

"Nothing is of greater value than the word of God, wife."

"And when we stand before the great Seat of Judgment, will God's verdict be rendered upon the evidence of what we have done, or what we have believed?"

"Who are we to know God's purpose?" Hoffman snapped, and Maria knew it was time to withdraw gracefully from the field of battle.

"As you wish, husband. Let us go no further."

Hoffman snorted in derision and strode from the room after shelving the old book, leaving Maria alone. She made her way upstairs to her private chapel and fell on her knees before the altar, her heart overflowing with gratitude, and at the same time full of trepidation.

From the moment she first saw it, she knew the ancient book was the treasure she sought, but to use it as she intended would mean stealing it.

"Holy Mary, Mother of God," she prayed under her breath. "If it be possible, intercede for me and expunge the sin I must commit. It is for Helga's sake I must take the book, not for mine. Nevertheless, if I must endure an eternity in hell, then God's will be done, for before all the saints I swear Helga shall not marry Peter Kopf."

Chapter Twenty-Two

Charles II of Spain stoically refused to die, even though he frequently seemed more dead than alive: his life confirmed only by his continuing to breathe. A new treaty was needed, and strenuous efforts to secure it began immediately.

In the gilded halls and mirrored salons of great houses and palaces, the powerful spoke of nothing but the Spanish succession. The common folk, caring nothing for the political niceties which occupied, if not obsessed, the mighty, simply lived with a reawakened dread of impending war.

Herr Wilhelm Kopf, meanwhile, had judged it prudent to undertake a journey to several countries for talks with his numerous partners, agents and representatives. He sought to lay plans in case negotiations should fail and war break out.

"I cannot say how long I shall be gone," he said to Hoffman during a dinner party, "but I beg you to postpone the wedding until I return. I am certain you understand. If there is war, we may all be ruined if proper precautions are not taken."

"But of course," said Hoffman. "There is much I must do as well."

And, he thought, *I am saved the dowry money a little longer.*

After the guests departed, Hoffman pulled off his heavy horsehair wig and sank gratefully into a chair.

"Dear Lord and Father, you cannot know how tired I am, wife."

"And I," answered Maria. "I had begun to fear they might never go. Elizabeth Schuler is my very dearest friend, but upon my soul I swear she cannot leave off talking once she has tasted a glass of wine."

"She would talk the leg off an iron pot," sighed Hoffman, tossing his wig onto a nearby table.

"Indeed she would," agreed Maria, with a smile.

"Herr Kopf is going away," Hoffman said, after a short pause. "Helga's wedding is postponed until he returns."

He looked narrowly at his wife, fully expecting another attempt at dissuasion, but she merely returned his gaze and said, "As you wish, husband. I shall tell Helga tomorrow morning."

* * * *

"All is in readiness, my dear," said Maria, after giving Helga the news, "but I adjure you to be prepared at a moment's notice for I do not know what warning we shall have."

"I shall," said Helga. "When I think of Peter, I am overcome with fear, stepmama. I grieve for his sad affliction, but surely he should be shut away as others like him are."

"The Kopf family will not permit it," Maria answered. "They pretend he is like other young men of his age, and say he is merely nervous or shy. Their feelings are understandable, I suppose, but creatures like Peter should be locked safely away where they cannot distress decent folk."

She kissed Helga on the cheek and patted her arm.

"But do not be afraid, lambkin. All will be well for you."

But not for me, I fear, she thought as she left Helga's room. *Helga is saved and I am lost. I may be forced to join her in her place of exile once I confess what I have done.*

* * * *

As the dawn of 1700 arrived, Hoffman and Kopf, who had returned the previous November, continued to plan their commercial venture and watch the political developments. Hoffman felt content, but Maria did not seem so.

"In God's name, woman," he barked, "can you not cease pestering? Do you expect us to hold a wedding in the teeth of winter? And for that matter," he went on, bending a suspicious look upon his wife, "it strikes me that for one so opposed to the union, you are uncommonly eager to set a date for it."

"I think only of Helga," Maria answered. "This indecision weighs heavily upon her, and I think it unfair."

"A date will be announced when we are ready to announce it, and not before," Hoffman declared. "We must be sure of the situation with

Spain."

"Spain, Spain, Spain," said Maria, holding up her hands. "Can no one think of aught but Spain? One cannot go to the closet these days but someone is talking of Spain."

Hoffman regarded her for a moment, his eyebrows raised, and then nodded.

"Spain is a carbuncle on the arse of Europe, I grant you, but thanks to her having a milksop of a king who lacked the foresight or vigor to provide a male heir, we are all obliged to pay attention to her."

April, however, brought news of a forthcoming treaty. A wedding date was announced for May and preparations began at once.

One day in the middle of the month, the Hoffman house was full of dressmakers and a small army of cutters and seamstresses. Hoffman growled at the noise and commotion as the bride-to-be, her mother and all of her sisters old enough to attend the ceremony were measured, fitted, primped and pinned.

"The entire place is nothing but swish and giggle," said Hoffman to young Richter who had come to visit his father-in-law. "I find an unruly house most disagreeable, not to mention the cost of all these new gowns."

He coughed and rubbed his chest.

"Come," he said, "let us go into the garden. Perchance we shall find some peace and privacy there."

Tulips and hyacinths bloomed everywhere, and the eight Hoffman dachshunds played and gamboled about on a patch of grass: a happy, panting tumble of long brown bodies, short legs and vigorously vibrating tails.

"My uncle says the new treaty will end the crisis," said Richter, as they settled themselves onto a wooden bench in the shade of an ancient oak. "It seems, after all, there is no appetite for war."

"Well praise God for that," said Hoffman with considerable fervor. "Is anything known of what this treaty will contain?"

"The contents have not been generally noised, but my uncle has told me the rough outline."

Hoffman thought again how useful it was to have a son-in-law who had an uncle.

"And?"

"The Archduke Charles of Austria is to have the throne of Spain, along with the Netherlands and all the Spanish possessions in the Americas. Philip of Anjou will receive Naples, Sicily and Milan, all of which have been territories of Spain since the Italian Wars of Emperor Charles V. The matter appears to be settled."

Hoffman nodded. In truth, he cared not one whit who received which possession, what city or whose loyalty, as long as stability was preserved and Bavaria was not disadvantaged commercially. As he listened to Richter's words, there unfolded before his happy eyes a vision of the prosperous future that lay before him like a long, sunlit road. All that was needed now was to cement the alliance with the Kopf family through Helga's marriage and he could sleep soundly. He turned his head and shouted over his shoulder for the butler.

"Peters. Two glasses and a bottle of the cellar's finest."

* * * *

The wedding had been appointed for May the thirtieth, and excitement ran high amongst the Hoffman children. The girls played at wedding ceremonies, taking turns being the bride, and teased their brothers about their new wedding finery: blue breeches, white wigs and embroidered coats.

Maria, watching it all, played her part in the preparations with mechanical detachment as though performing in a play. With each passing day she steeled and emboldened herself for the act of defiance that was to come.

On the night before the wedding, Hoffman and Maria hosted a sumptuous and glittering banquet in spite of the former's whining about the cost.

"Must there be so many invited?" he grumbled as he waited with Maria for the guests to arrive. "We shall be driven to bankruptcy."

"It is our duty, husband," she answered, "as well you know." Unable to help herself, she added, "Remember, this wedding was not my idea."

Hoffman glowered at her, but said nothing.

The night was a gala scene of revelry. There were vast quantities of food and oceans of wine, beer and sack. The great hall of the Hoffman house blazed with countless candles and in the minstrel's gallery, high above it all, a small ensemble played lively music. Hoffman himself possessed so leaden an ear he could scarcely distinguish the notes of a trumpet from the braying of a donkey, but as long as the composer was German, he was satisfied.

"We shall have none of that anemic Italian folderol," he told Maria.

Helga and Peter sat side by side with their parents on a raised dais at one end of the hall while a battalion of servants, many engaged especially for the occasion, ran hither and thither dispensing food and drink as the two hundred guests laughed and talked boisterously. Once again, Helga acted the shy bride as instructed and Peter gurgled and laughed, played with his food and clapped his hands in glee at the animated scene before him.

Maria, unfailingly gracious and elegant in a gown of purple silk, smiled and talked with her guests. About halfway through the evening she found her friend, Frau Schuler, and kissed her on both cheeks.

"All is prepared," Frau Schuler whispered. "I will slip away in a few minutes."

"I will await your signal," Maria answered.

The Kopf family was the last to depart. Hoffman, Maria and Helga stood outside to see them off. Their carriage was resplendent with decorations and ribbons befitting the occasion, and as his final act of bachelorhood, Peter brought up his dinner onto the cobblestones and over his father's silver-buckled shoes.

"Make ready," hissed Maria to Helga as they reentered the house. "We have not a moment to spare. Change your garments quickly and wait for me."

Saying nothing, Helga disappeared upstairs.

As Maria had anticipated, Hoffman imbibed freely at the banquet and he lurched towards his bedchamber without any suggestion they should bed together. She hurried to her own rooms, and after changing into an ordinary cotton gown, she opened the window a crack and sat down to wait.

After an anxious half hour, she heard a soft whistle from the street below her room, and taking up a small pebble, dropped it out of the window as a sign she was ready. She made sure the house was quiet and then crept, feather-footed, down the corridor to Helga's room and pushed open the door. As she did so, one of its iron hinges creaked with a noise that sounded to her over-wrought senses like the arrival of the apocalypse. She froze in terror. The silence of the house remained absolute, however, and after a momentary breathless pause, she whispered Helga's name. The girl materialized out of the darkness wearing a plain gown and carrying a small leather-bound prayer book and a silver crucifix.

"Have a care," whispered Maria, her lips close to Helga's ear. "We dare not use a candle."

The two stole downstairs and along a hallway, which led to the side door of the house. The way took them past the library, and Maria placed a restraining hand on Helga's arm before entering the room.

Picking her way cautiously in the silent darkness, Maria moved around chairs and tables to where she remembered her husband had left the gospel manuscript. She felt along the shelf, but it was empty.

Dear God, has he removed it? Where is it?

Panic seized her with frozen fingers, but she fought it down and explored the shelf above. A moment later her trembling fingers found the heavy leather binding with its brass straps. Relief washed over her like an ocean wave. She exhaled a long breath, and gathered courage for what she now had to do.

"God forgive me," she breathed, crossing herself. "I do evil, but only in the pursuit of good."

She eased the heavy book off the shelf and holding it tightly retraced her steps to where Helga waited in the corridor. They slipped outside and into the carriage drawn up in the street.

"Is all well?" Frau Schuler asked as the carriage moved slowly off. "You were not seen?"

"No," said Maria, reaching out to clasp her friend's hand. "God be thanked."

The coachman walked the horses until they were safely away from the house and then whipped them up smartly so that the carriage raced, swaying and bouncing, through the moonless, empty streets.

Maria remained in a torment of apprehension lest they be caught before reaching their destination. If their flight were discovered, Helga would be beyond all help.

"Everything is ready?" she asked. Frau Schuler nodded and smiled at Helga.

"They are expecting you, little one, and soon you will be safe."

"My dear Elizabeth," said Maria, "how can I ever repay you for your generosity and for what you have risked? As God sees me I swear no one shall ever know of your part in this."

"And what if they do?" scoffed Frau Schuler. "I would do it all again a thousand times to save Helga from a life of such horror, and I do not care who knows it."

Within a quarter of an hour, the carriage drew up by the high stone wall of a large building into which was set a wooden door reinforced with iron plates and ornately curved hinges. Elizabeth Schuler alighted quickly, knocked four times and waited. The night was impenetrably dark and not a soul stirred in the narrow street as she knocked again. Three this time. Immediately there came the clanking sound of bolts being drawn back, and the door opened, releasing a stream of lantern light into the street. Its warm yellow glow illuminated the diminutive, black-habited figure of a calm-faced, elderly nun.

"I am Sister Jubilata," she said in a tranquil voice. "Be welcome in the name of Christ."

Maria and Helga stepped into the pool of light, and the old nun smiled at Helga.

"And this must be our new young postulate."

"Yes, Sister," said Maria. "Fraulein Helga Hoffman, my stepdaughter."

Sister Jubilata took Helga's hand and drew her to the doorway.

"Come, my child, and now you must speak truly. I ask you to declare before God that you do come to this place and seek admission to this sisterhood of your own free will, coerced by none, and desirous of no worldly gain."

"I do so declare, Sister," Helga answered.

"Then enter in Christ's holy name and join us in the service of our Lord and Savior."

Helga embraced and kissed her stepmother and Frau Schuler, and then Sister Jubilata led her into the narrow passageway within. She stepped behind Helga as she entered, thus blocking the doorway as a symbol of acceptance and protection.

"And what do you bring in token?" she asked, turning to Maria.

"This," said Maria, holding out the manuscript. "An ancient gospel and prayers. I offer it as my token."

"Let it be so," said Sister Jubilata, taking the book and placing it on a bench against the wall of the inner passage.

With a blessing and a smiling nod of farewell, the old nun closed the door. Iron clashed against iron as the bolts were thrust home.

Maria closed her eyes and exhaled a long breath. It was done. Helga was now untouchable: still in the world, yet at the same time safely removed from it.

"Come," said Frau Schuler, taking Maria's arm. "You must return home ere you are missed."

* * * *

The following morning, as the entire household was abuzz with anticipation and preparations, the alarm was suddenly raised and word put about that Helga was not in her room. Her bed had not been slept in and she was nowhere to be found.

Maria, hearing the commotion, hurriedly finished dressing and sped to her husband's room in time to intercept a footman on his way to tell Hoffman his daughter had disappeared. She waved the young man away from the door, entered, and begged her surprised husband to listen to her words and try to understand.

"What can be the matter, wife?" snapped Hoffman, and calling forth from within her all the courage she possessed, Maria told her story.

"You what?" roared Hoffman, red-faced and almost inarticulate with rage. "You did what, you meddling cow?"

"I took her away," repeated Maria as calmly as she could.

"What do you mean, away?" Hoffman snarled. "Away where? Tell me, I command you. There may yet be time to fetch her back."

Maria shook her head.

"She is safely within the Convent of the Blessed Virgin. You cannot touch her there."

Hoffman stared at her, incredulous.

"Can you not comprehend?" Maria said. "I would not, nay I could not, allow her to be married to that idiot boy. I begged you, but you were blinded by your own ambition."

Hoffman spluttered in fury.

"God damn you, woman. After all my efforts. All my plans for business. All the money I have spent on the wedding, including the dowry I gave Kopf last night. How dare you defy my wishes and bring all this to naught?"

"The dowry was meager enough," said Maria. "I have no doubt we shall survive its loss."

He stood before her, half-dressed in his finest clothes, staring.

"I will be humiliated," he growled. "A laughing stock throughout the city. 'There goes Hoffman,' they will sneer. 'He tried to marry off his daughter, but his wife would not let him.'"

His words struck Maria's heart. He would indeed be scorned as a weakling, but such had been her concern for Helga the thought had never occurred to her. She felt a stab of pity for him, and fleeting shame.

"Good husband," she pleaded, "I sought only your daughter's welfare. I beseech you to believe I honor you and meant you no harm."

"Honor? No harm?" he shouted, striding towards her, his fist raised to strike her in the face. "By God, woman, I shall teach you what harm is."

She stood her ground, closing her eyes tightly against the expected blow, but it did not come. She opened her eyes and saw her husband standing before her, clenching and unclenching his fist in indecision. She waited, and saw his face darken still further.

"And how did you find the money for the offering in token?" he asked. "What did you sell? Some jewels at half their value, I suppose."

Maria, drawing strength from the thought of Helga's deliverance from hell, answered in a clear and steady voice, almost surprised at her own self-possession.

"No. Even had I been able to raise enough, money does not last, and so I did not offer it. I gave the sisterhood the ancient gospel you obtained

193

from Herr Zeller. It will be a treasure to the convent forever."

Hoffman cried out as though struck mad.

"My book?" His voice cracked into a falsetto shriek. "You gave them my wonderful book? How could—"

No further words came. His breath, suddenly harsh and rasping, was strangled from him as he clutched his chest. He coughed and gasped, his eyes wild and his mouth gaping. He swayed for a moment, and then staggered backward before toppling to the floor.

"Husband!" Maria screamed, but Hoffman was already dead.

PART SIX
England: The Present Day

Chapter Twenty-Three

As agreed, Randall presented his translation of the Bartoli testament to Brauer who promptly gave his permission for its use by Professors Rossi and Farina for whatever scholarly purposes they wished.

"Is the information in the document new?" he asked over dinner the night before Randall left Vienna.

"Actually it's not, really," Randall said, after a mouthful of excellent veal scaloppini. "Apart from some of the details about the siege of Sant'angelo, most of what he says confirms what we already know."

"But what is the book he speaks of at the end? The one he gave to the soldier. Do we know anything about that? It's a very strange story."

"Yes, we do. It was a gospel of St. John, early thirteenth century, and created in England."

Brauer's eyes narrowed slightly.

"The book is not a surprise to you, I think, Herr Doctor."

"No, although it was a surprise that Bartoli mentions it. He certainly seems to think it had a great influence on Clement. The fact is, you see, I've been looking into the background of that book lately, but it has no great historical significance in and of itself. What Bartoli says puts an end to the research, of course."

Brauer did not seem much interested in the gospel, and poured himself another glass of wine.

"Even if all it does is tell us a little more about the sack of Rome and provide an insight into the psychology of Clement VII, the document remains the only known work of the good Cardinal Bartoli, does it not?"

"Yes, it does," Randall said, "and I should tell you it needs professional attention. It's becoming very fragile."

Brauer nodded again, but remained silent. Randall took the last mouthful of veal and waited.

"I do not really need to sell it," Brauer said with a shrug. "I shall give it to the Vatican. They will know how to take care of it."

Randall's expression must have changed because Brauer raised his hand and smiled.

"I know, Herr Doctor. I am sure your university would give it an excellent home as well, but I think it belongs in Rome."

You can't argue with that I suppose, thought Randall, recalling the conversation with Brauer as he sat on the plane back to London. *It would have been nice to come home with a trophy, though.*

He spent the weekend with Katherine and told her how the gospel search had finally finished. She was almost as disappointed as he, but encouraged him to realize he had done all he could and traced the history of the manuscript from beginning to end.

"And that's quite an achievement," she said. "I'm proud of you."

* * * *

"You mean," Megan said, "this Bartoli chap just took the gospel out and gave it to some passing soldier?"

"That's what he says Meg, and I can't see any way of tracing it further. After all, there were thousands of soldiers rampaging through Rome, for God's sake. No pun intended. And, anyway, the soldier who took it may well have cooked his dinner over it as Bartoli suggests."

"Blast," she said. "After all that trouble."

"And speaking of trouble," Joyce put in, "I suppose nothing out of the ordinary happened while you were away?"

"Absolutely not," Randall answered. "I think we've no more need to worry on that score. And besides, once I start telling everyone the gospel's well and truly had it, the race to find it will be over. We can't decipher the illuminations if we can't find the book, so that's the end of the mysterious treasure of All Saints."

Joyce pursed his lips in thought for a moment and then said, "Perhaps you're right, but mind how you go all the same. There's still the possibility of sources other than the gospel, and if our man thinks you're still primarily interested in the treasure, whatever it is, he could still be dangerous. He's a murderer, don't forget, and one way or another I intend to get the bugger."

"Well then," Randall said, "perhaps I shouldn't tell everyone the gospel's lost. I could just say it disappeared during the sack so I'm looking in other directions or something like that."

"Good idea, George," said Joyce. "I'll check with Thomas, but if you're willing to continue being the target, so to speak, then that's the way we'll play it."

"Right," said Randall, "I'll improvise."

"Well for pity's sake be careful," said Megan. "This is still just as dangerous as it was before. Remember what happened in London."

"I promise."

"By the way, Pop," Megan said, "I haven't seen you smoking your odiferous pipe of late. Given it up finally, have you?"

"Er...yes," he said with a slight shrug. "Katherine doesn't care for pipes much, you see, and so...."

"Ah, I see," said Megan with a knowing nod. "Good for Katherine."

"Actually," Randall said in an injured tone of voice, "she said my pipe smelled bloody awful, and she almost never swears."

Megan was still laughing when she and Tony Joyce drove away.

* * * *

Summer found Randall at work in his garden, weeding, pruning and watching over his beloved roses with maternal care and attention. Although he was no longer on the hunt for the gospel manuscript, he continued to tell people he was interested in finding it, and this pretense had yielded results in the spring, the news of which came in a telephone call from Milan in April.

"Randall, speaking."

"Ah, George," replied the cheerful voice of Professor Farina. "I have some most interesting news for you, my friend. Yesterday, I have had a telephone call from a man named Clive Thatcher, a graduate student at the University of London. He said one of his tutors had suggested he speak to me about a manuscript called *The Haunted Gospel*."

"What?"

"Yes indeed," said Farina. "He said he had found a reference to it in

197

Vatican records, and his tutor told him I was researching it in cooperation with your good self. It is fascinating how quickly word gets around. No?"

"What did you tell him?"

"That the book was created in England but was lost in the sacking of Rome, according to the Bartoli testament. I told him there is no way to find it now even if it does still exist, which it almost certainly doesn't."

As soon as Farina hung up, Randall called a colleague at London University.

"Sorry, George," was the response, "there's no Clive Thatcher here. Are you sure you got the name right?"

"Must be a mistake of some sort," said Randall, trying to keep his voice casual. "Don't worry about it."

It has to be Mike's killer, he thought. *He's still on my heels.*

"Look, George," his friend was continuing, "as long as you're on the blower, there's something I want to let you in on. It's a bit hush-hush for now, but you'll get the official word fairly soon."

Randall listened with mounting astonishment. *Incredible,* he said to himself as he replaced the receiver. *Completely incredible. This could solve all our problems.* He wanted to call Katherine immediately, but restrained himself. *I need to be sure this is real,* he thought. *There's no use getting all excited and going off half-cocked.*

Joyce was jubilant when told of the call to Farina from the non-existent graduate student.

"Good stuff," he said to Randall. "We might just have a viable lead now."

"It's a damn shame he didn't visit in person," said Randall, "or we'd have a description of him to boot."

"Not likely," said Joyce. "He's already taken that chance by going to the British Library. The last thing he wants to do now is show his face to anyone."

"Yes, I imagine you're right."

"I don't suppose he left a phone number with Farina, did he?" asked Joyce in a tone of artificial optimism.

"Fat chance," Randall grinned.

"Right, but we'll get hold of the phone records. I daresay quite a number of people knew you were going to Milan, did they?"

"It wasn't a secret," said Randall.

"Just checking."

"And speaking of checking," said Randall, "you were checking out John Archer, weren't you?"

"Yep, and all I found was a minor traffic violation a couple of years ago."

"Not exactly a hardened criminal, then," grinned Randall.

"No," said Joyce. "Anyway, back to this phone call. Assuming this mystery caller is our boy, which seems highly likely, he now knows the gospel's probably lost forever, but you're telling people you're still after it, aren't you?"

"That was the plan, yes."

"So that may well encourage him to think you know something he doesn't, right?"

"Could be," said Randall. "What are you getting at?"

"Just thinking out loud really," said Joyce. "Anyway, I'll let you know as soon as we have anything on the call to Farina."

"Okay."

If he really does think I'm a step ahead of him, Randall thought, *I wonder what he'll do. If he needs the information he thinks I've got, how can he get it? Directly from me? By intimidation? Threat? That means he'll have to make contact. But,* and the thought brought him up sharply, *what if he doesn't need the information at all? What if he's the one who's a step ahead?*

* * * *

"Since it's a murder case," Joyce told Randall a couple of days later, "I got the boss to ask for some help from the Italian police via Interpol, and they found out the call was made from a mobile phone. I got onto that and traced the owner who lives in Cardiff, no less. It turns out the phone was swiped and the call made before the account could be deactivated. Unfortunately, the owner isn't certain of exactly where or when the theft occurred, which is a pity. Whoever nicked the phone probably chucked it into the sea or smashed it to bits as soon as he'd finished with it."

"Well, unless he's privy to sources I don't know about," said Randall, "he's not going to get any further in finding the gospel or the treasure than I did."

"Maybe, maybe not," said Joyce, "but he may be convinced the gospel survived the attack on Rome in spite of what Farina told him."

"Yes," answered Randall, "I've been thinking about that. What if somehow he knows the manuscript survived?"

"How could he know?"

"I don't really know; perhaps he's found out something new."

"On the other hand," Joyce suggested, "what if the manuscript isn't the real object? What if he's only after the treasure?"

Randall sighed.

"I always rather discounted the treasure possibility, as you know, but now I'm beginning to think there must be something in it after all."

"Yes," Joyce said, "and as we mentioned before, if he has another source, it must be one that told him about the treasure before he read Bartholomew. That's assuming, of course, the treasure was the motive for Mike's murder, and we don't actually know that for sure."

"Well," said Randall, "even if I accept the proposition there's a treasure at All Saints, I still think it's unlikely to be the silver and gold variety."

"But it could be, couldn't it?" said Joyce, "and what if our man actually *knows* it is? That would explain why he's still after it and is worried you may be as well."

Randall paused a moment before answering.

"You may be right I suppose, but All Saints was a small enclave, and certainly not wealthy. If they had some sort of a traditional treasure, then what the hell was it and where did it come from?"

Chapter Twenty-Four

In late July, Randall journeyed to London to meet Katherine and they departed for a summer holiday. They boarded the Eurostar at the newly renovated St. Pancras International Terminal and streaked across the sunlit countryside of southeastern England before plunging into the Channel Tunnel. After twenty minutes, their train burst out into daylight in northern France and hurtled on to Paris.

After a few days in the City of Lights during which they visited the Louvre and other celebrated attractions, they hired a car and drove south to the Côte d'Azur and then eastwards along the Mediterranean coast into northern Italy. They viewed the ruins of Christopher Columbus' house in Genoa, and had dinner with Christina and lunch with Farina in Milan.

For Randall, they were days of contentment. Katherine was relaxed and radiant. Her career was a demanding one and he sensed in her a great relief at being free, albeit temporarily, from the pressures of the office. They shared the driving, stopped wherever they chose, stayed wherever they liked, moved on whenever they pleased. Katherine called it a gypsy holiday and said it was a travel style she had always dreamed of trying.

Randall felt as if the tribulations of the gospel search were behind him. The manuscript could not be found, and he had decided the mysterious treasure was probably a misnomer after all. He acquired a sense of security he had not known for some time, but he would later say such complacency had been seriously ill-advised.

They crossed from Italy into Austria over the Brenner Pass and stopped in the town of Steinach Am Brenner, securing a room at the Steinacherhof Hotel in the Bahnhofstrasse. Tired and travel-stained after hours on the road, they had dinner in the hotel restaurant and then fell gratefully into bed.

Over the next couple of days, they explored the town and marveled at the surrounding mountain scenery. Randall wrote a postcard to Megan from the hotel describing the Tyrol as one of the most beautiful places he had ever seen.

On their third day, they hiked up into the lower mountain pastures and as the sun declined, they found a wooden bench, which some charitable soul had placed at the top of a long hill. Before them, a broad vista of green meadows and forest thickets rose into the distance to a backdrop of high, rugged peaks.

"This is a magical place," murmured Katherine. Randall nodded just as his mobile phone rang. He answered, listened, spoke briefly and then thanked the caller before flipping the phone closed and turning to Katherine.

"Katherine," he said in an excited voice, "there's something marvelous I want to tell you."

"Well out with it then," she smiled. "You look ready to burst."

"When I called to inquire about that non-existent graduate student at the University of London, I spoke to an old friend of mine who gave me the inside track about a professorship coming up. Apparently, some benefactor died and endowed a new Chair in Medieval History in his will. I didn't want to tell you until I was sure about it. The appointment is by invitation only, and he told me I was front-runner. I told them I was going to be away and gave them my mobile number. That call was a confirmation from them inviting me to take up the position and giving me a full three months to let them know. So what do you think of that?"

"Congratulations, George," she said, hugging him tightly. "That's absolutely wonderful. I'm so proud of you."

"But, good grief," he said, untwining her arms and looking into her deep hazel eyes, "don't you see? This means I can come to London."

"Oh my God," she said as realization dawned, "Yes, but…."

"What?" he said, his eyebrows raised.

"It would mean leaving Megan, leaving your home, your seniority at St. Arthur's."

"You're right," he said in a deliberately pragmatic tone of voice. "Forget I mentioned it."

She put her hand on his arm.

"No, no, I didn't mean—"

"Listen to me, Katherine," he said, taking her hand. "Megan is a grown woman and she'll be just fine, especially now it seems she's found a partner. London is a wonderful university and the position is a very senior one. As for leaving home, my home is with you. If you lived in Tibet, I'd try to find a job at the University of Lhasa, if there is such a place."

He paused. This was the moment he had looked forward to and planned for. He had to get it right. He wanted it to be perfect.

"Katherine, will you...I mean...would you...?"

He floundered like a mackerel on a fishmonger's slab.

Katherine, coming to his rescue with a smile, leaned forward and kissed him.

"Of course I will."

He exhaled voluminously.

"Thank God."

"You're delightfully inarticulate when you try not to be," she giggled.

They walked back to their hotel, Randall in a state of surpassing happiness, with Katherine wearing the ring he had bought in London a week before they left and which he had been carrying with him since their holiday began.

By the time they reached the hotel it was dusk, and as Katherine asked for their room key, the sharp-eyed young desk clerk noticed the new ring. He offered profuse congratulations, and when they went down to dinner, a bottle of champagne was delivered to their table with the compliments of the house.

After dinner they retired to bed in utter contentment, but by midnight their world had been turned on its head.

As they lay in bed, their tranquility was abruptly shattered by a strident peal from the phone on the bedside table.

"Oh no, not now," said Katherine as Randall grunted in annoyance and reached for the receiver.

"Hello," he mumbled, more than half expecting it to be a wrong number or something equally inane. The voice that answered was controlled and somber.

"George? It's Tony."

Alarm pierced Randall like sharp thorns.

"Tony? What is it?"

"There's been an accident, George."

Alarm turned to fear.

"Accident?"

"It's Megan" Joyce said, and hurried on before Randall could speak. "She's all right, George. She's in hospital, but she's going to be absolutely fine. There are no serious injuries."

"Dear God," Randall said, "not Megan."

He felt ill. His throat constricted and made breathing difficult. He became aware of Katherine's hand on his shoulder and her voice from behind him.

"George, what is it?"

"What happened?" asked Randall when he had found his voice again.

"The minivan lost its brakes."

"How is she?"

"Cuts and bruises and a bump on the head," said Joyce. "She's going to be fine; the doctor is sure of it. Megan told me not to tell you and spoil your holiday, but she's had a very nasty shock and I know she'd appreciate your being here. I'd appreciate it as well."

"We're on our way," said Randall, "and thanks for letting us know."

They pushed clothes into suitcases as quickly as they could, checked out—much to the consternation of the hotel staff—and set off with Randall driving. As they left Steinach and joined the autobahn, he stepped on the accelerator. They sped through the night with the great mountains lowering above them, their snow-capped summits glowing pale silver in the moonlight against the deep purple darkness of the sky.

"I'm sorry about this," he said after a long period of silence. "Our holiday's sort of had it."

"Don't worry about that," said Katherine. "We'll just have to come back next year and pick up where we left off, that's all."

"We can dump the car at the Innsbruck airport," he said. "If we can get a flight to London in time, I might just manage to catch the noon train home. I'm afraid that will probably mean leaving you to get home on your own, though."

"No, George," Katherine announced with complete finality, "I'm coming with you. They're not expecting me in the office for at least another two weeks and there may be something I can do for you or Megan."

"You don't need to feel—" he began, but she interrupted.

"Megan's going to be my stepdaughter, George," she pointed out, "and I want to help if I can."

"I'm sure everything will be okay," he said. "You ought to go home and relax."

"No," she said. "My mind's made up. I want to be there for you and Megan."

Randall had seen this stubborn streak in her before.

"Oh, I know," Katherine went on. "Megan's an independent adult and all that, but any traffic accident, even a minor one can be very unsettling and she might appreciate a bit of mothering for a while. I only hope she won't think me too presumptuous. I mean, she doesn't even know we're going to be married."

"Actually she does," said Randall, without taking his eyes off the road. "I showed her the ring right after I bought it."

"Did you indeed?" she said, her eyebrows arched. "There's cheek for you. You were darn sure of yourself, weren't you, Professor?"

"Yes, I suppose I was," he said, with a sidelong glance at her, "but when it came time to actually ask, I was petrified you might say 'no.'"

* * * *

They reached St. Arthur Newtown in the late afternoon and Joyce met them at the station. After introductions, he suggested they go and have a coffee.

"I'd like a word before we go to the hospital," he said, but he would not elaborate until they were seated in a restaurant around the corner from the station.

"What's going on, Tony?" Randall asked. "Did they underestimate the extent of Meg's injuries or something?"

"No, no," said Joyce, raising his hand for emphasis, "nothing like that at all. She had a slight concussion, which she shook off in record time, and her left ankle is badly twisted, but aside from those things, it's only cuts and bruises as I told you. They say they're going to give her a

205

pair of crutches and send her home tomorrow or the day after at the latest."

"Good news," said Randall in profound relief. "Then why are we here instead of on the way to the hospital?"

"Well," said Joyce, "first of all in all this upheaval I clean forgot to congratulate you both. Megan tells me you're going to be married."

"And she's as cheeky as her father," said Katherine with a smile as she allowed Joyce to admire the ring.

"Excuse me?" he said.

"Never mind," said Randall, "we'll explain later. Just tell us what's going on."

"All right," said Joyce, slipping into his professional voice. "Here's the situation. The van went right into a lamppost, but fortunately, Meg wasn't going very fast. There was lots of traffic about and she simply put her foot on the brake at a red light. She said the brakes caught at first—things might have been much worse if they hadn't—and then just disappeared. She went through the junction—the cars coming across were able to avoid her—and then had to swerve and mount the curb to avoid going into the back of a lorry. Next thing she knew, she was in an ambulance."

"Good Lord," breathed Katherine. "She could have been killed."

"Well," said Joyce, taking a deep breath, "that was probably the intention, I'm afraid.

"Oh my God, " said Randall. Katherine put her hand on his arm.

"I had the van checked over, of course," Joyce continued, "and the brakes had been messed with. No doubt about it. It wasn't a professional job and forensics found it in no time."

"God damn," Randall exploded. "The bastard couldn't get me, so he's gone after Megan. That's what this is, isn't it?"

"It looks that way," agreed Joyce.

"I take it you've got Megan under guard at the hospital then?" said Katherine. Joyce shot her an approving glance.

"We certainly have. There's a man outside her door and no unauthorized person gets in, but Megan can't see him and she doesn't know about the brakes yet."

Randall nodded.

"Okay."

"But couldn't it just have been some shoddy work by a garage mechanic or something?" asked Katherine.

Joyce shook his head.

"Don't I wish."

Randall tried to take a mouthful of coffee, but his hand trembled so violently he was obliged to put down the cup.

"It's going to be all right George," said Katherine. "Megan is quite safe now, and whoever or whatever this demon is, it won't bring us down because we won't allow it to."

They drove to the hospital where the uniformed constable outside Megan's room stood aside smartly at the sight of Joyce's warrant card. Inside, they found Megan sound asleep, a large white sticking plaster on her forehead, her injured ankle bandaged and elevated off the bed.

"We shouldn't wake her," whispered Katherine.

"Just a minute," said Joyce quietly. "When she finds out I've brought you all the way back from Austria she's going to be hugely upset with me, but now you're here, I know she'll want to see you."

Randall relaxed and grinned at Joyce. He felt glad, almost comforted, to see how well the young man knew Megan. He looked at his daughter lying asleep in her stainless steel hospital bed complete with wheels and side rails. She wore a standard-issue gown with little pink flowers on it. There was an IV tube in her wrist and he noticed a purple and yellow bruise on her left forearm.

Who's doing this, for God's sake? he asked himself. *What do they want? Is that bloody manuscript really behind all this? I wish I'd never heard of the thing.*

Joyce awakened Megan with the utmost gentleness, and she opened her eyes and tried to focus, looking groggy and disoriented.

"Tony?" she murmured, "I fell asleep...."

Randall leaned over and kissed her on the forehead.

"Hello, sleeping beauty."

"Pop?" she said, coming back to full awareness. "What...?" She turned to Joyce. "I said I'd kill you if you told them."

"And I'd have killed him if he hadn't," retorted Randall. She smiled up at him from the pillow.

"Thanks ever so much for coming, Pop, and this must be Katherine, at long last."

"I'm sorry we're meeting for the first time in these surroundings," Katherine said. "People aren't really at their best in hospitals are they?"

They chatted for a short while before an officious, middle-aged nurse hurried in and told them all to leave Megan alone to rest.

"The best thing for shock is undisturbed sleep," she said, as if she were talking to a group of children. "Come along now, off you go."

They said hasty goodbyes to Megan, who grinned at them all and thanked them for coming.

"See you soon," said Joyce, and he kissed her on the cheek.

Katherine went in search of a cup of tea, leaving Randall and Joyce alone in one of the visitors' lounges. After some discussion, they agreed that when Megan was discharged she would go to stay at Randall's house where Katherine could help look after her and Joyce would not have to worry about her being alone. He told Randall he would have the house watched for a few days, and asked him to look out for a message.

"Message?" said Randall.

"Yes. It may be this lunatic will contact you this time to warn you off. He's taken this to a new level now."

"But he didn't contact me before; why would he do it now?"

"If he'd killed you," Joyce said, "that would have been that. He could then have hunted for the gospel by himself. To have contacted you earlier would have sent a signal that someone else was after the gospel and would also have risked intensified interest from the law. But I suspect that now he's changed his strategy."

"But," Randall objected, "he heard from Farina that the gospel is pretty well lost for good. Why go after Megan at this point?"

"Because when you came back from Vienna you let it be known you were still looking for the manuscript. We hoped to lure him out."

"Yes, and that seems to have backfired on us, to Megan's cost. I didn't dream he'd go after her, but now he has, I'm going to make it clear I've given up altogether. I'll announce the manuscript was destroyed in 1527 and that'll be the end of it."

"No," said Joyce in his official voice. "I still think the best way is to go on giving everyone the impression you're still looking for leads. I think this attempt on Megan indicates increasing desperation, which could well cause him to make a mistake and give himself away. Desperation often leads to carelessness."

"It's much too dangerous," said Randall. "Putting me in his sights was one thing, but the game is entirely different now. And besides, I can't go on pretending forever. The gospel is gone and I might as well just say so."

"We thought you could sort of…make something up," said Joyce. "You know, invent a lead."

"We?"

"The boss agrees with me on this one and that's what we'd like you to do. I promise we'll keep Megan safe."

"Tony," Randall said, fixing the young man with a steady stare, "after my broken arm, you promised Meg no one else would get hurt, and now she's lying in this place."

"Don't remind me George. You've no idea how God-awful I feel."

"And what about Katherine?" asked Randall.

Joyce gave a small sigh, and Randall could see the weight of responsibility and worry that bore down on him.

"Yes," said Joyce, after a short pause. "I must admit that's a problem."

"I'll say," said Randall. "You said yourself whoever shoved me at that bus must have known where I was in order to follow me. This chap must know about Katherine and where she lives, although God knows how." Randall shook his head. "It's too risky. I won't endanger them."

"Look George," said Joyce. "I don't think your feelings for Katherine could be any stronger than mine are for Megan. She's the very best and most wonderful thing that's ever happened to me. Do you seriously think I'd suggest this if I had another choice?"

"It's all so ironic," said Randall. "In order to get the person who tried to kill Meg, we have to put her in danger all over again."

"Appearing to go on with the search is the only way I know to get him. God knows I wish we had an alternative." Joyce paused and looked hard at Randall. "But we don't."

He's right, thought Randall. *Do I want to get Mike's killer off the streets or not? And now he's gone after Megan. He's got to be stopped.*

"All right Tony, I'll do what I can on one condition. Megan and Katherine must agree. I won't make that decision for them. We can look out for Megan here, but Katherine will be on her own in London."

"Fair enough," said Joyce, "and there's one more thing."

"Which is?"

"We're going to behave as if the crash was a complete accident. There'll be no public statements about alleged criminal activity."

"Why not? I say let's put the heat on him."

"No. The incident is of no value to him if it's seen to be an accident. He needs to make it known that he's responsible. We want to force his hand; make him get in touch with you. Get him out into the open if we can."

Chapter Twenty-Five

After two days in hospital, Megan was taken to Randall's house where she began her convalescence. She could go nowhere without her crutches, but apart from that impediment she rapidly returned to good health. Katherine assisted with calm and capable skill and, to Randall's intense pleasure, she and Megan found much in common and soon became good friends. Joyce and Randall explained the plan to them one evening after dinner.

"I'll try and invent some decent-sounding lead to tell people about," Randall finished, "but we won't go ahead unless you both agree. I'm adamant that this has to be your decision. There's obviously danger to all of us now."

"I say go ahead," said Megan immediately.

"Are you absolutely sure?" asked Randall.

"Yes I am," she said. "This despicable little toad has to be found," she said, and Randall raised his eyebrows at the vehemence of her tone.

"Well, damn it all, Pop," Megan went on, her eyes bright with anger. "He's tried to kill you, he's tried to kill me and on top of all that he's completely buggered up my lovely van. If I ever catch him I'll string him up by his—"

"Thank you," Randall interposed with a grin, "I think we get the picture."

"Katherine," said Joyce, "what about you? You'll be by yourself in London. I can't offer you any sort of protection, I'm afraid, beyond some off-the-record phone numbers of one or two mates of mine who've agreed to help if needed. The big problem is our man appears to know where you live."

She said nothing for a few moments, and Randall could tell her mind was hard at work. He had long since learned the signs: a very slight frown, lips lightly compressed.

"Tony," she said at length, "are you honestly able to say this tactic is all you have to suggest? It didn't work the first time, you know. We didn't learn anything about this maniac or come even close to finding

211

him, and that's when George actually *was* looking. And now you want to try again, when he's only pretending to look?"

"I know it sounds lame, Katherine, but I swear it's all we've got."

"Very well," she said. "I agree with Megan. I want this business ended as soon as possible, so let's do it. Here's an idea. I have a cousin, Lucy, living just outside Wimbledon and she's been after me for months to go and stay with her for a while. She's no family at all—bit of a recluse actually—and lives by herself in an old pile of a house about twice the size of a super-tanker. I'll make arrangements with her before I leave here. Lucy will be delighted. I won't be found in Wimbledon, and I'll go straight there from here without going to my flat."

"Bravo," said Joyce.

"But I'm sure this character knows where you work," said Randall. "He'll simply watch for you there when he sees you're not coming home. I still don't like it much."

"I can do a great deal of work without ever going to the office," Katherine said, with perfect composure. "And if I do go—which I very much doubt—I won't use the bus or the Tube. I'll hire a car and drive from Wimbledon. There's underground parking at the office and the entrance is at the back. If this creep knows as much about me as you think he does, then he'll know I don't have a car of my own. *Ergo,* he won't be watching the parking garage."

"Excellent," said Joyce with a nod.

"But what if people call you at the flat?" asked Randall.

"They'll think I'm still away. All my friends knew we were going on holiday, don't forget."

"And your colleagues at work? What about them?"

"I'm the senior partner, George," she said with a smile. "My money helped found the firm. If I say I'm staying with a relative and working from there because I don't want to be disturbed, no one's going to press the point."

Randall sighed, still uncertain, and Katherine put her hand on his arm—a now familiar gesture of affection.

"Don't worry, my dear," she said. "I'll be all right. Let's get this over with, once and for all."

He knew that once again her mind was made up.

"You're a treat, Katherine," said Joyce with a grin.

"But there's one condition," said Katherine. "I realize the need for secrecy, and I'm sure Lucy won't be a problem, but I must tell Donald where I am. Once he knows what's going on he won't divulge anything to anyone."

* * * *

Randall decided the most plausible story he could use was simply to say he was looking for clues to the gospel's whereabouts in Germany. Given what he knew from Bartoli, it seemed workable and had a certain logic to it. Once back on campus he began to spread the story.

"Many of the soldiers who attacked Rome in 1527 were German Protestants," he told Max Thoroughgood, "and we know that a good deal of plunder was taken out of Italy in the months following the sack. I've got a couple of potentially good possibilities."

He knew it sounded a little thin, but it seemed to satisfy the curious and there was renewed interest in *The Haunted Gospel*. Since the so-called leads were spurious, he avoided having to explain them in detail, but the first part of the story was perfectly true. Looting had been rife, but even so, Randall did not truly believe the gospel had been taken north. He was unable to imagine an old Latin text being seen as valuable by a marauding horde of German Lutherans. Books, parchments and manuscripts had been destroyed wholesale when the Vatican was ransacked by the Colonna family's army in 1526, and he could see no reason why things should have been different the following year. In his view, the gospel had most likely been used to start a fire, just as Bartoli reported.

Notwithstanding his personal doubts, Randall faithfully maintained the story of the fictitious leads, while at all times remaining alert for the message Joyce hoped would come from the murderer: a message, which finally arrived two days after Katherine left for Wimbledon. Randall answered the phone in his office, and after a click, a synthesized voice spoke to him.

"Forget the gospel. Next time your daughter won't be so lucky."

He made a few quick notes and then telephoned Joyce.

"It was a computer voice," he said. "I imagine whoever it was simply made a recording of his computer speaking the sentence he'd written. It's not hard to do."

"Recording?" asked Joyce. "Why not just let the computer speak down the phone?"

"He could have done that," said Randall. "Only he used a public call box. I could clearly hear traffic noise and outdoor sounds. He'd have wanted to get the call over with as quickly as possible with a minimum of fuss so as not to attract the attention of anyone who might afterwards remember seeing him. Using a small digital recorder wouldn't be noticed at all, but manhandling a laptop would have been too conspicuous, I think."

"Okay," said Joyce. "We'll make a copper of you yet."

"No thanks," grinned Randall.

"We're still in a bind with this, though," said Joyce. "We've no voice to work on. Cunning bastard. I suppose we may be able to find the call box. We'll have a look at the phone records."

"I can tell you one thing straight away," said Randall, unsuccessfully attempting to keep the smugness out of his voice, "although you'll soon find it out from the records. The call came from Lincoln."

"How the hell do you know that?"

"Elementary, my dear Joyce," said Randall. "After I hung up I wrote the message down so as not to forget it, and then I went over and over everything I could remember about what I'd heard or impressions I'd had, and wrote all that down as well."

"Good for you," said Joyce. "Are you sure you don't want to be a copper?"

"Just before the message started, I heard a voice in the background shout, 'Meet you up Steep Hill at the Wig.'"

"And what's that mean in English?"

"Steep Hill is in Lincoln; leads up towards the Cathedral. The Wig refers to The Wig and Mitre which is a pub near the top of Steep Hill."

"How do you know all this?" asked Joyce.

"I used to go to Lincoln a lot in my student days. I had a girlfriend there and we used to frequent that pub; dates from the fourteenth century actually."

"The pub or your girlfriend?"

"Twerp."

"That's it then," said Joyce. "Well done, George, and don't tell anyone about this."

* * * *

By late autumn Megan, her crutches long since abandoned, had returned to her own home. Joyce had sold his flat, and he and Megan had set up permanent housekeeping together. Randall was more than pleased with this arrangement, because not only was Megan very happy, she was also afforded a good measure of protection as well. Joyce drove her to and from work and she never went out alone at night.

Katherine, unable to impose indefinitely on her cousin, close friend though she was, had suggested she might return to her flat since all appeared to be quiet, but Randall and Joyce would have none of it. At their insistence, she moved into a small flat in Horsham. She did not have a landline connected for the phone and only used her mobile. In response to any of the locals who happened to ask, she concocted a story about her own home being too noisy and uncomfortable due to renovations being carried out in the flat directly above. The work was expected to take several months.

Police investigations in Lincoln had proved fruitless. The call box was easily located, but individual fingerprints were impossible to isolate. Potential witnesses working in nearby shops and offices could remember nothing.

"Small wonder," said Joyce. "Who takes the time to study a bloke making a call from a public phone in broad daylight on a busy street corner?"

The new term had begun and Randall was busy with his teaching and other duties. He had an excellent crop of students again and he derived much satisfaction and intellectual stimulation from overseeing their study and research.

He maintained the appearance of continuing the gospel search, but the longer it went on and the more questions people asked him, the more

215

difficult it became. *Oh, what tangled webs we weave, when first we practice to deceive,* he reminded himself.

He went to see Katherine as often as he could; carefully observing Joyce's instructions to avoid being followed, but those occasional meetings were a poor substitute for a life together. As soon as Megan was out of hospital, he wrote to the University of London to say he would be honored to accept the position offered to him, but he had heard nothing from them for weeks apart from a rather flowery missive of acknowledgement and thanks.

There had been no further messages from Lincoln or anywhere else, but the silence did not comfort him; on the contrary, he found it unnerving, almost eerie. The killer was out there somewhere, and Randall never felt free of his malignant influence. The strategy of continuing the hunt did not seem to be working as quickly as they had hoped, so he and everyone else did the only thing left to them. They waited.

Christmas came and went without incident, but February saw a wholly unexpected change that brought the gospel search squarely back into Randall's life once again.

On a cold and miserable day at the beginning of the month, Randall sat in his office evaluating a proposal for a doctoral dissertation on the economic structure of fifteenth century Cistercian monasteries. He had just begun to write his critique and recommendations when his phone shattered his concentration.

"Damn," he muttered, reaching for the receiver without taking his eyes off his computer screen.

"Randall, speaking."

"Professor Doctor George Randall?" said a loud voice with a German accent.

"Speaking."

"Ah, excellent. Professor, my name is Zeller, Edward Zeller, and I am calling from Linz, Austria."

"I'm sorry, Herr Zeller," said Randall, reluctantly turning from his computer. "I don't believe I know you."

"You don't," said Zeller, "but I have your name and phone number from a good friend of mine, Herr Wolfgang Brauer of Vienna."

"Oh, I see," said Randall. "Is there something I can do for you, Herr Zeller?"

"I am told you are in search of a Latin gospel of St. John that disappeared from Rome during the Protestant Wars of the sixteenth century. That is correct, *ja*?"

"Yes it is, but—"

"It may be the same one I am looking for, Herr Professor."

Randall cleared his throat to allow himself time to recover from the shock of Zeller's words.

"You're looking for a gospel of John, Herr Zeller?"

"*Ja*. I happened to mention it to Herr Brauer—he and I are both collectors—and he told me immediately of your translation of the Bartoli document and the clue it contained for you, and perhaps for me also."

"You mean the fact that Bartoli gave the book to a soldier?"

"*Präzisieren*, precisely. And that soldier may quite possibly have been my ancestor."

"Your ancestor?" echoed Randall, in astonishment.

"Yes, Herr Professor. You see, I believe that gospel of John once belonged to my family, and I should like to retrieve it, or at least to know where it is now. Perhaps we can work together, *ja*?"

"Yes, of course," said Randall, but Zeller was still in full spate.

"I will come to London to meet you. Would the weekend of March second be convenient?"

Arrangements were quickly made and Randall then went round to Max Thoroughgood's office.

"It's unbelievable," said Thoroughgood. "To come out of nowhere like that."

"Well," said Randall, mindful of his cover story, "I have been following up some leads in that general direction."

"I know," said Thoroughgood, "but this has been handed to you on a plate."

"Pretty much, it seems. Zeller hasn't found the manuscript, though. However, according to what he says, the book that once belonged to his family was brought from Rome at the right time."

Thoroughgood shook his head.

"It's a remarkable coincidence."

"I thought so at first," said Randall, "then I got to thinking. There can't be that many people interested in collecting medieval manuscripts and able to afford to do it. In a world that esoteric and rarefied, the fact that Zeller knows Brauer, isn't really all that surprising."

* * * *

On the evening of March second, Randall and Katherine met Edward Zeller at his hotel. Zeller was a silver-haired man of about sixty, slim, and wearing a very well-tailored and expensive-looking charcoal gray silk suit. He carried a highly polished, black leather briefcase that he kept a firm hold of at all times.

After introductions, for which Zeller did not shake hands but bowed stiffly from the waist, he conducted them to the private dining room he had reserved for their dinner. After the briefest glance at the menu, he snapped it shut and gave his order curtly, without looking at the waiter. Randall and Katherine quickly made up their minds, and after the waiter departed, Randall offered to contribute a bottle of wine to the meal.

"I do not drink alcohol," said Zeller, and by his expression gave them to understand the subject was closed.

"So, Herr Professor, shall we turn to business?"

"As you wish," said Randall, uncertain how to respond to Zeller's abruptness.

"My family has an illustrious history, Herr Professor," Zeller began, ignoring Katherine altogether. "Let me tell you a little of it. The Zellers were originally cloth merchants and clothiers who reached the zenith of their prosperity in Vienna in the last half of the eighteenth century. Business suffered greatly in the Napoleonic Wars, however, and two Zellers were killed in 1805 at the Battle of Austerlitz. Their deaths signaled the decline of the family as a commercial power."

Appetizers were served, but Zeller carried on without interruption.

"The family was not Viennese, you understand. At the end of the seventeenth century, they were in Munich where they had achieved a modest success but then they fell on hard times through the dishonesty of one of their business partners. I am not certain of the exact date the family left Munich, but it must have been around the turn of the eighteenth century, give or take a year or two, and they went to Innsbruck. They managed to reestablish themselves there and as they grew richer they decided to move to Vienna."

Zeller paused for a few quick mouthfuls of his *fois gras,* and then continued.

"So now we come to the point, Herr Professor. Financial troubles forced them to flee from Munich, but they did their best to settle what debts they could before leaving by selling or forfeiting much of what they possessed. Many things were lost in this way."

Zeller reached for his briefcase.

"Now let me read something to you."

Zeller opened his briefcase and produced a thick wad of papers secured with a heavy elastic band.

"This manuscript is an English translation of a family history written in 1811 by my ancestor, Manfred Zeller. Listen to what he says.

One such family treasure lost was a very old handwritten book in Latin. It was a gospel of St. John and had prayers added at the end. It was much prized by my great-grandfather who frequently lamented its loss. It had been in the family for nearly two hundred years, having been brought by one of our ancestors from Rome during the time of the Protestant invasion and destruction of that city. The book was given to Herr Carl Hoffman in Munich in settlement of a debt immediately prior to the family's departure for Innsbruck, and although I have myself made many attempts to retrieve it and restore it to our family once more, I can find no trace of it."

"Good Lord," said Randall, "that could be the manuscript I've been looking for all right. This is quite amazing Herr Zeller. According to what you say, we now know the gospel—if it's the one we want—came into the hands of the Hoffman family of Munich around 1700 or so."

"Absolutely fascinating," said Katherine, but Zeller continued to ignore her.

"Quite so, Herr Professor, so here is what I propose. From today, you will devote your full time to the work of finding the book. I will finance your search. If you find the gospel, you will tell me first. Later, if you wish, you may write some sort of scholarly paper about it, or an article, or whatever you will call it, but you will agree that neither you nor your university will make any attempt to purchase or otherwise obtain the book."

Randall was completely unprepared for such an ultimatum, but the answer was clear and he strove to be as diplomatic as possible.

"Herr Zeller, your offer of financial support is very generous, but I can't agree to your terms. I am unable to give my full time to looking for the gospel manuscript because I have ongoing responsibilities at my university and obligations to my students."

Zeller waved an impatient hand.

"Come, come, Herr Doctor. Arrange for a leave of absence or something; a sabbatical. I am a businessman and have no skills for such a search, but you are an historian and researcher; it is eminently logical that you should undertake the work and I am prepared to make that possible. How can you refuse?"

"I can't get any sort of leave at this time," Randall persisted.

"So," said Zeller, frowning, "you are refusing my offer?"

"Yes and no," answered Randall.

Zeller put down his fork and fixed Randall with a gimlet-eyed stare.

"And just what, Herr Professor, is that supposed to mean?"

He appeared to be losing patience, and Randall hurried to explain.

"If you will allow me to use the information you've just given me, I'm quite prepared to continue the search for the gospel on my own time and without your financial assistance."

"What information in particular are you referring to?" Zeller asked.

"The information that the gospel came into the possession of the Hoffman family in Munich. I'll research the history of that family if I can find it, and perhaps learn what happened to the gospel."

Zeller shot Randall a shrewd glance.

"And you will inform me first if you find it?"

Randall paused for a moment.

"Perhaps we can compromise on that. I assure you I have no personal wish to acquire the manuscript for myself—and I couldn't afford it even if I had—but if I find it, I give you my word I will inform you when I inform my university. I doubt they will want to buy it either, but you will have an equal chance with them if they do. After all, they have invested a certain amount of money in the search already."

Zeller drew a long breath and exhaled slowly. From the firm set of his mouth, Randall expected him to refuse, but when he spoke it was with surprising geniality.

"All right, Herr Professor, I believe I can trust you. Continue the search and I shall await news from you. But," he added, raising a forefinger, "mind you keep your word."

They continued the meal and Zeller smoked a huge Cuban cigar while he dominated the conversation with stories about his collection of rare books, his numerous business interests, his stable of racehorses and the problems he was having finding good jockeys.

"If they can sit on a horse," he declared through a billowing cloud of blue smoke, "they think they can race a thoroughbred. I despair, I really do."

It was nearly eleven o'clock before Randall and Katherine were able to escape.

"What a strange man," said Katherine in the train back to Horsham. "He didn't say a single word to me all evening. I don't think he even knew I was there."

"Pompous ass," said Randall. "And that dreadful cigar."

"A respirator would have been a great help," Katherine nodded, "but it was no worse than that old pipe of yours."

* * * *

"The book he speaks of sounds like the one we're after," Randall told Tony and Megan at home the next day, "and assuming it is, it brings the chronology forward from the mid-sixteenth century to the beginning of the eighteenth. It also confirms the manuscript wasn't chucked into a fire."

"That's terrific, Pop," said Megan. "I told you something might turn up, didn't I?"

"And you can talk this lead up all over the place," said Joyce, "but don't give away all the details. If our man had found Zeller for himself somehow, it's unlikely Zeller would have come to you, so I think it's safe to assume this clue to the gospel is yours alone. If you make it known this is a good, solid lead, without saying too much more, it may tempt this bloke out from under his rock so we can get a look at him. Be on your guard, though."

"I will."

"And be sure to tell everyone there's someone new in the race for the gospel. It will add to the pressure on our man and it might just cause him to make a mistake."

Randall immediately began to let everyone know what was afoot. After bringing Dean Thoroughgood up to speed, he ran into John Archer talking in the hallway to Professor Bill Fellows and told them.

"That's bloody marvelous," enthused Archer. "Good for you, sir."

"Thought you'd pretty well given up, George," said Fellows.

"No fear, Bill," said Randall, "and certainly not now."

PART SEVEN
Germany: 1944

Chapter Twenty-Six

As Marta and Konrad Fischer sat at breakfast in their small house
on the outskirts of Munich on June the sixth, they knew nothing of the
fighting that raged on the blood-steeped beaches of northern France that
morning. They basked in the glow of their impregnable faith that the
Third Reich would last for a thousand years, and could not have
imagined that thousands of Allied soldiers were storming ashore in
Normandy like steel-helmeted harbingers of doom to bring an end to
Nazi Germany.

They sat opposite each other at their dining table chewing stoically
at the dry amalgam of flour and sawdust that Propaganda Minister Josef
Goebbels was pleased to call bread, and in between mouthfuls of this
desiccated concoction, they sipped at cups of a hot liquid whose only
resemblance to coffee was its color.

A loud knock on the front door made them look at each other in
surprise, and Konrad frowned.

"Now who the devil can that be?"

He rose stiffly from the table—the shell fragment lodged near his
right knee since 1917 still pained him—and went to answer the
summons, returning a few moments later bearing a small, brown
envelope.

"It's a telegram, my dear," he said, stone-faced, "from Waffen-SS
Reich Headquarters in Berlin."

The color fled from Marta's face and she dropped the slice of bread
she had been eating.

"Oh my God, not Paul."

Konrad sat down, tore open the envelope and unfolded the small
sheet of flimsy, gray paper it contained.

"Well now," he said, his face relaxing. "Just listen to this."

"What is it?" asked Marta, fear still haunting her blue eyes.

"I am proud to inform you," Konrad read, "that your son, Paul Ernst Fischer, has been promoted to the rank of *SS-Gruppenführer*, and has been awarded the *Ritterkreuz* with oak leaves and swords for conspicuous gallantry in defense of the Fatherland on the eastern front.

Heil Hitler."

"Wonderful," exclaimed Marta with a radiant smile. "A Major-General *and* the Knight's Cross. Oh, Konrad, how truly wonderful."

"And that's not all," said Konrad, looking up from his reading with an awed expression on his face. "This telegram is signed by *Reichsführer-SS* Heinrich Himmler himself. This is a great honor, my dear."

"It's overwhelming," breathed Marta, her eyes full of joyous tears.

"You see, Marta," said Konrad. "We've been right not to believe the cowards and defeatists. Germany *is* prevailing against the Communists, no matter what people say. Herr Himmler doesn't promote officers who are in retreat, or decorate soldiers for losing battles. All this talk of Russian success is nothing but scurrilous gossip. These rumormongers are traitors and should be arrested and sent to Dachau."

Marta nodded, but her thoughts were still with her son.

"I wonder if Paul will be allowed some leave now," she mused. "It's two years since we've seen him."

"I doubt they can spare him," Konrad answered with a shake of his graying head, "but it would be splendid to have him home for a few days, wouldn't it?"

"I'd love to see him, even for one day."

"So would I," said Konrad, finishing his ersatz coffee with a barely stifled grimace, "and I'd like to ask him how to send that old book I found to Herr Goebbels."

"You mean the one you salvaged from the convent?"

"Yes. I know the *Reichsminister* will appreciate it. He's a highly educated man."

"That may have to wait for a while," said Marta, and then she sighed with pride. "Think of it. Such a distinguished officer. Our little Paul."

"He isn't our little Paul any longer," chuckled Konrad. "He's thirty-eight years old."

"I know, I know," said Marta waving her hand, "but he's always our little Paul to me. I was so proud the day he joined the Hitler Youth and they made him a drummer. And then the SS. Do you remember the first day he came home in his new black uniform? So handsome and proud."

"I remember it well," Konrad said with a smile. "It was a great day for all of us."

"And I'm sure there will be greater days to come," said Marta. "I wonder what Herr Himmler has planned for Paul now. Something glorious, Konrad, you can be sure of that."

* * * *

A week before Marta and Konrad received the news of their son's promotion, *Reichsführer-SS* Heinrich Himmler, *Reichsmarschall* Hermann Goering, *Reichsminister* Josef Goebbels, SS-Lieutenant-Colonel Adolf Eichmann and eight other senior officers, had managed to subdue their personal animosities long enough to participate in a gathering to discuss what Himmler termed "their future." This select group assembled, thanks to the hospitality of Goebbels, in a bunker deep beneath the buildings in Berlin occupied by the Propaganda Ministry.

"Gentlemen," said Himmler, "if you would—" A series of muffled thuds from overhead cut him short. "If you would be seated please," he finished, raising his voice a little.

"That's the damned RAF," Eichmann muttered, "and the Americans have only just left."

The company took their places around a large dining table set with silver and crystal, and a dinner of roast venison with fresh vegetables was served, followed by strawberries and cream. After the white-jacketed stewards had cleared the table and left cut-glass decanters of cognac, Himmler rose to his feet and cleared his throat.

"Gentlemen," said Goebbels, tapping his wine glass with a teaspoon. "Silence please."

"Thank you all for coming this evening," said Himmler as the talk died away. "I believe that what we will do here tonight will be of the greatest importance to each of us."

He paused, took off his small, round pince-nez spectacles and cleaned each lens methodically with his linen napkin. Men squirmed in their seats. Eyes rolled and impatient fingers drummed on the snowy tablecloth before he finally replaced the glasses on the bridge of his nose.

"Before I go on, I must ask you all to respect the absolute confidentiality of this evening's proceedings."

"Yes, yes," snapped Goering. "Get on with it, for God's sake."

"I think it's true to say," Himmler resumed, after a baleful glance at Goering, "that while our personal loyalty to the Fuhrer remains absolute, we are forced to admit that Germany's victory in the war is no longer certain. More specifically, our agents in England assure us an invasion is imminent, and we cannot assume it will be repelled, especially since we are not sure of precisely where it's to be staged."

"The Fuhrer's astrologer says it will come at the Pas de Calais," Goering snorted.

"It wouldn't be coming at all if your Luftwaffe hadn't allowed itself to be shot from the skies by the Royal Air Force," said Eichmann in a steel-edged voice. Goering's fleshy face turned scarlet with fury.

"How dare—"

"Listen to that up there," Eichmann interrupted, pointing to the ceiling. "You hear those bombs? Where are your night fighters now?"

"Gentlemen, gentlemen," put in Goebbels, pouring oil on troubled waters in spite of his personal loathing of Goering. "Now is not the time for recriminations and childish squabbles; it is a time to consider reality."

"Indeed it is," said Himmler in a voice like that of a pompous schoolmaster. Goering and Eichmann subsided, their expressions cold.

"You are all aware," Himmler continued, after a sip of cognac, "that plans are being made to propose reconciliation with the Western Allies that will allow us to join forces with them against the Russians—our real enemy. Those plans are our political and military priority, but I wish to talk about a very different matter tonight, and it's this. All of us here are lovers of art and antiquities. We all possess collections, some of them very large, which, to be perfectly frank, have been obtained for the most part in an unorthodox, or at best unconventional, manner. Now, assuming Germany doesn't find itself able to sustain a war on two fronts following the invasion, and further assuming the Western Allies reject our overtures regarding joint action against Russia—which they may well do—we are all left in a somewhat delicate position, are we not?"

"Come to the point, can't you?" said a ribald voice further down the table. "The cognac won't hold out indefinitely."

Eichmann smirked as Himmler compressed his thin lips in annoyance.

"The point is simply this, gentlemen. If we, ourselves, are to escape in the event of Germany's collapse, we can't expect to do so carrying our art collections on our backs." He raised a forefinger. "Thus, I propose that as soon as possible we ship our collections safely overseas, probably to Argentina. They will be awaiting us when we arrive later on. In years to come, we may need to sell some of our pieces to provide income, and it is therefore imperative the collections be safe from harm."

"You forget one other important assumption," said Goebbels, "and it is that we, ourselves, will even be able to escape to Argentina, or anywhere else. I find it somehow difficult to imagine that the Allied leaders will wave us off at the pier."

"I've taken the liberty," Himmler continued, ignoring the faint rustle of laughter from around the table, "of drawing up a plan for the accomplishment of what I propose. A small, but very select, SS unit will be formed under the command of a senior officer who will report directly to me. That unit, in secrecy, will assemble our collections and store them somewhere near Berlin, safe from Allied bombing. After that, they will be taken to Lubeck, from where a ship registered in a neutral country will carry them to South America. It's actually quite a simple proposition. All you'll have to do is tell me where and when your collections are ready to be picked up, and my men will do the rest."

Himmler sat down with a smile and drained his glass of cognac, but a *Kriegsmarine* rear admiral spoke up at once, barely concealing his contempt. Many career officers had little respect for Himmler, regarding him as a play-actor, a pretend soldier, whose background as a chicken farmer and Nazi Party bureaucrat had done little to qualify him for the position of Supreme Commander of the SS, a rank he had held since 1929.

"*Herr Reichsführer,*" he said, "I'm afraid you're a little out of date.

The port facilities at Lubeck have been flattened by the British and Americans. My own ship was sunk there. Bremerhaven is no better off. Perhaps we should think again."

"No matter," Himmler answered, bristling at the man's tone. "A mere detail. I am sure we can find another place at which to embark our cargo."

"It all seems like a lot of trouble for nothing," put in an army brigadier-general, pouring himself another drink. "Why not just take the whole lot to Switzerland? The Swiss have been extremely helpful one way and another, particularly the bankers in Zurich. Sales could be arranged through Swiss dealers as necessary in the future."

"My God, Herr General," Goering burst out, "can't you understand? The Allies will say our collections have been stolen, and it's entirely possible that the museums, art galleries, churches, et cetera from which we took them may soon be in a position to demand them back. If pieces do have to be sold, it can only be on the black market, and nowhere is the black market in artworks better organized today than in South America. I have a Rubens in my collection, which I obtained from the Polish State Gallery in Warsaw. Do you seriously imagine I'd be able to contact a Swiss art dealer, tell him to sell it on the open market and send me the proceeds in Buenos Aires?"

"We can forget about the Swiss altogether," said Eichmann. "If Germany is defeated, the Swiss will make great haste to dance to the Allies' tune and will be useless to us."

"And furthermore," Goebbels chimed in, "it's not only from occupied countries that our collections have been gathered. I'm a particular collector of rare books and old manuscripts, and I have accumulated my collection largely from within the Reich itself. Many items were confiscated from Jewish families and book dealers who have been sent to concentration camps, and it could prove extremely awkward to say the least if that fact came to light. Our collections cannot possibly be left behind anywhere in Europe, and there's an end to it."

"The *Reichsminister* makes a very good point," said an SS-major-general. "Let's also remember it's not only *objets d'art* we're concerned with here. Most of us have a certain amount of foreign currency and gold, which will have to be shipped as well. I, for one, don't intend to arrive in Argentina as a pauper."

Amid nods and murmurs of agreement from around the table, Himmler rose again, displaying himself like a peacock.

"I take it, then, my little suggestion is accepted. Therefore, we come to the question of the officer who will command the SS unit I referred to."

"We need a damn good man," said Goering.

"There is an officer who I believe will be ideal for the job," Himmler said. "His name is General Paul Fischer, and he has just been awarded the Knight's Cross with Oak Leaves and Swords. He has an illustrious background in the SS, having joined in 1926 when he served as one of the Fuhrer's personal bodyguards. He showed himself a natural leader, and when the *Waffen-SS* was formed, he entered and rapidly advanced to his present rank. I've taken a personal interest in his career. He's utterly devoted to the Fuhrer, an exemplary National Socialist and has an absolute genius for organization, logistics and strategy."

"Do we not need such men on the battlefield just at this moment?" someone asked, and Himmler bent a glacial, narrow-eyed stare on him before replying in a tone of heavy sarcasm.

"What we need, *just at this moment,* is the right man to work for us."

"Is this Fischer at the front now?" Eichmann asked.

"No," said Himmler. "On my personal orders he's on his way here to Berlin."

"You're sure of yourself, aren't you?" Eichmann muttered.

"*Herr Reichsführer*," said Goering, "may I suggest we have an opportunity to interview General Fischer before entrusting him with this responsibility? There's a great deal at stake here."

"My dear *Herr Reichsmarschall*," Himmler answered, looking down on Goering's more-than-ample figure in its light gray uniform, "I assure you this was not a choice lightly made. General Fischer is a man of unimpeachable qualifications. He is a fellow citizen of mine from Munich—the very birthplace of National Socialism—and his father, Major Konrad Fischer, is a decorated veteran. He's a brilliant officer, and in order to provide him with even greater authority and freedom of action on our behalf, I have authorized his promotion to major-general."

"We can settle this with a vote," said Goebbels in a business-like tone. "I ask for a show of hands. Who is willing to leave this matter to the *Reichsführer* and accept his nominee?"

"Good," said Eichmann, as hands went up. "We don't have a lot of time; the invasion may come at any moment."

* * * *

Waffen-SS General Paul Fischer stared in disbelief at the written orders, which had just been delivered to him by a mud-spattered motorcycle dispatch rider. *This can't be,* he thought. *Berlin? Of what earthly use can I be in Berlin when the military situation here in the Ukraine is so critical?* He shook his head and reread the message, but the words had not changed.

Fischer stood in the front room of the small wooden farmhouse he had occupied as his temporary headquarters. Maps were spread out in front of him on a large trestle table strategically placed to avoid the steady rain falling through a ragged hole in the roof at the far end of the room. From his earliest days as a field commander he had always led his men at the battlefront, never directed them from the rear, and so the farmhouse was as close as possible to the fighting. The sound of machine-gun, mortar and artillery fire was everywhere, and from time to time, the house shook with the thunderous impact of a Russian shell. His four staff officers winced involuntarily, but Fischer was oblivious to it all as he continued to stare at his orders.

He knew of several high-ranking officers, mainly field marshals, who had been ordered to the rear to avoid capture, but here was Himmler personally ordering him all the way back into Germany. He looked up to see his officers looking at him in silent curiosity.

"Gentlemen," he said with crisp authority. "*Reichsführer* Himmler has ordered me back to Berlin. I'm leaving immediately. General Jurgens will arrive shortly to replace me here, and in the meantime, my orders of this morning will continue to stand. Good luck, and thank you all."

Ignoring the questions and expressions of regret at his going, Fischer returned the salutes, turned on his heel and made for the door.

"Oh yes," he added, turning back for a moment. "The message also tells me I have been promoted to major-general."

Followed by a chorus of congratulations, Fischer strode outside into the rain to where his staff car stood waiting on the muddy country road. His personal kit was already in the vehicle because these days he was never in one place long enough to unpack it. His driver, Corporal Ulrich Huber, ran around from the back of the house hastily jamming on his cap, jumped behind the wheel and started the engine.

"Berlin, Corporal," said Fischer from his place in the back seat, and Huber turned to him, wide-eyed.

"Sir?"

"You heard," Fischer answered, grinning at the young man's look of consternation. "I've been ordered to Berlin, and so to Berlin we must go. I thought of requisitioning a plane, but I'm assuming the High Command wants me there alive, so we shall drive."

"But, sir, the fuel," said Huber. "Where can we get the fuel?"

"We are heading for the rear this time, Corporal, not the front. We'll be all right."

I hope, he added to himself as the camouflage-brown car accelerated away down the wet, bumpy road and turned towards the Czech frontier only a few kilometers to the west. *I wonder what the High Command has in store for me.*

"Do you go to take up a new command, sir?" asked Huber, as if reading his thoughts.

"Your guess is as good as mine, Corporal," Fischer answered.

"What about France, sir?" asked Huber. "Field Marshall Rommel is in France and everyone knows there are thousands of SS troops there with him. I hear the 12th Panzer is in Normandy, and many other famous Divisions as well."

"You are well informed, Corporal," Fischer said, "but I would rather take all those men back to the Ukraine with me and throw them against the Russians. Perhaps I'll do that once we've driven back the invasion everyone seems so worried about."

"Of course, sir," nodded Huber, deftly steering the car around the putrefying carcass of a horse in the middle of the road. "And by that time we shall have the new super-weapons the Fuhrer has promised us."

"You mean high speed aircraft that fly without propellers and rockets that will carry powerful bombs made with heavy water, whatever the hell that is?"

"That's right, sir. We'll need those planes and bombs."

"Those are rumors," he said. "That's all. Don't put your faith in them. It'll take a lot more than rumors to slow the Allies. We'll need good planning, sound strategy and, above all, brave soldiers."

"Christ," gritted Huber through clenched teeth as the car bucked and rattled from the deafening explosion of a Russian shell falling into the road and digging a deep crater not fifty meters behind them.

"Good timing Ulrich," Fischer called, as mud and stones rained down, drumming on the car's canvas top. "If the Reds come after us, at least the bastards won't be able to use the road."

As they continued towards the frontier, the noise of battle gradually diminished and they drove through burned fields and deserted, bombed-out villages: lifeless ruins and devastated countryside. From time to time they encountered lines of refugees carrying whatever they could in handcarts or on their backs. Huber nosed the car through the straggling processions, revving his engine and blasting the horn, but the weary nomads only shuffled on, blank-faced, through the rain and the cold, clinging mud. In the course of the war, Fischer had seen countless multitudes of such displaced wanderers. It seemed to him they were always there, trudging endlessly towards a destination they never reached. At first, he had wondered what would become of them, but now he no longer cared. Of what possible concern were these nameless Slavs when his brave men, his loyal warriors, were fighting and dying for Germany?

They crossed into Czechoslovakia, found a supply depot a few kilometers east of Presov and then set out again into the gathering darkness and hammering rain towards Bratislava, the car loaded with forty-liter cans of fuel and as much food and water as it would carry. The headlights, mere slits to avoid being seen from the air, were of almost no use. Fischer concluded Huber must be driving more by instinct than by sight.

"Now what, for God's sake?" muttered Huber, slowing the car as a soldier with a lantern stepped into the road and flagged them down.

"We're only three kilometers from Bratislava."

"Checkpoint," said Fischer. "Something's up."

Huber rolled the window down and the young soldier, his uniform sopping wet and his helmet shiny in the lantern light, looked into the car.

"Identification please."

He examined Fischer's card by the light of his lantern and handed it smartly back before saluting.

"I'm sorry, Herr General," he said. "Czech partisans are operating in Bratislava and in the countryside to the north of the city. We are advising all traffic to go no further."

"I can't stop," said Fischer. "I'm on my way to Berlin. If we can't go on through Czechoslovakia, we'll go through Austria. Do we still hold the Danube bridges?"

"Yes, Herr General, so far as I know, but it's very dangerous in the city."

"We'll have to risk it," said Fischer. "Let's go, Corporal."

"We can cross from Austria into Bavaria, sir," said Huber, working the clutch and gearlever as he pulled out into the road again. "But it will take a little longer."

"Can't be helped," answered Fischer. "But this way we'll go through Munich and I can see my parents."

"A good plan, sir," smiled Huber. "Now let's hope we can get through Bratislava in one piece."

When they entered the city, they found all was calm apart from some sporadic gunfire. It appeared the German army had regained control. As they cautiously approached one of the bridges across the Danube, Huber pointed to a column of five tanks looming out of the rainy darkness in front of them, squeaking and clanking as they lumbered ponderously along the road.

"Look, sir. King Tigers."

"I don't believe it," said Fischer. "We could have put those to good use in the Ukraine, but here they are instead playing nursemaid to the damn Czechs."

And what good are they in the city anyway, he thought. *The King Tiger tank was designed for open terrain, not narrow streets and blind corners. Who the hell's making these decisions?*

They crossed out of Czechoslovakia without incident, and after a few hours rest, continued westward. Daylight had brought a merciful end to the pelting rain, and on Austria's paved roads, unhampered by refugees, Huber made good time. As they drove on, Fischer pondered the possibility of his being posted to France, and his thoughts turned to the present military situation so far as he knew it. The Allies were moving rapidly northward up the Italian peninsula, the Russians were closing in on the east and the Luftwaffe had long since lost air superiority. The U-Boat campaign in the North Atlantic had not starved the British into submission as Grand Admiral Dönitz had predicted it would, and the few surface warships of the *Kriegsmarine* that remained operational were no match for the combined naval forces of Germany's enemies.

And what of the occupied countries? If the tide of war can't be turned, those territories may well rise in revolt and turn their city streets into rivers of German blood. A second front in the west could be disastrous, he thought, clenching his fist. *Unsustainable. If the invasion comes, we must throw it back.*

Gott mit uns, he reminded himself. *God with us.*

* * * *

Shortly after four o'clock on the afternoon of June the seventh, they entered Munich. As Huber drove through the bomb-ravaged streets, Fischer was overcome by horror and fury at what the Allied air forces had done to the city he loved.

He had not seen Germany for more than two years, and he was unprepared for the devastation he now witnessed. Great heaps of broken stone and brick rubble stood everywhere, and ruined buildings, their windows blasted out, stared mutely back at him like eyeless skulls.

God damn them, he raged to himself, his teeth clenched so tightly his jaw hurt. *I'll see all of England flattened for this, and Churchill shot dead like a dog.*

The thought struck him that his parent's house might have been hit, and his stomach convulsed in fear. He became suddenly desperate to reach home.

"Get a move on, Corporal," he snapped, more harshly than he had intended.

They pulled up outside his parents' house twenty minutes later. Fischer was overwhelmed with relief to see it was undamaged. Situated well away from factories and similar targets, it had escaped the attention of the enemy.

"Welcome home, Paul," said his father, ushering him into the house and shaking hands with all the formality Fischer had expected. "I'm glad to see you."

Marta, overjoyed at the sudden and unexpected arrival of her son, hugged him and wept.

"I think you are more handsome than ever," she said, her clasped hands pressed against her chin.

"Well," Fischer smiled, suddenly conscious of his stained field uniform and stubble-covered chin, "I could certainly do with a wash and shave."

In the prewar days, Fischer had been fastidious in his attention to his uniform, but once on the battlefield, he had quickly learned that what a man did was more important than how he looked. He had often wished his appearance matched the Aryan ideal a little more closely, but that no longer troubled him. He understood the establishment of a Greater Germany must come first, and he knew selective breeding programs were already underway in Denmark and Norway to begin what Herr Goebbels called "the purification of the Aryan race." But although not the best Aryan specimen, he was nevertheless reckoned a good-looking man. He was just under six feet tall and of stocky build. He had brown, curling hair above a wide, sharply chiseled face with dark, penetrating eyes set under thick brows. His troops called him *der Bär:* the Bear.

"You're in luck," said Konrad. "The water has been off for five days, but they turned it on again yesterday morning. The mains were broken in an air raid."

"Right," said Fischer. "I'll get my kit from the car."

He made for the door, but stopped abruptly.

"Do you think one of the neighbors could put my driver up?" he asked. "The poor fellow's dog tired. We can only stay for tonight."

"Only tonight?" wailed Marta.

"Sorry, Mother," he said, with a rueful smile.

* * * *

As soon as Fischer reappeared in a clean uniform, his Knight's Cross at his throat, his father led him outside into the dusk of early evening where he was greeted by a spontaneous burst of cheers and applause from a large crowd of neighbors. A young, serious-faced member of the *Hitlerjugend* in a gray uniform and peaked cap stepped forward.

"Herr General," he said, with a sharp salute. "On behalf of us all here and on behalf of the Munich Hitler Youth Brigade, I welcome you home and offer you our congratulations."

To the young man's unparalleled pride, Fischer returned the salute with equal precision and then addressed the crowd.

"My fellow citizens," he said, "thank you for this warm welcome. It's good to be home. I can assure you all that our soldiers are fighting bravely, and will not allow the honor of the Fatherland to be tarnished. *Heil* Hitler."

He was answered by a forest of stiff-armed salutes as well as more cheers, and he felt gratified by the impromptu reception as he reentered the house. Morale on the home front seemed high and that was a good sign.

He and his parents sat at the dining table and enjoyed a meal such as they had not seen for some time. Enthusiastic neighbors who were happy to have so distinguished a soldier in their midst, opened their secret stores of food, meager though they were, and donated generously. There were two eggs for each of them, some dried horsemeat Marta boiled for nearly an hour and even a piece of sausage. As they ate, they talked of the glory days: the rise of the Nazi Party and the re-imposition of law and order following the riots and street battles of the 1930s, which Konrad avowed had been instigated by the Communists.

After the meal, Konrad brought forth a half-full bottle of schnapps from its hiding place beneath the cellar stairs.

"Watch carefully," said Marta, with a smile. "Your father is about to decant the last half of the last bottle of schnapps in Munich."

"How goes it against the Russians?" Konrad asked after they had drunk a toast to victory.

How goes it indeed, Fischer thought. *Unless replacements and better equipment appear very soon, it may not go at all.*

"There have been some setbacks," answered Fischer, quoting the official line. "But the fight will continue. Surrender is unthinkable."

"Excellent," said his father. "And the Allies cannot keep the war effort going much longer. Churchill is a hopeless alcoholic, you know, and Roosevelt is a cripple on the point of death. And as for Stalin," he added with a snort, "he has syphilis, which is only to be expected."

"Where did you hear all this?" asked Fischer.

"*Reichsminister* Goebbels, of course."

"But these dreadful air raids—" Marta began, before Konrad cut her short with a dismissive wave of his hand.

"A temporary inconvenience, nothing more."

"They terrify me," said Marta. "I hate them."

"Now, my dear," chided Konrad with a slight frown. "I've told you we must be strong and courageous. This is not 1918 and we will not be humiliated this time."

Marta sighed and nodded, but Fischer saw in her eyes the strain she was enduring. He had not seen it before, and it caused him concern. What was Germany's civilian population really thinking behind its outward show of determination?

Soldiers live with death every day, he thought, *but must their mothers be asked to live with it as well? And for how long?*

"But speaking of air raids and the *Reichsminister*," said Konrad, interrupting Fischer's thoughts. "Your cousin Belinda's husband is a member of Herr Goebbels' personal staff, you know, and has told me the *Reichsminister* collects old books and manuscripts. I think I may have a gift for him if you can carry it to Berlin."

"You have a gift for the *Reichsminister?*" asked Fischer in surprise. "What on earth is it, and what has it to do with air raids?"

Without answering, Konrad disappeared from the room for a few moments, and returned carrying a large, leather-bound book which Fischer saw immediately was very old. His father set it on the table and resumed his seat.

"I'm too old to fight," he said. "More's the pity, and I have this damned shrapnel in my leg, but I do whatever I can to help. I go out after the air raids and help rescue people trapped in buildings or shelters. Two months ago, after a daylight raid by the Americans—we shot five of them down, by the way—we discovered the old Convent of the Blessed Virgin had taken two direct hits. The nuns were all killed, and in the ruins of the library, I found this old Latin book. I thought of Herr Goebbels at once. I'm sure he'll appreciate it and if he has it, it will come to no further harm."

Fischer opened the book, its pages creaking as he turned them carefully, and looked at the painted illuminations in gold and silver and the slightly faded black lettering. The book's thick leather covers were studded with gold and bound with brass, and although scuffed and scratched from their recent misadventures, they had performed their function well and protected the book itself from damage.

"It's a miracle it survived," Fischer said. "Presenting it to Herr Goebbels will be an honor for our family. I had no idea he collected such things; he should be more than delighted with this. I wonder how old it is."

"Books like this haven't been made for centuries," said Konrad. "There was no one left alive at the convent to tell me anything of its history, but there are names and dates in it going back hundreds of years."

"Fascinating," said Fischer. "What a treasure."

Chapter Twenty-Seven

Fischer had not been in Berlin for almost three years, and he found the city much altered. Not only were large portions of it now standing in roofless ruins, but the people themselves were not as he remembered them.

On the surface, morale was high. Flags flew bravely from housetops and even from the summits of great piles of rubble, and everyone proclaimed their resolve to fight on to victory. But below the surface, carefully concealed from the light of day, Fischer could sense the same strain he had seen in his mother's eyes. There was fear as well: an infectious, corrosive fear that gripped the populace with strong, cold fingers. Although not yet officially acknowledged, the news of the June sixth invasion was everywhere, yet to speak of it openly as anything other than a temporary impediment to final victory was to court the danger of denunciation to the Gestapo as a defeatist, or worse. Those who dared think of defeat, however, prayed that if Berlin were occupied, please God let it be by the Americans or the British, not the Russians.

After his arrival in the city, Fischer was accommodated at an SS Barracks in the southern suburbs, and as he settled into his quarters, he felt secure in a world he understood and believed in.

The SS won't fail, he thought. *It still stands firm and strong: the defender of the Fatherland and a bulwark against our enemies.*

A young corporal brought him verbal orders requiring him to report to *Reichsführer-SS* Heinrich Himmler's office at nine o'clock the following morning.

"I am ordered to tell you not to be late, Herr General," he added, with some diffidence.

"Yes, thank you," said Fischer, returning the salute.

"*Reichsmarschall* Goering and *Reichsminister* Goebbels will also attend the meeting," the messenger finished.

Now why, Fischer asked himself, *would the Reichsminister be invited to a military conference? What can he have to do with my new command, whatever it is?* Fischer shrugged. *Anyway*, he thought, *I can take him the book.*

* * * *

Himmler occupied a spacious suite of offices in a bunker beneath the SS Headquarters, and it was there Fischer presented himself, on time, the following morning. He carried the old manuscript with him wrapped in brown paper and left it with the receptionist before being ushered into Himmler's presence.

It was well known Himmler suffered from a chronic stomach disorder, which often left him irritable and dyspeptic, but today he seemed in excellent health and greeted Fischer warmly.

"Welcome, Herr General." He smiled, rising from the chair behind his desk. "It's good to see you again, and please accept my congratulations on your Knight's Cross and promotion."

Fischer saluted, removed his cap and remained at attention.

"Thank you, *Herr Reichsführer*. I am greatly honored."

"Be seated, General," Himmler said. "*Reichsminister* Goebbels and *Reichsmarschall* Goering will join us presently."

Coffee was ordered, and Himmler settled himself behind his large polished desk once more while Fischer sat in a capacious armchair, which enfolded him in a soft comfort he had not experienced for months. The coffee was served, and as he drank, Fischer noted the difference between it and the pallid, artificial brew he had tasted in Munich with his parents. *But*, he thought, *who would expect one of the most powerful men in the Reich, the commander of the SS and Gestapo, to drink ersatz coffee?*

They talked of Munich, family and home—everything, in fact, but the situation on the eastern front and the invasion, until the two other members of the group arrived. The four of them adjourned to a small meeting room adjacent to Himmler's office, and seated themselves around the table. An armed SS man was posted outside the locked door. Fischer waited expectantly. Since the Allied invaders had obviously not been thrown back into the sea after all, he was now virtually certain his new command was to be in France, although he remained mystified as to why Goebbels was present.

"No one else from the High Command will be joining us, General Fischer," said Himmler. "And the orders you receive today must not be discussed with anyone apart from ourselves and the staff you will meet shortly. Do I make myself clear?"

"Perfectly clear, *Herr Reichsführer,* but if no one else is to be present; I take it this is...."

He was about to say "not a military matter," but bit off his words. He had no right to presume anything.

"Is what?" snapped Goering.

"A matter of some delicacy, *Herr Reichsmarschall,"* he improvised.

"Correct," said Himmler. "It's extremely delicate, but it's a project requiring military precision, which is why you're here, Herr General."

Himmler then outlined the plan and gave Fischer his orders. He was to assemble the collections, arrange for safe storage, design and maintain an inventory process to ensure nothing was lost. Articles not already packed were to be crated; everything labeled innocuously as "personal effects" and prepared for shipment out of the Reich to a destination in South America which would be given him in due course.

Fischer listened, incredulous. Art collections? Was Himmler serious? What sort of responsibility was that for a fighting soldier?

"This is a matter of the highest importance, General," Himmler finished. "Have you any questions?"

"Only to point out with the greatest possible respect, gentlemen, that I'm unsuited for this assignment. I am a battlefield officer, and I wouldn't know a piece of fine art from a garden ornament."

"At least you're honest," smirked Goebbels.

"It's not necessary that you should," said Himmler. "We will all make arrangements to have our collections ready in certain locations, and all you have to do is pick them up and ship them away. It's more a logistics and organization problem than anything else. As to your being a field commander, I remind you it is we who decide how best to use the manpower at our disposal. In our view, you're the best man for this assignment and your duty is to follow your orders."

"Yes, *Herr Reichsführer,"* said Fischer, feeling slightly resentful that Himmler had felt it necessary to remind him of his duty. *I've followed orders all my life and Herr Himmler knows it.*

"Be clear about one thing, General," said Goering. "Once you've taken charge of the collections, you bear the responsibility for their safety. Make no mistake about that."

"I understand that, of course. How many men can I have, if I may ask?"

"A staff of reliable men has been assigned to you," said Himmler. "One of them, Corporal Vogel, is an art historian and conservator who can advise on technical matters of storage and so on. There are also two transport specialists. Other men and any equipment you might need can be requisitioned directly from me."

"This work is all the more urgent now the invasion has come," said Goebbels.

Now the invasion has come, Fischer thought, *shouldn't I be with my men in the Ukraine or with Rommel in France? Surely that would be of more help to the Reich at this moment.*

"I can tell what you're thinking, Herr General," said Goebbels, with a humorless smile. "So let's be perfectly frank, shall we? A war on two fronts is a significant risk, especially with the United States involved. Italy is useless, and Japan is not in a position to help us here in Europe. Whatever happens, however, the Fuhrer's work for the future of the world must and will be carried on. It may become prudent for those of us in senior positions to leave Germany to continue the Fuhrer's work from elsewhere, and if that's the case we'll need our collections close by. We, as individuals, and the National Socialist Movement itself will require financing. Our collections guarantee that financing."

So that's it, Fischer thought. *All right, then.*

"I understand," he said. "Your collections will be safe in my keeping, gentlemen, and you may rest assured they will reach their destination safely. I am honored to play a part in this historic venture."

When they reentered Himmler's office, Fischer excused himself and quickly retrieved the paper parcel from the receptionist.

"If you'll permit me, *Herr Reichsminister,*" he said, swiftly unwrapping the parcel. "I have the honor to bring you this from Munich with the compliments and respects of my family. I believe it's most appropriate for the occasion. I trust it will meet with your satisfaction and be added to your collection."

He handed the book to Goebbels with a small bow.

"Undoubtedly medieval," said the *Reichsminister*, carefully turning the pages of the manuscript, "and in excellent condition. Beautiful. Very beautiful. I am grateful, Herr General. Many thanks."

"A splendid gift," said Himmler. "Most admirable."

"Can you read it, though?" asked Goering, leaning over for a better view and holding the page open with the end of his ornately carved ivory and gold baton.

"It's a gospel of St. John, my dear *Reichsmarschall,*" said Goebbels, proudly vaunting what he always considered his intellectual superiority, "with special prayers to the saint included. It's in Latin," he added, his voice heavy with condescension, "and for God's sake be careful. Poking away at it like that. You'll damage it."

Goering grunted and withdrew his baton. The darkening of his heavily jowled face clearly showed his understanding of the insult as he waddled to the door.

"I prefer something I can hang on my wall," he said, turning and pointing his baton at Goebbels. "Something everyone can see and admire. Not something that has to be shut away from the light of day like your precious dusty old books and documents. You just hide all by yourself and gloat over them. It's perverted."

The atmosphere in the room still crackled after the *Reichsmarschall* slammed the door behind him, and no one spoke for a moment or two until Goebbels snorted in annoyance.

"That fat—"

"*Herr Reichsminister*," Himmler interrupted in a sharp warning tone. Goebbels stopped, cleared his throat and turned to Fischer.

"Since you'll now be looking after all these things for us, General, I want you to retain charge of this book and see it's shipped with the rest of my collection. I have no time to study it at present."

"You may rely on me, *Herr Reichsminister*," said Fischer. He was about to take the manuscript back when Goebbels hesitated.

"I see there are some names here on the first page."

He placed the volume on Himmler's desk and took a gold fountain pen from his inside pocket.

"There are Vatican seals here," he said, "and then the name Zeller, but it seems the last owner was a certain Carl Hoffman who acquired the book in 1700."

"It was found by my father in the ruins of a convent," said Fischer, "but I have no idea how it came to be there."

"Well, they didn't sign it," said Goebbels. "Not that it matters now."

Goebbels wrote his name under Hoffman's, added the date and handed the book to Fischer.

"Look after it well, General."

"And I want a progress report from you at least once a week," Himmler added.

* * * *

One of Himmler's aides took Fischer to the room assigned to him where he met the five SS men who were to be his direct subordinates: a major named Klein, a lieutenant, two sergeants and Corporal Vogel. The narrow, windowless room was poorly ventilated and barely large enough for the six men who were to occupy it. There were three desks along one wall, two along the other and a double row of filing cabinets back-to-back down the middle. With the men seated, Fischer would have to squeeze behind their chairs to reach the small cubicle at the far end that was to serve as his private office. Two filing cabinets, a desk and two chairs had somehow been made to fit into this cramped space.

"Excuse me, sir," said Major Klein when Himmler's man had left them. "We're all wondering if you can tell us why we're here."

"We have a special mission," he said, and then went on to outline the job he had been given. "We are all SS men here," he finished, "and we will carry out our orders to the best of our ability and ask no questions. Is that clear?"

The five men came to attention as Fischer turned and made his way to his office. Once there, he lowered himself gingerly into the swivel chair behind the desk and called for *Sturmbannführer* Klein to join him.

Klein, a man of about Fischer's age, entered the office and stood at attention.

"Sit down, Major," said Fischer. "Although I hate to say it, it's obvious we shall all be living far too closely together to observe most of the normal formalities. We've been given a job to do and only a cupboard in which to do it, so let's make the best of it, shall we?"

"Thank you, sir," said Klein, settling himself into the one remaining chair.

Over the next hour and a half, Fischer and Klein, whose background was in the *Reichspost*, the State Postal Service, laid all the preliminary plans they could.

"Right then," said Fischer when they had finished. "Let's get moving on stage one. You start working on the design of an inventory procedure and begin arranging for the transporting of the collections from their various locations. I'll get together with young Vogel and we'll see if we can find a storage facility."

"Very good, sir," said Klein rising to his feet, but Fischer motioned him back into his chair.

"One more thing, Major. I'm officially appointing you second-in-command. I'll inform the *Reichsführer*, but I'm sure he will have no objection. We are still at war, and if something happens to me, you'll take over. Understood?"

"Yes, thank you, Herr General.*"

"And now," said Fischer, "I want some information. I've been on the road for several days and a bit out of touch. What are you hearing about the military situation in France?"

The major hesitated.

"Come along man," said Fischer. "We're both soldiers and loyal to the same Fuhrer."

"I only know what I hear, sir."

"Then tell me what you hear."

"Well, the word is the Allies arrived in overwhelming strength and established a beachhead by the end of the first day. However, I'm told that our troops have been reinforced by several panzer brigades and infantry divisions from the Calais region as well as from the south and southeast, and the Allied forces are now trapped with their backs to the sea."

"Excellent," said Fischer, driving his fist into his palm. "Excellent."

"Let's hope it's true, sir."

After Klein's departure, Fischer considered the question of what to do with Goebbels' book, and decided that for the time being it could not be any safer than right where it was. He locked it in the bottom drawer of the desk and then turned his attention to the practical matters of finding a place to store the collections, the agreed-upon code name for which was "Supplies".

* * * *

For the next week, Fischer and Corporal Vogel reconnoitered Berlin and its environs in search of a storage facility. A surface building was useless since the Allies had almost complete mastery of the sky and bombed the city more or less at will, so they searched for an alternative, which ultimately revealed itself in a somewhat unexpected form.

"It's a disused railway tunnel," he told Himmler in the *Reichsführer's* office. "It's about five hundred meters long, dry, and there's electricity close by. One end has been sealed by a landslide and the other closed off with a wooden barricade. It will be a simple job to replace that with a pair of steel doors."

"Very good," said Himmler. "When will you be able to begin bringing in our collections?"

"I estimate two weeks, *Herr Reichsführer*. I recommend a squad of at least fifty of the best men we have be assigned to guard the tunnel. The only drawback to the location is that it's not quite as remote as I'd like. There's no doubt our activities will be noticed immediately by those living nearby."

Himmler gave his approval to everything, and handed Fischer a list of where the various collections were located.

"Draw up a schedule for pick-up," he said, "and give it to me. I'll pass it on so everyone can be ready."

Fischer returned to his office and told his staff. Klein, with the help of the two lieutenants, coordinated the job of assembling a fleet of lorries. Vogel prepared a list of materials he would need in the event some of the pieces collected needed repacking or any sort of additional care.

Vogel was an energetic young man, a recent graduate of the University of Freiburg and a dedicated member of the Nazi Party. At first, he seemed overawed by having to work so closely with an officer of such senior rank, but he grew in confidence once Fischer demonstrated his intention to consider his advice seriously. Fischer quickly came to enjoy Vogel's company a great deal, and respected the young man for his knowledge and sincere love of art.

After returning to the operations room one day, Fischer showed Vogel the gospel.

"It's a great treasure, sir," said Vogel is a subdued tone of admiration. "The illuminations are exquisite. It's a shame it can't belong to the whole world, but I trust Herr Goebbels will keep it safe."

"I'm sure he will," nodded Fischer, but he was far from certain. He had quickly learned that much of Goebbels' supposed refinement and cultural sensitivity was mere sham.

A fortnight later, Himmler sent information to all concerned regarding the dates and times when their supplies would be collected, and Klein's lorries began fanning out from Berlin to all parts of Germany.

"The storage depot is receiving shipments on schedule, *Herr Reichsführer,*" Fischer reported in mid-July. "All seems to be going smoothly."

And then came July the twentieth.

* * * *

At noon on July the twentieth, Fischer was in Leipzig, collecting supplies belonging to Goering. Most of the *Reichsmarschall's* collection had been at his house on the Obersalzberg near Berchtesgaden where Hitler had his private retreat, but he had removed the best pieces to an underground vault in Leipzig following the first Allied air raid on the mountain. The *Reichsmarschall* had insisted Fischer supervise the transportation personally and with what he described to Fischer as the utmost discretion. This unexpected order puzzled Fischer, until Vogel told him it was rumored Hitler had ordered Goering to destroy a number of nineteenth century French masterpieces the Fuhrer deemed degenerate. The *Reichsmarschall* had disobeyed the order and kept them for himself.

By now, it had become common knowledge the invading armies had not been contained after all, much less flung back into the sea, as Goebbels had once proclaimed in a radio broadcast. The specter of defeat haunted Germany, and it made Fischer's masters even more desperate to know their collections were safe.

As Fischer was about to leave his temporary quarters in the Leipzig SS Main Barracks, Vogel, newly promoted to *Unterscharführer*, appeared, white-faced and trembling.

"What on earth's the matter, Sergeant?" he asked. "You look as if the Russians had just dropped in for lunch."

"Sir," Vogel stammered. "The Fuhrer…the Fuhrer…has been assassinated at Rastenburg. A bomb, this morning."

As Fischer stared at Vogel, dumbstruck, the phone on his desk emitted a harsh peal and he seized the receiver.

"*Gruppenführer* Fischer."

"Herr General," said one of Himmler's civilian aides, "do you recognize my voice?"

"Yes I do Herr Kuper. What—"

"It is my duty to inform you that the Fuhrer is dead. *Reichsführer* Himmler has left Berlin for an undisclosed location for his personal safety."

Fischer's mind raced, his immediate concern for the military consequences of this barbaric act overshadowing his personal shock and grief.

"It's vital I know who controls Berlin, Herr Kuper."

"We are not entirely certain, but it appears someone, perhaps General Fromm or General von Beck, has started moving units of the Home Army into the streets to maintain order. I can tell you nothing further. I must go. Goodbye, Herr General."

Fischer replaced the receiver and exhaled a long breath as he tried to marshal his thoughts. *Who's in command?* he asked himself. Goering was Hitler's designated successor, but if the transfer of power was not clear and immediate, the chain of command would be in danger of collapse. He wondered where the *Reichsmarschall* was. Had he been at Rastenburg? Had he assumed command of the armed forces already? Did he even have freedom of action, or might Germany already be descending into a civil war that would assure the Allies a speedy victory? And what then? Fischer felt cold and sick. With the death of its leader, the military edifice he had served and been a part of for so many years had suddenly ceased to exist. Where could he turn?

Think, man, he urged himself. *Think.*

Control of Berlin was a strategic necessity for whoever assumed command, and Kuper had said at present it was either Fromm or von Beck. But which? They were two very different officers.

No soldier in his right head would follow Erich Fromm to the latrine, let alone anywhere else, he thought with a grimace. *But Colonel-General von Beck is a distinguished soldier who could conceivably command the respect needed. It all hinges on who's behind the assassination. I need information, but I don't know who I can trust.*

He became aware of Vogel, still ashen-faced, staring at him.

"We must finish here and return to Berlin as quickly as possible," he said. "What's our situation, Sergeant? Give me a report."

The crisp authority in Fischer's voice brought Vogel back to the immediate task.

"We're still loading the *Reichsmarschall's* supplies, Herr General. I estimate we could leave here in a little over two hours."

"I want to be on the road in ninety minutes, Sergeant," he snapped. "Ninety minutes, do you hear?"

"Very good, Herr General."

* * * *

Fischer's convoy of three lorries and his staff car moved northward towards Berlin making the best time it could, but on several occasions, they were obliged to stop and take cover from marauding Allied fighter planes. They pulled over to the side of the road and, leaping from their vehicles, flung themselves headlong into ditches or behind hedgerows as the attacking aircraft swooped and screamed along the roadway, guns hammering.

Fortunately, neither men nor vehicles were harmed, apart from Vogel who was cut on the forehead by a piece of flying debris. To Fischer's relief, however, the wound was not severe and a simple field dressing stopped the bleeding.

On the morning of the twenty-first, the convoy stopped to refuel at an army storage depot. Fischer was told by the commanding officer, a pensioned-off colonel too old for combat duty, that Hitler had survived the bomb blast meant to kill him and had made a radio broadcast to the nation.

"He said he had been spared so that he might fulfill his destiny."

"Thank God for that," said Fischer as vast relief swept over him. "Have the assassins been arrested?"

"The ringleaders were caught last night and summarily executed by General Fromm."

"Who were they?"

"I am not certain Herr General," the commandant answered. "I know only that the one who planted the bomb was Graf von Stauffenberg."

"Good God," said Fischer. "Stauffenberg?"

He had met Stauffenberg socially on several occasions, but not recently. Count Stauffenberg had been born into one of the most distinguished families of the Swabian aristocracy, and it was difficult to imagine him capable of so monstrous an atrocity. Fischer remembered Stauffenberg as a tall man, resplendent in his tailored uniform and impossibly handsome. How could this man, indeed how could any man, contemplate murdering Adolf Hitler? Such an act flouted every oath of loyalty, every military tradition and precept, every ideal of National Socialism and Aryan nationhood.

* * * *

Once back in his office, Fischer made sure Goebbels' book was still safely locked in the desk, and then prepared a report for his superiors. Goering would be anxious, if not fuming and dithering with impatience, to be certain his precious supplies were safe in the storage tunnel, and Himmler, now back in Berlin, would require the usual detailed account of Fischer's activities.

At ten o'clock the following morning, he presented himself at Himmler's office and saw immediately that all the staff, military and civilian, were new. He was asked to show identification and then thoroughly searched by a young officer wearing the skull and crossbones insignia of the *Totenkopf,* the SS Death's Head Brigade, above the peak of his cap. It marked him as one of Adolf Eichmann's élite.

"We have our orders, Herr General," said the young soldier. "Things are now very different, as you may imagine."

To Fischer's surprise, Himmler sent out a message telling him to leave his report and return to his duties. The new military staff saluted, and then watched in stone-faced silence as he left. The civilians paid him no attention at all.

Chapter Twenty-Eight

By early September, Fischer was moving his assignment into its final and most crucial stage while all around him the Third Reich was dying. The Allied armies were smashing their way towards Germany from every side, crushing all resistance underfoot. The thousand-bomber raids continued to visit apocalyptic destruction on German cities, and their people went through it all in bewilderment and confusion.

"Where is the Luftwaffe?" they asked. "The Fuhrer said this would never happen."

In an effort to bolster morale, *Reichsminister* Goebbels conjured up fiery orations about ultimate victory and the triumph of Nazism over Russian Communism and western Zionists, but Fischer could spare no time to listen to them. He was pushing his men as hard as he dared in making final preparations for shipping the art collections out of Germany. The railway tunnel had been emptied and its contents loaded into railcars and lorries under Major Klein's watchful eye. *The sooner I finish this,* Fischer told himself, *the sooner I can return to battlefield command.*

"You still have a job to do," Himmler reminded him during one of his now rare interviews, "so I suggest you attend to it. The military situation is not your concern at this moment."

"Yes *Herr Reichsführer,*" he said, but as he was rising to go, Himmler motioned him back into his chair.

"Tell me something, Herr General," he said in a confidential tone, "how well did you know Admiral Canaris and General von Beck?"

"Not well at all, *Herr Reichsführer,*" Fischer answered, somewhat puzzled at the question and completely missing its implications. "I met them socially once or twice some years ago, that's all."

It did not occur to him to wonder how Himmler knew of his acquaintance with the two officers, brief though it was.

"You know they were convicted in the Stauffenberg plot, don't you?"

"Of course, *Herr Reichsführer,* and I find it almost impossible to believe. They were both distinguished officers."

"They were traitors," snapped Himmler. "Murderers. Don't talk to me about distinguished officers."

"Indeed, *Herr Reichsführer*."

"Well," said Himmler with a shrug, "the conspirators we've arrested so far have all paid the price for their disloyalty, as have their families." Fischer knew it was true. The Stauffenberg family in particular had been decimated. Those conspirators not executed by General Fromm had been tortured to extremity by the Gestapo and then hanged with piano wire; their death agonies recorded on film, which was shown throughout the armed forces once Hitler had seen it. Von Beck, however, had been given a pistol and allowed to commit suicide. The Fuhrer had become almost apoplectic with rage when told of it.

When he returned to his office, Fischer found Vogel awaiting him.

"Excuse me, sir. I am just finishing work on the inventory of Herr Goebbels' supplies. Do you wish me to take charge of the manuscript book now?"

"Good idea, Sergeant," said Fischer, unlocking the desk drawer and handing over the leather-bound volume. "Take good care of it for God's sake," he grinned, "or we'll all be shot."

Vogel left the office carrying the book and Fischer turned his attention to some travel warrants Major Klein had left for his approval. As he signed the last of them, he was startled by a harsh and peremptory voice from behind him.

"General Paul Fischer?"

"Yes?" he answered, turning in his swivel chair to see a small man in a black raincoat standing in the doorway.

"Gestapo," said the man, briefly showing an identity card. "You are under arrest."

"Arrest?" Fischer scoffed. "You can't be serious. What's the game?"

"Treason and murder are not a game," said the sharp-faced Gestapo man.

"Treason?" Fischer burst out, jumping to his feet. "How dare you? I insist on seeing Herr Himmler. He'll soon clear up this nonsense."

As he took a step towards the door, he was shocked to see three

Totenkopf soldiers with their Bergman submachine guns leveled at him. He fixed the Gestapo man with a cold and narrow-eyed stare.

"What the hell is this?"

"You are under arrest for your part in the plot to murder the Fuhrer. I have six more men with me in addition to these three, so I strongly suggest you refrain from any stupid heroics."

Rough hands pulled him bodily from his office and bundled him past his astonished staff.

"Major Klein," he shouted, "tell—"

"Shut up," barked the Gestapo man, as Fischer was pushed out of the room.

Outside, he was thrown into the back seat of a car where he sat numb with shock, a soldier on either side of him. Could they actually believe he had some hand in the attempt on Hitler's life? It was beyond all comprehension, but, ludicrous or not, it seemed to be the case. The guns digging into his ribs were very real.

Fischer had no great respect for the Gestapo, believing too many of them were simply ill- disciplined thugs, but they wielded enormous power and influence notwithstanding.

I've got to get word to Himmler, he thought, *but I can't do anything until I get out of this damn car.*

In addition to commanding the SS, Himmler commanded the Gestapo, and he would end this stupid farce in short order.

After only a few minutes, the car drew up outside an imposing gray stone and concrete building, which had thus far escaped the Allied bombs. His captors pushed him unceremoniously through a pair of heavy steel doors and into the granite-floored entrance hall of Gestapo Headquarters. Two soldiers took hold of his arms, propelling him towards a wide staircase at the far end of the foyer.

"That's enough, dammit," he shouted, but the soldiers ignored him, and he was manhandled up the stairs, across a hallway and into a large room, sparsely furnished with a few wooden chairs and a black desk. At gunpoint, he was ordered to come to attention and then the two soldiers backed away a few paces, leaving him standing alone facing the desk.

Overwhelmed by the monstrous predicament in which he found himself, Fischer tried to understand what was happening. Not half an hour before he had been in his office attending to the work assigned to him, and now he was under arrest for a crime so far beyond his imagination as to be preposterous.

I can't just stand here, he thought, his anger rising. *I've got to do something. Now.*

"I am your superior officer," he said through clenched teeth, turning to his guards. "I'm ordering you to return me to the *Reichsführer's* headquarters immediately, and I'm very sure you know the penalty for failing to obey an order."

"Face the desk and shut up," sneered one of the soldiers. "You give no orders here."

The insolence of the man's tone startled Fischer, and he saw in that instant the extreme peril of his situation. God alone knew what reason they had to suspect him, but his life could well be at risk. He knew he was about to be interrogated, but in relation to what? What was their evidence?

He heard a door open somewhere to his right and he turned his head to see a man in a dark uniform and polished jackboots approaching the desk. He had a high, wide forehead above narrow-set dark eyes and a thin, small mouth. He was expressionless as he seated himself behind the desk and regarded Fischer with unblinking eyes. Fischer recognized Heinrich Mueller, Chief of Operations of the *Geheimestaatspolizei,* the State Secret Police; the Gestapo.

"I see you know who I am," said Mueller, his voice as expressionless as his face.

"Yes, Herr Mueller, and I wish to say—"

"Silence," shouted Mueller, bringing the flat of his hand down on the desk with a sound like a gunshot. "You will answer my questions when I ask them, and that's all. Do you understand?"

Listen to the questions, he told himself. *Find out what's behind this and deal with it logically. You're a General. Act like one, for God's sake.*

He drew himself erect and cleared his throat.

"What do you wish to know? I have nothing to hide."

"That's better, Herr General," said Mueller, with a mocking emphasis on Fischer's rank. "You met the traitor Stauffenberg many times. Correct?"

"No. Perhaps three times."

"Where?"

"In Frankfurt last year at a military conference, I think, and in Munich three or four years ago, but I—"

"Shut up," roared Mueller. "I told you. I ask the questions, you answer. You met the traitor Stauffenberg in Frankfurt. Why didn't you say you met him with former Colonel-General von Beck at the home of former Admiral Canaris? Both traitors as well. Why leave that out?"

Fischer started to say he had not been asked who else had been present, but Mueller interrupted him again.

"Save your lies. We know you were there. We found it in Canaris' diary. See." He took a small book from the desk. "Here it is. Let me read you a most interesting passage.

April 25th, 1943. A most pleasant dinner party this evening. Count von Stauffenberg was there, dazzling the ladies, General von Beck, General Fischer, briefly returned from the eastern front, and several others. Fischer, von Beck, Stauffenberg and I enjoyed a long and confidential chat after dinner and found we were in agreement on many things."

Mueller tossed the diary onto the desk.

"A long and confidential chat," he sneered. "*Agreement on many things.* A cozy little talk with Canaris, von Beck and Stauffenberg. The three ringleaders. How *very* fascinating."

Fischer remained silent, appalled at what he heard. Why the hell had Canaris chosen those particular words? He remembered the occasion, but that was all. He could not recall what they talked about, and he knew Mueller would never accept that excuse.

After a moment's silence, the expected questions came.

"What did you talk about, and was anyone else with you?"

"We talked about the military situation on the eastern front and what might be done about it," said Fischer, as forthrightly as he could. It was a contrivance, but it might work. "No one else was with us for most of the conversation, but it was a large party. People came and went."

"You're lying," snapped Mueller. "Do you really expect me to believe you discussed military affairs? Do you take me for an imbecile? Admit it. They enlisted your support for the assassination plot, didn't they? That was what you *agreed* on."

"No, Herr Mueller, it was not."

The interrogation went on and on. Mueller hammered at him repeatedly for information on the conversation and Fischer strove to maintain his mental equilibrium, although the rapidity and intensity of the questioning made it difficult. Everyone had heard of Gestapo interrogation methods, and Fischer now found himself trapped as a result of a few poorly chosen words about an innocuous conversation at a dinner party fifteen months before.

At one point, he reminded Mueller of his rank and asked to speak with Himmler, but Mueller was relentless.

"I'm not interested in your rank. Officers more senior than you have already been executed for their complicity in this despicable and squalid conspiracy."

Mueller had been walking around the office hurling questions at him from this side and that, from behind him and in front of him. The man seemed to be everywhere, but Fischer was forced to stand rigidly at attention and remain facing the desk. His feet and ankles ached, and yet if he so much as shifted his weight a little, he was ordered to keep still by one of the armed *Totenkopf* soldiers who stood at the door.

Fischer held doggedly to his assertion that he, Canaris, von Beck and Stauffenberg had discussed nothing beyond the military situation in the Soviet Union. It was all he could think of. Whatever they talked about, he knew damn well it hadn't been the assassination of Adolf Hitler!

"All right," said Mueller, unexpectedly dropping into the chair behind his desk. "Send for a glass of water for the General and bring him a chair."

Fischer settled himself stiffly onto the straight-backed wooden chair and gratefully stretched out his aching legs. A thickset man in civilian clothes entered the office and thrust a glass of tepid water into his hand and he gulped it down in one long draught. Mueller's endless harangue and the physical discomfort imposed on him had combined to create a sense of disorientation, but he knew that was exactly what Mueller had intended. *Be careful*, he told himself, but he was completely unprepared for what came next.

"Look, I'm sorry about all this, Herr General," said the Gestapo Chief. "But after all that's happened, well...." Mueller sighed and spread his hands in a gesture of helplessness. "When that diary surfaced we simply couldn't overlook it. I'm sure you understand our position. I've been ordered by the Fuhrer himself to root out all the conspirators, and if I miss even one you know what'll happen to me, don't you?" He jerked his forefinger across his throat.

"Even so, Herr Mueller," said Fischer, "I am a senior SS officer and Knight's Cross, not a traitor or an assassin. I most strongly protest against this maltreatment and disrespect. I have admitted that some of the conspirators were once friends of mine, but I despise and disavow everything they stood for."

"Of course, of course," said Mueller, waving a dismissive hand. "Don't you think I know that, Herr General? But we can't take chances. The Fuhrer is greater than all of us; he is the Fatherland itself, and we must find all the traitors, even if we seem a little, shall we say, heavy-handed, at times."

Fischer grunted and regarded Mueller with a baleful stare. In spite of the outrage he felt at having his loyalty to Adolf Hitler and the German Reich called into question, he could see Mueller's point. The war was probably lost, but as long as Hitler was Fuhrer, the Reich would remain unified, and there would exist the possibility of salvaging the situation in such a way as to prevent the complete humiliation of the nation.

Mueller leaned forward, his forearms on his desk and spoke in a confidential tone.

"It's been hell around here since July, General Fischer; everybody running around in a panic. We're completely satisfied here that we've got all the conspirators, but *Reichsführer* Himmler is keeping the pressure on. We hardly have time to get any of the real work done."

"And speaking of work," said Fischer, "when can I go back to mine? You're no doubt aware the *Reichsführer* is not a patient man."

"I've noticed that, yes," said Mueller with a smirk.

"So if we're finished here, can I go?"

"Of course. I'll provide a car for you if you like?"

"Thank you," said Fischer, rising and grimacing as his feet protested again. "You'll forgive me if I don't say the meeting's been a pleasure."

Mueller snorted with laughter and then leaned forward again with an earnest expression on his sharp-featured face.

"Herr General, just to clear the air before you go. I want you to know I have the greatest respect for you, and I believe you completely when you say the eastern front was all you talked about that evening with Canaris and the others."

"Actually," said Fischer, with a rueful smile, "I don't really remember what we talked about."

Mueller shot to his feet, shouting, "Get him!"

Immediately Fischer felt himself being seized from behind.

"I thought so," Mueller roared, jabbing an accusing forefinger at him, "you *were* lying. I knew it, you vermin. You cowardly assassin."

Fischer struggled as he was pushed towards the door, but three more soldiers had burst in and he could do nothing but curse his own stupidity. The oldest trick in the book, a deliberate trap, and he'd missed it completely.

"Take him downstairs," Mueller shouted. "They'll get the truth out of him soon enough."

"Take your hands off me," Fischer shouted at the soldiers. "I am SS Major-General Paul Fischer, and I'll have you all shot."

"Get him out of here," roared Mueller from behind him.

"I demand to speak to *Reichsführer* Himmler," Fischer shouted as the soldiers pushed and kicked him out of the room.

"Save your breath," sneered Mueller. "He already knows you're here."

* * * *

For the next three days, locked in a small room in the cellar of Gestapo Headquarters, three thugs kicked and flogged Fischer until he passed out. They revived him with cold water and then locked his hands into a machine that slowly drove steel spikes into the ends of his fingers, one by one, and into the bone as far as the second joint. He screamed until only a hoarse croaking sound came from his gaping mouth. Throughout his excruciating agony, a relentless barrage of questions was hurled at him: how many times had he met the conspirators, where had he met them, what had they said and what did he agree to do? But, most of all, they shouted at him to admit he had known about the plot to kill Hitler.

Sometime during the afternoon of the third day, he must have said something that satisfied his tormentors, although he was totally unaware of having done so. The torture stopped abruptly, and he was flung into a dank cell where he lay groaning on the wet stone floor, blood oozing from his wounds, under the glare of a naked light bulb hanging from the ceiling. He was no longer the master of his own mind, and his thoughts whirled and spun in a hallucinatory vortex as he drifted in and out of consciousness. At one moment he believed he was at home, at another, he was with his men on the battlefield, and at yet another, he was with Sergeant Vogel in the storage tunnel.

He had no idea how long he had been lying in that cold cell when he suddenly became aware of rough hands hauling him to his feet and dragging him up a flight of stairs out into the daylight. His body still on fire with pain, he was tied to a post where he hung limply against the ropes, his head lolling forward, only dimly aware of where he was.

Stand on your feet, man, he told himself. *Stand up.* But he had no strength to do it.

He heard someone speaking to him as if from a great distance away, but although he struggled to understand the words, he could not follow them. He heard marching feet, orders being shouted, rifle bolts clattering and his pain-befuddled mind seized hold of the long-familiar sounds.

The Russians, they've broken through our lines. He struggled against the ropes around his body. *I've got to rally the men.*

"For God's sake, where's our artillery?" he mumbled, but he heard no reply as an instant later he died in a storm of gunfire.

* * * *

260

About two hours after Fischer's life had been wrenched from him, his parents, Marta and Konrad, bewildered, terrified and pleading for help, were flung from the back of a lorry inside the main gate of the Dachau concentration camp, not ten kilometers from their home on the outskirts of Munich.

PART EIGHT
England: The Present Day

Chapter Twenty-Nine

As soon as the university term was finished, Randall set about the gospel search once again. Thanks to Zeller's revelation, he now knew a manuscript, reportedly brought from Rome, had been in the possession of the Hoffman family of Munich around about 1700, and he felt he might actually be closing in on the elusive book.

Tony Joyce believed this reinvigorated search might well tempt Michael Stuart's killer out into the open, but that prospect caused Randall concern because of the threat it posed to the safety of Megan and Katherine. In spite of all the precautions being taken, he did not feel totally reassured.

He kept in close touch with Joyce, and one afternoon they went into The Sword and Trident, a small, crowded pub near the campus, known throughout the university community as The Knife and Fork.

"Any word on the post in London, George?" asked Joyce, and Randall shook his head.

"So far I've heard precisely nothing beyond the excuse that the setting up of the endowment and establishment of the new Chair are taking far longer than anticipated. However, the plan remains that assuming they do get their act together, I'll move to London as quickly as I can."

"Well, I hope it works out sooner rather than later," said Joyce. "Life for you and Katherine seems to be on hold these days."

"Still nothing from the Lincoln phone call?" Randall asked, sipping his Guinness.

"Nothing."

"It's amazing," said Randall. "This fellow never seems to leave a trail of any kind."

"Copper's worst nightmare," said Joyce. "But no one's infallible. If we keep at it, we'll get him eventually."

"Let's hope so."

"Any luck on the Zeller-Hoffman connection?" asked Joyce, finishing his drink.

"I can't do much from here," answered Randall, "so I've decided to go to Munich. I contacted the museums, libraries and galleries to see if, by any remote chance, they had a gospel of St. John dating from the thirteenth century, but no one had anything to offer. I called several dealers as well, and they know of nothing in private hands either."

"What will you do in Munich, then?"

"I'm not entirely sure," Randall admitted with a slight frown. "I'll have to play it by ear, but I thought of a visit to the university, perhaps talk to some collectors if I can find any. I also thought of doing a little more research on the Hoffman and Zeller families, and check if there's anything in the city archives or elsewhere. All I can do is hope I'll be able to spot a clue when and if I see one."

"I didn't know you spoke German, George," said Joyce, in some surprise.

"I don't really, but I can read it fairly fluently. Done a lot of research with German documents and manuscripts over the years, you see. I've always been interested in German monasticism and its influence on the monastic movement in Britain."

"And Katherine's going with you to Munich, I trust?"

"Unfortunately not," said Randall. "Too much work. She's going to see if her friend Christina can get me a good hotel, though."

As it transpired, Christina's firm did no business in Munich, so upon his arrival he took the thirty-minute taxi ride from the airport to the Holiday Inn on the Leapoldstrasse where he had secured a room for six nights.

Next morning he sought information from the city archives on Hoffman families living in the city in the late seventeenth and early eighteenth centuries. Based on the information obtained from Zeller, he concentrated on the name Carl, but although he found three living in the right time period, they evinced no apparent connections to anyone named Zeller. He did find out one of them had been the center of a scandal resulting from his attempt to marry his daughter off to what was termed "the idiot son" of a wealthy merchant in order to further his business interests, but the episode did not seem to lead anywhere. It had no connection to the manuscript that he could see, but he was intrigued by the human drama. Hoffman's wife apparently spirited the girl away the night before the wedding and when Hoffman found out the following morning, he fell dead from an apoplectic fit of some sort. The event had been a sensation at the time.

Sounds like an eighteenth century Bavarian soap opera, he thought with a grin.

Turning his attention to families named Zeller, he found references to four, although none of them were mentioned as going bankrupt or moving to Innsbruck. Legal records of 1696 and 1704 showed an Ernst Zeller had been hanged for murder and a Friedrich Zeller had been pilloried for publically calling the *Bürgermeister* a jackass, but neither of those incidents was helpful. It appeared the well was dry.

The archivist who helped him, commiserated on his lack of success, and asked if perhaps he would like him to contact a professor of history at the Ludwig-Maximilians-Universität. In the absence of any other clear option, this seemed a positive step and within a couple of hours, Randall was seated in the office of Professor Wilhelm Schwimmer discussing the history of Munich.

Schwimmer was a man of about sixty-five, wearing a dilapidated brown suit and a vivid yellow tie with the knot askew. He had a wild shock of unruly gray hair, and Randall thought he looked as if he had been dragged backwards through a hedge. He greeted Randall warmly, and in very creditable English announced he had heard of him and read three of his books, including the two on German monasteries.

"There they are," he said, pointing to one of the crowded bookshelves. "But what may I do for you, Professor Randall? What brings you to Munich?"

Randall explained his quest.

"The evidence suggests the strong possibility that the manuscript was here around 1700 or so," Randall finished, "in the possession of a family by the name of Hoffman. I spent some time in the city archives this morning and came up with nothing that tied any Hoffman to a manuscript or to anyone named Zeller."

Schwimmer shook his tousled head slowly and closed his eyes in thought.

"Hoffman is not an uncommon name and there are many in Munich. Also, I fear I have not heard of any *Haunted Gospel* or *Norwich Gospel*, nor of anything such as a manuscript brought here from Rome in the sixteenth century. I'm very sorry."

"I suspected as much," said Randall with a rueful smile. "I think all I can do is conclude that for the time being anyway, the trail's cold."

Schwimmer made sympathetic noises but offered no suggestions.

"There was one interesting item, though," Randall grinned, "about an arranged marriage between a Hoffman daughter and an apparently slow-witted young man."

"Ah." Schwimmer chuckled. "I know that one. That particular Hoffman family is still extant here in the city. In fact, I know Eva Hoffman very well. She's assisted me many times over the years. Would you like to meet her? It can do no harm, and she's a living history book. She's getting on now, but she was a professional genealogist and researcher for many years until she retired. She never married."

The offer was irresistible to the historian in Randall.

"That would be very interesting. I'm sure I'd enjoy talking to her."

The following afternoon, therefore, thanks to an introduction from Schwimmer, Randall found himself sitting on a rather hard sofa in the small living room belonging to Eva Hoffman engaged in a somewhat difficult conversation.

Eva was a very elderly woman, diminutive, and bent, with white hair and wrinkled features. Her English was poor, and what there was of it was all but submerged in so strong a German accent Randall had to concentrate hard to understand her. She was, however, as Schwimmer had promised, a veritable treasure house of family history and liked nothing better than talking about the lives and times of her seemingly innumerable ancestors.

"*Ja*, Herr Professor," she said, in answer to Randall's question. "That is a famous story in the Family Hoffman. A long time ago it was. *Dreihundert Jahre,* or how you say?"

"Three hundred years," said Randall, and then took a chance on getting the conversation turned towards the gospel search.

"Can I ask if anyone in your family has a library?"

"*Bitte*, please? A what?"

"*Bibliothek*," said Randall. He knew there was more than one word for library, but that one came to mind first. "Does anyone have a collection of books, particularly old ones?"

"Oh *ja*," she answered with a bright smile. "Many, many books. But all gone now."

"Lost?"

"*Nein, nein*. All given away. In 1935. Given to, how you say, the State *Bibliothek*. In Berlin, *ja*?"

"Really?" said Randall. "And there were many books, you say?"

"*Ja*. I am only ten years old at the time, but I remember all the books. In fact, it was Carl Otto, the famous one, who started the Hoffman library. A list was made of all the books."

"You wouldn't happen to have that list by any chance, would you?"

Eva shook her white head.

"It is *kaput*. Years ago."

"Well, do you remember if there were any very old books in the collection?" Randall made writing motions in the air. "Books written by hand?"

"*Ja*," said Eva, "many old ones. But written by hand? I don't know. I can't remember."

There was more than one Carl Hoffman, thought Randall, *but how many of them, I wonder, were lovers of old books and had large libraries? If this one loved books that much, he might just have accepted an interesting old one to settle a debt as the Zeller family history recorded. And if that book had survived, it might have gone to Berlin along with the rest of the collection.*

He asked several more questions, but could get no further details from Eva, and after a few minutes, he offered sincere thanks and took his leave. Eva, complaining bitterly of her arthritis, creaked stiffly to her feet and insisted on showing him out.

"Thank you for visiting, Herr Professor," she said as he walked down the outside steps to the sidewalk. "I hope you will find what you are looking for."

Randall hailed a taxi and went back to his hotel. He had a quick dinner and then sent emails to Megan and Katherine telling them he was not coming straight home, and going instead to Berlin to follow up a possible lead at the State Library. He then called the Lufthansa reservations office and rearranged his ticket to accommodate the additional sector to Berlin.

Lying in bed that night, however, doubts began to stalk him like a pack of jackals. Surely it was too much to hope that of all the Hoffman families in Munich today, Schwimmer should know a member of the right one. Furthermore, just because the family had once possessed a library, who was to say it contained the gospel? And even assuming it was the right family and the manuscript was in their library, the book could have crumbled into powder years ago, been devoured by rats, stolen, sold, given away. Anything.

But, he countered, *there've been long shots before now, and some of them paid off.*

* * * *

The hopes and misgivings persisted throughout the seventy minute flight from Munich to Berlin-Tegel Airport, whereupon he found himself and his suitcase outside the Arrivals Hall, and realized to his chagrin he had forgotten to make hotel arrangements. By asking a passing porter, who hovered about in anticipation of a tip like a vulture waiting for an animal to die in the desert, he discovered the Holiday Inn Berlin-Esplanade was less than two miles from Tegel. He thanked the porter for a second time, returned the man's scowl with a cheerful smile, hailed a taxi and was transported, at prodigal expense, to the Rohrdamm.

He secured a room for two nights, confirmed his flight back to London, and then headed for the library. A few minutes work on the Internet the previous evening had told him he wanted the branch on the Unter den Linden, so he once again took a taxi and tried without success to ignore the cost.

At the library's information kiosk he showed identification, explained he was there for research purposes, outlined his interests and was shown to a desk in a small alcove. After a short wait, an attractive woman in her late thirties with long blond hair arrived, introduced herself as Magda and said in impeccable English that she was a specialist in medieval books and manuscripts. She sat opposite him, smiled and waited for him to speak.

"I'm looking for a thirteenth century Latin text," he said after introducing himself. "It may have come to the library as part of a large collection donated by the Hoffman family of Munich in 1935. Is there such a thing as a list of the books contained in that collection?"

"Not any longer, I'm afraid," said Magda. "There's been a war since then, don't forget. Partition and reunification as well. Some of our holdings are still in libraries in Eastern Europe and we're trying to get them back. However, if the book came to the library at one time we should be able to trace it. If not, we can access other data banks and see if it's cataloged elsewhere. What's the title or the nature of the text?"

"It's a gospel of St. John," said Randall, "with prayers, or suffrages, to the saint appended. It's illuminated. Parchment or vellum, I'm not sure; most likely parchment. English production. Early twelve hundreds. It's the work of a copyist named Robert, to be precise."

"Oh yes," said Magda, without taking her eyes from her computer screen. "First time lucky, Dr. Randall. I know the one."

"I beg your pardon?" said Randall, uncertain of what he had heard. "You say you know it?"

"Yes indeed," said Magda, with a bright smile. "It did belong to the Hoffman family, but it didn't come to the library at the time of the original 1935 donation. It came quite recently, and only on loan. It's most interesting to know you're aware of it. I assume you saw it in London, did you?"

"What do you mean, *London*?"

"Some restoration work was done on the book about six years ago before we sent it to the British Museum for a special exhibition on the history of books in Western Europe. It's an absolute masterpiece, you know."

"It went to London?" said Randall, incredulous.

"Yes, for six months. I was responsible for taking it there, supervising its placement, and also for bringing it back at the close of the exhibition."

"Good Lord. This is incredible."

"During the cleaning of the last page," Magda went on, "our conservators discovered a colophon bearing Robert's name. Also, the name Hoffman appears on the first page along with the names of other owners. It must be the book you're looking for."

Randall stared at Magda, momentarily speechless.

"You look pleased," said Magda, with a dazzling smile.

"I am indeed," he said. "It's been a long search. Would it be possible for me to see it?"

"It's not here, I'm afraid," Magda said. "As I said, it came on loan. It was never part of our collection."

Randall's heart sank.

"It was brought to the library about eight years ago by its owners because it was in need of restoration. We asked them to lend us the book for purposes of the exhibition in London because it was such a fine example, and they agreed. Once the exhibition was over, we returned it to them. We tried to persuade them to allow us to keep it, but they wouldn't hear of it, sad to say. I would love to have it in our collection."

"Well can you give me the name of the owners?" Randall asked.

"Our regulations insist on confidentiality in cases like this," Magda said, with a shake of her golden head, "for security, you understand. I can call and ask if the owners are willing to show it to you. They may not wish you to know its location, but if so I'll suggest they bring it here.'

"I would truly appreciate that," said Randall. "Thank you very much."

Magda flashed him another brilliant smile and picked up the phone on the desk.

"One moment please."

She entered a number and then spoke in German. Randall could not keep up with it, but he gathered she was explaining who he was and his interest in seeing the manuscript.

Magda replaced the receiver.

"It's very good news. They're happy to show you the book, and you can go to see it at their home. I'll print out the address for you. You're going to see Mrs. Gertrude Auger."

She keyboarded quickly and a moment later took a sheet of paper from the printer and handed it to him.

"Her apartment is quite close. Good luck."

* * * *

A woman of about sixty, with iron-gray hair and wearing a plain green dress, opened the door to Gertrude Auger's apartment. She smiled broadly and ushered Randall into the small, somewhat threadbare living room where a very elderly man sat in a worn leather armchair.

"Welcome, Professor," she said in accented English. "This is my father, Herr Alric Vogel."

Vogel remained seated, but smiled and extended a bony hand to Randall.

"My father speaks no English," said Gertrude, "but I told him why you were coming and he's delighted that someone is interested in seeing his ancient book."

"I'm looking forward to seeing it," Randall said.

"When my husband died two years ago, I moved here to take care of my father. As you can see, he's very frail now and his mind is slipping just a little, God bless him. He has trouble remembering what happened yesterday, although he remembers every detail of the war. I've heard the story of the book many, many times, but if you would be kind enough to let him tell you everything in German, I'll translate for you afterwards."

"Thank you," said Randall. "I wish my spoken German was better."

"Please sit," said Gertrude, "and I will bring the book."

She left the room but returned in a few moments carrying a leather-bound book whose thick brown covers were heavily studded and whose spine was reinforced with metal straps. Herr Vogel nodded and smiled and his eyes shone with pleasure. He spoke in German and Gertrude translated.

"He says it is a beautiful object."

"It looks magnificent," said Randall.

Is this The Haunted Gospel? Randall thought. *Is this actually it?*

She placed the book carefully on a low coffee table in front of Randall and opening it, pointed to the bottom of the first page.

"These are the names of the people who once owned the book, but I am not sure what these seals are."

"This is the seal of the Bishop of Norwich," said Randall, pointing. "And that one is the Vatican Library, which dates it to the reign of Pope

270

Gregory IX in the thirteenth century. And this is the seal of Pope Clement VII from the early sixteenth century. Zeller and Hoffman are previous owners as well. I know of them through my research, but I can't read the final signature. It's a real scrawl."

"Josef Goebbels," said Gertrude.

"Good God," said Randall. "That's astounding. How on earth did he get hold of it?"

"It's all in the story my father will tell you," answered Gertrude with a smile.

She told her father what they had been saying, and while she did so, Randall noted the date beside the name of Hoffman: 1700. That was dead right, but he had to check one final thing.

"May I see the last page, please?"

"Of course," Gertrude said, and with Randall's help, turned over the thick pages with great care.

"According to the woman at the State Library," he explained, "there's a colophon at the end."

"Please?"

"I'm sorry," he said. "A colophon is a short piece of writing put in by the scribe who created the manuscript. It's a sort of prayer or blessing, and the scribe adds his name to it."

Gertrude turned over the last page and there it was.

"Amazing," he murmured, and then thought, *I wish Mike were here to see this.*

"What does it say?" asked Gertrude. "I was taught Latin in school, but I can't remember a single word now."

"I'll read it to you," said Randall.

"Glory to God and peace to all who read His word herein set down. The scribe has but a short life, and when his bones are become dust, he is gone. But this writing shall not perish, but live forever to speak praise to Almighty God. I, Robert, Brother of All Saints and obedient servant of the Most High God, made this book."

The scribe has but a short life, mused Randall. *Sadly prophetic words, Robert, old chum.*

271

Gertrude translated for her father, and the old man smiled and nodded again.

Thanks to the restoration work done by the State Library, the colors of the illuminations were once again as brilliant as they had been when Robert applied them, and the gold and silver glowed as if burnished only yesterday. As Randall looked through the ancient book, it took his breath away.

As he arrived at the final chapters and suffrages, he saw how the illuminations changed from the more traditional religious themes and took on a unique character. Were these the keys to the so-called treasure Brother Bartholomew had written about? He found a small representation of a building, clearly a monastic structure, and before it stood a team of oxen yoked to a cart. Here, in an initial, were several men digging, but they were not monks, nor were they in a monastic garden. They were inside some sort of room, and they were dressed like thirteenth century men-at-arms. A little further on, a design ran across the top of a page, but in amongst the twining vines, bell-shaped white flowers and emerald green leaves he could make out those same soldier figures carrying what looked like bales or boxes. Finally, almost lost in the elaborate designs and patterns in the initial that began the final prayer, he found an exquisite miniature: a scene of monks sitting at work copying sacred texts. Beneath their feet was a red rectangle, in the center of which he saw a tiny crown—a masterwork in brilliant gold, perfect in every detail.

"That's it," he said. "That's absolutely it, by God. Whatever it is, it's under the scriptorium."

He looked up to see Gertrude and her father regarding him with amused curiosity and realized he had no idea how long he had been absorbed in his study. He had virtually forgotten they were there.

"Oh dear," he said, with a sheepish smile, "please forgive me. It's just that I've been looking for this book for several years and it's hard to believe I've actually found it."

Gertrude translated and she and her father smiled at him.

"Please," said Randall, "let me tell you the book's history as far as I know it and then perhaps you'll tell me how it came to be in your possession."

272

With Gertrude translating, he went through everything he had found out about the gospel and its journey through the years, ending with Carl Hoffman at the beginning of the eighteenth century.

Vogel shook his head as Randall finished and spoke to his daughter. "He says it's a most wonderful story."

Gertrude served coffee and Vogel spoke for almost fifteen minutes without interruption, his voice becoming weak and tremulous. When he fell silent, Gertrude summarized the story of SS-General Paul Fischer, the art collections and the gospel manuscript.

"Goebbels signed the book, as you have seen," she finished. "Then General Fischer kept it for him. General Fischer was later implicated in the Stauffenberg plot against Hitler and shot, but just before his arrest, he gave the book to my father with orders to add it to Goebbels' collection. That collection fell into Russian hands when Berlin was occupied, however my father managed to retrieve the book and keep it hidden. After the war, he contacted many churches in Munich without success. No one knew anything about the book. The convent was never rebuilt and so he kept it himself. Perhaps he should have given it to a museum," she added, "but he loved it too much by then."

Randall sat enthralled throughout the story, and apart from not explaining how the manuscript got to the convent, it traced the final chapters in the gospel's history. *Maybe the Hoffman family just gave it to the convent,* he thought. *Who knows? At least it's here now.*

"You know," he said, as Gertrude poured him another cup of coffee, "it would be a wonderful gesture on your part if you placed the book in the State Library. People would be able to see it there, and scholars could make use of it as well."

"It's my father's greatest treasure," said Gertrude. "He sees it as a great work of art, and I think he values it more as a link to his youth and his glory days in uniform. It was difficult even to persuade him to take it for restoration. It took him weeks to decide to allow them to send it to London, and I don't think he slept a wink for the entire six months it was gone."

"I don't blame him," smiled Randall, "but it's one of the world's treasures as well, and it should be kept safe. Money-wise, it's worth a fortune, of course, especially with Goebbels' signature in it. You met

Magda at the library and you know they're completely trustworthy. Please let me call her and arrange for you to take the manuscript in. Just call it a permanent loan if you like. I'm sure you'll be able to see it whenever you want, and they'll take the best possible care of it. It could begin to deteriorate at any time, even though it seems fine just now."

Eventually Vogel gave in, saying he would do it only because the Herr Professor advised it, and Randall made the call. Magda was at the apartment within thirty minutes and the formalities were quickly completed.

She spoke to Vogel in German as she and Randall prepared to go, and the old man nodded and smiled, albeit wanly.

Magda and Randall rode down in the elevator together, Magda carrying the gospel in a padded leather case slung over her shoulder.

"What did you say to him, if I may ask?" said Randall.

"I told him we are honored to have the manuscript and extremely grateful for his generosity."

"Good," said Randall. "I got my chance to look at it, and it's now in the right hands. I'm glad it all worked out."

"Thank you so much, Dr. Randall," she said. "We wouldn't have this wonderful book if it weren't for you."

"Not at all," he replied, thinking to himself that not only was the gospel now safe, Vogel and his daughter were as well.

* * * *

Katherine stood waiting for Randall when he arrived at Heathrow. He thought how lovely she looked and to be with her again made the world a perfect place.

"I found it, Katherine," he said after a long embrace and a kiss. "It's in Berlin. I saw it. I read the owners' names. Robert's colophon as well. It all fits."

"That's absolutely wonderful, George," she said, kissing him again.

They took the train and then a taxi to her temporary flat, and as they prepared a late lunch, Randall excused himself and picked up his mobile phone.

"I just want to give Tony a buzz and tell him the news, and I ought to see what he wants me to do now I've actually found the gospel."

He rang through and to his relief Joyce was at his desk.

"Hello, Tony," he said, deliberately keeping his voice neutral and calm. "I've found it."

"Found what?"

"What do you think?" he laughed. "*The Haunted Gospel*, of course. It's in Berlin."

"My God. That's bloody marvelous. Congratulations, George. Good on you."

"I looked at the illuminations and I'm pretty sure I know where the stuff is, or was, but I'd rather not go into that on the phone."

"Right you are," agreed Joyce. "Have you told Megan?"

"No. I'm going to call her straight away, but I need to know what you want me to say to people from now on so I can put her, and Katherine, in the picture."

"I think—" Joyce began, but Randall interrupted.

"I've told Katherine, of course."

"That's okay," said Joyce, "but let's keep it to the four of us for now. Don't tell anyone else until I've had a chance to talk to Thomas. I'll see you tomorrow."

Randall called Megan, and she squealed with delight at the news.

"I'll meet you at the station tomorrow, and you can tell me all about everything," she said. "It's so exciting. It's wonderful, but…." Her voice softened. "I wish Mike…."

"Me too," he said. "Perhaps he does know. Meg. I hope so anyway."

Katherine set out sandwiches and coffee and they sat down at her small table.

"So," she said, "how did you finally find it, and how on earth did it get to Berlin?"

He told her the story of Munich, the Berlin State Library and the culmination of the search in Vogel's apartment.

"Good Lord, George," she said when he finished. "You mean it was once actually owned by Josef Goebbels?"

"I saw his signature on it, but he only owned it very briefly. Vogel said Himmler and Goering saw it as well."

"The mind boggles."

"And whatever the treasure is, or was," he added, "it was originally buried under the floor of the scriptorium at All Saints."

"You deciphered the illuminations?"

"Truth to tell," he said, "there was no deciphering to be done really. When I got a look at the illuminations, I could pretty well see the story in plain pictures. It wasn't Da Vinci Code stuff at all, although it wouldn't mean much to anyone who didn't know what to look for."

"Well," she said, "this certainly calls for a celebration."

"Champagne?" he asked, as she took his hand and led him from the table.

"That too," she said.

* * * *

The following afternoon, Megan drove Randall home from the station, and Joyce joined them shortly afterwards bearing a sumptuous order of Chinese food. While they ate, Randall went through all the details, and answered their questions.

"I've been thinking a lot about this in the past couple of days," he said, "and I've come to the conclusion that whoever killed Mike doesn't need to search for the gospel because somehow or other he already knows where the treasure is—assuming that's his motive."

"But he might just be biding his time," said Megan, and Randall shook his head.

"This occurred to me before, and I mentioned it to you, but I didn't think it through properly. You can't go searching for a thing like the gospel without people knowing about it. If he'd suddenly turned up asking all sorts of questions of different people the way I had to, he'd have given himself away. I've no idea what his source might be, but whatever it is, I'm sure he doesn't need the gospel. He just wanted to make sure I didn't find it because if I did, I'd know what he knows."

"Maybe he's seen the gospel himself somehow," Megan suggested.

"It's only been out of Vogel's sight twice since the war. Once when it went for restoration and once when it came to the British Museum, and both those events were long before all this business started. No, whoever we're looking for must have a source other than the gospel, but must somehow have known the gospel also held a key. If he didn't, he wouldn't have tried to stop me from finding it. We know Bartholomew wasn't his source because he read it too late. I'll bet he knows where the treasure was and maybe what it was as well."

"Can you speculate on what the source might be, George?" asked Joyce, and Randall exhaled, blowing out his cheeks.

"I suppose it's perfectly possible that another document could exist. Perhaps written by another monk, or perhaps recorded by someone outside the priory altogether. Bartholomew says the enclave was sworn to secrecy, but humans are remarkably fallible creatures."

"Well, second source or no second source," said Joyce, "things are different now you actually do know where the manuscript and treasure are."

"Precisely," said Randall, "and I say there's no more need for caution. Going after me, Meg, or Katherine is pointless now, not to say stupid as well. What I think I have to do is let all the world and his wife know I've found the gospel, and tell them it appears there may be some interesting religious artifacts buried at All Saints. Let's not call it a treasure, for God's sake."

"Dead right," said Joyce, "and Thomas said exactly the same thing. The idea is for you to go after the treasure yourself. That could make our boy desperate enough to make a bad move."

"He hasn't made one so far," murmured Megan.

"Okay," nodded Randall.

"So how do you go after the treasure?" asked Megan.

"I approach the archeology department at St. Arthur, tell them the whole story, Bartholomew and all, and see if they're interested in getting permission for an excavation to look under the scriptorium at what's left of All Saints. It could take a year or more to get the approval, though."

"And do you think they'll be interested?" Megan asked.

Randall chuckled.

"They won't be able to resist it."

"All right," said Joyce. "That's the plan. Let's see what happens."

* * * *

277

The next morning, Randall arrived at his office and began spreading the word. By lunchtime, the news was all over campus, and a steady stream of people visited him to find out more and offer congratulations. Max Thoroughgood's cherubic face fairly glowed with delight.

"But you must have contacted the Berlin State Library before, surely," he said. "They have a vast collection of manuscripts. It's an obvious place to look."

"Yes, I did," Randall answered, "but the gospel didn't belong to the library, you see. I asked if they had a thirteenth century gospel of St. John that was once in the Vatican Library, and, of course, they hadn't. The haunted bit didn't mean anything to them either."

Randall visited the archeology department and told them about the possible existence at All Saints of what he simply called "significant religious artifacts."

"Found the Holy Grail, have you, sir?" quipped one of the graduate students.

"I think so, yes," said Randall with a grave nod, and grinned at the young woman's look of astonishment.

Lengthy discussions ensued concerning the submission of documents necessary to secure approval for an excavation and the wheels were set in motion. The news traveled quickly and soon speculation was rife as to the nature of the artifacts.

Katherine moved gratefully back to her own flat with Randall's help and declared she had had quite enough of her cloak-and-dagger existence.

"It made an interesting change from my normal routine," she said, "but I've decided I rather like my normal routine after all. Besides, I missed the view from my dining room."

Randall continued to speak openly about the gospel and the possibility of an excavation, and in mid-February, he and Joyce met over lunch to take stock of the situation. Outside, the air was cold and as still as death. Snow fell heavily, and traffic had come to a near standstill.

"What are the chances of getting approval for an excavation?" Joyce asked.

"Well, given the new information we have, I'd say pretty good."

"New information?"

"Yes. During their preparation of the proposal, the archeology people checked up on any previous excavations—you have to do that—and apparently, there was one carried out in 1938 by Dr. Edward Callum from Oxford. He didn't publish anything about it before he died and it seems his records and notes were misplaced or destroyed during the war. So essentially, our excavation will be the first to be documented and that's the main point in our favor. I suspect Callum's was a fairly routine exploratory job that turned up little of significance. It may have been no more than a site survey for all we know."

"Would Callum have looked under the scriptorium floor?"

"I doubt it. Even if he exposed the floor, assuming it was still there to be exposed, there isn't usually very much underneath floors except tombs, and they tend to be underneath churches or chapels, not scriptoria."

"Okay. And there's been nothing going on where you're concerned that you can pinpoint? No one acting oddly? Asking too many questions? You know the drill by now."

"Not a damn thing," said Randall, signaling for the check.

"So you don't feel as if—what was it you said once—as if you have the devil at your heels?"

"No, thank God," Randall grinned. "Is there any progress from your end?"

"No," answered Joyce. "Nothing. The file stays open, of course, but it's virtually a cold case now. Unless we get some sort of break, we're potted."

"Yes," Randall said. "I was hoping this very public push for an excavation might flush him out, but no such luck it seems."

"He knows the risks of showing himself at this point," said Joyce. "If he forgets the treasure and just stays out of sight, we may never get him."

"I suppose not," sighed Randall.

"Is there any news on the Professorship in London?" asked Joyce as they ventured out into the polar conditions.

"It's all supposed to be laid on," answered Randall. "All I'm getting is apologies and bafflegab, though. Their problems with the endowment

279

have apparently escalated into the rarefied atmosphere of solicitors and court battles with family members disgruntled over their share of the estate, which I understand is enormous. I don't know what the specific issues are, but the uncertainty is very difficult to put up with."

Chapter Thirty

"Good Lord," exclaimed Randall as he opened his front door on a sunny morning in late April. "Donald. How very nice to see you. Come in, come in."

"Hello, George," said Crowley, stepping into the front hall and shaking Randall's hand. "Sorry I didn't call, but I'm just on my way to Cardiff to see a chum of mine for a few days, and I thought why not come up your way first. I enjoyed the drive."

"Well I'm glad you're here," said Randall. "Come and sit down."

"Congratulations again on finding the gospel, George," said Crowley as they settled themselves in the front room. "It's a great achievement."

"Thanks," Randall grinned. "I do feel pretty chuffed about it."

"Are you going to publish on it?" Crowley asked.

"Probably. If there's an excavation at All Saints, the story of the manuscript can be added to the report. I expect your mother's told you all about everything."

"The supposed treasure you mean? Yes, she has. It reminds me of pirates or the Holy Grail."

"Don't you start," said Randall. "I've had quite enough of that already, thank you very much."

He insisted on taking Crowley to lunch and they ate a pleasant and companionable meal in The Sword and Trident.

"I hope Megan is fully recovered," said Crowley.

"Absolutely," answered Randall. "It's long over and done with now, but thanks for asking."

"Good," said Crowley. "I was away for almost a month when it happened and I was pretty shocked when Mum told me about it afterwards."

"Cardiff again?" asked Randall.

"No, Lincoln actually."

They finished their lunch and Randall waved as Crowley drove off a couple of hours later. He stood staring down the street long after the car had rounded the corner and disappeared.

It can't be, he thought. *It's just a coincidence.*

He called Katherine that evening as usual, and told her about Donald's visit.

"He said he was on his way to Cardiff to visit a friend."

"Oh yes, that's Billy Compton. He often goes to see him. They've been friends since schooldays."

"He certainly seems to get about quite a bit, though," Randall said. "He said he was in Lincoln when Meg had her accident."

His voice sounded unnatural to him. Hollow and artificial. He was deceiving her, and he hated himself for it, but he could not tell her what he suspected. All he could do was hope he was wrong.

"What's wrong with going to Lincoln?" she asked in an amused tone. "Lots of people go there, George. It's not exactly the dark side of the moon, you know."

"Of course not," he said, perhaps a little too quickly. "Just interested, that's all."

As their conversation continued, Randall strove to keep his voice natural while his thoughts spun in a vortex of alarm and fear. The call ended and he replaced the receiver with an unsteady hand.

He called Megan, but all he heard was her well-modulated voice on the answering machine telling him "Megan and Tony can't take your call at the moment." He left a message and spent the rest of the evening in a state of desperate impatience. At about half-past ten, Megan returned his call.

"Sorry to be so late, Pop. We were at the theater with a couple of friends."

"It's all right Meg," he said, "but I must speak to Tony please. It's very important."

"Oh…okay. He's right here."

Megan sounded nonplused, but handed over the phone to Joyce.

"Hello, George," he said. "What's up?"

"Look here, Tony, I'm in a hell of a state."

"For God's sake, what's happened? Has whoever it is had another go at you? Have you heard from him again or something?"

"No," said Randall, hearing Megan's words of alarm in the

background. "Nothing like that. I just want to know the name of the bloke in Cardiff who had his mobile phone swiped. The one used to call Farina."

"Oh heck," said Joyce, "I'm not sure right at this moment. Why do you suddenly want to know that?"

"Was it Compton?"

Joyce paused for a moment.

"Yes, I believe it was. William Compton. Preferred to be called Billy. But how—?"

"Oh God," Randall said.

"George," said Joyce, his voice almost stern, "what the hell's going on?"

Randall drew a deep breath.

"Donald Crowley dropped in this afternoon. He says he goes to Cardiff a lot. He knows Billy Compton. And as if that's not enough, he was in Lincoln when I got the warning call after Megan's accident. What does all that tell you?"

Joyce was silent for a few moments, and when he spoke, his tone was cautious.

"It doesn't tell me anything at this stage. It's just a set of circumstances, but obviously we'll have to follow it up."

"It's probably all a coincidence, though," Randall said, his own voice sounding desperate to him. "After all, we don't know Donald was in Cardiff when the phone was stolen, and the call from Lincoln doesn't prove anything really, does it?"

"Hmm," said Joyce, more in thought than agreement. "It may all be coincidental, but on the other hand, it may not. I'll talk to Thomas and call you tomorrow."

Randall went to his office the next morning and acted out the routine of a normal day, but he could not concentrate on anything. *What if it is Donald?* he asked himself, time and again. *What will Katherine do? She'll be devastated. And what will I do, come to that?*

This is nonsense, he told himself. *It couldn't possibly be Donald. He isn't a killer, for God's sake.*

Midafternoon, Joyce called to say Thomas had decreed nothing would be done until Crowley had returned home to Norwich. Compton would be interviewed only after Crowley was back where he could be watched.

"If Donald is mixed up in this," said Joyce, "and we go to see Compton while he's there, he'll know we're on to him. If he does a runner, he could be impossible to find."

"All right," said Randall, "but, Tony, if it is Donald…."

"I know what you're thinking," Joyce said. "Let's not jump to conclusions. This is a matter of taking one step at a time, like any other investigation. What we have before us at this point is nothing more than a collection of circumstances, as I told you last night."

"But Katherine's been telling him everything all along," said Randall. "He knew everything I was doing, and what I was finding out. Even some of the details no one else knew, apart from you and Meg."

"I know," said Joyce, "but think for a minute. Since he knew everything, he'd have no need to call Farina, would he? We need hard evidence, George. We might possibly get that from Compton, but we can't be sure. Meantime, the strategy is wait until Crowley is home and cross those bridges only when we come to them."

* * * *

For the next week—the longest seven days of Randall's existence —he spoke each evening to Katherine, striving to sound his usual self. He loved and trusted her, but could not bring himself to tell her what was going on. He hoped his fears would prove groundless and then she need never know anything. He told himself repeatedly he was in fact sparing her what was quite possibly needless anguish, but it lacerated his soul nonetheless.

The call from Joyce came on Friday evening.

"Well, George, it seems Donald Crowley was indeed staying with Compton at the time the phone was nicked.

"Dear God," said Randall. "I can't believe this is happening."

"Hang on now," Joyce continued. "That fact by itself still proves exactly nothing."

"I know," said Randall. "That's what I'm counting on."

"We've found out something else, though," Joyce said. "Mike

Stuart went to Norwich to a conference several months before the gospel business started and we know Crowley attended the same conference. The Norwich department came up with that bit of intelligence a few days ago. It's circumstantial as well, of course, but they're going to use it as an excuse to drop in on Crowley and ask him a question or two."

"But I'm sure if Donald had met Mike, he'd have told me."

"Perhaps," said Joyce, "and perhaps not. If he is involved in this, he wouldn't want you or anyone else knowing he'd met Stuart."

"So is Donald a suspect then?" asked Randall.

"No, not yet anyway," said Joyce. "Obviously he's become a person of considerable interest. That's why Thomas got the Norwich department to go deeper into his background."

The next day being Saturday, Megan came round to see Randall and he poured his heart out to her.

"I had to tell Tony what I'd found out about Donald, but I haven't told Katherine in hopes it all amounts to nothing."

"As Tony said, Pop, Donald's not a suspect, so don't run away with the worst case scenario you can think of."

Randall sighed.

"And anyway," she added, "knowing Donald as you do, do you seriously imagine him capable of all these things? Do you really see him as a murderer?"

"No, of course not, but if this investigation comes between Katherine and me, I don't know what I'll do."

"There you go again with the worst case thing," she said. "If Donald is guilty, and please God he isn't, then there's no denying you and Katherine may be in for a rough ride, but if you both want to, you'll make it through. She'll know you did what you felt you had to do."

"I hope so," he said, with a sense of bleak foreboding in his heart.

"Buck up," Megan smiled. "Gloomy pessimism isn't your style, you know."

Randall nodded, but said nothing.

"There's something else, too," Megan added in a gentle voice. "If Donald is arrested and charged, Katherine will need all the love and support you can give her."

Megan gave him a hug as she left and told him she had complete faith in his honesty, his integrity and his strength.

"Katherine says those are only three of the qualities she admires and loves in you," she said.

"Oh really?" he said, raising his eyebrows. "And do you two talk about me often, then?"

"Constantly," she laughed as she went down the front path to her van.

"Constantly, indeed," he muttered as he went inside. "My own daughter."

He felt better following his talk with Megan, but Monday brought further disturbing news. Joyce had asked the Norwich police to verify Donald's whereabouts on the night Megan's brakes were done over, and they found he had not been at home in Norwich at that time.

"We know that already," said Randall. "He was in Lincoln."

"He was in Lincoln when you got the warning message," said Joyce, "although we didn't know when he got there. We wanted to know where he was on the actual night in question. His landlady says he was gone around that time for over a month. When asked, Crowley confirmed he was away but said he couldn't remember where he'd been that particular night. They helped his memory along by asking him if he'd been in Lincoln, and at first he said he hadn't, in spite of what he'd told you. He said he'd been here, in St. Arthur Newtown. Then he changed that story and said he'd been in Lincoln all the time but couldn't remember the exact dates. He said he'd been there with a friend."

"What friend?" asked Randall. "Compton?"

"There's the rub," said Joyce. "Crowley refused to give a name. Said unless he was actually being charged, he didn't have to say anything."

"And is that correct?"

"Technically, yes, but it doesn't make things look good for him."

Randall felt a coldness sweep over him. The worst seemed about to happen after all.

"It's not the behavior of an innocent man, George," said Joyce. "If he is in the clear he should be giving us all the cooperation he can, not playing silly-buggers about not knowing this and not remembering that and refusing to divulge the other. I really hate to say it, but I'm inclined to think we've probably found our man."

"Poor Katherine," said Randall. "I can't imagine what this will do to her. And what's she going to say when she finds out I'm the one who put you on to Donald in the first place?"

"Well," Joyce said, with careful deliberation, "we can conceal that if you want us to."

"No," said Randall. "It's very tempting, but I have to tell her. It's not in me to hide it. I'd feel I was living a lie. Besides, if Donald goes to trial, I'll be called as a witness, won't I, and it would all come out then? That would be even worse."

"True enough," said Joyce.

"But there's something else bothering me," said Randall. "You've said several times that the man we want is clever and covers his tracks and all that sort of thing."

"Yes?"

"Well, if Donald is guilty, why on earth would he have told me he was going to see a bloke in Cardiff? If he'd stolen Compton's phone and called Farina with it when he was there before, he'd have kept quiet, surely. It just sounds too careless to me. And why say openly he'd been in Lincoln if he'd made the warning call from there? It's not plausible."

"Well, George," answered Joyce, "I can't really answer that except to say that in doing those things he may have made the very mistake we were waiting for. Perhaps he became overly complacent, who knows? Maybe he thought the heat was off. Criminals can be damn clever, but as I told you once before, precious few of them are infallible.

Chapter Thirty-One

"George," Katherine blurted when he answered the phone, "I've just had a call from Donald. They've arrested him. On suspicion of tampering with Megan's van and killing Michael Stuart. It's an outrage. I can't believe it. Tony Joyce must be totally out of his mind."

Randall had been expecting and dreading this moment. He searched frantically for the right words, but Katherine rushed on.

"He said he'd been questioned a couple of times in the last week or so, but didn't tell me because he didn't want to worry me. I'm going to Norwich with Joseph Hardwick, my solicitor. We're leaving in an hour. He's already arranged for a Sir Oswald Prentice to meet us there. I've never heard of him, but Hardwick says he's a top man for this sort of thing. I want this nonsense sorted out, and sorted out now."

Her voice lost some of its stridency as fear replaced her anger.

"Oh God, George, how on earth could this have happened? I feel as if everything's gone out of control. It's a nightmare. Will you meet me in Norwich please? I need you with me."

"Of course I will," he answered. "I'll be there as quickly as I can."

He was in torment throughout the journey. *She needs my support,* he thought, *but what support can I possibly be once she hears what I did? I wish to God I'd just shut up. I should have left it all to the police.*

"I must tell her," he muttered under his breath as he parked at Katherine's hotel. "I won't go on deceiving her. Things are bad enough already."

He met her in her room and explained everything: his suspicions, his discussions about Donald with Tony Joyce, everything.

"I prayed it would never come to this, Katherine," he finished. "I'm most desperately sorry, but I tried to do what I thought was best."

She stared at him for a moment in stricken disbelief, and then hot fury blazed into her eyes.

"You believe he's guilty, do you? My son. You think he's a murderer? You actually talked to the police about him without telling me?"

He had never seen her so angry.

"It was a complete and utter betrayal of faith and trust, George. How could you? How dare you?"

He spread his hands in a gesture of helplessness and supplication.

"No one wants to believe he's guilty, Katherine, least of all me, for God's sake. But think how it looks."

"How does it look?" she snapped. "Just you tell me."

"Donald maintains his innocence," he said, "but he won't provide any information to substantiate it. He keeps saying he can't remember things. Whom he was with on particular days and nights. Why he went to Lincoln and Cardiff. Tony says that at one point he even denied knowing Billy Compton and then changed his mind. The longer he does this sort of thing, the worse it gets. I'm sure if he'd only cooperate, this could all be resolved."

She sat silent, her anger and hurt seeming to fill the small room.

"Listen Katherine," he said, without meeting her pain-filled eyes, "I can't believe Donald's guilty, and I thought I was doing right by not telling you what was going on. I fully expected to hear that Donald wasn't implicated in any way, and then you need never have known anything about it. Whatever the truth turns out to be now, I want us to try and face it together if we can."

"I still can't believe you put the police onto him without telling me. All those times we spoke on the phone and you said nothing. Nothing. I could tell something was bothering you. I'm not as complete a fool as you seem to think. But you wouldn't say, even when I asked. It was deliberate and calculated deception and dishonesty."

"For God's sake, Katherine," he said, stung by her words. "That's not bloody well fair, and you know it. What did you expect me to do? Call you one day and say, 'Oh by the way, Katherine, I think Donald might have murdered Michael Stuart so I'm calling the police?' I was trying to think of you above all else because you're more important to me than everything else. I tried to do what I thought was best for you."

"And I suppose you thought if you did tell me I'd put Donald on the first plane to South America, did you?"

"Oh don't be ridiculous," he said, feeling his own anger rise in spite of himself. "It's Donald we ought to be thinking about most of all. He has to start cooperating. Surely you can see that."

She leveled a steady stare at him for several long moments before answering.

"Donald was a friend of yours, or at least you said he was. You didn't believe he was guilty, yet you reported him to the police."

"You would have done the same thing if you'd been in my shoes. You would have done what you thought you had to do, and so did I. Maybe I didn't get it exactly right in the end, but I did the best I could, and that's the truth."

"I would have told you," she said, her words like sharp icicles. "I would have trusted you."

"All right," he sighed. "If I'd told you before I spoke to Tony, what would you have done?"

She answered without hesitation.

"Donald, you and I would have sat down and sorted out the real facts. If, after that, we felt Donald was vulnerable and needed further advice, we'd have gone to see Hardwick, examined the entire situation with him and made a decision on the basis of sound legal opinion. Perhaps we would have gone to the police voluntarily and perhaps we wouldn't, I can't say, but we would have made our decisions together, as we should have done."

Randall could not find words to reply. Viewed with the intense clarity of hindsight, trusting her seemed such an easy thing to have done.

As he looked at Katherine, sitting stiffly upright on the edge of her chair, he saw her expression change from indignant anger to weariness and dejection. He stood and took a couple of steps towards her, but she held up her hand, turning her face away.

"Leave me alone, George. Please, just leave me alone."

There seemed to be nothing more to say, and as he turned for the door, she called him back and handed him the engagement ring with a quick, firm gesture.

"And take this with you."

He left the room, closing the door quietly behind him; closing it on all the hopes and dreams he had cherished for so many months. Rain was oozing from a low, gray sky when he left the hotel, the large drops hissing as they struck the shiny pavement. He put his hands into the pockets of his raincoat and walked away along the High Street without the slightest idea of where he was going.

* * * *

Tony Joyce arrived the following day to question Donald Crowley before conveying him back to Yorkshire. Randall waited in his hotel room for news, mentally wringing his hands in anguish and nervous anticipation. He recalled Megan's words on the phone the previous evening.

"Of course she's upset and angry. She's probably terrified out of her life as well. Her only child is facing a murder charge. Don't give up on her, Dad. This one will take a bit of time."

"But she had a solution, Meg, don't you see?" he said. "She knew what we should have done. What I should have done. I should have gone to her the way people in love are supposed to. I feel like a fraud."

"Don't start second-guessing yourself, Pop," she said, "or you'll go bonkers. You did your best and that's all anyone can ever do. You told me that yourself after I came dead last in the egg-and-spoon race on Sports Day when I was seven years old."

As Randall sat turning and returning these thoughts over in his head, the phone on the bedside table suddenly rang, splintering the silence like a scream in a deserted house. His heart thundered as though to leap from his chest as he seized the receiver.

"Katherine?" It was almost a shout.

"Sorry, George," said the official voice of Tony Joyce, "it's only me."

"Tony! For pity's sake man, what's happening?"

"Crowley's made a statement, George," said Joyce. "And it's a real stunner. I need to come and see you."

Thirty minutes later, Randall opened his door to Joyce and the young detective entered and sat down.

"Is Donald our man, then?" asked Randall, sitting on the edge of the bed.

"His statement suggests he isn't, but we're not entirely sure yet. However, he's implicated someone else, and it's someone you know."

"Someone I know? Who?"

"The student you had working for you at one time, John Archer."

Randall was thunderstruck.

"How on earth is Archer involved in all this?"

"He's the one Crowley's been trying to protect with all his 'don't know' and 'can't remember' stuff. He's Crowley's boyfriend, you see. Crowley's gay."

"Oh my God," said Randall. "I wonder if Katherine knows."

"He says not," answered Joyce, "but he knows it has to come out now. He thinks it'll be fine once Katherine gets used to it."

I should be there with her, Randall thought, *but it's not possible now*. He wondered if she felt as bereft and isolated as he did.

"Let me fill you in on the rest of Crowley's statement," Joyce was continuing.

Randall exhaled a long breath.

"Okay."

"Crowley's been telling Archer everything you've been up to," said Joyce. "Apparently Archer always asked a lot of questions; Crowley simply put that down to curiosity and interest."

"But Katherine asked Donald not to pass on any information to anyone,"

"Archer was his boyfriend," said Joyce with a shrug. "He trusted him."

"I suppose he did." Randall nodded, and Joyce continued.

"The crunch came when Katherine moved, and we really stressed the need for secrecy. He told Archer she was moving, and when he wouldn't say where Archer got violently angry. That was when Crowley began to wonder about him. Apparently, Archer's got a hell of a temper when he gets going. Crowley was able to see a pattern of behavior, and although he didn't want to, he was forced to think Archer might have some involvement in what had been going on. Under questioning this morning, after a very well-timed warning from Oswald Prentice, the barrister, about the seriousness of his position, Crowley finally realized he couldn't go on protecting Archer any longer. At that point, he gave in and outed him, as they say on CNN. He went on to make a lengthy statement about his relationship with Archer, their visits to Cardiff and

Lincoln together along with all the relevant dates. Most notable of all, I think, was the confirmation that he'd been in St. Arthur Newtown staying with Archer the night Megan's van was messed with. Archer came home well after twelve that night saying he'd been out 'teaching someone a lesson.'"

"So what's Donald's situation now, then?" Randall asked.

"Well," said Joyce, "even if it turns out he's in the clear on everything else, there's still the issue of obstructing a police investigation."

"Can't you overlook that, Tony?" Randall said. "After all, he's made a full statement now."

"We'll see," said Joyce. "He did have a message for you, by the way."

"For me?"

"Yes. He says he fully understands why you spoke to us about him. Says he'd have done the same thing in your place."

"That's generous of him," said Randall. "I'd have thought he'd like to give me a swift kick right where it counts most."

"He may yet," Joyce chuckled.

"What's the next step?" Randall asked.

"We've asked the Newtown police to call on Archer and question him about his activities in Cardiff and elsewhere; the matter of Megan's van, and his whereabouts the night Michael Stuart was murdered."

"I can't believe young Archer would do anything like this," said Randall.

"We don't know he did yet," said Joyce. "Until we're certain, Crowley stays in the jug. I don't want to run the risk of Archer being tipped off. And," Joyce added as he rose to go, "there's still the possibility that the whole Archer story is an attempt by Crowley to save himself."

Chapter Thirty-Two

Donald Crowley was eventually released without charge. It took the combined persuasive powers of his lawyers, Hardwick and Prentice, to convince the police he was misguided rather than malicious in his attempt to shield Archer from prosecution. A month after Archer's arrest, Randall, Megan and Tony Joyce sat in Randall's bright living room while the dog, William Wallace, slept peacefully on the carpet in his accustomed place.

"Well," said Joyce, opening a blue file folder he held on his knee. "It's all over bar the shouting, and I've submitted the final report. Archer has been charged with manslaughter, attempted murder, assault and several other things, but here's the story."

He glanced at the file for a moment.

"Donald Crowley and John Archer met at a party in Norwich five or six years ago, and about a year after that they became an item or whatever you want to call it. It seems Archer had gone to Norwich to end an earlier homosexual relationship with a bloke who was related to a certain Dr. Edward Callum."

"Callum, the archeologist?" asked Randall.

"The very same," Joyce said. "He's the connection, the link, the key figure, as you'll see. Now as you told me once before, George, it was Callum who carried out the excavations at All Saints just before the war, but it turns out he was killed in the very first air raid on London and nothing was ever published because no one could find his notes on the dig after the war."

"Right," Randall nodded. "Flaming nuisance, actually."

"We now know all Callum's papers went to his widow, who didn't give a tinker's damn about archeology and had no idea what the papers and files might contain. Thank God she didn't chuck them all in the fire. She remarried in 1945, and the papers went to her son by that marriage and so on, until they fetched up in the possession of this chap John Archer was involved with before Donald Crowley. The notes on the All Saints excavation have now surfaced."

"Marvelous," Randall enthused.

"It gets better," Joyce grinned. "As a token of friendship, this chap, whose name is Gordon Bedford by the way, gave something to John Archer that he'd found amongst Callum's stuff and which he thought Archer, being a lover of history and all that, would like to have. Apparently Callum excavated part of the old cemetery at All Saints and found the grave of a monk named Gottfried."

"Prior Gottfried," Randall nodded.

"Right. He was buried in a well-sealed lead coffin and had been sort of naturally mummified. The lead had also preserved a parchment which had been buried with him. Callum had kept it in his files, presumably to disclose at some later date, but never get the chance, thanks to the Germans. So Bedford, who found it and had no idea what it was, gave it to Archer. Archer now refers to his erstwhile boyfriend as 'a stupid idiot' for not understanding the importance of the parchment."

"Well what was it, for heaven's sake?" asked Megan. "Don't keep us in suspense."

"It's a letter from King John to Gottfried, no less, royal seal and all."

"The King John letter," said Randall, with a snap of his fingers. "That's got to be it."

"Yes, indeed," said Joyce. "It was a letter asking Gottfried to hide the crown jewels at All Saints."

"The crown jewels," echoed Randall. "Good God. The conventional wisdom amongst historians has always been that King John lost them in the fen country around about 1216. This is astounding. If it's true, we'll have to rewrite those bits."

"He didn't lose them," said Joyce. "He ordered the monks to hide them, and so I think we can presume they're the treasure of All Saints Brother Bartholomew refers to."

"Must be," said Randall. "I thought the gold crown in the space under the scriptorium in the illuminations simply denoted something of value, but it actually represents the nature of the treasure. That letter must be the second source of information we were speculating about."

"Yes," Joyce continued. "Archer knew the crown jewels, or royal regalia, which is the correct term, I'm told, had been hidden at All Saints and he also knew Callum hadn't found them, so unless Henry VIII had come across them when he pulverized the priory, there was a fair chance they were still there. Only he didn't know exactly where they were—at least not at first."

"The plot thickens," said Megan.

"At this point, John enters St. Arthur University and takes a tutorial from Michael Stuart. He showed Stuart the parchment letter and asked him to confirm its authenticity. Stuart did that, and when Archer asked for it back, Stuart refused, saying it was better for him to keep it. Archer went to Stuart's house the night of the dinner party and demanded the letter back, but Stuart still refused. There was a brief argument, and then Archer lost his rag and hit Stuart with the poker, which he chucked into the river afterward. He took the king's letter off Stuart's desk and cleared off."

"My God," said Randall, "it's unbelievable. But I find it hard to think Mike would have essentially stolen the letter. That sort of dishonesty wasn't like him at all."

"Perhaps we didn't know him quite as well as we thought we did," said Megan.

"Perhaps not," Randall nodded.

"So was Mike looking for *The Haunted Gospel* to find out where the crown jewels were buried?" asked Megan.

"No," Randall interrupted. "That doesn't work, Meg. Unless Mike had seen Bartholomew's journal, he wouldn't have known about the gospel."

"Dead right," said Joyce, "and we know Stuart never did read Bartholomew."

"Then why was he looking for the gospel?" asked Megan.

"Because Callum did see Bartholomew and wrote about it in his research notes. He also wrote that he'd gone looking for the gospel in Vatican records and found references to a text called *The Norwich Gospel*. As he traced those references, Callum came across the now-famous note about *The Haunted Gospel* and correctly deduced the two names referred to the same document."

"As did Farina."

Joyce nodded.

"Correct, and not expecting Mike Stuart to cheat him, Archer told him the whole story."

"So Mike didn't actually find the reference himself, as he told me he had," said Randall.

"Nope. Archer told him about it."

"Well I'm damned," said Randall. "Mike and I were friends for years, and he didn't even tell me the truth. Maybe you're right, Meg. We didn't know him all that well."

"According to Archer, Stuart intended to publish the letter and the story of the crown jewels, and went to Norwich to see if he could find further information on All Saints or the gospel. He posed as a person from the University of Surrey, presumably because he didn't want anyone to know what he was up to."

"So," said Megan, "Archer knew about Bartholomew, the royal regalia *and* the gospel, all thanks to the notes of the late lamented Professor Callum."

"Correct," said Joyce, "but he didn't know the exact relationship between the three because Callum didn't specifically spell it out. Callum did say the Bartholomew journal was in the British Library, however, so after Archer killed Stuart, he took a chance and nipped off to London posing as Stuart to see if he could learn anything further. He used the introductory letter he simply happened to find with the King John parchment on Stuart's desk. Plain good luck. They were both in file number one. And after he'd seen the Bartholomew journal, he damaged it slightly in an attempt to keep it off the shelf in case anyone else asked for it. Like you for example, George."

"But what on earth was Archer thinking?" said Randall. "Did he seriously imagine he could just waltz into what's left of All Saints with a shovel over his shoulder, dig everything up and find the crown jewels? And even if he did, what was he planning to do with them? Sell them on eBay?"

"He hasn't said," answered Joyce. "Given his behavior, I'd imagine he had some sort of idea. Whatever else he is, he's a well-organized forward planner."

Randall shook his head in wonder.

"Now," said Joyce, "let me get to the heart of this. Once Archer got a look at Bartholomew and understood what the gospel contained, he realized he'd already seen it."

"Seen it?" echoed Megan.

"Allow me," said Randall, with a mock bow in his chair. "He saw it when it was at the British Museum."

"Exactly," said Joyce. "Give that man a cigar. He attended a lecture on the gospel manuscript given by one of the Museum's specialists, and the speaker pointed out the strange illuminations: men digging and all that. At the time, Archer had no idea what it all meant, however once he saw King John's letter and Bartholomew's journal he was clever enough to put two and two together. He figured out where the stuff was buried."

"That's a bit of a stretch, isn't it?" asked Megan. "Are you sure he's not having you on?"

"He couldn't have known what he does know except by seeing the gospel, but just to be certain I asked him where the regalia was buried, and he had it right. He even said there was a crown in the illuminations marking the actual spot."

"Bloody hell," said Randall. "And after all I went through to find it."

"Yes," said Joyce, "and that was the problem. Everything seemed to be fine until suddenly you 'stuck your nose in' as Archer put it. When you announced you were going after the gospel, things got a lot more difficult, particularly after you'd read Bartholomew. If you were successful, Archer foresaw the danger that you, too, would find out about the regalia's hiding place, even if you didn't know what the treasure actually was. He certainly didn't want that to happen, and he offered to help in the search so he could keep tabs on what you were doing. And he had an additional source of information in Donald Crowley, of course."

"Archer is a calculating little sod, isn't he?" said Megan.

"That he is," said Randall, "and he damn near killed you, don't forget."

"Claims he just wanted to scare you off," said Joyce. "That's why he sent you the warning message. Says he didn't want to kill Meg, but says he'd have been, and I quote…." Joyce consulted his file. "'…Happy to knock off old Randall.'"

Megan tried unsuccessfully to suppress a laugh as Randall spluttered with outrage.

"Old Randall?"

"He admits everything," Joyce said, closing the file. "Killing Dr. Stuart, trying to run you off the road, the phone calls when you were in Norwich, shoving you under the bus, chucking the boulder through your window, Megan's van. The lot."

"We've all been bloody lucky, Pop," said Megan.

"Anyway," said Joyce, "just to finish up. Donald Crowley wanted to introduce Archer to Compton, who is gay as well, by the way, so he took him to Cardiff. Archer took advantage of the opportunity to nick Compton's mobile phone and call Farina. Got his number off the Internet. He was more than pleased to learn you thought you'd hit a dead end and would give up the gospel search. When you began to tell everyone you were working on those so-called new leads, he got very worried again and when Donald told him about the meeting with Zeller he got really desperate. He was planning to kill you when you came back from Germany, but when you did, you told everyone you'd found the gospel. There was nothing he could do after that."

"Just as we thought," Randall nodded.

"What a bloody mess, though," said Megan. "This thing cost Mike his life, nearly cost you yours, Pop, put me in hospital and John Archer will be banged up for years to come. And for what?"

"Money, recognition, envy, jealousy, greed. Who knows?" said Randall. "All I wanted to do at first was honor the memory of an old friend, but it all became much more complicated than that."

Randall lowered his eyes.

"And it brought Katherine and me together and has torn us apart as well."

Epilogue

Ten months after John Archer's arrest, his trial concluded and he began serving the first of the fifteen years he was to spend as a guest of Her Majesty. Megan and Tony had presented Randall with a grandchild, whom they named George Anthony, and although Randall found himself the patriarch of a small and devotedly happy family, a dark and dispirited loneliness invested his soul. Even though Donald Crowley had not been prosecuted, Katherine remained unforgiving.

"She misses you as much as you miss her," said Crowley one afternoon. "I know that for certain. I've urged her to just reconnect with you and work things out. I know she wants to, but my God she can be stubborn sometimes."

Randall recalled that conversation as he sat in his study, a letter from the University of London before him on the desk. The letter informed him that after prolonged litigation, the university had finally untangled the intricacies of the endowment that was to fund the Professorship he had been offered. He reread the letter, but without enthusiasm. He saw little purpose in uprooting himself and moving to London if he could not be with Katherine. Life without her was a bleak prospect. He still carried the engagement ring about with him in its velvet box, loath to believe she might never wear it again. Although London University was pressing him for a decision on when he would take up the post, he continued to procrastinate.

He laid the letter aside yet again and went upstairs to pack a small suitcase. The excavation at All Saints had been approved and the archaeology department had invited him down to view the work. The British Museum had recently unveiled the hitherto unknown letter from King John, and the possibility of finding the long lost ancient royal regalia at the priory had focused considerable public attention on the excavation.

He left for Lincolnshire the following day, and upon arriving at the site parked next to the dozen or so vehicles belonging to those working on the dig. He stood in the sunshine looking over the site.

In half a dozen places, the turf had been cut away and large areas of bare earth exposed. Trenches and pits had been dug and the remains of stone foundation walls exposed along with the plinths of several columns and the flagstone floors of three buildings.

He was hailed by the dig's director, Professor Henry Cox, who conducted him to a particular spot where the foundations of a large structure with several rooms had been uncovered.

"Now, you see, George," said Cox, an enthusiastic young man of about thirty-five wearing brown overalls and a wide-brimmed straw hat, "according to old Callum's notes that we got from Bedford, we're pretty sure this over here on the left was the dortoir where the monks slept, and over there to the right was the scriptorium. Callum excavated this entire area, photographed it, logged in a few minor artifacts and then covered it up again."

They walked around the perimeter of the foundations and came to a place where the flagstones had been carefully removed, exposing a rectangle of bare brown earth some twenty by twenty-five feet in size. Near the middle of this area, Randall saw a pit about ten feet square and about seven feet deep.

"Callum didn't take up the scriptorium floor," Cox explained. "When he found King John's letter, and learned about the regalia, I imagine it never occurred to him it might be under this floor. He read Bartholomew only after he'd finished the dig, presumably in an effort to discover where the regalia was, but that didn't tell him anything, as we know. Anyway, once we got the flags out of the way we could clearly see that space in the middle had been disturbed. It was full of stones and rubble, not at all like the surrounding ground, so we knew it had once been dug out and later refilled. Then when we got into it, we found that at one time, probably originally, the hole had been lined and floored with wooden planks, and although we sorted and sifted every scrap of material that came out of that hole, there wasn't a jewel in sight. The only thing we did find—right at the bottom—was a gold ring which in all likelihood had fallen between the planks at some point and been overlooked. It bears King John's coat of arms."

"Well, that's of some significance," said Randall with a nod. "There must have been something there at one time."

"Unfortunately," Cox went on, "there was nothing in the pit that allows us to determine when it had been opened and cleaned out. However, given the ring we found, King John's letter to the prior, the gospel manuscript's illuminations and Bartholomew's writings, I think we can safely conclude the royal regalia was not lost accidentally as previously believed. It was stored here at All Saints, but has since disappeared anyway."

"Yes indeed," agreed Randall, "and we now know John did his best to keep it safe."

"Right," said Cox, "but if you'll come along with me, George, there's someone here I want you to meet."

Randall followed Cox to the far side of the site where a large tent had been set up. Inside he saw eight trestle tables on which were various artifacts, tools and pieces of equipment. Cox led him to the table against the back wall and then turned to him with a grin.

"Professor Randall, I'd like you to meet Brother Robert of All Saints. Robert, this is George."

Randall stared at the skeleton laid out on the table, the bones stained reddish-brown with darker patches of near black on the hands and feet.

"Is it really Robert?" he asked.

"Yes it is," said Cox. "Many of the bones, especially the extremities, show signs of having been burned, and you can also clearly see the depressed fracture on the left side of the skull. From its shape, it appears to have been made by a square-headed object of some kind. And what did Bartholomew say? 'The blow clave his skull, whereof he died.' The final proof is this, though."

Cox lifted a small clay bowl from the table.

"This was buried with him. We found traces of ink in it of the type used in the medieval period, and there was also a sharpened piece of charcoal. We've sent that off for radiocarbon dating, and I'll bet you a pint of Guinness it comes back as thirteenth century."

"My God," said Randall, and looked down at the skeleton again.

"Glad to meet you at last, Robert," he said. "You led me a hell of a chase, but I did see your gospel in the end and it's bloody marvelous."

Cox chuckled.

"We'll rebury him soon, but I wanted to let you see him first. I knew you'd want to."

"It's incredible," said Randall, "to think that's really him."

"I'll leave you to it now, George, if I may," said Cox. "We uncovered the kitchens and refectory yesterday which Callum never found. There's a lot of good stuff there."

Cox hurried away leaving Randall alone. After another long look at the skeleton, he murmured, "Rest in peace Robert, old chum, your gospel's safe."

He walked out of the tent into the bright sunshine and made his way back to the area of the scriptorium. He stood deep in thought, staring at the flat ground before him with the empty pit at its center. To his left there were large piles of sifted earth, stones and other detritus, and beyond them the flagstones from the floor, each carefully numbered according to its position, had been neatly stacked in preparation for eventual replacement.

So, he thought, *King John didn't lose the crown jewels, but they're just as gone as if he had. I wonder who dug them up and what happened to them after that. Perhaps the monks succumbed to temptation or curiosity after all. Perhaps Henry VIII's Commissioners found them. No, that won't work. If they'd dug up the regalia they certainly wouldn't have filled in the hole and put the floor back before destroying the priory. Did Callum find the regalia, then? No, that's impossible as well. He didn't run the excavation single-handed, and if something as momentous as a cache of royal gold and jewels had been found, it would have been impossible to keep it a secret.*

As he stood deep in thought, he heard footsteps approaching and assumed Cox was returning. He turned to greet him, but instead of the young archeologist, he saw Katherine, wearing a light blue summer dress, her face drawn and tired-looking. His heart leaped at the joy of seeing her again, but he said nothing as she came and stood beside him, not meeting his eyes.

"Any crown jewels, George?" she asked in a flat voice, looking out over the excavation site.

He did not look at her, but simply shook his head.

"How did you know I was here?"

"Megan told me. We've been talking a lot lately."

"Why have you come, Katherine? Do you want another apology after all these months?"

"No."

"What then?"

"Well," she said, turning to face him, "I hear from Megan, who is a wonderfully loving and perceptive young woman, that you're very unhappy and desperately lonely. So I thought I'd just come and tell you I am as well."

He looked at her, seeing not only the strain in her eyes, but something else as well: an expression that seemed to say, 'I've had enough. Here I am if you still want me, but I'll go if you don't.' He took her in his arms and held her tightly.

"Dear God, Katherine," he whispered, "I've missed you so much. I wish I'd trusted you as I should have."

"And I wish I hadn't been so judgmental and blind stubborn," she answered.

"What happened is past and gone," he said. "I'm sick and tired of carrying all that excess baggage, aren't you?"

"Utterly."

"So, shall we find a quiet place for dinner?"

"All right," she said, taking the hand he offered her.

About the Author

Retired from a career in post-secondary education, Charles now lives on Vancouver island on Canada's scenic west coast. He was born in England but has lived most of his life in Canada. Schooled in Canada, England and the United States, he is an anthropologist and historian by training and likes to use his background in the history and culture of China and Europe in the stories and novels he writes. He enjoys sailing the 24' sailboat he and his wife bought and re-fitted, or working in his garden. He also undertakes a large amount of volunteer work for the Canadian National Institute for the Blind. He says he is giving time to that organization in return for the help provided to him as a partially sighted person since the age of nineteen. When not writing, sailing, gardening or volunteering, Charles likes to read audio books, and plays classical and flamenco guitar.

MuseItUp Publishing
Where the Muse entertains readers!
https://museituppublishing.com/bookstore2/
Visit our website for more books for your reading pleasure.

CPSIA information can be obtained at www.ICGtesting.com
Printed in the USA
LVOW051735190812

294939LV00002B/281/P